Praise for
Dragonmaster

"Slam-bang excitement, lusty action, and military magic . . .
fast-paced and ferocious."
> —Julian May, author of *The Many-Colored Land*
> and *Ironcrown Moon*

"The characters are gloriously multifaceted. . . . Their histories make them deeper and more realistic. I fell in love with each and every one of them . . . a great read. At times you find your imagination taking off and flying with the dragons in the book. I loved it. Breathtakingly awe-inspiring."
> —SF Crowsnest

"Rich and convincing . . . will leave you eagerly awaiting the next installment."
> —*SFX Magazine*

"The action in this series opener is nonstop and violent. . . . Bunch's military background stands him in good stead as he concocts strategy and depicts battle in the air and on the ground. . . . A good bet for military SF and fantasy fans."
> —*Booklist*

"Fans of military fantasy and dragon lore should enjoy this fantasy adventure."
> —*Library Journal*

continued . . .

Praise for the novels
of Chris Bunch

"Bunch knows how to mold heroes . . . and how to create exciting scenes of battlefield mayhem." —*Publishers Weekly*

"Glorious swashbuckling . . . absolutely riveting." —*Locus*

"An excellent fantasy adventure."
—*Science Fiction Chronicle*

"Stirring." —*Realms of Fantasy*

"Powerful . . . a well-crafted universe that seems starkly real . . . will delight fans of military SF." —*Affaire de Coeur*

"Remarkable." —Michael A. Stackpole

"Bunch's battle sequences are second to none."
—*The Oregonian*

"Complex plots, intrigue, and great descriptive narratives of battle and combat." —SF Site

"Lovers of military science fiction could hardly find better fare." —Painted Rock Reviews

KNIGHTHOOD OF THE DRAGON

BOOK TWO OF THE
DRAGONMASTER TRILOGY

CHRIS BUNCH

A ROC BOOK

ROC
Published by New American Library, a division of
Penguin Group (USA) Inc., 375 Hudson Street,
New York, New York 10014, USA
Penguin Group (Canada), 90 Eglinton Avenue East, Suite 700, Toronto, Ontario,
Canada M4P 2Y3 (a division of Pearson Penguin Canada Inc.)
Penguin Books Ltd., 80 Strand, London WC2R 0RL, England
Penguin Ireland, 25 St. Stephen's Green, Dublin 2,
Ireland (a division of Penguin Books Ltd.)
Penguin Group (Australia), 250 Camberwell Road, Camberwell, Victoria 3124,
Australia (a division of Pearson Australia Group Pty. Ltd.)
Penguin Books India Pvt. Ltd., 11 Community Centre, Panchsheel Park,
New Delhi - 110 017, India
Penguin Group (NZ), cnr Airborne and Rosedale Roads, Albany,
Auckland 1310, New Zealand (a division of Pearson New Zealand Ltd.)
Penguin Books (South Africa) (Pty.) Ltd., 24 Sturdee Avenue,
Rosebank, Johannesburg 2196, South Africa

Penguin Books Ltd., Registered Offices:
80 Strand, London WC2R 0RL, England

Published by Roc, an imprint of New American Library, a division of Penguin Group
(USA) Inc. Previously published in an Orbit Books edition. For information address Orbit
Books, Time Warner Books UK, Brettenham House, Lancaster Place, London WC2E 7EN.

First Roc Printing, March 2006
10 9 8 7 6 5 4 3 2 1

Copyright © Chris Bunch, 2003
All rights reserved

ROC REGISTERED TRADEMARK—MARCA REGISTRADA

LIBRARY OF CONGRESS PUBLICATION DATA:

Bunch, Chris.
     Knighthood of the dragon / Chris Bunch.
         p. cm.—(Dragonmaster ; bk. 2)
     ISBN 0-451-46067-7
     1. Dragons—Fiction. 2. Human-animal relationships—Fiction. I. Title.

PS3552.U466K65 2006
813'.54—dc22   2005054426

Printed in the United States of America

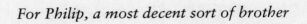

For Philip, a most decent sort of brother

1

The music crescendoed, then stopped abruptly; and the chatter was loud in the great hall, then swiftly muted.

Trumpets blared, and a leather-lunged herald shouted:

"Dragonmaster Lord Hal Kailas of Kalabas, Member, King's Household, Defender of the Throne, Hero of Deraine, accompanied by Lady Khiri Carstares."

The trumpets sounded again, and Hal bowed to Khiri, took her hand, and started down the long staircase to the dance floor.

"You barbarian," Khiri hissed.

"That's what the king pays me to be," Hal agreed amiably.

"You could have waited until after the ball," she whispered. "Or . . . or else seduced me earlier, and given me time enough to straighten up."

Hal leered at her.

"My lusty impulses couldn't be restrained."

"If the king asks why my hair's mussed—and . . . and other things are awry—what would happen if I told him the truth?"

"That you're a horny devil who can't keep her hands off

me?" Hal asked. "He'd probably chuckle in the beard he doesn't have."

"You!"

"I love you," Hal said.

"And I you," Khiri said. "Sex maniac. And at least we got you bathed enough times so you don't smell that much like a dragon anymore."

They were halfway down the staircase, and Hal looked out over the bejeweled crowd, most of the men in dress uniform hung with medals and ribbons, the women, save for a scattering of ranking officers, magnificently gowned.

Kailas was six feet, brown-haired with green eyes. His face, when smiling, could be attractive. But he smiled seldom these days. War had hardened his features. Seeing, and bringing, too much death had made his face cold, watchful.

Hal wore black thigh boots, tight white breeches, a red tunic, almost hidden by decorations, with gold epaulettes and shoulder straps as befitted his rank, and a very practical-looking dagger at his belt. Against regulations, he was bareheaded.

Hal Kailas was just twenty-four.

Khiri Carstares was nineteen, as tall as Hal, dark-haired, with violet eyes. She wore a stylish gown, with less of a flare than common, ending a handspan above the floor, green with minimal white lace piping, elbow-length gloves, and white slippers. A jeweled necklace cascaded around her neck, matched by bracelets on wrist and ankle.

The trumpets blared again behind them, and the herald called:

"Lord Cantabri of Black Island," and a host of decorations, "accompanied by his wife, Lady Cantabri."

Hal looked over his shoulder, saw the tall warrior with the hard yellow eyes of a hunting tiger and scarred face coming down the stairs, in full dress uniform. His wife was small, a few years younger than Cantabri, and was dressed simply and expensively.

Hal continued on down to the floor, still limping from his leg wound at the battle of Aude, stopped Khiri until Cantabri joined them.

"You look wonderful, Lord Bab," Hal said, still not used to calling the man by his first name.

"Maybe," Cantabri snapped. "But what are we doing here, dancing to the king's command, when we ought to be across the water, killing Roche?"

"Bab!" his wife said sharply. "Behave."

Hal almost laughed.

"Why," he said, "we're doing just as you said, dancing to the king's command."

A baron came up, and Kailas and Khiri moved away, as other notables were announced.

"Does he think about anything other than slaughter, ever?" Khiri wondered.

Hal pretended to think.

"Yes, actually. I once caught him in a light moment, musing about maiming."

He fielded two cups of punch, gave one to Khiri.

But Cantabri had asked a good question.

Aude had fallen almost two months earlier, after a brutal siege. The Roche forces had fallen back from the ruined city in order, and taken fighting positions only ten miles from the battleground.

Hal knew why Deraine hadn't continued the attack—the siege had been most expensive, and the first line troops had been decimated.

Replacements had been rushed in, most barely trained, and with them came supplies, including new dragons for the dragon squadrons.

But the Deraine army still held in place.

Then came the surprise—more than thirty of the highest-ranking officers had been ordered to leave their formations in the charge of their second in commands, and journey, with all haste, to Deraine's capital of Rozen, "to await the king's pleasure."

That had sent Cantabri off. "What, for more medals, and leaving the damned Roche to keep rebuilding their damned army? That's plain foolishness!"

Hal agreed.

But King Asir's ways were set, and so the officers, with a scattering of enlisted men who'd distinguished themselves in the siege, obeyed.

Surprisingly, some of those summoned were Sagene, Deraine's not-always-wholehearted allies, with the written approval of the country's Council of Barons.

All of them, enlisted to generals, were cosseted in their journey north through Sagene to the Free City of Paestum, across the Chicor Straits, and upriver to Rozen.

They were ordered, to their great surprise, to take quarters in the king's castle, a high honor, and to stand by for further orders.

So far, that had consisted of being commanded to attend this ball.

Hal had thought wryly of his estates granted by the king somewhere north, next to Sir Bab's own holdings. They purportedly included several thousand acres, included dairy land, some islands, half a dozen villages, fishing rights, as well as a mansion here in Rozen. He'd seen none of them yet—the war was an all-encompassing beast. The closest he'd come was being notified of his monthly rentals and profits, paid into an account at a merchant bank recommended by Sir Bab.

Someday, before he was killed, he hoped to see his lands.

But those were thoughts for another day.

Now he and Khiri, who had been orphaned by the war and owned estates far vaster than anything of Hal's, were here, in the palace.

Allowances had been paid for new uniforms, and gowns

for the ladies who might not be able to afford them. Tailors scuttled to the castle with orders to have their wares finished within two days.

Hal, who would have preferred to be back with his flight, training the new fliers and dragons, had learned to keep his mouth shut on occasion, and so put aside his impatience, and passed the time sleeping or dancing close attendance on Khiri.

Speaking of which, as the band started playing again, he took her by the hand and led her to the dance floor.

He was intercepted by Sir Thom Lowess, the taleteller who'd decided, some time ago, that part of his duties were to build Hal's reputation.

Sir Thom had also introduced Hal and Khiri, and so was very large in both their hearts.

He greeted them effusively, saying how glad he was that Hal had lived through the battle, and "covered yourself with even greater glory."

Kailas was embarrassed. Khiri tried to change the subject, saying perhaps they'd have a chance to have dinner with Lowess at his cluttered mansion.

"You might," Lowess said, holding back a grin. "You might, indeed, Lady Khiri."

"And what's wrong with me?" Hal asked.

"Nothing. Nothing at all," Lowess said, holding back a chortle. "Other than you'll notice the punch is remarkably weak, so even the hotheads won't have an excuse for their wits not being about them. Now, I must go."

He bustled away.

"That man and his trade are a perfect match," Khiri said. "He couldn't keep a secret if you threatened him with . . . with whatever you threaten a taleteller with."

"True," Hal agreed.

They both noticed something at the same time—equerries, in royal livery, were moving through the crowd, stopping here and there. Hal saw them pause at Cantabri, at Lord Egibi,

Commander of the First Army, Lord Desmoceras, Sagene Commander of the Second Army, other high-rankers.

One stopped at Limingo, the king's most talented sorcerer, who was accompanied by a lithe young man both Hal and Khiri agreed could only be described as beautiful.

Something besides a formal dance was transpiring.

Hal wondered how long it would be before he was told.

Kailas was rather astonished when one of the equerries came to him, bowed, and said, "His Royal Majesty summons you to an audience in the chamber beyond the green door."

He didn't wait for a response, but passed on.

"Interesting," Hal said.

"And there goes my dance . . . and romance," Khiri murmured.

2

The room was large, a grandiose living room, with comfortable chairs in a large semicircle, end tables next to them. Hal noted the tables had pitchers of iced water, nothing stronger.

Clearly the king had not summoned anyone for a celebration.

Around the room were the toughest fighters and most skilled commanders of Deraine's southern armies.

Something was very much in the offing.

Hal caught Limingo the magician's eye, raised an eyebrow. The wizard shook his head in equal ignorance as to what was going on.

The short, fat equerry Hal remembered from his ennoblement ceremony came into the room.

"All kneel for His Majesty," he ordered.

Everyone obeyed, except for the Sagenes, who, Hal was impressed to see, at least bent a knee as King Asir entered the room. It appeared the age-old enmity between Sagene and Deraine might be lessening.

Asir was short, stocky, and wore simple robes as was his style. Hal thought his eyes looked even more tired than the last time he'd seen him.

The war was grinding on everyone.

"Sit down," Asir said. "Thank you for attending me."
Behind him, Sir Thom Lowess entered the room, waited by
the door.

"What I'm going to tell you will, no doubt, displease some.
As well as," and he pointedly looked at Hal and Sir Bab,
"please others.

"This invitation was extended to all of you as part of a
grand deception.

"I know that some of you have been loud in your unhappiness that I have not ordered our armies to follow up on their
advantage at Aude." Again, he looked at Cantabri, smiled
slightly.

"That was not accidental. First, it was necessary to rebuild
the Deraine and Sagene units in the field, and give our soldiers
a bit of a breather. Second, it took some ambassadorial con-
ferring with the barons of Sagene until we were in full
agreement as to the next stage.

"But now our forces are strong again, and our soldiers
have had a rest.

"It is late summer, and the word is being spread that it is
too late in the season to be mounting another campaign, and
that we will be taking up winter quarters and securing the
supply line from the ocean down the Comtal River to Aude.

"In fact, shovels, canvas and other pioneering tools have
been loudly dispatched to Aude.

"Because of this planned inactivity, I decided to have a
grand award ceremony for my victorious soldiers.

"There *shall* be medals awarded, but all of what I just said
is a crock of shit."

There was a mutter around the room, a bit of laughter, a
bit of shock. There were those who weren't familiar with the
king's bluntness.

"My intentions are, in fact, to mount an attack on the
Roche positions beyond Aude, striking in a great crescent

with heavily guarded flanks. I intend to smash a hole in their lines, then turn left and right, turn loose my heavy cavalry and force their surrender.

"With that gaping hole, the way will be clear to the Roche capital of Carcaor, and the war's end."

There was a stir of excitement.

"Forgive me, Your Highness," a general said. "I applaud your audacity. But what does this attack have to do with us being here instead of with our troops?

"Did you want personal contact, to make sure we understand your orders?"

"Hardly," Asir said. "By this stage of the war, those who have trouble understanding are either serving in a rear echelon somewhere . . . or they're dead.

"You are the centerpiece of my deception.

"For those of you in this room, there'll be no comfortable rest here in the palace, although no one beyond these walls will know of it.

"The celebrating and feasts will go on, and those men still outside, and your ladies, will be my guests until the battle is mounted.

"Sir Thom, here, for those of you who aren't fortunate enough to be his friend, is probably the best, and most trusted, taleteller in either of our two kingdoms.

"I'm afraid that his credibility may be a bit shattered by what I'm requiring of him."

Lowess smiled, clearly not worried about that.

"He'll be putting out stories on a regular basis about the men and women he's interviewing, particularly our most steel-fanged heroes, some of whom are relaxing, more of whom are talking about their plans to wreak havoc on the Roche come spring.

"All—or as many as Sir Thom can connive—of your names will be taken in vain.

"Meantime, those of you here will be leaving before dawn

tomorrow, back for Sagene and your soldiery. Since the weather is portending storms, which Limingo and his wizards shall be casting, you'll travel in covered omnibuses, as if you were just another convoy of replacements, if a bit more heavily escorted than normal.

"My equerries have already gone out to your units, and have provided them with written orders, which they are then instructed to return to the bearer, which shall give them an understanding on what is planned.

"I want the attack mounted within two days, no more, after your return to Aude."

A general whistled.

The king nodded. "Not long at all. And we shall attack without warning, without any probing attacks.

"This is the chanciest part, that the Roche may have prepared surprise defenses, although I'll have Limingo, and a small task force, journey south with you, with orders to magically search the Roche lines."

"But won't we be missed here?" an elderly general asked, a trifle plaintively.

"No," the king said. "There'll be soldiers wearing your uniforms, accompanying your wives or . . . or friends, that'll be seen from a distance."

The older man looked worried.

"I'll add," the king went on, "that all of them have been ensorcelled so there won't be any possibility of . . . problems."

Evidently the older man had, or thought he had, a wandering wife, for he visibly relaxed. Again, there was a bit of laughter from those who seemed to know.

"Obviously," the king said, "you can tell your wives, since we need their cooperation, although you must swear them to complete secrecy, for millions of lives, and perhaps even the fate of the kingdom, depend on this deception being carried off."

"I'll add," Sir Thom put in, "that there'll be no chance—or almost no chance—for any gossip to spread the tale. The king has officially told me that this gathering is intended to give his generals complete relaxation, and they are not to be burdened with any cares of the outside world."

"Easy to say, Sir Thom," a lord said. "But you don't have my wife, who'll kill anyone who tries to stop her from shopping, now that we're in the capital."

"Some of our most exclusive shops will be bringing their wares to the castle," Sir Thom said. "I doubt if anyone will be angered by the fact the tradesmen with them may not be as knowledgeable about silks and such as they should, because in reality they're disguised members of the royal household, since the items offered will be heavily discounted."

"Also," the king said, "the humbug will only last for five, perhaps six days, until you've returned to Aude, and battle is joined.

"I shall not keep you from the dance. Enjoy yourselves as best you can, but please don't tell anyone until you've returned to your quarters.

"You'll have enough time on the journey to study the plans that've been drawn up for you.

"Oh. One small thing. I know it won't alleviate your ladies' rage at me, but there'll be large amounts of leave after the battle. That's all."

He stood, and again the soldiers knelt or bowed.

"Lord Cantabri, Lord Kailas, if you'd remain for a moment?"

The king waited until everyone had left.

"Your orders are a bit different from the others.

"Lord Cantabri, I require you to remain in readiness at the armies' headquarters. Your unit has already been turned over to your subordinate for the nonce.

"Your duties during the battle are to watch closely for any hesitation, malfeasance or loss of command in any of the units, including the Sagene.

"You will have written authorization from me, and from

the Council of Barons, to take over any faltering unit, Derainian or Sagene, and to relieve any officer you see fit.

"I am very damned tired of our plans being ruined by the hesitant or the timid."

Asir didn't wait for Cantabri to say anything, but turned to Hal.

"Your orders are somewhat simpler. I know your flight was badly stricken during the battle, and the new fliers I had sent to you are hardly combat-ready.

"I want you to take over three other flights—I've specified them in my orders to you—and provide aerial security all along the front. I don't want any Roche peepers overlooking our plans for the offensive.

"If they present themselves, make the new black dragon formations and their commander, Yasin, a particular target. We must have, and keep, command of the skies.

"When the attack is under way, you're to revert to normal duties, and provide reconnaissance for our advance, plus, with your added strength, defense for other, smaller flights.

"I know your formation won't be fully trained for what I require, but I have full confidence that you'll fulfill your duties.

"I promised you a great squadron of dragons that I simply haven't been able to provide.

"These four flights, once the battle is over, will be the formation of that squadron. At present, that is the best I can do."

The king smiled wryly.

"I hope that the war will not last long enough beyond this coming victory for you to accomplish that.

"Do either of you have any questions?"

Cantabri and Hal shook their heads.

"I'll give you a further order, but hardly in writing. Neither of you has my permission to get killed. I'll need both of you in the days to come. "That is all."

*

"You swear," Khiri said fiercely, "you didn't know anything about this little game of the king's?"

"I swear."

"You swear you're not going to do anything dumb like get killed?"

"I swear. The king personally forbade it."

"You swear you'll be making love to me enough, for the rest of the night, to make me think you never left when you come back?"

"Uh . . . I swear."

"Then come here. And one more thing. You'd better be thinking, while you're off getting all dragon-stinky again, about doing something wonderful for me when you get back."

"Like what?" Hal asked.

"You just think about it."

3

Hal heard the eager honk of a dragon before he came in sight of his base. His horse reared at the sound, and he quieted it.

"If you're going to be dragon-shy," he said, "you'd best learn different . . . or think about becoming glue."

The dragon, a single rider aboard, passed about twenty feet overhead. It was green, with broad red streaks across its belly, and a male.

The monster was fully grown, almost fifty feet long, with twenty feet of that in its lethal tail. On the ground, it would stand around twelve feet tall. Its wings stretched wide, almost a hundred feet.

A dragon, in spite of its size and wingspread, could fly primarily because of its light bone structure, although it preferred, in its wild state, to spend as much time gliding as working its wings.

The warm-blooded creature had a heavily armored body, slightly less on its stomach.

Second only to man in its lethality, the dragon's weaponry was considerable: the head had twin horns, with impressive fangs, and spikes on either side of the snaky neck.

Its most deadly weapon was its tail, which the dragon cleverly used as a flail, a bludgeon, or a strangling cord.

At the neck's base rose a carapace, and behind it a flat area suitable for riders. "Tamed" dragons had holes drilled painlessly in the carapace for saddlery to be bolted into.

All four of its legs had three-taloned claws. There were also talons on the forward edge of the leathery wing.

No one quite knew how intelligent dragons were. In fact, no one had the slightest idea how to measure that intelligence. Everyone agreed they were smarter than dogs or apes, but as smart as a child? Some said they were, others said they were merely quick to learn.

Hal thought dragons were very smart at being dragons, and he didn't try to measure them against men.

Secretly, he thought that if he did, man might come up a bit short.

From here, Hal could smell the musky odor of the animal after it'd passed, and he grinned slightly, remembering Khiri's words about him getting dragon-stinky. Although there were other times she said she liked the faint smell that hung about him, times that made his body stir a little.

He put those thoughts aside as he turned off the "main road," just a rutted highway along the Comtal River, up a bluff to his landing field.

A few miles east, on the far side of the river, was the half-ruined city of Aude, and, beyond that, unseen, the front lines.

Hal hadn't recognized the dragon's rider, guessed he or she must be one of the three new flights he'd been given.

That might present a problem, he knew. He wouldn't have time to evaluate the other three flights, let alone put his stamp of command on them before this, hopefully war-winning, battle began.

Which brought up the idle thought—what would Hal propose doing when the war ended?

That begged the probability that he'd die before it was

over. He remembered the words of his first, real love, Saslic, who believed "there won't be any after the war for a dragon flier." She'd died in the disastrous invasion of Kalabas, and taken a piece of Hal's soul with her.

Hal caught his mind's reel, lashed it back into line. There were many things to worry about first.

Such as the crowded near-chaos he saw as he topped the rise and looked down on his command.

Actually, it wasn't that bad, considering that the art of dragon riding had only been accomplished in his lifetime, and the idea of using dragons for anything other than aerial stunting hadn't begun until after the first year of the war, not half a dozen years before.

Especially since he'd planned the field to not only harbor, but conceal, a single flight of dragons.

At full strength, a flight numbered fifteen dragons and their fliers, and eighty men and women whose only duties were to keep the dragons healthy and flying. There were teamsters for the huge oxen-drawn wagons used to move the dragons about when they weren't being flown, cooks, clerks, blacksmiths, orderlies, leathersmiths, veterinarians, and, Hal thought, provided grudgingly, a doctor to keep the distinctly secondary humans functioning.

Hal had been most proud of finding this spot, heavily forested, ideal to hide the huge dragon barns. He'd had the brush and smaller trees selectively cut, concealing the other buildings of the base, and the paths were laid out to hide the movement of men.

He knew what happened when a field was discovered by the Roche dragon fliers, and had wreaked revenge for such a bloody attack.

Now, four flights had been jammed into this field. Trees were being cut down, tents for humans erected and canvas being pulled over skeletal iron hoops to shelter the dragons.

Men and women scurried here, there, intent on their tasks

under shouting warrants, and dragons blared, some angry, some pleased, no doubt being fed, others just perplexed at being ripped from their homes to this new base.

A sentry blocked the road. Hal identified himself, and the sentry saluted smartly, and bade him welcome.

Very good, Hal thought. It appeared someone was in charge.

She was.

Mynta Gart came from under a dragon shelter. She was heavyset, an ex-seaman, the 11th Flight's adjutant, and a skilled combat flier. One of Hal's inflexible rules that he would be applying to the new flights was no deadwood. Everyone, no matter what his assignment, was expected to turn to and keep the dragons, and their fliers, ready for combat, and do whatever service required when they came back.

"Welcome back, sir."

"It's nice to be back," Hal said truthfully.

Gart smiled slightly.

"I think we're all doomed, for there's no place that calls home to us except this damned war."

"That," Hal said, thinking of his estates, his villages, and such, "is an unfortunate truth."

"We were told you were on your way back," Gart said. "Or, rather, I was."

"And given other information to boot?"

"Yessir."

"Let's talk."

"Yessir."

Hal followed her not to the shabby tent he'd been inhabiting before he left for Deraine, but to a large, double-walled pyramid tent, with a wooden floor.

Hal dismounted, slung his saddlebags over his shoulder, and Gart shouted up a hostler, who took the animal away.

"Quite a mansion," he said.

"Anyone who leads four flights deserves a bit of comfort," Gart said. "You'll note the shelving, the chairs, all made of packing crates."

"How are the other fliers?"

"I assumed you'd ask that," Gart said. "Equally posh."

Both of them were talking around what was foremost in their minds—the coming offensive. Hal told Gart to sit down.

"How ready are we?" Hal asked.

Gart considered.

"Overall, we're at full strength, men and dragons.

"The eleventh is in fair shape. I've had all of the replacements in the air as much as possible, and had the experienced fliers working with the new dragons. All of the fliers and dragons have had flights over the lines, and are, hopefully, learning to spot a dragon in the air, and a catapult on the ground.

"I've put Sir Loren in charge of the training."

"Good," Hal said. "He's easy with the ignorant. And speaking of ignorant—and the old crew—have we heard from Farren? How is he healing?"

"I don't know how he's healing, but he's here," Gart said. "And troublesome as usual."

Sir Loren Damian, with Mynta and Farren Mariah, had graduated from flying school with Hal and two others, now dead. Farren Mariah had landed on the Aude rooftop with Hal, and saved his life before going down wounded.

Hal had no idea what had happened to the other nineteen graduates of the school and assumed the worst.

"If you agree," Gart said, "I'll have the trainees fly in pairs, new with old, when the attack starts."

"Fine," Hal approved. "At least, as long as it's a standard recon. Don't put any of the virgins on anything shaky. And I'll give orders for any of them to break for the camp if they encounter black dragons. Speaking of which . . . ?"

"We've sighted one or two," Gart said. "Well on their side of the lines, and damned skittish. I went after one, with three backups, and the bastard went for the ground and home. I turned back."

"Good," Hal said. "Maybe I got Yasin a bit twitchy when I shot him at Aude.

"Now, what about my new flights?"

Gart told him things were probably as good as could be expected.

"I can't really say, precisely, sir," she went on. "There's things I like, things I don't like, about all three of them."

"Details," Hal asked, then changed his mind. "No. I'll see for myself. First the dragons, then I'll meet with all four flights, then, this evening, with the fliers in—I assume it's still standing and you didn't put it off limits—their club."

"Off limits? Hah," Gart said. "Farren's decided he is the new officer in charge of the booze, so I think that shack is completely out of my—and probably your—hands."

"That's our Farren," Hal said. "Give me a moment to unpack my saddlebags, and then let's have a look at the shelters."

"Leave the baggage. I've appointed an orderly to take care of you."

"But—"

"But me no buts," Gart said firmly. "You've got over three hundred women and men to take care of. You don't need to be mending your own socks."

Hal didn't think that was very democratic, but conceded her point for the moment.

"I'll be back in a few minutes," Gart said, leaving the tent.

Hal got up, stretched, looking out at the bustle around him. He turned, trying to figure what he would do with an orderly, hoping Gart didn't mean for him—or her—to share the tent.

"Knock, knock," a voice said.

Hal knew without turning who it was.

"Enter, Farren."

"Arrh," the small, wiry man said, obeying. "Now that you're a full squadron commander, do I have to kowtow and genu-genu-genuflect?"

"I'll not hold my breath waiting for you to do that."

"That's wise, boss. Most wise," Mariah said. He looked around the shelves. "Yer back an hour, and there's never a bottle about. Th' damned king's gone and reformed you."

"I doubt that," Hal said. "How're your wounds?"

"Still stiff, still bothersome."

"Why didn't you stay in hospital, or on leave?"

"The thought occurred," Farren said. "Howsomever, there were ladies who seemed to feel marriage'd set right with Mrs Mariah's favorite son. Two of 'em."

"And so you fled?"

"Aye, back to the safety of the front. I don't mind a deal of grief when I go, but I'm not of a mind to start makin' widows and orryphins. At least, not by the set."

Uninvited, he straddled a chair.

"So, we're off to war, eh?"

Hal tried to hide his reaction, evidently without success as Farren snickered.

"What in the hells makes you think that?" Kailas tried, somewhat feebly.

"Ah, when you're supposed to be gone, livin' on the viands of His Royal Hisself for a couple weeks, and then, just after you're gone, all these couriers start zippin' up and down the highways, and Gart's bustling about making sure the pikes are all sharpened and the talons burnisheed . . . what's a poor lad to think?

"Although, bein' as how there's a grand collection of numbnuts about, I've said nothing, feeling there's none worthy of my wizardy talents."

Mariah did have a bit of the Talent—he claimed his grandfather, back in the warrens of Rozen, had been a notorious witch. And every now and then his spell-casting did work, most spectacularly when he managed to dump a wagon of shit on the dragon-fliers' school's most hated warrant.

"And you're making no move to dig in your duffle and buy me a congratulatory drink," he said.

"I brought no alcohol with me."

"For certain there's a battle brewing . . . not to mention your brain's a bit askew."

"Perhaps." Hal looked at Mariah steadily. "So what's your call on the squadron?"

Farren held out his hand flat, wiggled it back and forth.

"That good?"

"I'm a real old soldier now, you know," he said, "and there's none to match the old ones who've gone past and under."

Mariah turned serious.

"You know, your dragon, Storm's finally on the mend."

Hal hadn't wanted to ask about the dragon who'd saved his life time and again, but that was, of course, the reason he'd wanted to visit the barns first.

"He took a bad turn, but as soon as I got back, and put him on a diet of farmer s stolen pigs and the odd sheepdog, he started back to health, instanter. And I'll not say whether I cast a spell or six to help."

There was a moment of silence.

"All right," Hal said. "You've wormed it out of me with your wiles. We are going to battle. The day after tomorrow."

Farren made a noise.

"All that traveling up to Deraine was a deception," Kailas went on. "Now, secretly, everyone's back, and we're to attack at once."

"Without running patrols, or aerial searches?"

"Exactly."

"That," Farren said, scratching the top of his head, "will give a bit of surprise, I suppose.

"And we should be hopin' the Roche haven't got their own surprises."

"We'll be taking dragon flights up along the lines, as close to crossing as we can get, tomorrow morning," Hal said. "And by the way, you and Gart are grounded until the battle."

"F'why?" Mariah's voice was an outraged shriek.

"If you go down, you might be made to talk."

"Me? Course, if captured, I always planned on singing like . . . like one of those birds out there on the tree, assuming the dragons haven't snapped 'em all up for snacks. But Gart'll never talk.

"And you need me up in the skies, fightin' ready for good ol' Deraine. So you might want to be rethinking that order, or I'll sic a dragon on you."

Hal considered. He'd wanted them on the field to keep order, but if it was to keep the secret from leaking, why was he himself proposing to fly? Not to mention the probability that somebody in the ground forces would let slip, and the Roche would find out the secret.

Hopefully it wouldn't be believed by Roche headquarters, which, when Hal had gone north, had been commanded by Duke Garcao Yasin, head of the Household Regiments and, it was rumored with a snicker, Queen Norcia's "confidant."

Or, if it was, there wouldn't be time enough for the Roche to prepare their positions against the onslaught.

No, keeping Gart and Mariah in the rear, just for the stupid reason of giving them one more day of life, made no sense.

"All right," Hal growled. "Order cancelled. You'll fly with me, as my backup."

Farren grinned.

"I deserve no less. Dragonmaster and Companion of the King."

Hal threw a dagger, fortunately sheathed, at him.

Storm was indeed mending, kept in a pen by himself.

He recognized Hal's voice, staggered to his feet, and yawned.

Hal's stomach curled at the dragon's breath.

"We fed 'im a passel of geese an hour or so ago," the stableman said. "T'at hits 'im like a padded hammer."

The veterinarian accompanying Gart and Kailas nodded. "We use poultices, and let the dragon sleep as much as possible, then feed him the best. Your man Mariah's been most helpful."

Storm, having given Kailas recognition, curled around himself, flapped his great wings with a noise like leathery thunder, curled back up, and put a paw over his nose.

"When will he be flying?"

"Oh . . . short flights, no strain, maybe two weeks," the vet, whose name was Tupilco, said. "No combat for a month."

Hal turned to Gart.

"I assume you've another dragon for me?"

"Already chosen," Gart said. "You can take her up any time you wish."

"After I talk to the flight commanders."

They went on through the cavernous, if drafty, shelters. The 11th's older dragons were a bit battered, but all were well-fed and were stirring about, as if expecting the action to come.

The 34th's were almost as spotless. The 18th's were worn-looking, but Cabet's flight had seen much action. The 20th's were acceptable, although the stablemen could have done with a bit of a cleanup.

Hal's dragon, Gart said, was named Sweetie.

Hal winced.

Gart shrugged.

"A little letter came with her. She was hand-raised by some backcountry girl, then given to Garadice when he came through looking for remounts.

"You could always write a letter to the girl—we've got her address—telling her how fond you are of her dragon."

Gart snickered.

Hal gave her a hateful look.

"We'll leave that for Sir Thom, on his next pass through."

"And I'll make sure to tell him," Gart said, and burst into laughter.

"I'm delighted," Hal said, "to be taking charge of such a *cheerful* frigging squadron. I think I shall have all of you whipped."

Cabet was the first flight commander to arrive, which was just what Hal had expected. He was a small, precise man, with a small, precise mustache, and was known as a worrier. That may have hurt his digestion, but it kept his flight away from any foreseeable disasters, since Cabet managed everything very carefully.

Mariah had told Hal it was rumored that Cabet planned just when, and where, he would take his twice-daily shits, and was about to elaborate when Kailas told him to get out.

Pisidia, of the 20th, was the second. He was lean, with a hungry face and close-trimmed beard. He wore an eyepatch, from a wound early in the war, and Hal wondered how he was able to judge perspective with just the one eye. He, too, had a good reputation for taking care of his fliers and drag-ons, without much regard for the niceties of uniform and decorum the army preferred.

Last to arrive, announced by a booming laugh, was Richia of the 34th. He was heavy, with a jolly face, a booming voice, and ready laughter. It wasn't until you looked closely at him, and saw his eyes were hard, cold, those of a hunter, that you knew him to be a dangerous man.

"Sit down," Hal said. "You know who I am, and I know, at least by name, all of you."

He glanced out of his tent, made sure the posted sentry was just beyond earshot.

"I have no idea what you think of being put under my command, and don't, at least for the moment, give a damn.

"There is no time whatsoever for personalities."

He told them of the upcoming attack.

All reacted in their own ways: Cabet began scribbling notes on a slip of paper; Pisidia began stroking his beard, looking into nowhere, making plans; and Richia barked a surprised laugh.

"This could be a chancy thing," Cabet said, looking up.

"Very much so," Hal agreed. "Which is why I don't propose to make any changes in the way you gentlemen have run your flights, at least until this offensive is over.

"However, I will issue one standing order. I want your new fliers to be paired with experienced ones, as much as possible. I realize, Cabet, that you were badly struck during the siege, and won't be able to always follow that order, but do what you can.

"I'll also want a flight of four fliers on constant standby. We'll take one from each flight.

"This will be a reaction element. If any Roche dragons approach this field, this flight is to get in the air and climb for altitude, whether or not orders are issued, and engage the bastards.

"I don't fancy the thought of having any of *Ky* Yasin's black dragons springing a surprise on us.

"And, speaking of Yasin, any black dragons that are sighted on our side of the lines are to be attacked immediately, always in pairs or more, and hopefully will be outnumbered.

"I want any other Roche dragons to be treated roughly, and I have no interest in any fair fighting or dueling.

"Kill the Roche when we see them, don't let them escape, especially if they might have gathered any information."

"What about claims, Lord Kailas?" Richia asked.

"I don't understand."

"Say one flier attacks a dragon, wounds it. He loses the dragon for a moment, and another flier kills it. Who gets the victory?"

"It'll be split," Hal said, "and I'll let you figure out how you'll explain to your granddaughter that you killed half a dragon."

There were smiles.

"Whatever your policies are," Hal said, "you might know mine. The only dead dragon I care about counting is the last one of the war."

"So we've heard," Pisidia said. "I think getting numbers-happy does no good for a flight—or a squadron's—morale."

"And I quite disagree," Richia said. Cabet said nothing.

"Another thing," Kailas went on. "I don't much give a damn about titles, or even being sirred, except when things are formal or when there's outsiders about."

"Good," Pisidia said. "There's too much flumpf about this war already."

"Formality has its place," Cabet said.

"Agreed," Pisidia said. "In the king's court, not over here."

"Well," Cabet said, "my men and women will continue to show proper respect."

"Run your flights as you wish, as I've said," Hal said, standing.

"Now, before I talk to the squadron, I want to wring a few knots out, and make sure I still know how to fly."

"Well," Hal said, "let's see what we're made of." He shuddered a little. "Sweetie."

The dark red and brown dragon looked over her shoulder at him, blatted. Hal couldn't tell anything from that, but, since the beast seemed to know the name she'd been given, that meant he wouldn't be able to give her a better name.

He grabbed a scale, pulled himself up into the saddle, settled back and tested the reins. They were taut.

Kailas noted about half the squadron had drifted to the sides of the field, and were watching carefully, pretending to do other tasks.

This was part of the ritual of command.

If a dragon flier was worth a damn, he or she believed she was the absolute best. Around outsiders, a flier would swear that her flight commander was just a touch better, although that came from greater experience, not ability, of course.

So when a new commander appeared, it was expected that he would show his flying ability—unless he was one of those who led from the ground, which meant being held in complete, if unspoken, contempt.

It was stupid but Hal admitted to himself that he believed the same as any other flier.

"You're going to hate me before this is over," he said, and kicked the dragon in its slats.

It lumbered forward, lurching from side to side, its huge wings reaching out.

Then the awkwardness was gone as the dragon was in the air, wings striking down hard, lifting more slowly, and the ground shrank below Hal's boots.

He let Sweetie climb to about two thousand feet, then, using reins and feet at first, tapped her into a series of turns. She responded well, and Hal went through another series, this time just with the reins.

Again, the dragon obeyed.

Hal realized he shouldn't have been surprised—she supposedly had been trained by Garadice, a dragonmaster before the war, when the term meant a man who traveled about, giving rides, and doing stunts. Garadice's son had trained and served with Hal, and had been killed by Yasin's black dragons, during the siege.

He put the dragon into a gentle bank, first right, then left.

He was looking far out, beyond the torn city of Aude, beyond the ribbons of trenches, where far mountains were lined in pink and gold as the sun moved down the horizon.

He thought he would give almost everything to be over those mountains, with nothing but this dragon under him, perhaps a pack with necessities lashed behind him, Khiri clinging behind him, or even on her own, and no one and nothing to worry about, except where he might land, buy a sheep for his mount, and cook a sparse meal before laying out his bedroll. At the next dawn, he'd be flying on, into the unknown, day after day, until . . . until he didn't know when.

He brought himself back to the present.

"Now, let's see how you can work," he said.

The field was just below him. He put Sweetie into a steep dive with his reins, let the ground close a little, pulled her out at what he guessed was a thousand feet.

He sent the dragon into another, more gentle dive, brought her back, turning, almost flying inverted, leveled her on an opposite course.

"Good," he said. "You can have a pullet or something with your dinner. You didn't lose a foot of height."

Again, he sent Sweetie down and down, the ground rushing up at him, the wind whipping at him. The dragon honked protest, but didn't try to disobey.

At about three hundred feet he pulled back on the reins, and the dragon's wings flared.

As it pulled out, a bit over a hundred feet above the field, he tapped its left side, and, obediently, the monster banked, its great wing almost brushing the ground. He brought it out, then turned, and turned again, alternately left and right, then sent it down, and pulled hard.

The dragon's wings snapped out, and its feet reached for the ground, and they were on the ground.

Handlers ran up, and Hal slid from the saddle, tossing his reins across it.

He took a moment to pat the dragon's head as it snaked back, looking at him.

"Good," he approved.

His fliers were approaching, Farren Mariah at their head.

"Not bad . . . sir," he said. "I'd never trust a new one to be that well mannered."

"That's because you didn't pay close enough attention in dragon school," Hal said. "I don't have any trouble keeping my mounts in hand."

Farren sneered.

Hal had a wagon pulled into the middle of the field, and the flights surrounded him.

"Sit down if you want," he said, and did the same on the wagon's railing.

"Welcome to the First Dragon Squadron. We're trying something new, and I'll explain, later, just what I've got in mind. But I hope that my ideas are right, and this squadron is the signpost of the future.

"You know who I am . . . and I've yet to learn about you.

"Let's hope it's as pleasant an experience as it should be.

"We're going to be very busy for the next couple of weeks, which I can't tell you about yet.

"So the old bullshit about my tent's always open for anyone with problems can be set aside for a while. I'm going to be busy, and you are as well.

"There won't be any time for lollygagging or farting around for a while, so don't give me, my officers, and my warrants any grief.

"If you do, you'll reap the harvest you sowed.

"But I don't think there'll be any problems. You old soldiers know what's expected, and you new ones can study their ways and do the same.

"I don't expect anyone to have any questions this early in the game, and I'm not sure I've learned the answers yet.

"I'm not one who believes in speeches, and, as you've seen, am not worth much at making them.

"So fall out now for supper.

"That's all."

*

That night, Hal stood in a corner of the pilot's club, nursing half a pint of weak beer, and watching his pilots.

They were more than a little nervous. The braver tried to draw him out, into a drinking contest or a game. He smiled thanks at the offer, but refused.

The veterans he knew greeted him, and were bought a pint. In Sir Loren's case, that meant a mug of nonalcoholic cider. He was as abstemious before combat as always.

The replacements listened to Hal's easy banter with envy, and thought to themselves that they'd soon be considered worthy of equality as well.

Mariah was behind the bar with Chincha, and Hal was pleased they were still together and, frankly, still alive.

Hal and Gart talked briefly, and he knew the fliers were trying to figure out what they were discussing. If they'd known, they might've worried.

Hal was noting the fliers who were drinking heavily. It wasn't that he gave a damn how much someone drank—by this stage of the war alcohol was the only thing keeping some of the more worn fliers together.

But drink wasn't a good habit for a young flier to get into, unless he knew what he was doing.

The old hands could take care of themselves.

As a gentle guidance Kailas was scheduling all of the replacements who were guzzling heavily for a dawn patrol. They'd quickly learn that flying with a hangover wasn't the easiest way to spend a morning.

And he would be in the air with them.

Hal's orderly was a man old enough to be his father, named Uluch, who looked on anything and everything sourly. But he couldn't be faulted in his duties.

Kailas was quite grateful, especially in the mornings, he hadn't gotten some godsdamned chatterbox.

*

Hal desperately wanted to work his squadron to the bone, to make sure they were as sharp as possible before the battle.

But he knew better. An exhausted flier can be a dead one, very rapidly.

So he ran his patrols up and down the lines. There was only one fight, and he wasn't lucky enough to get in on it, and it was inconclusive, the two Roche dragons being chased back over Aude.

It seemed the Roche fliers were holding to their side of the lines as well.

Kailas wondered what orders they were under, but there were no clues.

"His" 11th Flight was armed with the repeating crossbows that Farren Mariah had designed. The other three had motley collections of conventional crossbows and short recurve bows. Hal hadn't the time to order the repeaters from Joh Kious's works far to the north in Paestum—yet another thing that would have to wait until after the battle.

So Hal stewed, and flew, and waited.

And then the day of battle came.

4

The Derainian and Sagene soldiers came out of their hides with a roar, just at dawn, running hard across the dead space between the lines, closing with the Roche.

From the Deraine lines, ballistae hurled boulders into the Roche, and catapults shot their great arrows at clumps of officers on horseback.

Hal's squadron had been in the air for an hour, and dawn had come first to them, while the ground below was still black, and shadowed.

He had the 11th, the best armed, at about three thousand feet, the 18th at the same level, the other two squadrons providing high cover two thousand feet overhead.

The replacements were gaping down at the battle, the first real fight they'd seen, in spite of orders to keep their eyes on the sky.

Sir Loren Damian was the first to spot the Roche dragons, half a dozen of them, scattered, climbing for height.

Communication on dragonback was done by trumpet. He blatted his horn twice—enemy in sight—and Hal replied with one long note—attack.

The dragons, wings partially folding, dropped on the Roche, talons working in and out, mouths open, hissing, screaming, at least as eager for a fight as any human.

Above and in front of the straggling Roche monsters were two black dragons, a third as big as the others, known for their ferocity.

Hal steered Sweetie down on the lead one.

He had his crossbow lifted, aimed, and there was nothing else in the universe but that black dragon, and its rider, who gaped up at him, then fumbled an arrow out, and nocked it on his bowstring.

But it was too late.

Hal's bolt took the rider low in the shoulder, almost in his heart. The rider screeched, dropped his bow, and lost his foothold in his stirrups. He swayed, feet flailing, grabbing for a handhold, forgetting the reins, and slid out of his saddle, and fell, twisting, toward the battleground below.

Then Hal was past and below the Roche. He fought Sweetie back up, toward the other black.

But Farren Mariah had sent a bolt into that beast's neck, and he lost interest in the battle, and dove for the ground and home.

The air was a swirl of color, red, green, yellow, brown, and then it was empty of the Roche.

There were three Roche dragons fleeing, and nothing in the air around but Hal's squadron. In the distance, near the flank of the attack, Hal saw other dragons swarming, other Derainian flights.

That was the first skirmish, and Hal did a fast count. He'd lost no one, and relaxed slightly.

He took Sweetie back to height, and then he could look down at the battle.

It was a swarming melee, already behind the Roche positions. Deraine and Sagene had driven the enemy back, and were pressing hard. Reinforcements were coming up from the

Derainian rear, and, on the flanks, the heavy cavalry was being sent in.

They cut in and out of the struggle, and again the Roche fell back.

But they fell back without panic, holding their formations, and the cavalry could do no more than nip at their heels, since horses will never charge into anything solid, whether a hedge or a spear-wall.

Hal didn't see any strong point he might take the 11th, the most experienced in ground attack, down against, so didn't consider wasting his crossbow bolts.

The Roche fell back and back, all that long hot day. Hal sent his dragons to the base in sections for the men and animals to feed, for no more Roche fliers came up to challenge them.

Hal had a bit of hope that maybe, just maybe, this attack would do what it was intended to, break the Roche, and the way would be clear for the Deraine and Sagene armies to close on Roche's capital of Carcaor, and end the war.

But that evening the Roche took up new positions, and Hal, swooping over them, saw the positions had been prepared earlier.

He was no general, but didn't think that boded well for the offensive.

His fliers were a chatter of excitement, not wanting to sleep, ready to fight their first battle over and over again. But Hal ordered them to eat and then to their tents, refusing Mariah permission to open "his" club for more than one beer per flier.

The next morning, they were up and in the air in darkness.

Below, Deraine and Sagene pressed the attack.

Again, the Roche fell back, still orderly.

By nightfall, the new line of battle was five miles or more into the Roche rear. But Hal had seen no sign of mass surrender, no sign of panic.

The cavalry tried to flank the retreating Roche infantry, but the Roche cavalry blocked them, and there were savage, inconclusive skirmishes.

Hal's fliers spotted Roche cavalry lying in ambush three times, dove, dropping streamers with notes wrapped around pebbles to give a warning.

Hal wished there was some way he could drop more than a pebble. A huge damned boulder on a Roche's head. But dragons couldn't lift anything that heavy, and it would take much training, even if such a device existed, for a flier to be able to hit a target.

Hal, feeling frustrated, with Mariah just behind him, went flashing over the Roche positions not fifty feet in the air. Heavy bolts from catapults flashed up at him, and he came to his senses and broke off the attack.

When they landed for a meal, Farren gave Hal a bolt almost as tall as Mariah, said he'd plucked it from the air at the top of its flight, and added, "Hee-roes might skedaddle along first in line, flashin' their cocks about, but it's their poor damned wingmates trudging along behind that give the fine target.

"No more showin' off, boss, unless there's something to shoot at, orright? That big damned arrow damned near put paid to your favorite flier."

Hal, grateful that Mariah had said this out of earshot of the other fliers, nodded sheepishly.

The attack went on, and every day the Roche fell farther and farther back.

Hal, isolated in his camp and in the sky, had no idea what the high command and Sir Bab thought was going on, but one evening, as he was making the last high patrol, it came to him.

In the distance, to the east, mountains rose, now no more than five leagues distant.

Hal suddenly thought he knew what the Roche intended: to

retreat on this open ground, which gave neither side the advantage, and take position on the mountains. They could hold the heights until doomsday, and let Deraine and Sagene waste their best trying to reach them.

He thought of darting back, and giving his illumination to Sir Bab, then caught himself. Cantabri was hardly a fool, and could read a map as well as anyone, even if he was deathly afraid of going aloft.

And even if Hal's surmise was a revelation, what could be done about it?

Deraine and Sagene were attacking as hard as they could, leaving a strew of bodies as they advanced.

What more could be done?

A week later, the dragon fliers were groggy with fatigue.

They still hadn't had any major engagements with the Roche fliers—their command seemed to be keeping them back, though for what end, Hal had no idea.

Kailas knew if the fliers were tired, even though they were able to land at a base every evening, eat hot food, and sleep in a bed, what shape could the poor damned infantry and cavalry be in?

He remembered his days as a light cavalryman, before he became a dragon flier, and how he and his horse would be staggering with fatigue after scouting for an advance and skirmishing around the battle.

The Roche couldn't be in any better shape. It was demoralizing to retreat, and retreat again, even though done in an orderly manner.

By now, it was indeed clear the Roche had a plan, and it was just as Hal had feared: pull back to the mountains, really not more than a low range of bluffs, and then bleed Deraine and Sagene.

So what if Deraine was occupying Roche territory?

Queen Norcia couldn't care much about this borderland,

sparsely settled and garrisoned by the occasional castle.

When Deraine came on one of these, rather than waste time with a siege, they bypassed the stronghold. They could come back later and reduce it.

The retreat went on. There were no surprises to be found from the sky, and, after each dawn's reconnaissance, Hal started taking his dragons low, as soon as the Roche moved back.

They shot down soldiers, got lucky from time to time and killed an officer or courier. Hal was doing this not only to do what little he could to help, but out of pure frustration.

Kailas was flying back to his base, the setting sun reddening his wind-battered face, when it came to him.

He realized, and felt like a dolt for his thickness, what Khiri might have meant, back in Rozen, when she told him that he would be expected to do something wonderful when he came back to Deraine.

He landed, turned Sweetie over to a handler, and hurried to his tent.

> *Dearest Khiri,*
> *First, I love you, and I'm glad that you love an idiot like me. When I return, would you grant me the greatest honor I could have, and agree to marry me?*

And then the ground began to rise, and, day by day, the Roche retreated less, and the Deraine and Sagene forces fought uphill.

There was no estimate of casualties so far, but there were rumors that entire Deraine units had been so decimated they had to be pulled from the fight.

And things could only get worse.

Then Hal was summoned by Sir Bab Cantabri to a conference.

It was short.

The attendees were commanders of units on the Deraine west flank. Hal noted no Sagene officers.

"This is a last ditch effort," Cantabri said, "that I'll take command of. We've got to stop the bastards short of the hill-crests, or this war could become even more of a stalemate than it's been."

He pulled the cover off a large-scale map. The canvas, as it fell to the dirt floor of the tent, rattled loudly in the silence.

"Our scouts have found a break in their lines, over here." He tapped the map.

"Our attack will be simple," he said. "We're going to feint on the right with cavalry, then hit hard on the left, here, into this break, with units we've moved away from the center.

"If we can break them, or round their flank, we can roll up their lines like carpets.

"If they stop us . . . Well, that's the end of campaigning for this year, and we'll be fighting them from here. But if we can smash them before they reach the top, before they start digging in . . ."

He didn't finish the sentence, nor need to. His hard yellow eyes gleamed.

Once more, Hal and half his squadron were in the skies before sunrise, but the hope that this attack would be the breakthrough had torn away their fatigue.

Hal had offered to recon the target area, been refused by Cantabri, who was afraid any extra attention in the area might tip off the Roche.

"Just like we'll attack without any magic. But once we start moving," he said, "anything you can give me will be appreciated."

Even this high in the air, Hal heard the thin blare of the trumpets as the attack was mounted.

Tired soldiery heaved themselves out of the temporary

shelters they'd found at the end of the previous day's fighting, started forward.

There was a first, then a second, then a third line of dirty, weary infantrymen who went in.

Hal heard a trumpet toot twice, looked over as Pisidia swung close.

"Down there," the man shouted. "Just in front of the point men."

Hal looked, couldn't see anything, cursed that a one-eyed man could see more sharply, dug his glass from a saddle boot, sent Sweetie around.

"There's a great cave down there," Pisidia shouted. "Or, rather, a whole bunch of 'em."

Then Hal saw the darkness of the entrances. Worse, he saw the flash of metal, and the flutter of banners as hidden Roche soldiers charged out into the midst of the Deraine formations.

"Son of a bitch!" Hal swore. "They've laid a trap. Pisidia, take the message back."

He blew four blasts—assemble on me—and his squadron, scattered across the front, flew toward him. It might be a waste, but it was the least he could do.

He blew two blasts, and, pulling back the cocking handle of his crossbow, let a bolt drop down into the track.

Hal snapped reins down on Sweetie's neck, sent her into a dive, aiming for the mouth of one cave.

Other fliers saw the targets, and followed him in.

Hal brought his dragon out of its dive low, almost at treetop level, spotted a man on horseback, shot at him, hit his horse. He let go the reins, and worked the slide of his crossbow, reloading it.

Maybe he should've listened to Farren's advice about trusting a new dragon too much, for as he looked for another target, holding on to Sweetie's sides with his legs, something startled the dragon, and she jinked sharply sideways.

Hal lost his balance, slid out of his saddle, dropping the

crossbow, grabbing for a hold on Sweetie's wing, scrabbling at the leathery skin, losing his grip again, and falling.

He dropped only about twenty feet, smashed into the top of a tree, tumbled, grabbing for branches, had one, and was safe for a moment.

Then the branch snapped, and dropped him, bruised, bleeding, ten feet to a soft landing on moss.

He rolled to his feet, reaching for his sword.

But there were five, no, a dozen, shouting Roche soldiers rushing at him, spears ready to be cast, arrows ready to be fired.

5

The two leading Roche soldiers skidded to a halt, seeing Hal's ready sword. But they were experienced soldiers. One nodded to his fellow, and they split up, coming in on each side of Kailas.

One chanced a lunge, and Hal's sword flashed out, cutting the spearhead off at the haft. The second struck at almost the same moment, and Hal barely jumped out of the way.

That man was muttering, "Dirty buggerin' dragon bastard, kilt my brother, kilt my brother, dragon bastard, cut your balls off an' feed 'em to you for supper."

Hal saved his breath.

The man drew back, then thrust with his spear, cutting an ugly gash in Hal's thigh.

His fellow had dropped his spear, had a sword out and was about to attack.

Kailas was surrounded by half a dozen soldiers, cheering for the two going in on Hal when a shout came.

"Stop!"

They pretended not to hear, and the one whose brother had supposedly been killed by dragons tried another thrust, which was parried, and then Hal counterthrust, and lopped the man's ear off.

"You heard me," the shout came again. "Stop and stand to attention!"

One soldier turned, reluctantly, reacted.

"Attention!" he shouted, and this time the knot of Roche froze as ordered.

A young officer—Hal didn't remember Roche ranks that well—pelted in. He carried no weapon, only a short stick.

"When I give an order, it's to be obeyed at once," the man snarled. "All of you are on bunker detail when we get to the top of this hill.

"Now, you, Teat, get your butt to the herbist, and tell him what you've got is only what you deserve, so he's not to worry about causing you a little pain.

"Move out!

"You, and you . . . You'll escort the prisoner—and I'll be with you to make sure you don't kill him 'attempting to escape'—to company central."

For the first time, he appeared to take notice of Hal.

"And you, drop that damned sword, and unbelt that dagger.

"For you the war's over, unless you keep trying to play hero."

Hal looked around, saw, high overhead, one of his dragons, swooping down, a hundred feet above, which might as well have been leagues.

He dropped his sword, unfastened his belt, and let it fall.

Hal Kailas, Dragonmaster, was a prisoner of the Roche.

But the officer was the only one who might actually believe Kailas's war was over.

The Roche company commander seemed not at all disturbed that his headquarters was no more than one guard, one warrant, two runners, and a tattered chunk of canvas tied between two trees.

"Your name?" he asked.

"Lord Kailas of Kalabas," Hal said.

One of the runners gulped, whispered "Th' Dragonmaster!" and got a cold look from the officer.

"Your rank?"

"Commander."

"Of what?"

"I'm sorry," Kailas said. "That's information I can't give you."

"No," the officer agreed. "But we read the stories your taletellers publish. I know you're the Lord Commander of the First Dragon Squadron, and far too rich a dish for peasants like us."

He looked at the officer who'd saved Kailas's life.

"You'll be commended for this. Now, take this man—and two more guards—and escort him back to regimental headquarters."

"Yessir."

The commander turned back to Hal, and Kailas knew what he was going to say before he spoke.

"Congratulations. Your war is over. And you'll be alive, if you cooperate, to see our great victory."

Hal didn't reply.

The young officer noted that Hal was limping.

"Can you walk?"

"I can walk," Hal said.

"If you're having trouble, I can assemble a party of litter-bearers."

"I can walk," Hal repeated.

Regimental headquarters was a collection of skillfully camouflaged tents in a wide ravine that had been covered with netting stuffed with branches that was just back of the military crest of the hill Hal had been attacking when he was brought down.

A beribboned officer whistled when he heard who Hal was, immediately relieved the young officer, and took charge.

Hal had wanted to get an address for the young man and, when the war was over, planned to write him a letter, thanking him for his life. But the man saluted, and was gone.

The ranking officer was about to ask Hal a question when he noticed the dark stain seeping through his trousers.

"You're wounded!"

Hal nodded.

"Then you're for hospital, at once. I'll have no one of your rank ever thinking we Roche are uncivilized."

He shouted for a sergeant, and bade him assemble stretcher-bearers.

"There," the man said. "There'll be an officer arrive in the hospital to interr—ask you certain questions.

"Man, you look pale. Sit down, here, on this stump.

"My leg *is* starting to bother me," Hal admitted.

"Our potions and spells are the best," the man said. "So, for you, the war is over."

Hal almost laughed at the stock chorus, but then noted the officer had spoken with an unconscious note of wistfulness.

Pain was starting to wash over Hal, but he forced alertness, trying to take note of everything as the stretcher-bearers carried him to the rear.

A great deal of the trip was done under cover staked poles, with camouflaged netting over them. Hal didn't know if the Roche did this because they thought Deraine and Sagene were barbarians who'd attack the wounded, or because they didn't want any aerial observers being able to make estimates of the casualty rate.

There'd been tales that the Roche were beaten, stumbling, on their last legs in this offensive.

Hal saw no evidence of that.

The troops were battered and their uniforms were worn . . . but no more than their enemies.

Kailas was able to verify his idea of the Roche plan—that they'd be holding, and fighting, from this hill range. He saw almost as many soldiers working hard with mattock and shovel, making entrenchments, as moving forward with weaponry into the dying battle.

There were no signs that the king's great offensive would end the war, or be more than another killing ground for both sides.

The hospital was a good ten miles from the front, exactly laid out rows of tents, with graveled walkways between them, and white-painted signboards. Orderlies came and went, and wizards, chirurgeons and what Hal heard called nursing sisters, women in a sort of uniform, a gray smock and cap.

He was being logged in, and questions asked, when, very suddenly, the world swam about his shoulders, and he sank into peaceful, pain-free unconsciousness.

Hal awoke to a throbbing pain. He must have moaned, for a voice said, "Ah. Good. If it hurts, it means your leg is yet alive."

He opened his eyes, saw a rather tubby man bending over him. He had a thin fringe of hair, a rather scruffy beard he was trying to grow long, without much success, and plain robes.

"I am Mage Nizva," he announced. "I am in charge of the healing spells in this and three other tents."

"And I'm—"

"Hush. Talk later," Nizva said. "Concentrate your attention on letting the spells I've cast, and the herbs I've poulticed your wounds with, take effect."

Hal lifted his head from the cot he was on. The light was dim in the long tent, seventy-five feet by about twenty feet. Every few feet was another cot, with another wounded man, and a scattering of women, on it.

Somewhere Kailas had lost his bloodied uniform, and wore only a gray ankle-length nightshirt.

Hal nodded understanding to Nizva, and sank back into a stupor.

Hal was awakened by the preposterous shout: "Lie at . . . attention!"

He lifted an eyelid, saw a host of medal-heavy officers stamp into the tent, dancing attendance on an even more beribboned man with a very impressive white beard.

"I am General Ottignies," he said. "And I greet you, honored warriors of the Roche nation, in the name of Her Most Blessed Highness, Queen Norcia, who this day has authorized me to provide you with rewards for your heroism."

He started down the row of wounded, two aides beside him. At each bed, he'd select a medal, say a few words, pin the medal to the soldier's blankets, salute, move on.

Hal couldn't believe what was evidently about to happen.

But it happened.

General Ottignies looked benevolently down at Hal.

"Healing nicely?"

Hal nodded.

"Good. Good. We need warriors like yourself back at the front, to ensure our great victory."

He took a medal, attached it to Hal's blanket, saluted.

Hal found strength, was able to feebly return the salute.

"Good man," Ottignies said, not understanding the uncontrollable grin on Hal's face, and moved on to the next hero.

Hal reached down, lifted the medal. It was a tasteful bronze medallion, with a ribbon of red and white. On it was scribed: HERO OF ROCHE: SECOND CLASS.

Kailas choked back laughter, wondered what he'd have to do to become a First Class Hero.

"Oh gods," Nizva breathed. "You're not one of us at all."

"No," Hal said.

"You're Derainian?"

"Yes."

"Named?"

"Kailas." Hal left the title off, thought of substituting Second Class Hero Kailas, decided that might not be the wisest.

"Kailas?" Nizva said. "The Dragonmaster? The one who seems to have disappeared here?"

"I haven't disappeared," Hal corrected. "I've been lying here quietly all the time, letting your potions heal me, as you ordered."

"Oh my gods," Nizva said again, and scuttled up the aisle.

So the easy days were over now, Hal thought. He'd been playing sickling for two weeks, and was far stronger than he admitted to the sisters or the mage.

Now it was time to plan his escape.

6

Hal knew little of the fine art of escaping. There were many classes required of the soldiers of Deraine, from saluting and recognizing your superiors to how to wash yourself.

But escaping wasn't on the list.

Hal growled at that, but realized the subject was fairly out of bounds, since no proper soldier even conceded the possibility of capture.

Nevertheless . . .

Hal had been told by someone, he disremembered who, that the best time to escape was the soonest after capture. The longer you were in captivity, the farther you'd be taken from your own lines, and, as likely as not, the worse physical shape you were in, since no army has ever fed its prisoners better than its own soldiery.

His wound had kept him from making an immediate break, but now it was healing nicely.

Now that he'd been discovered, no doubt the next step would be moving him into a proper prison.

Best he try to get away from this hospital.

The problem was finding a set of clothes. He had an idea

that wandering the roads of Roche wearing nothing but his damned gray nightshirt might make him noticeable.

Shortly before being unmasked, even though he'd not planned his hiding, he had noticed there were some civilian workers in the hospital, no doubt local farmers who were pleased to be getting paid while their fields were being plowed into wasteland by war.

The Roche being what they were, the civilians changed into gray coveralls, almost uniformlike, when they arrived for work.

Hal had realized this when he was up just at dawn, using the jakes, and saw the workers troop in to undertake their tasks.

The day after his uncovering, Hal slid out of bed before false dawn, and crept out of the ward. He was grateful that Nizva and the hospital authorities, whose strength was trying to heal, not play at war, hadn't gotten around to putting a guard on him.

The changing tent was next to the two cooking tents. Hal hid in the flies of a nearby tent as the sky brightened, and the day shift came in.

The night workers left a few minutes later, and Hal went into the changing tent, and looked for a costume.

It took only a few minutes to discover one that fit him quite well, and made him out to be a rural bumpkin, wearing a knee-length smock, short breeches, a hat that had seen better centuries, and a padded coat.

Unfortunately, its owner didn't seem to be that fond of bathing, but maybe that would be an advantage. If he was checked by a patrol, he would wave his armpits at them, and flee in the ensuing disgust.

Hal went out of the tent, and away from the hospital as quickly as he could.

He was pleased to see that his leg only troubled him for a short while; then the muscles loosened up, and he could travel easily.

He wanted to run, knew better, and so strolled along, a straw between his teeth, thinking farming thoughts, in the event some magician might be able to read his mind. That was an impossibility, he'd been told, but wizards were always coming up with new evils.

He spotted a pitchfork leaning against a fence and added that to his costume. In the event, it could also serve as a weapon. Kailas had no intention of returning to captivity without a fight.

He'd quickly oriented himself by the scattering of troops moving forward, and the sun. That gave him compass directions.

His plan, and he thought it idiot clever, was, rather than go directly for the front lines, to head east for half a day, then turn, depending on what presented itself, either north or south for a distance.

That wasn't the direction anyone would expect him to take, and, besides, it could be very chancy trying to creep through the battle zone, where both sides were keyed to kill any strangers.

Once he was wide of the battle area, then he'd turn back to the west, and make his way into Deraine/Sagene lines.

Or so he hoped.

Hal's stomach reminded him that he was escaping with his victuals a bit on the nonexistent side.

It was midday, and he'd only stopped twice for water at abandoned wells, and was feeling peckish. Some nice peasant bread and cheese would set right with him, or even some of that horrible broth the hospital had insisted was strengthening.

The lane he was following curved down into a village. Even though he didn't have any money, maybe there'd be a field with . . . with whatever was ripe. It was summer, so that should be almost everything.

He was halfway through the village, just short of a stone bridge over a small river, when he realized there was something strange about the hamlet. There was no one, not man, woman, child, about. Nor did he see any dogs or animals.

He was about to dart up a side lane, and skirt the rest of the village when a man came out of an alleyway, and shouted, "Halt! Drop that damned pitchfork!"

Since he had a drawn bow, aimed steadily at Hal's side, Kailas obeyed.

"Who're you?" the soldier said, advancing on Hal.

Kailas had spent some time coming up with a story.

"No one," he said, putting on a panicked peasant's fear-babble that wasn't really that much of a put on. "Or, maybe, I'm just named Haifas. Haifas. I went out from my home yesterday, wanting to join up, but they wouldn't have me, saying something about my heart's got an echo to it or something, and I'd probably fall over dead on them, so I guess I'm going back to the farm, and—"

"Silence," the soldier snapped. "You should have seen the sign, back about a mile, saying this road and the village have been sequestered by the army for quartering, and no civvies are allowed."

"Oh," Hal said. There hadn't been a sign.

"I saw something," he said. "But I've got no schooling. Never learned to figure."

"Ain't no excuse," the soldier said, coming still closer. "And you talk real good for somebody that's not lettered."

He glowered at Hal, and Hal tried to look innocent and doltish.

"C'mon," he said. "We'll go to my warrant, and he'll decide what to do with you."

Hal didn't think that was a good idea.

He snapkicked the soldier under the breastbone, and bow and arrow dropped in the dust of the road.

Before the soldier could recover, Kailas kicked him very

hard, twice, in the face. He heard the man's neck snap on the second kick.

Hal dragged the man to the bridge, hoisted him up on the parapet, then bethought himself.

He went through the man's pouch, found a few coppers, one silver piece. He thought about taking the soldier's dagger, or his bow and arrow, but knew that'd be grounds for instant execution if he was caught with them.

He tipped the body over, into the river, got the bow and arrow and tossed them over as well, then took off running.

He hoped that the soldier's warrant and officers would think the man had an accident.

But he didn't think that was very likely.

He chanced no more villages, even with his coins, trying to put as much distance between himself and his victim as possible.

Hal skirted villages, going through the fields.

Fortunately, the district had been pretty well cleaned out of civilians, with only a stubborn couple here and there holding to their farms.

Barking dogs alerted him to these.

At dusk, he was exhausted. He found a deserted farm, whose cornfields hadn't been totally stripped by foraging soldiers, got half a dozen ears.

He took those to a brook, stripped, washed, then thought about dinner.

He saw a few fish flicker, tried to grab them from beneath, the way he'd been told country boys did it. He had no success at all.

Which left him with the raw corn.

Hal wished he'd learned how to cobble fire up from a bow or sharp rock, but in his travels he'd always paid a few pence for a firespell.

The ears of corn sat there.

Hal realized that, for all his complaining, like all soldiers do, being in the army hadn't been the worst he'd had it.

Before the war, before he found a dragon flier to follow, and had been a wandering laborer, he'd eaten raw corn, stolen or begged from a farmer's field more than once.

And, he reminded himself, had the shits to go with it.

But there was nothing else, and so he ate, rather greedily, the six ears.

It was still light when he curled up. But there was a bit of a wind, and he wished he had a blanket or two to pull around him.

That, also, was missing.

Hal could've felt sorry for himself, but he took deep breaths of the air of freedom and forgot his complaints.

He closed his eyes, sure he'd be tossing on this bare ground for most of the night, but when he opened them, it was false dawn.

Kailas came to his feet, muscles screaking at him, did some stretching exercises after washing and defecating, wincing at the leaves he used to clean himself.

Then he moved on.

At the next crossroads, he decided he'd turn north or south, whichever looked easiest.

The area he was moving through must've been a long-term bivouac for the Roche army. The huts had been stripped, their roofs and the fencing around the neat fields used for firewood.

It was a desolation, barren of animals and people.

Hal knew this sort of desolation well—all armies brought that in their wake, little caring how the people of the district would live after the soldiers moved on.

He was about halfway across one such blasted heath when he heard the calloo of hunters.

But there was nothing to hunt around here.

Nothing but Hal Kailases.

The hunters were a formation of light cavalry.

There was another call, and the formation, almost a company, Hal guessed, lowered its lances and came after him.

Kailas wanted to run, but there was nowhere to run to.

He couldn't even put his back to a wall and go down fighting.

Hal waited, hoping the bastards wouldn't just lance him and ride on.

That would be a particularly pointless way to die, forgotten in this forgotten land.

The lead rider, an officer, reined his horse in short feet of spitting Kailas.

"And what," he said, voice mockingly triumphant, "do we have here?"

The cavalrymen trussed Hal like a shot deer, threw him over the back of a horse. Kailas bounced along until the horsemen found a camp of infantry, rode into its center, shouting for the unit commander.

When he arrived, they kicked Kailas off the horse.

"Got somebody for you," their officer said. "Either a deserter or maybe that escaped dragon rider everybody's hot after."

The infantry took him to the nearest town, turned him over to the authorities.

Two beefy officers frog-marched him into the tiny prison, opened a cell, pushed him inside.

One of them stared at Kailas consideringly, then, without warning, hit Hal in the stomach, very hard.

Kailas caved in.

The man picked Kailas up by the hair, and smashed his face into the stone wall.

That, for some time, was all that Kailas knew.

7

Kailas came to, slumped on one of the jail's iron cots. He sat up, tasting the cold iron of blood in his mouth. He checked his teeth with a probing tongue. The front ones were just a little wobbly, but would tighten up.

His nose . . . he was sort of glad there wasn't a glass in the cell because it felt like it'd been well and truly mashed. Oh well. Supposedly something like that made people think a man was more rugged.

He heard a laugh, looked up, saw the guard who'd smashed him into the wall.

"Damn Deraine!" the man snarled gleefully. "Ha'n't been for orders, we coulda done a lot worse."

Hal made no answer, just kept looking at him.

The man's grin twitched away; then he scurried off.

Hal dreamed of having five minutes alone with the bastard, knew it'd never happen, leaned back against the wall, began planning.

So he was caught again.

The next stage would be a transfer to a prison camp. Or,

perhaps, execution, but Kailas thought that was unlikely.

The best time to make another escape would be when he was being transferred, since the warders at a camp would be more experienced at dealing with prisoners of war.

There was a basin of water on the table, and he washed the blood off his face, rinsed his mouth, and spat into the chamber pot.

From somewhere, something he'd read or been told came to him: a prisoner of war is just a soldier in different dress, and it's still his duty to fight back, in any way he could.

Another, rather forlorn thought came, and he counted days. It would be just about today, or maybe the day before, when Khiri would be getting his proposal of marriage.

And then, no doubt, they'd announce he was missing in action. Hal didn't think any of his squadron had seen him once he'd landed in the treetops, and would most likely think him slain.

Poor Khiri.

Now, he thought wryly, what would happen to his estates, since he had neither kith nor kin, his only survivors his parents, far north in the bleak mining village?

Not that that mattered much to him. As tramps, wanderers and soldiers say, "I came into this world without a coin, and expect to leave it the same."

And he'd had nothing before the king's benisons, so what did it matter, anyway?

Now all that he could do was wait, and be ready to seize any advantage.

For two days, no one spoke to him, and he lived on the thin soup the jail served its prisoners.

He was the only prisoner of war, being fairly far behind the lines.

The guards regularly beat the other prisoners who came in, but they left Kailas alone. The other, civilian prisoners were whipped jackals or, at best, snapping terriers. Kailas was a crouching panther, and he made the guards—and the other prisoners—nervous.

He forced himself to hide his impatience, never pacing back and forth as his restlessness wanted, not speaking to anyone, trying to get as much sleep as he could, knowing he'd need it when he was out in the wilds again.

He was slightly proud of himself for thinking "when," not "if."

On the third day, he had two visitors.

He knew both of them, but in vastly different ways.

The first was a haughty-looking knight, wearing several decorations, who announced himself as Sir Suiyan Tutuila, by the grace of Queen Norcia, Respecter of Prisoners. Hal avoided a snicker. It was clear, from his expression, that Sir Suiyan thought prisoners could best be protected in a sealed dungeon, or, a little better, at the end of a rope.

He was the archetypal jailer Kailas had encountered in his prewar wanderings.

He glared at Hal with pursed lips, said no more for the moment.

The other man Hal knew, first from a card game years before the war, when his gambling-besotted dragonmaster, Athelny of the Dragons, had been euchred out of his flying show, and then his life.

The second time he'd seen him was over the rooftops of Aude, when his black dragon had swooped low, trying to kill Hal. Hal had sent a crossbow bolt into the man's shoulder, cursed at his bad aim.

He was *Ky* Bayle Yasin, a superb flier, the first, as far as Hal knew, to fly the dreaded black dragons into battle, and, unless he'd been promoted recently, Commander of the First Guards Dragon Squadron.

He was slender, a bit older than Hal, and when, before,

he'd had the fringe of a beard, now was clean-shaven. Hal noted he was starting to bald.

"Lord Kailas," he said. "It is pleasant finally meeting you."

He refrained from the obvious addition, "under these circumstances."

"And I feel the same," Hal said. "How is your wound?"

Yasin flickered slightly. "Quite healed, thank you."

"Pity," Hal said, in a way he'd heard the word used by a great lord.

"You will be silent," Sir Suiyan said. "It is not the place for a prisoner to jeer at his betters."

Hal didn't respond.

"*Ky* Yasin wishes to have a few words with you," Suiyan went on. "Privately.

"And of course, I'm pleased to grant a great *Ky*'s wish." He stood, his chair scraping on the stone floor, and went out.

"I wanted to see you for several reasons," Yasin said. "One is disbelief that you allowed yourself to be captured at all. Most of *my* fliers would prefer to die in battle instead of facing this humiliation."

Again, Hal held his tongue. If he hadn't learned some control at jibes after all this time in the army, he was a fool indeed.

"Another is to inform you that your secret weapon was captured as well, and is being duplicated by our craftsmen. I refer, of course, to that repeating crossbow.

"Still another is to warn you that you are potentially in desperate circumstances.

"There was a soldier killed the same day you made your escape from the hospital."

Hal pretended surprise.

"You were captured wearing civilian clothes. By any tribunal, a soldier so dressed is a spy, and qualifies for immediate execution. If he also has murdered a member of Her Royal

Highness's Armed Forces . . . the penalty could be adjudged in quite a severe fashion.

"Sir Suiyan wanted to bring you up before a tribunal right now, but I convinced him you were far too valuable to die a villain's death. I hope you prove me right.

"Of course you don't know what I'm talking about."

"I truthfully don't," Hal said.

Yasin smiled for a brief instant.

"I came here to offer you the chance of safety and life after the war. If you provide certain information to us—nothing that would cause any of your men or women to come to harm—I can guarantee this murder will be forgotten, and you'll spend the rest of the war in safety, in a rather comfortable detention camp."

Hal started to respond, but Yasin cut him off.

"Of course, I don't expect you to agree at the moment, but I wanted to put the idea in your mind. You may take advantage of it at any time you wish."

"Thank you," Hal said. "But I don't think I'll be accepting."

"Of course not," Yasin agreed, standing. "But keep my offer in mind.

"Something else. I thought you might appreciate news of the war. It is not going well.

"For Deraine and Sagene. Your idiot generals are persisting in attacking in the salient they were lucky enough to create.

"But our positions are completely impregnable, and Deraine and Sagene soldiers are being wasted trying to climb the heights.

"They will, no doubt, continue with their niggling attacks through the winter, weakening themselves, and then, in the spring, we'll mount a great offensive, and recover not only the territory we've lost, including Aude and the Comtal River to the sea, but drive a stake into Sagene, and convince Deraine that she has no interest in Sagene's fate.

"I'm hardly confiding any military secrets by saying that."

He went to the door, opened it, and Sir Suiyan came back in.

"I assume *Ky* Yasin has told you of the danger you're in," Suiyan said. "I can promise you that if I can get any evidence of the crime you committed, I'll gladly see you face the ax . . . or other forms of punishment that are even uglier.

"For the moment, though, I can tell you that you will not continue to be lodged here."

"Just when I was starting to enjoy country life."

Tutuila's lip twitched.

"You might just be able to escape, and a man of your rank, holding information that Roche could well use, cannot be treated in such a casual fashion.

"Roche has several prison camps that are much harder to escape from.

"And one that is impossible."

Yasin broke in.

"It's far to the east and north, up an estuary. Its name is Castle Mulde. There we've sent prisoners who've successfully escaped other camps, high-rankers such as yourself, and dragon fliers, whose value is incomparable."

Hal suddenly remembered the late traitor Nanpean Tregony, who'd claimed to be in such a camp before making his escape from the Roche, and thought perhaps that part of the man's lies might just have been truth. Or maybe Tregony had only heard of Castle Mulde.

"I could be melodramatic," he went on, "and say that you'll rot there. But that's not the case. Nothing so exciting ever happens. There you can sit and wither, while life—and the war—goes on around you.

"I understand, from captured broadsheets, that you are the favorite of a certain noble popsy," Yasin went on. "I wonder how long it'll take her to find another bedmate.

"Or bedmates.

"I, frankly, have learned never to trust a woman alone for more than a few weeks."

Without bracing, without any giveaway, Hal kicked Yasin in the balls.

Yasin howled, clutched at himself.

Tutuila shouted for guards.

Hal was going after him, rounding the table, when three men burst in.

The one in front was the guard who'd broken Hal's nose.

Hal forgot about Sir Suiyan, and rolled across the table, on his back.

He kicked out, very hard, his feet together, and caught that guard in his chest. Kailas heard ribs crack, was off the table, and stamped on the man's face as he fell.

Then the guards were on him, beating him down.

He went into a ball, dropped to the floor.

Eventually they got tired of kicking him, and dragged him back to his cell.

It had definitely been worth it.

8

They took no chances with Kailas.

When they were ready to move him to Castle Mulde, a wizard and a blacksmith appeared. Black bands were wrapped around his ankles and wrists, and the magician cast a spell that "soldered" them in place.

Kailas was told, cheerily, that none of his escort had any idea of what the counterspell was. Only the mage of Castle Mulde knew.

They chained him to the bed of a wagon, with four guards, plus the teamster and his assistant. Behind that wagon was another, with twelve more guards in it, changed every three hours. Then came a supply wagon.

Twenty light cavalrymen rode in front and behind the convoy.

They set out, from the village Hal had never learned the name of, east, then turned north.

It was still summer, but Hal felt a chill as they continued on. It might have been his imagination.

Twice he saw dragons overhead, and once they were blacks. He assumed Yasin was keeping track of him.

At night, the convoy either stopped in a Roche army camp, or in open country, never chancing an inn or a city.

The head of the escort was a Lieutenant Hoj Anders.

He was solid, big, and his face looked like he'd placed second in several rough-and-ready brawls.

But there was intelligence behind the scars.

And training and experience.

He rode, contentedly, casually, beside Hal's wagon.

Anders was quite talkative, although his eyes never stopped sweeping the countryside and the escort. The slightest mistake by a guard, and the soldier would be ordered off his mount or his wagon, his wrists tied with a long lead to the back of a wagon, and he spent the rest of the shift trying to keep up, stumbling, running, sometimes falling and being dragged.

Anders' conversation was about Castle Mulde, and how incredibly secure it was, Roche's inevitable victory, and how Hal would do himself good by cooperating with the Roche.

"There's half a dozen guards to every prisoner at Castle Mulde," he said. "And they're carefully chosen for intelligence, alertness and patriotism."

"Pity they're not on the front lines," was Hal's reply. "Helping to fight the war, instead of scrounging about the rear."

That got a quick wince from Anders. But he persisted.

The castle was guarded not only by the visible bars and chains, but by magic as well.

"It has a great magician, who's completely devoted to keeping the prisoners secured."

"Therefore one that's not casting spells against our army," Kailas came back.

He may have been chained, only allowed to walk about for an hour in the morning and evening, when he washed and did his ablutions, but Hal kept fighting.

A broken piece of harness, and Hal would loudly sympathize about the poor quality of the Roche leather, and whether the maker wasn't secretly in league with the forces of Deraine, as so many sensible Roche were.

The soldier who cooked for the formation couldn't, and so Hal would lovingly describe how well Deraine, and especially Sagene, soldiers ate, making up the most absurd menus from meals he'd had with Khiri or Sir Thom Lowess.

But it was hard to keep cheerful as the miles creaked past, and they moved deeper into Roche.

Hal kept himself alert not only by chivying the guards, but by studying and memorizing the land they passed through, mostly farmland, with scattered forests.

Kailas had no idea who or what lived in those forests, but they appeared untouched by man, with never a forester or woodsman to be seen. The soldiers became nervous each time the road narrowed and great trees reached high overhead, a seemingly perpetual wind soughing.

Kailas inquired as to the horrid monsters living in these woodlands. Anders told him to shut up, would say nothing else.

In the open country, they passed many small villages, and, at regular intervals, strongly built castles.

Sometimes someone would ride out from them, and be greeted by Anders, and be warned to stand clear, that there was a dangerous man, the Dragonmaster, in the wagon, and they were entitled to cheer him on his way to a lonely doom.

Few did.

All of them were frantic for news of the war and, when told Roche was holding firm, cheered.

Kailas noted there were few noblemen coming out to greet them, mostly women and children.

Similarly, he saw only a scattering of men working the fields. Roche had combed the north well for soldiery.

Anders told him they were bypassing the area's cities, "although there are not that many in these northlands.

"The people are Roche now, but they still remember when

they were but savage tribesmen, before we brought them the benefits of civilization."

"I don't doubt that," Hal said. "Most people value their freedom. That's why we're fighting you, you know. When the war is over, you'll learn about freedom, and that your ruler doesn't always have to keep her boot at your throat."

Anders grunted, kicked his horse to the head of the column.

That was one small victory for Kailas.

But it was hard keeping his morale up.

Hal dreamed, and it was a strange dream, for it was completely real.

He was flying, but he wasn't on the back of a dragon, nor was he suddenly able to fly on his own. He'd had those dreams before, and woke sadly, realizing the limitations of his body.

It took a few moments for him to realize he was no longer a man, but a dragon. A real dragon, for his wing was sore, from a healing injury, and he had other, almost-vanished wounds on his back. He remembered the black dragon that had given them to him, fighting over a collection of stones that man built.

But there were no men on his back now, and he was floating happily in a strong wind.

Below him was the sea, the beginnings of a storm building, the waves white and gray.

He banked, feeling the air, the free air, rush past.

Behind him was land, square fields almost to the edge of the cliffs.

Here and there were small cubbies that Hal, dreaming, recognized as the huts of peasants, huts he thought he'd seen before.

Then there was a huge collection of piled stones, just at the cliff's edge.

Hal recognized it, with a great start.

It was Cayre a Carstares, one of Lady Khiri's holdings on the west coast of Deraine.

It was here that Hal had come to let his wounds heal, where he'd been nursed by Khiri, and where they'd fallen in love.

Hal dove, rolled into a ball, and dropped toward the ocean.

A dim memory came, from the time he was a very young dragon, floating on the current, the storms wailing about him, toward a new land. There had been other dragons around him, young, old.

Now Hal flattened, spread his wings, and the wind coming hard from the sea lifted him almost as high as he'd been.

Again, he was looking out to sea, and he knew what was across a vast ocean, a land where there was death and pain, a land he'd fled when he was a kit.

Then his wing began throbbing, painfully.

Very suddenly, Hal knew who he "was."

He was Storm, his battle dragon, wounded at the siege of Aude. But Storm, the last Hal had seen him, had been recovering from his wounds in a tent across the river Comtal from Aude.

How had he reached Deraine?

But there were more important things, such as a live sheep and some hot mash he had been promised in his comfortable, solitary barn, within the castle walls.

Far below was a tiny dot.

He knew who it was, and dove, then pulled out of his dive, circling.

The dot was a man, a female man, waving at him, and calling.

Hal/Storm brought his legs out, flared his wings, coming in for a landing.

He recognized the female.

It was Khiri, somehow now his keeper and guardian.

Very suddenly, Hal jolted awake in his wagon, feeling silent tears on his cheeks.

He managed to wipe them away, so the bastard Roche wouldn't see them, and mock him.

Hal Kailas slept no more that night, for something in his mind was telling him an obvious lie.

That hadn't been a dream, but for a few moments he'd been Storm, been in his head.

That was quite impossible.

No man could share thoughts with a dragon, nor an animal, any more than a man could read another's thoughts or command his actions.

But those moments of freedom, when he was Storm the dragon, with no rider, no one his master, stayed with him as they traveled on.

For the first time, they entered a smallish city, but moved directly through it to the docks. Here, amid fishing boats, light transports and a scattering of pleasure boats, they boarded a single-masted, large wherry.

There were staples in the deck, an overhead for his shelter. There was a cuddy forward and another overhead at the stern, around the long tiller.

Hal was unchained from his wagon, and his manacles refastened to the wherry's deck.

There were ten sailors, and half of the escort, including Lieutenant Anders, on the boat, when the mooring lines were brought in and the wherry slid off into the sullen waters, letting the current carry it north.

They raised a sail in midriver, let that move them faster toward the sea.

The river, named the Zante, felt hostile to Kailas, brooding, angry, and the small villages they passed were filthy.

Hal noticed, the farther north they traveled, that the villages had palisades around them, but were open to the river. Then the palisades had guard towers at them.

Kailas chanced asking Anders.

"I told you the people of this region were once Roche's enemies. Now, those who've become sensible are regarded as enemies by their once-brothers in the wilderness, particularly when these peaceful peasants are prospering under Roche rule, and are frequently attacked by the savages."

Hal didn't think the villages looked that prosperous, said so.

Anders snorted.

"Perhaps not by your nobleness's standards . . . but they're doing very well compared to the forest barbarians."

"Would you believe," Hal asked, "that before the war I was a destitute commoner, no more than a wandering farm-worker?"

Anders gave him a look that said, very clearly, he certainly wouldn't.

Hal went back to studying the terrain around them as the boat rode downstream toward the sea.

There were marshes, or, once away from the river, heavy forests that seemed to stretch on forever.

The river grew wider, then wider still, almost half a mile from bank to bank.

Once an arrow arced out of the wilderness and splashed down close to the boat.

The soldiers pulled on their armor, and crouched behind the wherry's high bulwarks.

But nothing came out to attack them.

"We shall reach Castle Mulde tomorrow," Anders said.

"A pity," Hal said. "I could travel like this, an endless vacation, forever, in the charming company of you and your fellows."

Anders gave him an odd look.

"By the way," Hal asked innocently, "how far is the castle from the sea?"

"A day's sail," Anders said, then caught himself. "But you

do not need to be knowing anything about the castle's sur-
roundings, for you'll never see, until we are victorious,
anything but its stone walls.

"Or unless," he added, "you decide to accept *Ky* Yasin's
generous offer."

"How could I ever forget," Hal murmured.

They sailed all that night. Anders said the shores were most
hazardous.

"Particularly since," he said with an unpleasant grin, "we
pay fifty pieces of silver for any prisoner captured alive, a
hundred for one dead."

"Silver, eh?" Hal said, seemingly undisturbed. "Too cheap
to afford gold?"

At dawn, they rounded a bend. The Zante River divided into
two channels. In the center, a stone island stood five hundred
feet above the water.

From its cliffs rose Castle Mulde.

A high curtain wall, with a balustrade along the top, circled
the inner wall.

Inside the keep, a central building, six stories high, with
peaked roofs jutting here and there, stood.

Three towers rose from the keep, and there were guards
posted atop them.

Hal saw warders pacing the wall, at close intervals.

All was gray, dripping, lifeless stone.

This was a place that could erode a man's soul, make him
give up his courage, his allegiance, maybe his life.

Hal glanced at Anders, who was staring up at the ominous
castle. For once, he didn't chide Kailas about the impossibility of escape.

He didn't need to.

The sailors manned the wherry's oars, and rowed it out of
the current, to a small dock, where they tied up.

Two soldiers struck off Hal's chains, and helped him onto the dock.

Steps led upward, to the castle's heavy gate.

Hal took the first step, and a gong rang across the valley.

He started, looked at his guards.

They, too, had heard it.

Hal took another step, and another, more dissonant gong came.

Then a third and a fourth.

The instruments, if that was what they were, sounded, booming across the river, at each step as he walked to the gates of Castle Mulde.

9

And then the spell broke.

Raucous laughter rang down, and grinning faces peered over the battlements. The men, and a scattering of women, wore motley, or the remains of Deraine/Sagene uniforms.

"A proper greetin' for the Dragonmaster," a shout came.

Then came a BRRAAACCCK as someone blew a typical flier's welcome through his lips.

Hal recognized the man, vaguely. He'd been one of the dragon fliers lost, feared killed, during the Aude siege.

There was another familiar face, and a third, and then fuming, sputtering Roche guards were muscling the prisoners away from the walls.

There was the rattle of chains, and then a door was unbolted.

Half a dozen Roche soldiers rushed out, surrounded Hal, and bustled him into Castle Mulde.

His escort was taken in another direction, and he lost a chance to throw a final insult at Lieutenant Anders.

A rather large, white-bearded man, wearing the carefully

kept, if tattered, uniform of a Derainian general, stood there, flanking a stone-faced Roche officer.

"Take the prisoner into processing," the Roche ordered, and Hal was muscled off.

He ended up in a small cell, looked about, assuming this would be his new home.

Then a tall, cadaverous-looking man, wearing robes, came into the room. A small wormy sort, wearing Derainian uniform, came in behind him, carrying a case and a wand.

"I am Ungava," the tall man said. "I am the wizard for Castle Mulde. It is my duty to ensure you'll never be able to escape. You'll be moved from here to a proper cell as soon as I've taken care of a couple of matters."

Without looking back, he held out a hand, and the small prisoner smacked the wand into it.

Ungava bowed his head over Hal's chains, muttered a phrase, struck the manacles, and the chains fell away.

Hal felt a moment of hope.

Ungava reached inside his robes, took out an atomizer.

He sprayed Hal with its contents.

Hal held back a coughing fit. Whatever magical items the atomizer held, all of them stank.

Ungava motioned with the wand to the four points of the compass, then began chanting. Hal could make out only a few of the words:

> . . .
> *Bind, bind . . . hold fast*
> *Swirl about . . . there is no north*
> *You cannot see . . .*
> . . .
> . . .
> . . .
> . . .

Hal lost the last four lines completely.

Ungava did all this with an air of boredom, as if this were a spell he cast every day.

He handed the wand back over his shoulder, looked at Hal expectantly.

Hal stared at him.

Ungava smiled tightly.

"Think of north, and then face in that direction," he ordered.

Hal took a moment, closed his eyes, thought. He'd come in, then a left, then a right into this cell. So north should be over . . .

Sickness caught him, almost like vertigo, which, as a flier, Hal had never felt.

He stumbled, almost fell.

The prisoner caught him.

Ungava's smile grew broader.

"This is what binds you to Castle Mulde, more than any guard, any stone wall, any chain. You, and the other prisoners, are held by confusion, so that even if you were able to physically escape the castle, which you'll learn is an impossibility, you'd still never be able to find your way to your own lines.

"Now you can join the others."

He nodded abruptly, wheeled, and stamped out. The small prisoner looked back at the door, smiled sadly, and winked.

Hal didn't know what that meant, if anything beyond a slight bit of encouragement.

Waiting outside the cell was an officer in Derainian uniform who wore the dragon emblem on his chest. He limped over, saluted Hal and introduced himself as Lieutenant Sir Alt Hofei, formerly executive officer of the 66th Dragon Flight, with Second Army.

"But now," Hofei said, "I'm like all the others in here, rattling my chains and watching the world go past. Can't even escape, thanks to my damned leg. Tell me, sir," he said eagerly, "how goes the war? We get no news here . . . which is quite deliberate on the part of our peerless warder, Baron Patiala.

"It's like that damned spell," he said. "I saw Ungava the wand-waver go past a few moments ago, so I assume you're ensorcelled like the rest of us."

"It works as he said it does?" Hal asked.

"It does," Hofei said.

"Do we have any magicians here?"

"None," Hofei said. "And if there's any with a bit of the Talent, they're very damned quiet about it.

"You see, sir, Castle Mulde is for special cases. High-rankers, generals, noblemen . . . and fliers.

"There's hundred and forty-four—now a hundred and forty-five, counting you—fliers here. As for wizards, all of us were asked if we knew anything about magic when we were first told off to go to this damned place. I surely don't, but there were some who claimed they did.

"They were separated from the rest of us, and supposedly taken to a 'special camp.'

"Nobody knows for sure, but there's a cheery minority who think they were taken behind the nearest barn and had their neck stretched.

"Nice war we're having."

Hal nodded. "It is that."

"I've orders to show you to your room, sir," Hofei said.

"Room?"

"High-rankers such as yourself, Lord Kailas, rate a room, with but one or two mates." Hofei leaned close. "Although let me give you the warning, small rooms make a good place to start an escape from."

For the first time, Hal smiled.

"Escape, eh?"

"There's none of us . . . at least none of us who're fliers, who aren't always thinking, planning, maybe even trying something."

"Good," Hal said. "By the way. Since I'm a flier, like you said, we can eliminate the lord business."

"Yessir," Hofei said. "I assume you'll be taking over as senior officer."

"You may assume," Hal said, a bit astonished, "but I know nothing of that."

"A lord outranks a general, even if he is a sir, I'd guess," Hofei said. "So you'll most likely replace Sir Treffry, who'd like to see you as soon as it's convenient."

"Treffry? That heavyset one with grandfather whiskers?"

"That's him, sir. But don't think he's an ass, though he seems determined to make you think so, sometimes. Poor bastard was captured right at the start of the war. Tried to escape twice, captured twice, one of the first to be purged to Castle Mulde.

"Since then, he's made four more attempts. The last made it beyond the walls, and had the beastly luck of running into a Roche cavalry patrol."

Hal was grateful for Hofei's warning.

He'd known men like Sir Sen Treffry before the war, when he was a wandering farm laborer. They were bluff, hearty sorts, seemingly more concerned for their prize bull or racing stables than anyone who worked for them, although they could show surprising interest in their workers. Certainly Hal had never been cheated of his wages by one of them, which hadn't been true of some other country gentry.

"So I s'pose you'll be the new 'un in charge, Lord Kailas?"

"Not a chance, sir," Hal said. "You know the ins and outs better than I do."

Treffry humphed, grunted.

"I s'pose that's a compliment," he said. "Although heard good things about you, from fliers that've come in, even though none of 'em have the slightest idea of discipline.

"I do wish you'd take command, though, to be selfish."

Hal waited.

"We've got a rule here," Treffry went on. "All escape plans have got to be registered with either myself, m' adj'tant or Lieutenant Hofei, whose main detail is head of the escape group. That keeps tunnels from running into each other and such.

"That means, course, that neither of the three of us can make a runaway of our own without steppin' down for a month or so. Keeps us honest, and from sneakin' others' ideas.

"Y'sure you wouldn't like the task?"

"You just made me even more so," Hal said.

Treffry huffed through his beard.

"Since there's times the walls appear to be listenin', I'll not draw the obvious conclusions from that.

"But I s'pose you'd like a briefing on what you're into."

"I would."

There were 309 prisoners in the castle, over half Derainian. There were three generals, "includin' m'self," twenty-one noble officers, nineteen noble civilians, "poor sots who got caught tourin' the Roche lands when the war started, and now they're mewed up like so many hawks, nobody quite knowin' what to do with them," seventy-one soldiers who'd made thorough pains of themselves by repeatedly attempting to escape, "fifty poor sorts of infantrymen, none escapers, who've been detailed off as batmen who also do scut work for the Roche, under protest," and 145 dragon fliers, all of whom had tried and failed to escape.

"Y'can, if you wish," Treffry said, "think of this damnable castle as a sort of academy, and the other prisoner of war camps as primary schools. If you escape, and make it home, you've graduated.

"Failures are sent here, where they can try and try until they go quite mad."

Hal remembered something the traitor Tregony had said

about being in a camp full of fliers, asked about him.

Treffry shook his head.

"Never heard of the wight. Friend of yours?"

"No," Hal said, then chanced again: "What about a woman flier, named Saslic Dinapur? Maybe killed, maybe captured, wounded, down in Kalabas?"

Saslic had been his first great love, had fallen into a melee of Roche soldiers, was presumed killed with her dragon.

"Don't b'lieve I have," Treffry said. "Though there's other camps for fliers who're better-behaved guests of the Roche."

A last feeble hope died in Hal. If Saslic had lived, she would undoubtedly have tried escape. So she was truly dead.

Then he felt senseless guilt, thinking of Khiri.

Treffry noted his expression, turned away.

"We've all lost someone," he said heavily. "Some of us more than one someone in these stupid damned times."

Hal asked about letters.

"None in, none out," Treffry said. "That's another burden Baron Patiala works on us.

"Speakin' of whom, I'm supposed to take you to him. Then young Hofei'll show you to your chambers.

"By the way. He' s a very good man, and the current head of the Escape Committee."

Baron Patiala considered Hal icily.

He was about Hal's height, in his sixties, and wore a dress uniform with only one decoration on it. Hal decided, remembering a phrase of Farren Mariah's, that Patiala wouldn't say shit if he had a mouthful.

The commandant's office was in one of the castle's towers, and overlooked an exercise yard, and beyond the walls, a small patchwork of fields.

"I have always believed that you Derainians should be considered as nothing more than criminals for starting this war in the first place."

Hal suppressed a start.

"Oh yes," Patiala said. "Were it not for your country's refusal to consider reasonable demands from Queen Norcia, we would all be at peace.

"Instead, you chose to company with the loathsome Sagene . . . and now you are paying the price.

"You should be aware, Kailas, that your escort brought full details of your murderous behavior in your escape attempt, and the only thing that would please me more than to turn you over to a military court would be being permitted to execute you myself for murdering that poor soldier."

Hal said nothing.

"Be advised, Castle Mulde is run firmly but fairly. We do not torment our prisoners, unlike what I have heard your warders do to our soldiery.

"You are advised to follow my rules precisely, and, even though I consider you a common criminal, you will be treated as an equal with the others.

"Break my laws, and, at the very least, you'll be moved into a solitary cell.

"Obviously, any attempt to escape will be met with harsh penalties, and if, impossibly, you make it beyond these walls, the loyal Roche in the countryside will ensure your recapture."

Baron Patiala allowed that to sink in.

"You're dismissed."

Hal nodded curtly.

"So I am. Patiala."

He omitted a salute and the man's title, but didn't wait for a reaction.

Kailas spun, and stamped out of the office, determined, more than ever, that he would escape, and do it very damned soon.

10

Hal's room—cell—was halfway up one of the towers, and overlooked the river. He had two knights, captains, for company. They were out at the moment, Hofei said, "farming."

"Beg pardon?"

"Did you see those little fields when you were in Poophead Patalia's den? We've been given permission to work them, and harvest what we will."

"Hasn't anyone made a break.

"We're on parole when we're out there."

"Which nobody breaks?"

Hofei shook his head.

"You people are a great deal more moral than I am," Hal said. "But I suppose I'll have to go by custom."

Hofei took him out into the corridor.

"Treffry told you who I am?"

"He did."

"That's another point of morality we have," Hofei said. "All escapes get registered."

"Mmmh," Hal said. "How many successful getaways have there been?"

"We're not sure," Hofei said. "Six prisoners have gone out that've never come back. Whether they were killed or died in the forest, or what, we've never heard.

"We like to think the best."

Hal was about to tell him that, when he was captured, there'd been nothing heard about Castle Mulde. He would've expected to have heard something, considering his rank and the number of fliers imprisoned here.

But he said nothing.

Nor did he ask how many failed escapes there'd been.

The dank stone, the cold rain, and the mere fact of being prisoners was demoralizing enough.

"One caution I've given everyone, so there's no offense meant, sir," Hofei said. "Ignore anything that isn't your own business. It might be part of an escape.

"Treffry says that if anyone sees him walking around naked, with his buttocks painted purple and a broomstick stuffed up his arse, no one had better flicker, because he's on his way."

Hal managed a grin.

He went to the window.

"Don't, by the way, put any leverage on any of the bars around here," Hofei warned. "They've probably been chiseled loose by someone."

"Ah." Hal peered out, and Hofei limped to the window.

"Can you get ropes?"

"We have made them from thread, other materials," Hofei said, a bit proudly.

"Long enough to get out from here, then down to that rooftop, and from there . . ." Hal puzzled for a farther route.

"That roof you want to get to is one of the guards' barracks," Hofei said. "That route hasn't been tried since last winter, when three went down a rope from a floor below, then made a snow tunnel, trying for the wall.

"They were doing fine, until someone slipped, and they

avalanched down to the courtyard. Two broken legs, one broken arm, and three months in solitary.

"But there's no reason, come winter, someone who's a little defter might not make it."

Hal nodded. He had no intention of waiting until winter.

Hal's two roommates kept very much to themselves, showed Kailas formal courtesy, but seemed uninterested in making friends.

Hal had his feelings slightly hurt, then realized the two men were most likely up to their armpits in some sort of escape plan, and didn't need or want a third along.

The prisoners ate twice a day, generally a soup called stew, that once a day had some bits of pieces of meat in it. Bread was baked by the prisoners, and shared with the guards.

The rest of the meal came from the gardens beyond the walls.

There were six prized hens, bought from the locals, and there was a drawing for the eggs.

It wasn't much, but just enough to keep from starving.

Just.

The eleven women prisoners in Castle Mulde were assiduously courted by the others. But there were very damned few places to be alone, and it took some arrangement to find an empty cell.

The second problem was avoiding pregnancy, which, so far, hadn't happened.

Baron Patiala had sworn that any woman getting pregnant would never be freed, and she and her "spawn" could keep on rotting where they were.

There would be no mercy, he said, until the Roche standards flew over Sagene's capital of Fovant and Rozen.

*

While Hofei was showing Hal around the castle, they encountered a man on a landing, in deep conversation with himself, talking, laughing, seemingly content.

When they were out of hearing, Hofei said, "One of our madmen. He's harmless. There're three others we keep in cells who want to do damage to others . . . or themselves."

"Can't you get a magician in to try to straighten out their minds?"

Hofei snorted.

Late that night, Hal heard the screaming of one of the madmen, echoing up the stairs from the cellars.

Hal's first lesson as a prisoner was finding some way to pass the time.

His first attempt was to sleep, the customary pastime of any combat soldier. He knew Patiala and his guards were watching him closely, and thought it might be wise to appear docile until they grew bored waiting for him to do something.

But, impossible as it seems to serving soldiers, it *is* possible to catch up on all the hours missed on detail, night guard, or action.

Eventually, Hal could sleep no more, and sought another way of passing the time.

As yet, no brilliant ideas had come that shouted "this is the way out."

So he set about learning Castle Mulde from top to bottom.

Hofei eagerly showed him plans the prisoners had drawn up, and Kailas memorized them.

But still, nothing came.

Once again, witless, he noted the pastimes of the older prisoners—some taught anything they knew, from the art of fishing with a net to history to music to blacksmithing to embroidery, which was taught by one of the Derainian generals.

Others took every "course" they could, even though this

schooling might be no more than one man talking to another man in a corner of the courtyard.

The cell doors were magically locked at nightfall, unlocked at dawn, and the guards didn't bother the prisoners much, other than making irregular sweeps, looking for anything.

The unconfirmed story was that the guards had been chosen for a bit of prescience.

No one knew if that was true, but when a Roche passed, prisoners made an effort to think and talk about things other than escape.

There was a morning and evening assembly, but no more.

The occasional working parties were quickly volunteered for, doing various tasks in and out of the castle. They, too, helped the time pass.

"Interesting thing you might not be aware of," Treffry said one morning. "This castle had another face, once."

Hal brushed raindrops away from his eyes. The two were walking up and down a chill battlement, which was better than the rather smelly confines of the castle, and, best yet, fairly lonely.

"Let me guess, sir. A civilian prison."

"Close," Treffry said. "But not quite. It used to be a mad-house."

"*Used* to be?" Hal asked.

Treffry chuckled.

Hal noted another solitary man, except that he was clearly not mad. His name was Goang, and he spent most of his day-light hours outside, regardless of the weather, studying the birds of the castle, swifts, swallows, ravens, others.

When he was asked, Goang said he would, one day, when the war was over, write a complete history of this building, seen through its birds.

In the evenings, Goang would drift to the fringes of one or another of the dragon fliers' groups, and listen quietly, once in a while asking a technical question about the nature of flying.

The man seemed harmless, and was sort of accepted as an odd hanger-on, no more.

Summer was almost over and still Hal fretted for a plan, even an idea.

Hofei said there was a plan afoot that could use another man.

"Doing what?" Hal asked, knowing nothing is free.

"Well, digging."

Hal went with the lieutenant to the castle's former meeting hall.

There were prisoner guards at regular intervals on the way, each scanning his own sector for a sign of a Roche.

In the assembly hall, a huge table had been levered up, and stones pried out of the floor.

Hal looked down into the cramped space, felt his stomach clench, forbade it recognition.

A prisoner with a fat lamp on a perch beckoned him down.

He slid through the entrance, down a rope ladder a dozen feet, past the prisoner.

"Now," the prisoner told him, "go on your knees, and duck your head. You'll see the tunnel mouth. Go on up it to the face of the digging. The only problem you'll have is about ten feet in, where there's this great godsdamned boulder you have to weasel your way under.

"It took us three weeks to dig under that."

Hal crouched, peered into the tunnel, saw, far ahead, a flickering where diggers would be at work.

He started into the tunnel, and clammy sweat came.

Panic tried to take him over, but he fought it down.

He took half a dozen deep breaths, but he felt no calmer, remembering the deadly hours, back at the beginning of the war, when he and others stood watch, during the Roche siege of Paestum, far underground, listening to diggers undermine the wall, waiting for the boulders to groan and bury him alive.

And he remembered the mines of his native village, and how, every now and again, there would be a cracking roar, and there would be screams, and other men with picks and shovels tore at the smoking earth, hoping to save their brothers, buried in a cave-in.

Sometimes they succeeded, and white, trembling men were pulled to freedom.

But more often there was nothing but despair, and a burial ceremony with never a body, and the next day, another shaft would be driven.

Hal straightened, went up the ladder without looking in the prisoner's face, pushed his way through the entrance.

He was sweat-soaked.

Hofei helped him to his feet.

"Don't worry, sir," he said. "I can't stomach tight spaces, either. Maybe that's what made us fliers."

Hal nodded, unwilling to speak, and reluctant to admit what he felt was cowardice.

One thing that was guaranteed to stop a conversation among the dragon fliers was the sight of a dragon.

Sometimes it was a wild monster, banking and swooping in the late summer winds above the castle.

Sometimes there was a man aboard, and the watchers' expressions would grow hard, envious.

Twice black dragons dove low over Castle Mulde, and Hal wondered if they were from *Ky* Yasin's group, keeping track of their prized prisoner.

The only hobby almost every prisoner had was alcohol.

A bit of fruit, water, perhaps some grain, warmth, and the

beginning of a tremendous hangover was under way. Some called the result beer, others wine; the more sensible just used the generic label of headsplitter.

Bottles of any size were at a premium, and Hal could never figure out where they were coming from.

But every prisoner had one or two, and when the sun was warm, in this dying summer, the bottles would line the parapets.

Surprisingly, at least after first consideration, the Roche made no attempt to stop the various home brewers.

Then Hal realized that of course they wouldn't. A prisoner obsessing about his jug of hooch or sprawled in blissful unconsciousness or crawling around the floor in the throes of what was considered the worst hangover in the world was not as likely to be making trouble or trying to escape.

Hal had no idea how, but somehow, without ever a word being said, "everyone" knew there was an escape about to happen. Who, where, how, no one knew, or those who did weren't talking.

Then another rumor went out—three men were gone. Where, how, the details weren't there yet.

But the guards had been, were still, completely fooled.

Then, after a week, someone slipped, and Patiala and his guards called for assembly after assembly after roll call. Ungava stalked the corridors of the castle, flanked by his woebegone little prisoner, but found nothing.

Little by little, word came out.

The escaped prisoners had been on parole working their tiny fields. But parole did not apply when they were recalled, and roll was taken outside the castle's entrance.

Three men, two Sagene, one Derainian, had ducked away, after other prisoners staged a phony mass fight. They'd gone over the balustrade behind the gate, then down the rocks, across the river, and hopefully away.

It took another two days before their method of covering was revealed: plaster dummies had been cast of the three escapers' heads, and mounted on boards. The plaster was painted precisely, using charcoal from the stoves, paint base for faces, scraped from the mortar holding the stones together, pigmented with various spices or substances from the castle kitchen.

When the melee had ended, the casts were draped with overcoats, and the boards put on adjoining prisoners' shoulders.

The head count was just that, and so the guards came up with the appropriate number.

Hal wished he knew of some reliable gods to pray that the escapers would succeed.

There weren't any benevolent gods in this part of Roche, at least not this year.

Two weeks after the escape, grinning hunters came to the castle, with slung, stinking, burlap bags.

The prisoners were assembled, and the bags dumped.

Out rolled the heads of the three escapers, and the hunters collected their bounty.

One of the hunters chortled, "Like huntin' blind pigs. We watched 'em stumble in great circles, lost as bastards, for half a day afore we got tired an' went in an' kilt 'em."

Ungava preened.

His spell of confusion was, truly, the greatest guardian Castle Mulde had.

Hal could feel the souls of the men watching collapse.

But at that instant, very strangely, Kailas felt the plans for his own escape click together.

11

"So what will be your escape route?" Sir Alt asked.

"I won't tell you," Hal said, "because it's one that only I can use."

"Those tend to be the riskiest," Hofei said.

"I'll tell you . . . in time," Hal said. "I just wanted to tell you that I'm planning something. Right now, I need some things: pen, ink, paper."

"Easily done."

"Then I need to know who're the traitors in here."

"We have none," Hofei said, a bit snippily.

"Come now," Hal said. "Someone—most likely several someones—have got to be talking to Patiala, or one of his men, in exchange for better quarters, food, or whatever. Let's not call them traitors, but, maybe, people who aren't as strong as they should be, or maybe aren't aware they're being played like a fish."

After a moment, Hofei grudged, "We have two . . . perhaps three."

"Who're their best friends?"

"No one with any decency will associate with them."

"You're doing it wrong," Hal said mildly. "You should have your people start cultivating them. It's always good to have some kind of subtle line in that you can use to your own ends."

Hofei looked at Kailas carefully.

"You're not just a dragon flier, are you?"

"I'm somebody who plans on being alive when all this is over," Kailas said. "And I'll use any talent I can think of to make sure of it."

Hofei nodded slowly.

"I have some strong-stomached men—and a woman—in mind."

"Good," Hal said. "I'll want them to leak something scandalous in time."

"What?"

"In time," Hal said. "And the second thing I need is any prisoner who knows anything about magic."

"We have no one," Hofei said. "All wizards—or anyone with any Talent—were purged before they got here."

"There's always somebody," Hal said stubbornly. "I have a man in my squadron who's a bit of a witch. His grandfather was a full-fledged one. Sometimes my man can cast a small spell, sometimes nothing happens. But he'd never claim to be a wizard. That's the sort of person I'm looking for."

"I honestly don't know of anyone," Hofei said. "If there is, he or she is bound to be keeping it secret. But I'll see what I can come up with."

"Good," Hal said. "Now, if you'll get me my writing materials, I'll set to work."

"Might I ask what you're going to be writing?"

"My confessions."

He smiled sweetly.

A day later, the writing materials were delivered, and then Hal set to work, spending hours sitting in his cell, writing away.

He told no one what he was writing, other than this was his after-the-war money machine.

Since diaries and such were forbidden, Hal hid the paper in a hollowed-out leg of his cot.

Some of the noble prisoners sniffed—a man who'd been so favored by the king with vast estates should hardly be worried about gold, as if he were no better than a tradesman.

But they kept their councils to themselves . . .

"I think I may have someone," Hofei said. "One of our civilian internees has an interesting background. You might be interested in talking to him."

"I am, indeed," Hal said, and the next day Sir Alt brought the man by. He was young, thin, quite tall, most shy, and looked as if he'd be happier as a priest, or perhaps an archivist, Hal thought.

The man was Mav Dessau, eldest son of Baron Dessau of Anhewei, a title even Kailas had heard of.

"I don't know if my father still lives," Dessau said. "He was doing poorly when I left on my travels. Have you . . . ?"

Hal said, apologetically, that he knew little about the nobility, and hadn't kept up with their lives.

"So I suppose I'll continue on as the eldest," Dessau said. "No more. Which doesn't displease my father, since he considered me a bit of a disappointment."

"Ah?"

"I love to study, to learn," and enthusiasm glowed in Dessau's voice.

"At one time," and here he looked about Hal's cell, as if there were an eavesdropper crouched under the wooden cots, "I wanted to be a thaumaturge.

"They said I had a bit of the Talent, and I'd been accepted by a tutor. When my father heard of this, he raged, and cut off my allowance, and swore he'd disinherit me. I should have told him to make one of his prize bulls the next baron, for it mattered . . . matters . . . little to me.

"But I'm afraid I'm a coward. I suppose any of us who come from wealth are always terrified that we'll be cast loose on our own, and that our devices shall not be sufficient.

"So I dropped that field of study, and decided that I would become an architect, a master builder, and that there might be a future amalgamating the styles of Deraine, Sagene and Roche.

"I was studying in Carcaor when the war started. Since my father is one of King Asir's strongest supporters, Queen Norcia thought I would make a good hostage.

"And so here I am, with nothing more to study than a damned monolith like this swamp of a castle."

"I think I might have something more for you," Hal said. "Something in the way of wizardry."

"Magic? As I said, I know very little, although I've read much, but haven't the training. And—" Again came the frightened look. "I do not wish to be sent to . . . to wherever the captive wizards were sent.

"To be eaten by dragons, I suppose. Or demons."

Dessau took a deep breath.

"But I suppose I have no choice. Patriotism, and all that.

"So I'll try to do whatever you wish, although you'll most likely be disappointed by my best.

"And I'll ask but one favor. If you make good your escape, would you mind visiting my father? Or my brothers, if the baron has passed on?"

"I'll do better than that," Hal said. "If I make it back to Deraine, I'll hunt the baron up and tell him that it was your magical abilities that made it possible to escape."

Dessau smiled.

"Thank you. I'd just like to be there to see his face when the Dragonmaster, Lord Kailas, tells him that."

Sir Suiyan Tutuila came to the castle, summoned Hal, asked if he wished to confess, saying if he did, Tutuila and *Ky* Yasin would intercede at Kailas's trial, assuming he was willing to cooperate.

Hal made no response, just stared at Tutuila until the exasperated inquisitor ordered him returned to his cell.

The next part of Hal's conspiracy was having the little prisoner of war who was Ungava the magician's reluctant servant visit his cell.

"Ah knows nofing, nofing, about magic, or magicking," the man, who had only the single name of Wolda, swore. He was very nervous, hardly used to being in the company of a noted nobleman.

But Kailas hadn't been a cavalry warrant and then a unit commander without learning a few ways to put men at their ease.

He drew Wolda out about the small island he'd grown up on, off the west coast of Deraine, where he'd fished before deciding to join up, to end up on a coastal patrol boat.

Hal told him about Khiri's estates, and her village fishermen, although, of course, without sounding like he'd ever lorded it over them. He told Wolda about seeing the flotillas of dragons, on the water with their wings folded over their heads like tents, coming from the west.

"Ah've seen them too," Wolda nodded. "We used to try to reckon what they were comin't frae, where they was goin't, with not a clue."

Hal told Wolda about the time he'd tried fishing for a living, and how it was too much for him, and after the small man recovered from his surprise that a mighty lord had ever baited a hook, let alone run one into his palm, and said, "Ay, they say'n you're t'be born t'it. An' Ah'm hopin't Ah lives, an' gets back t'it. Ah misses th' sea."

Wolda recovered a bit of his suspicion, and asked Hal why he'd summoned him.

"Because I'm hoping you'll help me get off this damned rock," Kailas said.

"Ah doubt there's aught Ah might do."

"You're Ungava's assistant."

"On'y 'cause Ah was told to it."

"I need to know a couple of spells," Hal said.

"Nah, nah. Ah'm no wizard."

"Do you remember what Ungava says, when he takes the irons off a new prisoner?"

"Cours't. Tha's simple. He rubs oil, which Ah've got in a vial, on his fingers, not lettin' anyone see it. Then he whisper't, 'Chain, bend, steel, work, uncoil, uncoil.'"

"That seems simple," Hal said. "Could I work it?"

"He told me once't Ah could, so Ah'd wager so," Wolda said. "Course, y'd need a bit of th' oil."

"Could you steal some of it for me?"

Wolda looked frightened.

"He tol't me once if Ah did him false, he'd change me int' a sea monsker." Wolda took a deep breath. "But Ah'll help. Th' oil, for your learnin', is made of some kind of rock serpent from th' east."

"That's one thing I need," Hal said. "The second is the spell he casts to keep us confused."

"Ah'm noo lyin't," Wolda said. "Ah dinna know it. He whispers it close."

Hal made a face, and his hopes sank. Then he had an idea.

"You know what hypnosis is?"

"Cours't," Wolda said. "Afore m'boat sank, and th' Roches caught me, went to a turn one night, an' they had a woman. Fair, she was, and she put spells, but said it was hypnotizing, on m'mate, and made him think he was a woman, and should be kissin't th' skipper.

"Fair laughed till Ah 'most pissed myself, Ah did."

"Would you be willing to be hypnotized," Hal said, "and have somebody ask about that spell? They say everything you hear, or see, gets tucked away in your mind, and needs only a little prodding to come out."

"Ah dunno," Wolda said. "I don't think—"

Hal cut him off before he could refuse.

"Go think about it. And remember, if I get out, you'll be one step closer to being home, and back on your boat, fishing."

Wolda licked his lips, looked piteously at Hal, but Kailas bustled him off.

"I don't suppose," Hal asked Dessau that evening, as they strolled along the battlements, "you happen to know anything about hypnosis?"

"I read a book about it once," Dessau said. "Seems fairly simple, assuming you've a subject who doesn't object to the idea.

"And you know, of course, that nobody will do anything they don't want to when they're hypnotized, so you can't get one of the guards to open the gates for you."

"I just want a simple bit of remembering," Hal said.

"I'll give it a try," Dessau said. "But no guarantees."

"I've been a soldier too long to expect anything like that," Kailas said.

"Ah've thought," Wolda said. "An' Ah'll let y'try wi' th' hypnotizin't."

"Good," Hal said. "This evening, before lockup, after assembly."

"All right, Wolda," Dessau said in a soothing voice, tucking the bit of stolen oil into a pouch. "Just relax, lean back, and watch this medallion."

"Ah'll try."

There was no one in Hal's cell but the three of them. Hal had run his roommates out, thinking, the less confusion, the more likely this might work.

"See how it turns," Dessau said. "See how it spins."

"Ah do."

"Now, don't talk," Dessau said. "Just watch the medallion, and listen to my voice."

Dessau kept talking, about soft, gentle things, and always, always, the gold medallion he'd gotten from somewhere kept turning.

Wolda looked quite alert.

Hal felt himself getting sleepy, wondered how long Dessau would keep trying, wondered if Wolda had a godsdamned mind to hypnotize, got sleepier, and suddenly realized Wolda might not be going under, but he surely was.

Kailas looked at the ceiling, afraid to move as the voice wove on, talking about home fires, with the rain and wind beating against the window panes, and a good meal warm inside, and the fire crackling, and then Hal got his shin kicked.

He looked back down, and Wolda had his eyes closed, and a happy smile on his face.

"Can you still hear me?" Dessau asked.

"Aye."

"Do you want to tell me some things?"

"P'raps."

"Do you want to tell me some things about Ungava?"

"Do Ah have to? He' s tryin' t' take me away frae m'fire."

"I'll not let him, and soon I'll leave you alone to toast your bones. Ungava is a magician."

"Aye."

"An evil magician."

"Aye."

"He uses a spell to keep prisoners from being able to escape."

"Aye. A secret spell."

"But you've heard it."

"Aye."

"Would you like to tell it to me?"

"You'll not let Ungava turn me int' a sea monsker?"

"No."

"Th' spell goes," and Wolda' s voice took on a singsong, and deepened, to match the Roche magician's:

> *Spinning compass*
> *Bind, bind, hold, hold fast*
> *Swirl about with my wand*
> *There is no north*
> *You cannot see clear*
> *There is no south*
> *No east, no west*
> *All is fog*
> *All is lost.*

"An' he tap't wi' his damned wand afore in all directions, sprays wi' that evil shit, an' as far as Ah know, that's all."

"Good," Dessau said. "Go sit by your fire."

Wolda fell back into unconsciousness.

Dessau motioned to Hal to follow him out of the cell.

"Well," he said, "I guess I'm a real hypnotist.

"I was hoping there'd be herbs, or something else," Dessau said, "that Ungava uses to lend the spell power. But there's nothing but that damned wand of his and whatever's in the atomizer.

"I don't think it's just the words."

"Try it," Hal said. Dessau handed him the tiny vial of oil, and Hal put a bit of it on his face. It stank as badly as he remembered.

Dessau, face most skeptical, chanted the spell.

Hal turned to the setting sun, knew that as west-north-west by knowledge, felt for north, found nothing.

"No," he said. "You're right. It needs the wand. I hope nothing more."

"So all we need to make the thing work is to steal Ungava's magic stick, we hope," Dessau said. "Something tells me that might be a bit of a challenge."

Hal nodded, gloomily. Then an idea came.

"Maybe not. You said that you can't make somebody do something he doesn't want to do."

"Right," Dessau said. "At least, that's what I've read."

"But what about something he might want to do, if he had the courage?"

Hal explained.

"Mmmh," Dessau said. "I'll give it a try. I just hope it works . . . and that our poor little fisherman in there doesn't get turned into a sea monster.

"Although I've never seen any magician with that kind of power."

The next day, Ungava the wizard was stalking through the prisoners' areas, peering about, looking for anything resembling an escape attempt.

As always, he was flanked by his small prisoner aide, Wolda, carrying a bag of sorcerous implements and, in his other hand, Ungava's wand.

They rounded a corner, and a prisoner cannoned into Ungava, sending him flying back into Wolda.

Wolda fell heavily, the wand under him.

Unexpectedly, it shattered like glass.

Ungava shrieked like an impaled baboon, knelt over the broken remains of the wand.

Wolda tried to help, chattering that it wasn't his fault, and please, please, don't transform him.

Ungava ignored him, came to his feet, and started screaming at the prisoner, who'd been supposed to grab the wand and run, flattened against the wall as if being beaten.

Ungava ran out of words, and stalked away, Wolda, carrying the bag and the bits of the wand, scuttling after him.

Later that afternoon, he gave the bit of the wand he'd hidden to Kailas.

"Let's see now," Dessau said. "You're properly oily.

"Now we point at the four compass points with this little piece of whatever the hells it is . . . damned glad you drew the headings on the floor, since I can't tell direction any more than you can, and then . . ."

And then he muttered the spell.

It was if a fog had cleared.

Hal knew north, south, the other directions, had a vision of a crude map, with the Zante River and the castle, and, a bit to the north, the welcoming ocean that led to the Chicor Straits and home.

His eyes were moist.

"It works," he managed.

"Good," Dessau said. "Now, what about the rest of that oil?"

"I'll give it to Hofei," Hal said. "There'll be other escapers after me. I hope."

Hal saw the next escape in the making.

He was finishing up his "diary," and enjoying a rare, sunny day, a nice breeze from off the river cooling the castle's hot stones.

He heard a small crash, looked up.

A slate had fallen from one of the turrets. Then he saw a hand, carefully taking other slates inside, until there was a sizeable hole in the turret.

Other prisoners had seen the same thing, and Hal noted the eeriness—no one shouted, or did anything more than find a vantage point where he could unobtrusively watch whatever was happening.

The hole grew, and then a prisoner clambered awkwardly out onto the roof.

Hal recognized him as Goang, and thought for a moment the man was about to jump, suiciding down on to the flagstones of the courtyard below.

Others must have had the same fear, for prisoners began moving toward the steps into that turret, hoping to stop Goang before he jumped.

But Goang wasn't suicidal—at least, not directly.

Two other prisoners handed something out to him, and he fitted them together.

Hal saw that they were wings, made of paper, he guessed, glued onto thin lathes.

The wings were curved back, like a swift's.

Goang attached them to a harness he'd made, and Hal marveled at the amount of work the man must've gone through, first studying the birds until he understood their wings, then making his own.

Goang braced, then jumped, and now there was a sound from the watching prisoners, something between a hiss of surprise and a gasp of fear.

The wind caught Goang, and lifted him.

Now a guard saw the flier, and shouted an alarm.

Goang was pulling on lines that led to the front of his wings, forcing them down, and he dove at an angle.

Hal figured he would just clear the castle walls, and then have a fair shot at being able to fly over the river.

What Goang would do then, Hal couldn't think, since he saw no sign of the weapons, food or clothing Goang would need to evade the hunters and make his escape.

The wind eddied, and Goang's left wing dipped.

He was just over the wall when his wingtip caught a battlement.

Instantly what had been a birdlike thing of grace and beauty, collapsed, and Goang was falling.

But he was able to reach out at the last minute, and grab that same battlement.

He slipped, almost fell, then had a firm hold, and pulled himself up, onto the parapet, just as half a dozen guards had him.

The bits of his bird machine were ripped apart, and Goang hauled off to the baron, and from there to a solitary cell.

But his failure gave the prisoners a bit of hope, and something to talk about.

Hal wondered why it had taken a nonflier to come up with this idea, decided he would think more about this device.

But that was for the future.

Now, he was finally ready to go.

Within a few days, the story of what the Dragonmaster had been writing so laboriously was all over the castle.

It was the story of his capture, and imprisonment, supposedly complete with details of Castle Mulde.

Some said that Kailas was keeping this diary to stay sane, others for it to be used as evidence in the trial of Baron Patiala, after the war, "for surely the bastard has to be tried before we can hang him."

Hofei whistled.

"Now I understand why you refused to tell me your escape plan."

Hal shrugged. "It was the only idea I could come up with."

"But what happens if it fails, anywhere along the path?"

"Then," Hal said, trying to sound nonchalant, "they'll hang me. Tell mother I died game."

The guards burst into Hal's cell just before dawn.

Very efficiently, they bundled him out of bed, and put him against the wall while they searched his meager possessions.

Kailas noted that they deliberately behaved as if this were a blind search, and they "just happened" to come on the hollowed-out cot leg.

Obviously Patiala had no intention of exposing the big mouth or traitor who'd passed the story about Kailas's manuscript along.

The guards dragged out the manuscript and, whooping with glee, hauled Kailas off to one of the solitary cells.

"One thing that has always pleasured me about life," Baron Patiala said, "is that villains will out."

He reached out and tapped Hal's manuscript, lying on his desk.

Hal tried to look like a not particularly bright villain, caught red-handed.

"Not only did you have the cold-blooded ruthlessness to murder one of the queen's soldiers, but you were stupid enough to brag about it, even after you'd been warned both by *Ky* Yasin, Sir Suiyan Tutuila and myself that you were being watched, and would face prosecution for this capital offense as soon as adequate proof was amassed.

"Truly, you played into our hands, and now you shall pay.

"I have sent word of your idiotic behavior to Sir Suiyan and *Ky* Yasin, and that you will be escorted, on the morrow, from Castle Mulde to Carcaor, where you shall be court-martialed, as common law admits, and then punished, I hope to the fullest extent of the law.

"I knew it was just a matter of time."

Hal didn't know any of the guards detailed off for the escort.

All he was permitted to take were the clothes he'd arrived in, now somewhat more worn in the months he'd been prisoner at Castle Mulde.

The prisoners turned out to watch him leave.

No one spoke, and few could meet his face.

Most of them had heard the tale of Hal's stupidity, writing about what he'd done after escaping from the hospital, and thought while Kailas was most certainly brave, they agreed with Patiala, and considered Hal a fool.

Ungava put the spell of the chains on, after the limber metal strips had been wound about his ankles and wrists. Hal felt them clasp him tightly.

He was half-carried, hardly able to stagger, back down the hill, to where a boat waited.

The warrant in charge of the escort laughed harshly as the boat was pushed away from the dock, and the guards started working the sweeps, driving the small craft back upriver.

Hal looked once at Castle Mulde, and spat into the water.

He waited until near dusk, just before the boat's commander would be looking for a place to beach the craft before dark.

The boat had passed three fishing villages since leaving Castle Mulde.

Then he knelt, and whispered the counterspell over his leg irons, hoping that Ungava hadn't been lying to Wolda when he said that spell could be worked by anyone.

He hadn't been lying. The metal uncoiled like a snake, and clattered to the deck.

Hal quickly whispered the spell again, near his manacles, and they, too, fell away.

The clank was heard by a guard, some yards away.

He spun, saw Hal, standing free, and his mouth fell open.

Before he could shout, Hal kicked off his boots, dove off the boat, disappearing in a swirl.

Then there were shouts, orders, and the boat spun in the current, coming to a halt as guards dropped their oars, strung bows, nocked arrows, and had spears ready for the cast.

But there was nothing but the eddying, muddy waters of the Zante River to be seen.

12

Hal swam underwater as deeply and as far as he could, then came to the surface slowly, turning on his back, and letting only his mouth appear long enough to gulp air.

Then he dove again, and kicked for the river bank.

He had to surface for air twice more, the second time staying up long enough to look at the bank, and pick his landing place—where thick brush grew into the water.

He surfaced in this thicket, and finally let himself look back at the boat.

They were rowing in circles, still watching the water, waiting for either Hal or his body to surface.

Hal slid out of the river, and crawled into the bush. On its far side, he came to his feet.

Sooner rather than later, the Roche would be checking the shoreline, and he thought he'd rather not be there.

Hal started downriver as fast as he could travel on bare feet. He'd deliberately left his boots off as much as possible over the last month, trying to harden his soles.

But it hadn't done much good.

By the time he'd walked a third of a league, he was starting to limp.

And, as it grew darker, it was getting cold.

Fall was definitely either here, or about to arrive.

But he was free!

That thought, and the sight of the first village, drove his aches away.

He wanted to enter the village and beg a handout, but rather appreciated his head being attached to his neck.

Also, this village, even if they didn't kill him for the reward, would be the first the Roche soldiers would go to, looking for additional searchers.

Besides, the next village held his dream.

He skirted the village, and went on.

There was a rough cart track behind the village.

Kailas knew he shouldn't use it, that he should be deep in the bush.

But he figured that, with no alarm out yet, he'd most likely hear any oncomers before they saw him. As for the hunters that were his real fear—they'd be working the brush, since game animals quickly learned to avoid anything of man.

It was well after dark, and both moons had risen when Hal came on the second village.

He crept down to the water, and slid into it. It was very cold, and he tried not to shiver.

Hal swam out, let the current take him for a bit, washing him past the outer palisade into the village's heart.

He'd spotted, going upriver, several skiffs pulled up on shore.

Hal swam hard for the bank, keeping his hands and feet below the surface.

He came up on the bank in the middle of four boats.

The village was still alive, with two fires in the squares, and most of the huts still lamp-lit.

Hal wanted to grab the first boat, and pull away.

But he made himself take a bit of time, and found one with an unstepped mast with a sail furled around it. None of the boats had oars in them, which he hadn't expected, and "his" boat had, at least, a long pole.

There was a locker in the bow, but he wasn't calm enough to see what it held.

Instead, he crawled onshore to that boat's painter.

Hal grinned. For the first time, he had a bit of luck.

The painter was a bit frayed.

Hal saw a jagged rock at water's edge, used it to saw the painter away.

That was good. With luck, the boat's owner would find the end of his moorings unraveled, and curse his carelessness, never thinking of a thief.

Especially not a dragon-riding thief.

Hal went back into the water, and slowly eased the boat off the bank.

It floated free.

Hal looked around for any guards, sentries, afoot or on the walls, saw none.

Perhaps they had magic wards set.

He shuddered, preferring the thought that they were just careless.

The current was pulling at the boat, and Hal let it take the craft, staying in the water and holding on to the stern.

There were no shouts, outcries, but he waited until the village was round a bend before he clambered aboard.

The boat rocked, and Hal almost went overboard. It would be just his luck to lose the boat and drown now.

But he didn't.

The boat was traveling smoothly downstream.

Hal could relax for a moment, and in that moment he realized there was a chill wind coming upriver.

He had no time to be cold.

He went to the forward locker, opened it.

There were some net floats, some bits of wood, rope, oakum for leaks, fishing lines, and the great discovery—a long, sharp, fish knife.

Hal, armed, felt quite cheerful.

Now, for that sail.

He stepped the mast, and unfurled the sail.

At that point, his luck ran out. The sail hadn't been raised in too long a time, and was mildewed, rotting. It tore apart at the first gust of wind.

Probably just as well, at least for the moment, since Hal hadn't the slightest idea of how to tack back and forth in a river.

He found and mounted the rudder, and let the river take him.

Hal passed the third village at midnight, and there were no lights or other signs of life.

Something loomed, rushing up at him. Hal thought he was being attacked by some kind of river monster, readied his knife.

The something was a huge tree trunk, its branches reaching, menacing. But as long as he stayed clear, the log seemed to offer no harm, and went past him.

After it was gone Hal realized, that if he were a true riverman, he would've tied up to that log, and let it carry him down to the sea.

But he wasn't, and so forgot about it.

Just at dawn, Hal passed Castle Mulde. He tried not to look at it, tried to think like an innocent fisherman, out early to check his nets or whatever sort of fishing they did on the Zante River, in case Ungava was mounting his own form of guard.

He was hard-pressed, as Mulde fell behind him, to not cock a snook, or even show them his bare arse.

But he didn't, and then the castle was swallowed up by the dawn mist.

Hal, yawning mightily, feeling like he was almost truly free, was swallowed by deep fatigue.

He had to sleep, had to be alert when he reached the river mouth.

He saw a small islet, managed to use his pole as a crude oar to close on it. The boat was pulled under an overhanging branch, and Hal had the branch, almost lost his boat, then hand-over-handed it to the shore.

He pulled it up on to the bank a few feet, thought he was adequately hidden, curled up in the stern sheets and was instantly asleep.

He wasn't sure what woke him, but something said to lie very still.

Hal peeled an eyelid back, saw it was midday at least.

He waited.

Then he heard a whisper, and the squish of river mud.

From his right.

He braced his left leg, and his right hand found the fish knife.

Dark hair lifted over the boat's gunwale, and he saw a pair of eyes.

No more, for Hal was up, rolling, his knife in his left hand, and lunging.

He caught the man just below his chin line, driving the blade into his neck almost to the hilt.

The man gargled, fell back.

Hal came over the gunwale, into the mud, ignored the man bleeding to death at his feet, saw the man's companion, frozen in horror.

Then he came alive, lifting the crossbow he carried.

But it was too late.

Hal dove across the five feet between them, blade first. The knife took the man just below his rib cage, and he screamed in agony.

Hal whipped the knife free, had the man by his greasy hair, and drove him face first into the muck, and held his thrashing body until the convulsions stopped.

Then he was awake, throwing up, and his body shook.

After a while, he recovered.

The two men were dressed in heavily patched and mended hunting garb. Both of them had crossbows, skinning knives at their waists.

Hal ignored the bodies for a moment, went around the small island. He found the men's boat, not much more than a skiff, on the other side.

Maybe the hunters were good fellows, and had come to see if the occupant of the boat was in distress.

Or maybe they thought they could steal an abandoned craft.

Or maybe word was out, and they were looking for an escaped prisoner.

It didn't matter.

He went through the boat, found, to his great pleasure, blankets tied in sleeping rolls.

And there were oars.

There was also food, loaves of bread with meat stuffed in them, and flasks with beer.

Very good.

He went back to his boat with the blankets and food, and carried the bodies to their boat.

Hal was winded by the time he finished. Not only was he out of shape, but he'd lost a lot of weight as a prisoner.

No mind. He'd gain it back once he reached Deraine.

One of the hunters was about his size, and so Hal stripped off his outer gear, took the other man's coat. He found two very heavy rocks, stuffed one in each of the hunter's clothes.

The current was pulling at that boat. Hal stabbed its hull

four or five times with his fishing knife, kicked it off into the current.

Then he went back to his own boat, pushed it into the river flow.

It caught him, and he was swept away.

He looked back at the sinking skiff near the islet.

With any luck, it'd go down quickly, and the bodies would sink, and all there'd be was another mystery.

If they were found, what of it?

Hal was already a self-confessed murderer, he told his uneasy conscience.

Hal used one set of blankets to make a crude sail.

He used fishing line to make awkward locks for the oars.

Now he was very close to the ocean, tasting salt when he dabbed a finger into the water.

He heard the ocean's roar growing louder as he neared the ocean.

Hal desperately wished he had Mynta Gart with him, or even that he'd listened more to her sea stories.

But what he had, he had.

It was late afternoon, and he dreaded going out into the ocean at dark.

But the tide was at full ebb.

There was a tiny settlement at the river's mouth, and there was a speck of bright color on its beach.

The figure waved, and Hal waved back, having no idea if the person was being friendly, or trying to warn him.

The river grew choppier, tossing him about.

Hal lashed himself to a thwart with a bit of rope, began rowing hard.

Ahead was the bar, a line of white solidly across the river's mouth.

Hal's mouth was very dry, but the river had him firm, and pulled him hard toward the waves.

One caught him as it broke, and white water drenched him.

Hal ignored the water, pulled even harder.

Another wave lifted him, and his boat almost capsized.

He was caught in a current-swirl, spun, spun again, and then another wave took him high, and he could see all the way back to that tiny settlement.

He teetered at the crest, then slid down its back, and was rowing even harder.

Now the ocean had him, trying to overturn him, but the river current was still strong.

Hal, gasping for air, pulled hard at the oars, caught a crab, almost lost an oar, then recovered his stroke.

He rowed endlessly, afraid to stop, not sure whether he was safe or not.

Then exhaustion caught him, and he could do no more, collapsing over his oars.

His wind came back to him, and he looked around.

He was well clear of the river and the shore, and the swells around him were those he remembered from being at sea.

He'd made it.

Now the worst that could happen to him was drowning.

No, he thought. The damned Roche must have patrol boats out.

But the hells with it. He had two crossbows, and three knives.

He'd not be taken again.

Hal restepped the mast, watched his blanket sail as the stiff wind tried to tear it free.

But it held, and bellied out.

West, there, into the setting sun, and steer a bit north.

North for Deraine.

North for home.

13

Hal, hardly a seaman, didn't know if the weather was supposed to get worse the farther he drew away from the Roche shore, but it did.

He'd been on ferries, and on dragon transports, but seldom this close to the heaving ocean.

He didn't understand it, didn't like it.

With full dark, the world closed in about his tiny boat. The night was as black as any he'd experienced. But maybe that was just as well, he thought. He didn't have to see the waves that rushed on him.

They lifted and dropped his boat, and the wind screeched like a fishwife. His mast was bending, creaking, and he thought he'd better take in some of his blanket/sail. With the sail down, the boat pitched worse than it ever had.

He remembered one of Gart's stories, about having been caught away from her coaster in a small boat when a storm hit, and she set something called a sea anchor.

Hal grudgingly tied the other set of blankets into a bundle, and lashed rope around them. He'd freeze, but he'd rather be cold than drown.

He couldn't remember whether the sea anchor was supposed to be tied to the stern or the bow, decided the stern had to be more logical.

That seemed to help a little, holding the little boat's prow into the oncoming waves.

There wasn't anything he could do, and so he secured the oars, and crept up into the bow, trying to cram as much of his body into the tiny cuddy.

It started raining, but it took a while for him to notice it, since there seemed to be as much spray as air for him to breathe.

He felt miserable, but not that miserable.

Then he remembered the sandwiches, and dug one out, keeping it under his coat.

The meat was unfamiliar, but that didn't bother him. He inhaled the sandwich and half of one flask of beer.

The beer also tasted strange, and he wondered if it was some kind of bark beer that he'd heard peasants made.

He hadn't had alcohol in some time, not being much at stomaching the home brew the prisoners made, and found himself a little tipsy, and singing.

Maybe it was as much being free and feeling defiant as the brew.

At least he wasn't getting sick from the boat's motion, and as soon as that thought had come, he regretted it, swallowing mightily.

But the meal stayed down.

Hal was afraid to go to sleep, but his body would have none of that, and his eyelids sank, opened, sank, and then it was gray twilight out, and he discovered he'd been right not to want to see the storm around him.

Everything was gray, except the white froth atop the monstrous waves that the wind took and whipped along the water's surface.

But at least it wasn't raining anymore.

And he thought the wind was dying.

No doubt it was his damnable optimism.

But, some time later, he realized the wind *was* lowering, and the storm was passing.

He chanced putting the sail up, and caught enough of the sun glow through the clouds to get a rough idea of which way he should be sailing, again, into the choppy seas.

The wind held strong, but the waves died, and he was cutting through a gray, calm sea.

He remembered the sea anchor, and brought in the sodden blankets, spreading them across the thwarts to dry out a bit. But they were wool, and still would hold warmth, even wet.

He treated himself to half a sandwich and the rest of the first flask of beer.

Finally, Hal Kailas had a chance to take stock.

He wondered how many days' sail it would take to reach Deraine, hadn't a clue. He knew small boats didn't sail as fast as big ones, but didn't know much more.

He also realized he itched.

Kailas felt a deal less sympathy for one of the men he'd murdered, whose coat he'd taken. The bastard had fleas.

Oh well.

It wouldn't be the first time he'd had armor-clad dandruff in this war.

Three days later, Hal had long finished the soggily stale sandwiches. He'd been able to nurse the beer along, since it rained daily, for which he tried to feel grateful.

It had cleared on one day enough for him to improvise a sun compass, and get an accurate reading for north.

To his considerable relief, his instinct had been true, and he had been sailing in the direction he wanted, not, as he'd feared, either in circles or back toward Roche.

Deraine was out there.

Somewhere.

*

Hal was awakened from his drowse by a mournful honk that brought him fully alert.

The honk could have come only from a dragon.

He sat up, and saw, about twenty yards distant, a dragon, dark and light red, bobbing in the mild seas like a cork, its wings folded.

It had been tamed—its breastplate was drilled for a saddle, and the remnants of harness dangled down across its side. Reins had also been torn away, maybe by the dragon itself?

Itself?

Herself, Hal realized.

The dragon saw Hal was alive, honked again.

Hal saw the monster had scars along one side, and the rear of one wing had been torn.

A dragon flier's mount.

The flier must have been killed, and the dragon fled the battleground.

Hal made a tentative noise, comforting.

The dragon replied equally tentatively.

Its huge tail lashed back and forth on the water's surface.

Hal reached slowly for an oar, and began to canoe-paddle toward the beast.

Froth appeared at the dragon's chest, hindquarters, as its talons back-paddled away from this unknown man.

Hal tried more soothing noises.

The dragon waited.

Hal paddled closer, and again the dragon swam away from him.

Hal cursed.

He paddled closer, very slowly.

The dragon bellowed, and its wings unfurled.

"No, dammit," Hal said. "Don't . . ."

But the dragon's wings were flailing at the air, and its talons digging into the water. It skated away from him, bounced off a wave crest, crashed through the crest of another, and was in the air, climbing toward the clouds.

Hal slumped back.

The dragon circled him once, curiously, then set a course.

Hal didn't need the compass he didn't have to tell its course.

North. Due north.

Toward Black Island and the far northern tundra.

Hal dangled one of the lines over the side, wishing he'd saved something for bait.

But it didn't seem necessary.

A fish, a large fish, Hal didn't know what sort, but it looked edible; he took the hook as if it was the only edible thing in this ocean.

Hal grinned, started hauling in, hand over hand.

Then a bigger fish, almost as big as the boat, came from nowhere, and took fish, hook and line away with it.

"Son of a bitch," Hal said sincerely, and found another line.

Another fish took the hook, and Hal jerked the fish out of the water into the boat, just as that monster predator came back for seconds.

Hal sneered at the beast, then regretted it, as the huge fish, with far more teeth than any creature not a demon had a right to have, kept circling him, eyeing him as he cut the fish open, gutted it and then devoured the rest.

It appeared as if this great fish thought Hal now qualified, having kept the fish, for the monster's dinner.

Hal thought of potting it with one of his crossbows. He found it mildly funny that he knew exactly where to hit a man or dragon for a killing shot, but no idea whatsoever for a damned fish.

It was a day and a half before it gave up, having chased all other fishes away.

*

There was nothing Hal could do but keep on his course, and try to keep his mind busy.

He started thinking about Khiri, and his base intentions, but that didn't go very far, considering his rather malnourished condition.

Meals were better dreams, and, even though he'd never been much of an epicure, he planned enormous menus that he and Khiri would inhale, and then he would work his wiles on her, given more energy.

Then an idea came, pushing food and sex out of his mind.

He became very busy making a plan, and deciding how he would broach it to the king, and perhaps Sir Bab Cantabri might be willing to involve himself.

Hal was so busy plotting it took him almost an hour to recognize the thin dark line on the horizon as land.

He closed with the land, dropped his sail a half a mile from shore, when he realized what he was looking at was great cliffs, with never an inlet to be seen.

Hal guessed that he was somewhere on the southeastern coast of Deraine.

Or, rather, he hoped, since that was the only part of Deraine that had steep cliffs.

That he knew about, anyway.

Otherwise, he might have been cast far into the seas, and might be about to wreck on some unknown land.

Hal guessed what he should do was bear south or north, looking for some sort of port, or, even better, encountering a friendly ship.

Then he saw a bobbing dot, about a mile away.

Very awkwardly, he managed to steer the boat in its direction.

It was another boat, smaller than his, with two men in it.

Fishermen in oilskins, working what looked like crab pots, very close to the surf line.

They saw him, waited.

Hal didn't really know what he should say.

"Ahoy," was what he settled for.

"Eee-yup," was the response.

"I need help," Hal said.

"Looks like," the other fisherman said. "You one of them Roche spies?"

"No," Hal said. "I'm an escaped prisoner."

"Eee-yup," came back. "Who's the boat belong to?"

"Nobody," Hal said. "I mean, nobody now."

The two fishermen looked at each other.

"What sort of rewards they give for prisoners?" the first asked.

"Damned if I know," the other one said.

"Bet they're not as good as for spies," the first said.

"Look," Hal tried. "Help me ashore, and I'll give you this boat. Free. And gold, when I'm able."

Both fishermen looked interested.

"Don't know about gold," the first said. "Everybody's always been promising me some of that, and nobody ever came through."

"You think we could use something like that boat?" the other asked.

"Dunno," the first said. "But spies don't give things away. They need all kinds of things for their deep, dark doings."

"Guess he might be telling the truth, then."

"Maybe so. Welcome to Deraine, mister. We'll take a claim on the boat before we take you ashore. People forget, sometimes."

14

The fishermen searched Hal, took away his weaponry. Then they pulled their nets, keeping a careful eye on Kailas, put him in their smaller boat, took it in tow, and rowed south, rounding a promontory after an hour, and entering a cove with a tiny village nestled in it.

The village had one warder, who also ran the general store and tavern.

Hal introduced himself, and the warder gaped.

"But . . . you're dead!"

"If I am," Hal said dryly, "then I'm a damned solid ghost."

"But . . . what . . . If you're the Dragonmaster, what do you want me to do?"

"Nothing," Hal said. "Especially not let anyone else know who I am."

He was about to give instructions, when one of the fishermen ostentatiously cleared his throat.

"Oh," Hal said. "First, bring me pen and paper. I've a deed to write."

The warder, still in shock, obeyed.

Hal wrote out a bill of sale, signed it, gave it to the fisher-men.

"Now you've got the start of a fleet."

One of the fishermen thought things were amusing.

"If you're some kind of muckety," he told Hal in a low voice, "then you're the most important person who's come here since . . . " He had to think.

"Since that duke who got lost, whatever his name was," his partner put in. "Back when we were toddling."

"That was the man."

Hal asked them not to say anything to anyone, hoped they'd keep their word, since he'd promised to send them gold. But it didn't matter that much. If important people didn't come to this nameless village, it was unlikely to have a cell of Roche agents, either.

He asked the warder to ride to the nearest duty station and arrange for a coach to pick him up.

"Make it a prison coach," he said, thinking he was used to that. "There'll be no wonderment about a mere prisoner being transported."

The warder nodded jerkily, bustled off, utterly perplexed about the situation, and forgetting about whether Hal was who he said he was, and if he wasn't he should be secured somehow.

In fact, he left Hal with the keys to the tavern.

Kailas made himself at home. The warder was single, so there was no family to explain himself to.

He sorted through the man's wardrobe, found pants and a jerkin that weren't too impossibly large.

Behind the house was a large vat. Hal lit the stove in the kitchen, heated buckets of water from the well, and stripped naked.

He ceremoniously burned the clothes he'd worn in the warder's backyard, not much caring if there were holes in the fence around it and peepers behind every hole.

Then he bathed.

He'd been happily torturing himself staring at the man's larder, but at last could hold back no longer.

There was smoked fish, and a large ham.

There was half a loaf of bread, country butter, and Hal carved slices off the ham, sipping at a flagon of the warder's strong beer, real beer, made from grain and hops, not the Roche bark—or whatever-it-was brew.

He fried some of the ham in butter, seasoning it with herbs from the cupboard, then sat down at the table. He just stared at the meal for awhile, not remembering when he'd been able to eat so well.

Then, like a worried cat, glancing around him, as if afraid someone would take this feast from him, he set to.

Fatigue took him after that, and he found blankets, and spread them on the floor.

It took him only seconds to fall asleep.

When he awoke, many hours later, it took him some minutes to remember where he was, that he wasn't still in Castle Mulde, waking from a most elaborate dream.

He ate, slept, ate, and then the carriage came back.

With it was the warder's commander, and four guards, none of them at all sure Hal was who he said he was.

It didn't matter.

Now he was bound for Rozen and the king, and it didn't matter what anyone thought of him.

One thing was solved at their first stop: a warder who'd been discharged, wounded, remembered Hal from the Kalabas campaign, so there was no longer any question as to his identity.

The man was sworn to secrecy.

Hal asked the warder's commander to continue the pretense.

The man was puzzled.

"Why, Lord Kailas? You deserve, and you would undoubtedly get, an escort to the capital more in keeping with your fame. I know that any of the nobility still living in Deraine, who aren't abroad with our fighting forces, would give their left arm to so honor you."

"Thank you," Hal said. "But there are reasons."

The warder waited, but no explanation was forthcoming.

Hal gave him further orders: once they reached Rozen, they were to take him to the town house of Sir Thom Lowess.

"The taleteller?"

Hal nodded.

"But . . . if you wish your presence to be secret, then why . . . ?" The warder broke off, realizing this question would most likely go unanswered as well.

"Great gods in heaven," Sir Thom said. "So you weren't killed at all."

"I was not," Hal said, his mouth full of roast. He'd been lucky, and Sir Thom was in-country, and it was just dinner time.

"Oh, what a story, what a story," Lowess said, rubbing his hands together. The last time he'd said it was when Lady Khiri and Hal declared their love affair.

"My fellows will give half their pay for this, but it's mine, mine, all mine."

"No," Hal said. "It's not all yours. At least, not yet."

Sir Thom goggled.

"I want no one—and I mean no one—to realize I've escaped and come back to Deraine. Except for the king. And . . . where's Lord Cantabri?"

"He's afield. Still with First Army, still battering their heads against the heights beyond Aude."

"I want an audience with the king, as soon, and as secretively, as possible."

"There should be no problem with that. What else?"

"Nothing. Except nobody can talk about me. This is very important, Sir Thom."

"What about Khiri? Lady Carstares?"

Hal hesitated. He wanted to see her in the worst way.

"I can't chance it," he said. "She'll have to remain a widow for the moment."

But Sir Thom noticed the hesitation.

"Let me see about the king," he said. "In the meantime, you should concentrate on putting some weight on those bones of yours."

"I can do that," Hal said. He smiled, but it wasn't much of one. He damned his dutiful soul to several perditions, thinking about Khiri.

Two days later, Hal was sitting in Sir Thom's library, sipping mulled wine, finishing a letter to his land steward, sending a fairly astonishing amount of gold to the two fishermen. It would be taken to the steward after Hal's plans were either denied by the king, or granted and set in motion.

But his mind kept drifting to the map on a nearby table. He finished the letter, sanded and sealed it, and his mind forgot about it, and leapt to his plan.

He went to the map, going over, not for the first nor the tenth time, a map.

His plan, his scheme, did have a chance, he thought, then bent over the map again, looking to see if there was anything that could go wrong.

Everything could go wrong.

But maybe, for a change, it wouldn't.

He didn't notice the soft click of the door behind him closing.

"I assume," Lady Khiri said, "there's some good reason for you avoiding me."

Hal spun, tried to say something, saw tears in her eyes, and was in her arms. He was quite amazed at the feelings—very well, use the word love—that swept him.

"I'm really glad you're still alive," Khiri said.

"So am I," Hal managed, picking her up in his arms and carrying her to a window seat. "So am I."

"I think," Hal said, "you're more beautiful naked than with clothes on."

"I will not allow you to talk to my dressmaker," Khiri said.

Hal had explained his plan, why he was staying hidden.

"And you don't think I can keep a secret."

"No," Hal said. "It's not that. It's just that—"

"That somebody might see me walking about with a great happy smile, instead of the gloom I've been broadcasting for the last several months."

"Well . . . yes."

"Hmmph. Well, for your information, I brought suitcases. Sir Thom said I'm not permitted to leave this house without your permission."

"Which you won't have," Hal said. "Not when I think about how much I love you, how much I've missed you."

"Well then," Khiri said, rolling on to her stomach, "start making up for your absence."

Hal moved over her, nuzzled her shoulder.

"A day at a time?"

"An hour," Khiri said throatily. "Perhaps even a minute."

"I guess," Khiri said, "you really do love me."

"Of course," Hal said.

"You haven't asked about your damned dragon that I so carefully stole from the army and moved to Cayre a Carstares, where he's getting fatter and stinkier by the day."

Hal thought of telling her about his dream of being Storm, which had just proved itself truer than he thought, but for some reason didn't.

*

It was after dinner that night, and Khiri, wearing a dressing gown, was wrapped around Hal. Rain was tapping at the window.

Sir Thom beamed at them, and poured himself another snifter of brandy.

"I suppose one should ask," he said, "when you plan on uniting your holdings, to put it as coldly as possible."

"He hasn't asked me," Khiri said.

"I've been afraid you'd turn me down," Hal said.

"Coward."

"I am that."

"Screw your courage to the sticking point, young man," Sir Thom said. "What, after all—"

His butler entered.

"A visitor, sir. Three of them, in fact." His voice was a little shaken.

Sir Thom got up.

"All right. You two upstairs, and I'll make sure there's no suspicion . . ."

His voice trailed off.

In the doorway stood King Asir.

"I dislike being out on a night like this," he growled. "But it's easier than trying to slither you into the palace without notice."

Hal, Khiri, and Sir Thom were on their knees.

"Get up, all of you," he said irritably. "Someone pour me a drink, old brandy by preference, and make sure my equerries have one, too."

The butler scampered out to obey.

The king shed his cloak, unbuckled a sword belt and slung it over a chair.

"I shall be damned glad when this war is over, and I can stop carrying real weapons about. Too damned heavy. No wonder they say that soldiers are more than thick, wanting to lug all that iron about."

He took Sir Thom's snifter and drained it. The butler came back in with a decanter, and King Asir refilled the snifter, made no motion to return it to Lowess.

"Now," he said. "You wanted to see me?"

"I'll be upstairs," Khiri said, and was gone.

"And I'll find some business of my own," Lowess said.

"Good people," King Asir said. "They know when to vanish.

"First, my congratulations on being alive, and escaping from whatever hells the damned Roche had you mewed up in.

"Now, I assume you're ready for a good long leave before we figure out what job you'll be suited for next."

"I know what job I want, Your Highness," Hal said. "The same one I had before, and maybe now there'll be enough men for me to build the full squadron that we talked about.

"But I don't want any leave.

"That's why I made sure I came back to Rozen as secretly as I could.

"I want to put together a raiding force—maybe with Lord Cantabri as its commander—and go back to Castle Mulde.

"There's more than three hundred men and women I want to set free."

The king reacted, started to down his drink, thought better, and set it down.

"I assume you have a plan?"

"I do, sire," Hal said. "And I think it will work . . . if it's mounted quickly enough."

"Ah," the king said. "And that explains why you're being so secretive."

"Yes, sire. If the Roche find out I escaped . . . they might start taking precautions."

"Over three hundred men and women, you said," the king said thoughtfully.

"Yes, sire. And many of them are fliers. Or noblemen."

"At this point in the war," King Asir said, "I can do without nobility. But dragon fliers are another story.

"I think we'd better send for Bab Cantabri at once."

It was suddenly obvious that all of Hal's careful arguments he'd prepared on his sail for home wouldn't be needed.

He was going back to Castle Mulde.

This time with sword in hand.

15

A grim Lord Bab Cantabri arrived within the week. His bleakness lifted a bit when told of the upcoming raid, and he and Hal set to, looking for men and units.

Hal asked him how badly the battle was going.

"Worse than you can imagine," he said. "Lord Egibi doesn't seem to have any better ideas than to keep hurling his forces up those damned mountains."

Lord Egibi was Commander of the First Army.

"The problem is," Cantabri went on, "neither does anyone else.

"Those mountains we're hitting," he went on, seemingly irrelevantly, "nobody knew their names when we first attacked them, although I suppose the Roche maps called them something.

"They've got names now: Desperation Rise. Bloody Nose Hill. Slaughter Vale. Massacre Mountain."

Hal winced.

Cantabri shook his head.

"Ah me, ah me. One of these centuries the war'll be over, and we can sit on our estates, phoomphing at each other and talking about the good old days when we weren't bored orry-eyed."

"What a future you predict," Lady Khiri said, coming in with a tray of sandwiches. "It's time to feed the inner warrior."

After some debate, it'd been decided by the king that the planning headquarters for the raid would be at Sir Thom's mansion. His staff had been handpicked for their discretion, and would not talk.

Lowess and Carstares had both been told the secret. They were used as couriers to the palace, which lessened the number of uniformed messengers going back and forth.

Hal picked up a sandwich, pointed at the map.

"If we could take the—"

"Stop that," Khiri said firmly. "Meals are important. Both of you get away from that damned map, and concentrate on eating. Otherwise you'll get ulcers the size of your heads, and be worthless to anyone."

"She's right, you know," Cantabri said.

The two men went to a table, and sat down.

But Hal found his eyes creeping to the map, and he was eating faster than he should.

He caught himself, shook his head.

"I wonder if we'll ever be worthwhile as people, once the war's over?"

Cantabri glanced to make sure Khiri had left the room.

"Don't worry about it," he said. "Neither of us are likely to make it that far."

Hal shivered a bit, remembering Saslic's words, "There won't *be* any after the war for a dragon flier."

"The most important thing," Hal said, "is speed. If we fart around, and piecemeal our troops together, and then they're inspected, and every hinky little lord and lady gets to visit our camp, we might as well let the prisoners in Camp Mulde rot, because we'll be on a suicide mission.

"Not to mention the godsdamned Roche could well do something nasty, like massacre everyone in the castle before we take it, if they hear about the raid."

There were only two men in the room—Cantabri and the king.

"I must say," King Asir said, "I'm not used to being preached at."

"I'm sorry, Your Majesty," Hal said.

"No, no," Asir said, and his voice was tired. "I said once, a long time ago, that people like you are sometimes uncomfortable to be around.

"You're living up to your reputation."

Hal desperately wanted to bring his own First Squadron back from the front for the raid, but knew that could well be a red flag to the enemy.

Instead, a rather battered pair of flights from Second Army, due for a rest, were rotated back to Paestum, and two freshly trained green flights went back in their place.

Cantabri pulled a battalion here and there until there were three waiting in a camp west of Paestum for orders.

That should have made 1500 men. But that would've been in peacetime. There were only a few more than 700 infantry for the raid.

"Wouldn't it be nice," Hal said, "to have a special unit, a Raiding Squadron call it, on standby for things like this?"

"Maybe," Cantabri snorted. "If they had a good commander, who had enough clout to keep them from being thrown into the line any time some lord wanted reinforcements or line troops. And if . . . higher-ranks . . . realized what they had, and kept them from being wasted."

Hal knew Lord Bab meant the king.

"And there'll still be the drawback . . . these elite men might have gotten higher rank, and medals, and accomplished more, staying in their base formations.

"Not to mention things like morale," he went on. "What do you think the average infantryman, or cavalryman, is going to think of himself and his own unit when he keeps hearing of the King's Own Specially Dangerous Guards, or whatever they'd be called?"

"Still," Hal said, and let the conversation drop.

Maybe Cantabri was right. And maybe all that Hal wanted was first line, rested troops, instead of the tired warriors he was getting.

And on the other hand, he also might want solid gold toenails, and they weren't forthcoming either.

"You know, Lord Hal," Limingo the wizard said, "there are other magicians in the king's service who can be volunteered for your dirty deeds, many of whom are no doubt better than I am."

Hal grinned. At least in the field of magic he was getting the best.

"It's just that you're like an old shoe," he said. "You get more comfortable the more I'm around you."

"Oh, thanks ever so for the compliment," Limingo said. "I wish I knew a spell that would give warts."

"No you don't," Khiri said. "For I'd put sand in your lubricant."

Limingo looked shocked.

"Well, I never. Well, hardly ever, anyway.

"And so to business," he went on. "I assume you want the usual spells of confusion, multiplication of forces, and such."

"I do," Hal said. "And I'll want a big spell . . . It's not just the folks in the castle who should be confused, but the people in the area around aren't exactly well-disposed."

"Let me consider," Limingo said. "Perhaps there's something better I can come up with for them."

*

"Do you remember," Khiri asked, "back a couple of weeks or so, when the king came in on us, to our great surprise?"

They were lying in bed, spooned together.

"I do well."

"Do you remember what we were discussing when he did?"

"Uh . . . yes. Marriage."

"Sir Thom probably thinks it's very romantic that—what I hope, at least—a marriage proposal was interrupted by royalty. Or was I mistaken about your intent?"

"Well . . . I've never been married," Hal said.

"Neither have I, dummy."

"Well, then, would you like to try it?"

"Gods," Khiri said. "How romantic."

"I'm new at this," Hal tried to explain.

"You're supposed to be on your knees, looking deep in my eyes, clasping my hands in yours and vowing eternal devotion," Khiri said.

"Oh," Hal said. "But that floor's cold."

Khiri didn't say anything.

"All right," Hal said, and got out from under the covers. "I'll do it the way I'm supposed to."

"That's far enough," Khiri said. "I just wanted to see if you'd do me right sooner or later."

Hal gratefully dropped back down into bed, and pulled the heavy comforter over them.

There was silence for a bit, then:

"Well?" Hal asked.

"Well what?"

"Godsdammit, do you want to marry me?"

"Of course," Khiri said, her voice sounding a bit choked. "I thought you'd know."

"I don't know anything."

"You'll make a wonderful husband, then," she said. "Easy to train."

"So when do you want to do it?"

"If it's marriage, then after you get back from playing hero. And then you'll take some leave, and we'll finally do the Grand Tour of your estates.

"But if you're thinking of some other sort of it . . ." She rolled over onto her back.

"Seize the moment, as they say."

Ships were assembled, including the ex–horse transport *Galgorm Adventurer*, the wallowing tub that had been converted to a dragon carrier.

The story around Paestum was that the two dragon flights were being taken back to Deraine, for rebuilding and further training.

Certainly no one thought they'd be thrown back into combat.

Much the same story was passed around about the three battalions of battered infantry, who were loaded on common ferries, and transported across the Chicor Straits.

But they didn't land in any of the normal ports, but were taken north to a patch of bare ground, near an abandoned village, where nothing waited but rows of tents, fresh uniforms and supplies.

The wiser ones moaned when they saw the twenty new warships anchored, waiting for them.

The dragons were fed, but not offloaded from the *Adventurer*. Their fliers went ashore, and waited.

The soldiers were landed, escorted to their assigned tents. Enormous vats of hot water and soap waited for them, and, once they were bathed, shaved, and clean, they were formed up in a large open area.

It was an overcast day, almost winter, and a chill wind was blowing off the sea.

Most of the troops knew the two men waiting for them on a crude stand, and now all of them knew they were not coming home for a rest.

They were called to attention, then given "at ease."

Cantabri walked forward. He needed no magical implements for his voice to carry to the rear ranks.

"Good afternoon. I assume you know who I am.

"I'm the one—and this other man, here, the Dragonmaster—who's been lying to you.

"Not to your faces, but it might as well have been."

There was a ripple, half astonishment, half amusement, from the troops. Generals didn't usually talk to common swordsmen like this.

"We pulled you out of the lines, and let you think you were due home leave.

"You'll get it . . . after one job."

There was an incoherent shout from the ranks. Outraged warrants moved to find the man, and have him skinned. Cantabri held up his hand.

"No. He's right to be doubtful.

"Lord knows people like me've been lying to him, either directly or otherwise, since the war started.

"So I won't add to the bullshit.

"Here's what we're going to do.

"There's a Roche prison somewhere behind their lines.

"Lord Kailas was a prisoner there until six weeks ago. Then he made his escape, swearing to go back and rescue the other prisoners.

"There's at least three hundred of them, some who've been caged up since the war started.

"We're going to set them free.

"Then you'll get your leave . . . and have a story to tell your children's children."

He stopped. There was silence, except for a forlorn dragon bleat from the *Adventurer*, and the whisper of the wind.

A soldier stepped out of ranks.

"What are our chances?"

Cantabri nodded to Hal, who came forward.

"If the Roche haven't magicked this secret out, fairly good," Hal said. "Your warrants and officers will be given everything we know, when you board ship again, and you can judge for yourselves."

"I've been in too many fights where everything was a secret," the soldier shouted. "And then the godsdamned Roche were there, waiting for us."

Hal nodded.

"I have, too.

"But think about this. If everything does go wrong," and his voice dropped, so that the soldiers had to lean forward to hear his words, "is there a better reason to die than rescuing your brothers?"

16

Eighteen dragons dove out of a thick fogbank on Castle Mulde. Each was heavy-burdened with three passengers, two unarmored infantrymen, and a flier, sometimes a woman.

Hal Kailas was at the head of the ragged V formation.

It was false dawn, and the Roche guards on the walls goggled at this attack from nowhere.

They goggled, and then died as the fliers pincushioned them with crossbow bolts.

Hal wished he'd had some of Joh Kious's repeating crossbows, but there was no time to have them made, and so the fliers were armed with everything from standard crossbows to short bows.

Hal forced his dragon down, toward an outer battlement. The dragon shied, and he cursed, and kicked it.

It grudgingly grabbed an allure, and the two soldiers behind Kailas leapt onto the wall walk.

Around Castle Mulde, other dragons were being forced to land long enough for their passengers to jump off, or even balk with their wings flared and give the archers time to slide off.

Then the dragons, like gigantic, multicolored crows, dropped down toward the river, and vanished into the fog.

The thirty-six volunteers held to the heights as the alarm was shouted, and half-awake guards stumbled out, buckling on armor.

One of the volunteers was one of Limingo's assistants, who paid no attention to the battle, but busied himself casting a spell.

Most of the Roche warders died before they could fight back.

The prisoners were coming awake, banging at their cell doors.

Then the wizard's spell worked, just as Limingo had guaranteed it to, and doors banged open, and the prisoners streamed out.

In his turret, Ungava screeched disbelief, and tried to cast a counterspell to lock the cells up again.

Then, below, on the river, twenty warships appeared, backing sail, and dropping anchor.

Two were bold enough to close on the tiny jetty, and Derainian soldiers poured off.

It was just a week since the small armada had set sail from Deraine.

The soldiers had been transferred from the secret landing to the warships, and the ships set sail north by northeast, arcing up into the northern sea before turning south for the Zante River.

No one had been allowed to lollygag about.

Hal spent the time taking his two undermanned and -dragoned flights off from the *Adventurer*, teaching them to fly formation with each other, trying to get the two flights to fly a common track, and then, hardest, making the dragons land within a small space, the barge the *Adventurer* towed alongside, touching their talons to the wood, then scrabbling back into the sky.

He also sent them off in foul weather, getting them used to the idea of flying when it was somewhat blind out, using homing spells devised by Limingo, and careful compass reading.

Volunteers were called for, with only a handful standing forth until Cantabri, in some disgust, promised gold and decorations.

"Damned sure wouldn't have had to beg for men back when the war started," he snarled to Hal.

"No," Hal said. "But all those eager young bodies are dead now. Dead, crippled or maybe a few learned better."

Cantabri gave Hal a dirty look.

"Are you sure you're a soldier?"

"I'm damned sure I'm not one," Hal said. "At least, if that means marking time and saying yessir, nossir to every idiot idea that comes along. *Lord* Bab."

Cantabri had the grace to grin ruefully.

These "volunteers" became dragon riders, such as Hal had used years ago in the battles around Bedarisi, armed with bows or crossbows.

The *Adventurer*'s barge became a target range on clear days, at least until one particularly inept bowman put an arrow in the *Adventurer*'s helmsman's leg. After that, empty wine barrels were cast loose for targets.

The assault troops were also trained as thoroughly as it was possible to do aboard ship—being rousted around the decks by their warrants, singing, exercising to exhaustion.

They'd found a map of the Zante River mouth in the royal archives, used that to make models of the area.

Hal had sketched, growling at his inability as an artist, Castle Mulde. From that, Limingo and three assistants had made five scale models of the castle, which Hal critiqued over and over, and new models were spell-cast. Then they were taken from ship to ship, and every soldier had to memorize his individual and group's mission.

"This," Hal said, "is the way soldiers should fight, not charging blindly ahead at some hilltop or other."

"Here's your special Raiding Squadron again," Cantabri said. "Which is starting to sound like a good idea. I assume you'd like to be put in charge of it."

"Not a chance," Kailas said. "I leave it for one of nature's noblemen—you, for instance—while I flit about above the clouds without a care."

Cantabri growled, and went looking for an erring junior officer to savage.

Certain soldiers, considered by their officers to be more intelligent than the common spear-carriers, were given special training in the handling of prisoners, and then, one wintry day, the coastline of Roche was in sight.

It was too rough for fishermen, which was a blessing for Deraine.

A small pinnace was sent into the river's mouth, to track the changes of the tide.

Three days later, just as the tide began to flood, the ships sailed into the mouth of the Zante.

As they did, Limingo's fog bank roiled up from the surface of the sea, and moved inland.

Limingo had considered his other spells, including the standard fear and confusion incantations. But he decided not to use these, since any combat soldier might recognize the castings, and assume there was an attack in the offing, no matter how far behind the lines the Zante River was.

Instead, he cast a spell of general malaise: the weather was foul, so of course animals wouldn't be out, and, for some unknown reason, the fish probably wouldn't be biting.

It would be exhausting, he told Hal, because it was a piece of "soft" magic, relying on the magicians' forced moods to "color" the spell, and repetitive chanting rather than herbs or forbidden tongues to give it strength.

Hal, remembering his own travails in a tiny boat, admired

the skills of the warships' captains and master's mates, especially in the fog, as the ships went upriver in short tacks.

They didn't anchor that night, but pressed on, and, just when the sky began to lighten in a gray sort of way, Hal took his dragons and riders aloft.

He wished he was riding Storm, instead of the rather battered, sour monster he was aboard, whose name he kept forgetting, but that, like bringing the First Squadron up, was a chance he couldn't have taken.

The two dragon flights followed the river to the heights that marked Castle Mulde, struck hard, dropped off the troops, then flew back to the *Adventurer*, landing and taking off in rapid succession. When a dragon landed, a bundle of swords was slung over his carapace, and the monster was back in the air.

There was a collision, dragons crashing into each other just above the barge, spitting, striking with their snaky necks, and rolling into the river.

But they recovered, splashing about angrily, and neither rider drowned. After the rest of the flights were gone, they were derricked aboard the *Adventurer*, and sent off again.

Again, the dragons came on the castle, and dove low, letting the bundled weapons thud down into the courtyard.

Even a hundred feet in the air, Hal could hear the shouts of glee as the prisoners armed themselves.

An arrow screeked off his dragon's carapace, barely missing him, and he quit mooning about, and climbed for altitude.

A handful of dragon volunteers fought their way down to the courtyard, armed prisoners joining the fray, and they made the main gate.

Half of them were down, and there was a hacking melee around the gate tower; then, with a great crash, the gate slammed open.

There were Roche guards on the wall walks, firing down at

the Derainian soldiers making their way up the winding track to the main gate.

Hal blasted a command on his trumpet, and his dragon fliers sent their mounts spiraling down, shooting as they went.

They weren't very accurate, but the very idea of being shot at from the skies sent many of the guards pelting for the stairs and cover.

There were Derainian troops running hard, through the gate, into the castle, and boats were landing reinforcements.

That was enough for Hal.

He sent his dragon skittering down toward a wall walk, sliding out of his saddle as the beast closed on the castle.

It was against his orders, but Hal cared not a whit.

He jumped, landed hard, rolled, and his dragon flapped upward, to go wherever he wished.

Hal had a crossbow in hand, and a man was running toward him, waving a spear.

Hal sent the bolt into the man's abdomen. He screamed, clutched himself, fell. Hal tossed the crossbow away, drew sword and dagger, found a stairway, went down into the battle.

He saw the diminutive Wolda, screaming joyfully at the top of his lungs as he hammered Ungava's corpse with a balk of wood, ran on.

He went up other stairs, into the heart of the castle. Here was a knot of guards, holding the doorway to the central keep.

Then arrows whistled, and the way was clear as the Roche fell.

Hal was the first through the door, went down a familiar corridor, and smashed into a closing door.

There were two men in the room—one of the guard warrants, and Baron Patiala.

The warrant had a halberd, swung it at Hal.

Kailas had no time for such nonsense, lopped the halberd's

head off, and smashed the warrant's face in with the butt of his dagger.

Patiala had an old-fashioned broadsword out and, recognizing Kailas with a start, jumped toward him, swinging the blade.

Hal parried, struck back, missed.

Neither man spoke, intent on the other's death.

Patiala lunged, and Hal kicked him in the forearm.

The Roche shouted in pain, and the sword spun away.

Hal slashed the man's throat open with his dagger, let him fall.

That was one payment made.

He heard shouting, went back into the corridor, saw a man in an ornate uniform running.

An archer slammed Hal out of the way, and sent a long shaft into the running man's back.

He screamed, contorted, went down, and rolled over.

Hal went to him, and saw, with near infinite glee, it was Sir Suiyan Tutuila, the "Respecter of Prisoners," and Hal's would-be hangman. He must've chosen to visit Mulde at precisely the wrong time.

Now the screaming and shouting were dying away. Guards were either surrendering, the surrender sometimes accepted, lying in their blood, or scrambling down the rocky sides of the island and diving into the water.

Hal doubted if the local hunters would have any objection to them as prey, even if there wasn't a bounty.

Hal saw a jovial Treffry, a bloodstained sword in hand. Flanking him was Sir Alt Hofei, beaming as if it were his birthday.

Warrants and officers were shouting for order, and slowly the blood rage died.

Some of the prisoners were ecstatic, others were in complete shock.

This had been allowed for.

The trained men escorted them out of the castle, not listening to their pleas to go back to their cells for anything, not letting them retreat into numbness.

Within two hours, the castle was empty. Even the madmen were taken, with infinite care and pity, to boats, secured against themselves and taken to the warships.

The raiders returned to their ships.

They'd lost only thirty men killed, twice that wounded, a more than acceptable price.

Castle Mulde's gates hung open, ripe for the looting.

Carrion kites were already circling overhead, under the dragons' constantly circling umbrella.

One of the riders swooped low, where Hal had been signaling from the boat landing.

Hal pulled himself up behind the rider, and the dragon's wings beat, beat, and they were climbing as the sorcerous fog lifted.

"What happened, sir? Did your dragon get hit?"

"I had some business to take care of," Hal said.

He looked back at the gray stone nightmare that had been his prison, wishing that stone could be burnt.

Then he forgot about Castle Mulde, and started considering what would be the most spectacular wedding in the history of Deraine.

17

It had begun snowing gently just after dawn. But the weather was warm, and so the snow melted as it struck the ground.

The king had proclaimed the wedding day a royal holiday, and cheery crowds packed the streets along the route the broadsheets had announced.

They were held back from the great square the great temple stood in by dress-uniformed cavalry.

Bands and street performers entertained the throng as they waited.

A keen-eyed little girl saw it first—a dot, high in the sky, spiraling down toward the square.

She squealed, and everyone looked up.

Hal Kailas brought his dragon, Storm, down in a glide. Its claws skittered on the cobblestones, and it was down. Before Hal had returned from the raid, it had been arranged by Khiri to bring Storm from her castle to Rozen.

He was most unhappy until he saw Hal, then tried to larrup him with his great tongue.

Storm's breath hadn't improved in his convalescence, but Hal was quite used to the various odors dragons emitted by now, and hoped that Storm felt the same about human smells.

Kailas slid down from Storm, and a man ran out and took the dragon's reins.

Hal wore a white tunic, with his decorations on a dark blue sash. Blue breeches, bloused in black thigh boots, complemented the sash, as did his gloves. He wore the red forage cap of the dragon fliers.

Kailas was armed, not with a ceremonial sword, but with the long, single-edged, most functional dragon flier's knife at his waist.

He was cheered by the crowds as he waited, standing not quite at ease, not quite at attention.

There was more cheering, coming toward the square like a wave, and a carriage, drawn by eight matching white horses, appeared.

Hal had been warned by Sir Thom to expect surprises, but not this.

The carriage was the royal carriage, an old-fashioned box on iron springing, all red and gold leaf.

It drew up in front of the temple, and King Asir got out.

The crowd gasped, and went on its knees, as did Hal.

Asir was a rather remote king, especially since the war had started, and so most of the throng had never seen him.

He looked around in approval, and motioned the crowd back to its feet.

They slowly got up as he handed Lady Khiri Carstares out of the carriage.

She was utterly gorgeous.

Her close-fitting wedding gown was pewter satin, with a lace bodice. Tiny gems, given a spell, flashed in many colors on the bodice and in her long, dark hair. She wore a short lace jacket over the gown.

Hal thought he'd never loved her more.

She grinned at him, and the king took her arm, and led her

up the steps. The train of her gown had evidently been ensorcelled, for it waved as she walked, a bit like a dragon tail.

Hal thought this was a bit much, but didn't say anything.

The square was a boil of cheering as he followed Khiri and
the king up the broad flight of stairs into the temple.

Music swelled out of the huge doors.

The crowd tried to push forward, but was held back.

The temple was quite packed. Every nobleman and -woman
not off fighting had been wrangling for an invitation for
weeks to this, certainly *the* social event of the year.

Khiri and the king, flanked by a gaggle of bridesmaids,
were moving slowly up the aisle toward the altar.

Hal was met by Lord Bab and Sir Thom.

"Since your lady is an orphan, the king thought it might be
appropriate for him to present the bride," Sir Thom whispered.

Hal bobbed his head.

It wasn't as if anyone would gainsay the monarch.

Lord Bab nudged Hal with his elbow, and the three of them
started up the aisle, as the music soared around them.

In the third aisle from the front were Hal's parents, Faadi
and Lees.

Hal hadn't planned on inviting them, and Khiri had torn
into him like a drill field sergeant, asking if he didn't love
them . . . Well, yes, of course he did, but he really hadn't gone
to see them in the hated tiny northern village of Caerly, even
after the army had given him enough rank so he had the freedom to consider it. And why not? Hal wasn't sure. He'd
always sent them money, and, after the king had ennobled
him, and given him estates, he'd written them, asking if they
would accept a house on his property. He'd wondered why he
felt a bit relieved when they wrote back, saying they'd prefer
to stay in Caerly minding the tavern they'd always had. Hal
had immediately bought the building the tavern was in, and
deeded it to them.

Why he felt a bit uncomfortable thinking about them, he could not figure. Perhaps, the thought came once, he felt he'd failed them somehow in getting involved in the brawl that had forced him to run away. Or . . . or perhaps something else.

He didn't know.

But he did feel that he'd done right in obeying Khiri, and sending them the invitation to the wedding, as well as dispatching a carriage and outriders to bring them to Rozen.

He shut off that line of thought, concentrating on Khiri, waiting for him.

The king nodded to Hal, then, quite against protocol, left Khiri and went up to the altar. The high priest behind it raised an eyebrow, but it was, again, certainly the king's right to do this.

"Please stand," the king said, and all obeyed.

"I wish to invoke the blessings of the gods on the man and woman about to be joined in matrimony, and that their union be long and fruitful.

"But beyond this, I request the blessings of the gods on our war efforts. Some think that it is not right to call to the gods when the cause is bloody.

"But I deny this, for our cause is for freedom, and against tyranny.

"Our people, and the men and women of Sagene, have bled too long in this nightmare, and I require the gods to see the justice of our fight, and to give us their aid.

"I ask this in the name of the people of Deraine."

Hal noticed that the king, unlike the others in the temple, didn't bow his head when he prayed, but stared up, as if demanding what was rightfully his from equals.

He wondered, wryly, not only if there were any gods, which wasn't the first time he'd had the thought, but if the priests of Roche made similar prayers, and if Queen Norcia also laid her demands on the heavens.

He decided that if he were a god, he'd have done with

humanity, at least until the slaughter ended.

Then he wondered why his mind was coming up with such cynicisms on a day like this.

The king stood aside, and the priest began the ceremony.

Hal's mind went blank, and he lost track of the words.

Khiri kicked him in the shins, and he realized he'd been asked the question.

"Yes," he said, as memorized, "I, Hal Kailas, Lord Kailas of Kalabas, welcome pairing in holy wedlock with this woman, Lady Khiri Carstares."

The question was asked of Khiri, who suppressed a giggle, and agreed.

Hal wondered why women always seemed to be able to handle things like this better then men.

Then, hearing snuffling, he wondered why women also seemed impelled to cry at weddings.

He withdrew the thought, realizing it was Sir Thom Lowess leaking the tears.

"You are as one," the priest said, and Hal kissed Khiri.

She was very chaste, and kept her lips closed.

They bowed to the priest, to the king, then turned and bowed to the congregation.

Hal's mother was crying . . . as was his father.

Local lad makes good, he thought, keeping a pleasant smile on his face as Khiri had told him to.

He realized, very suddenly, why he was bearing such cynical thoughts. He was scared silly at the idea of getting married and, more immediately, at being in the middle of all this ceremony which he felt so very insecure in.

He would never make a courtier.

But the pair made it back down the aisle, and then outside, where a real surprise waited.

Since this was sort of a military ceremony, he'd half expected something like crossed sabers to walk under, or something.

Something turned out to be six dragons drawn up, three on either side of the temple steps. Hal had no idea how the hells they'd been maneuvered into position without him hearing it from inside.

But there they were, heads snaking back and forth, fangs occasionally bared. They clearly didn't like being in the middle of this city, and surrounded by people.

Then Hal recognized the riders:

Farren Mariah, Myna Gart, and Sir Loren Damian sat the closest three. Behind them were Cabet, Richia, Pisidia, his flight commanders.

Hal had a moment's wonder at who was running the squadron, realized that was belittling.

Khiri was goggling at the huge beasts as they walked under the moving necks.

It was that moment that caught Hal, and made him start crying. He fought the tears back, tried to look properly martial.

On the other side of the dragon row waited the royal carriage, and, nearby, Storm.

Hal and Khiri got in the carriage.

Storm blatted disappointment. Evidently he thought he should be the honeymoon transport.

The carriage horses, restive at being around dragons, were held in control by footmen, then led away until the driver could take firm control.

As the carriage moved out of the square, there was a commotion behind him.

Hal craned to see what it was, but Khiri jabbed him in the ribs.

"Try to look noble, milord," she said.

Hal obeyed, putting that pleasant smile back on, and moving his hand back and forth, as they moved down the packed streets toward the royal palace, where the wedding celebration would be.

He thought it was snowing harder, realized there were flower petals falling from the sky, coming from nowhere.

That would be Limingo's wedding present.

The crowd's roar washed over them.

Hal leaned over for a kiss, got a return peck.

"That's the best you can manage?" he said.

"Behave yourself," Khiri said.

Hal's grin changed to an evil one.

"I am thinking of you, lying on a bed," he whispered. "You're naked, and your hands are tied with a silk scarf to the bedstead, and your legs are apart—"

"Stop that," Khiri hissed.

Hal didn't.

By the time they reached the gates of the palace, there was a fine bead of sweat on Khiri's brow.

"And you said you had no talent as a taleteller," she whispered.

"At the clean stuff, none," Hal agreed, then leaned close and put his tongue in her ear.

"I said behave yourself," Khiri said. "And if you go and get yourself drunk like my father did at his wedding, after making all these cheap promises, I swear you'll be a capon before dawn."

"I promise to be good," Hal said.

The king made the opening toast, to the couple.

Hal, making the royal toast in return, barely sipped the wine.

Others were not so decorous.

The members of Hal's squadron in attendance had evidently sworn an oath that Kailas was not to be permitted to walk to the marriage bed, but would have to be carried.

But Hal evaded their efforts.

He'd slipped a gold coin to one servitor, and told him to pour him nothing but charged water, no matter what he or others asked for.

Before things got too drunk, he made a point of introducing his parents to the king, who chatted with Faadi and Lees until they lost a bit of their awe.

"I'll never forget this," Lees said to Hal.

"I hope not," Hal said. "I only plan on doing this once."

"Good," Faadi said. "I made the same promise."

Lees glowed, and hugged her husband.

Then they were swept away in the throng.

Farren Mariah was there, holding out a glass.

Hal took it, pretended to sip it, put it behind him on a table.

"What," he asked, to disguise his duplicity, "was all the excitement about when we were leaving the Square?"

"Aarh, it was your dragon," Farren said.

"Is he all right?"

"*He's* fine," Farren said. "He saw some old fat sort with too many jewels on her dress, and didn't like her on sight, I guess. She had some little white dog in her arms who kept yapping at Storm."

"What happened?" Hal asked.

"Nothing to worry about," Farren said. "The woman's healthy. Storm just ate her dog, was all."

Hal let himself be dragged away by Lord Bab, who wanted to drink his health.

Kailas circulated around the huge room, only sipping at his glass.

After an hour or so, he found Khiri, and jerked his head toward the stairs.

She looked momentarily disappointed, then started making her apologies.

"Were you a good boy?" Khiri said, then hiccuped.

They were in the apartment the king had given them for the night.

"I was . . . and am," Hal said.

"I wasn't," she said, looking not a bit ashamed. "I thought you might be interested in a bad girl tonight.

"Not that it matters," she went on. "All I have to do is lie here . . . if you'll give me a hand with this dress.

"And you'll find a scarf in the top drawer of my trunk . . . the biggest one.

"This bedpost looks strong enough.

"Just take off that damned uniform first. I've got enough creases from dancing with enough generals with their damned medals."

The first half of their honeymoon was spent touring Hal's estates, the first chance he had to travel their vastness. The people in the villages greeted him with a bit of caution to their exuberance.

But Hal made no mistakes, no missteps.

By the time the pair left for Khiri's own holdings, the people had decided Hal was worthy of their fealty.

They were especially taken that the Dragonmaster had brought Storm.

Hal had asked Farren Mariah about Sweetie, the dragon who'd dumped him into captivity, had been told the dragon never came back to the base. Hal knew better than to think dragons could have guilty consciences, hoped mildly that Sweetie had gone back to the little girl who'd supposedly raised her.

He rode Storm daily, and even enticed Khiri aloft once or twice, when the winter winds died, and it was calm.

She swore she enjoyed it, but Kailas wasn't sure she wasn't just being in love.

In the west, on Khiri's lands, Hal had already made his name, and the time there was unrestrained joy.

One thing that happened, Kailas would always remember.

Dressed warmly, they were on the winter beach below Cayre a Carstares, Khiri's great castle on a promontory.

Chunks of ice were being washed ashore by the tide, and it was a bleak day, the sort of day Hal loved.

Hal saw, not more than half a league to sea, four tented shapes—dragons, their wings over their heads.

They were being carried north-northeast by the currents.

"One of these days," Hal said, "I'd like to travel west, and see what the dragons are fleeing."

Khiri shivered.

"I suppose I'll have to go with you," she said. "And keep you from the clutches of the princesses of those lands."

Hal watched them, until they were out of sight, dimly aware that he'd made a promise to someone . . . himself, perhaps?

Their time together ended, and now Hal had to make his squadron into the mailed fist he'd dreamed of.

18

Khiri had wanted to come back to Rozen with Hal, but he'd asked her forgiveness, and said that he would be too busy to give her any attention, let alone the amount she deserved.

She sniffed, complimented him on getting a bit more politic, stayed at the castle.

Hal returned to Sir Thom's, and was immediately just as busy as he thought he'd be.

He'd requested Farren Mariah and Mynta Gart to stay on when the other dragon fliers returned to the squadron, which the king had ordered withdrawn from the lines until Hal returned to duty.

His dream of a fully-manned unit, made up of the best fliers, had been approved by the king more than two years earlier. But shortages in both men and dragons, plus the devouring offensive east of Paestum, had prevented him bringing the dream alive.

Now Hal had enough of equivocating, and used every bit of clout he had with the king to obtain one weapon.

It was a parchment scroll, in Asir's own hand, ordering

that the bearer, Lord Kailas, be given anything he requested, or face royal displeasure or worse.

That was a start.

Hal, sadly familiar with the ways of the army, knew there would still be many who'd find a way around the order, never quite refusing cooperation, but never giving it, either.

The second weapon was a tale for the broadsheets, carefully crafted by Sir Thom.

It announced that Lord Kailas of Kalabas, the Dragonmaster, was building a super squadron, intended to take on anything the Roche could put in the air, and that this would be the spearhead for the inevitable spring offensive.

Volunteers were being accepted immediately.

The trick, Hal told Sir Thom, was that he wanted to attract the best, but without slighting other fliers who weren't good enough, or, Hal said grimly, "without enough of the killer in them."

Also, other flights couldn't be made to feel inferior. Morale was low enough as the endless war dragged on.

Hal's plan was simple—he would fly south, calling on every Deraine dragon flight. He knew commanders would try to shuffle their worst and slackest fliers on him, in the manner of every army formation in history. But he knew enough names, and fancied himself a good enough judge of fliers, if not necessarily men and women, to bring only the best back with him.

One thing he had to take care of in Rozen was tracking down Goang, the prisoner who'd built a glider and tried to escape Castle Mulde.

He found him after some effort—he was a civilian, Lord Callo Goang. He'd been studying the chants of certain Roche hill tribes when the war caught him up. The Goangs were a famous family in Deraine, so naturally he became a hostage in Castle Mulde, where he made four unsuccessful escapes.

He was the darling of his family, who tried their best to keep him safe from the batterings of the world.

"I don't understand, Lord Kailas, just why you want me to join your squadron, although of course I'm more than flattered."

"You don't think like the rest of us," Hal said.

"Beg pardon?"

"A castle full of fliers, yet you're the only one who studied birds and tried to fly out."

"It seemed quite obvious to me."

"Exactly."

"I certainly had no interest in the war, but I must say I have developed a certain dislike, even before the fighting started, for the bullying ways of the Roche. I do not think the world would miss the absence of their form of government at all.

"Besides, until I'm able to travel the hills of Roche freely, my studies are at a halt."

"Good. I'll give you the rank of lieutenant, at first," Hal said. "And the minute the war ends, you'll return to civilian status."

His family was horrified that Kailas was putting their jewel in harm's way, and Hal swore he had no intention of letting anyone harm him.

Goang settled the matter by saying he was joining, and that was that.

Hal felt a bit like a kidnapper, taking Goang from the heart of his family. The man left burdened with packages, warm clothes, advice and money.

It was very different, calling on Mav Dessau's father, Baron Dessau. The student of architecture and magic had survived the raid, but just after returning to Deraine had fallen ill, and died within a week.

Hal, as he'd promised Mav, called on his father, a bluff, boisterous country man. He didn't seem much interested in Hal's account of his son's help, nor of how he clearly looked up to his father.

The man offered Hal a drink, then said, "Well, I suppose

I'm glad you came to call, Dragonmaster. But I'm sure you'll have to admit that Mav's help was purely accidental. You could hardly call him worthy of soldiering, now could you?"

Hal set the untouched drink down, looked coldly at Dessau, and said, "Baron, you may be a big supporter of the king, but I'm sure you will have to admit you're more than a bit of a shithead, and damned unworthy of having a son like Mav."

Dessau goggled. Clearly no one had ever, or not within memory, had the temerity to call him that.

He glared at Hal, considerably smaller than he was, and reached for a coach whip hanging on the wall.

Then he noted Hal's hand was on his dagger, the catch of the sheath unsnapped, thought better of doing anything, and stamped off.

Hal let himself out, rode away, trying to think that he'd somehow revenged Mav, but knew the dead could never be avenged.

Hal was summoned for a final audience with the king, who gave him only one instruction: that he was to visit all Sagene dragon flights as well as those of Deraine.

Asir had already gotten permission from Sagene's Council of Barons for such an irregularity.

"And," he added, "be sure to pick more than a token number of Sagene. You, by the way, will be flying a dual banner of both countries' standards when you take the field."

Hal was starting to realize there was a great deal more to high command than merely bashing the enemy.

He picked up his cap, clapped a hand to his chest, was about to back out of the royal presence, when the king held up a hand.

"One other thing," Asir said. "I know Baron Dessau is a shithead. In fact, I'd most likely call him worse names. But to myself.

"That's all."

Hal found a frizzy-bearded man with a sad face waiting at Sir Thom's.

It was Garadice, chief dragon trainer, who'd withdrawn to a secret base with some fifty black dragons, gathered in the raid on Black Island. His son, Rai, had trained and flown with Hal and had been killed in the siege of Aude.

"I have a small present for you," Garadice said. He attempted a smile, failed. Hal wondered if he'd ever smile again. "The rest of the army will think me a villain, and you a conniver who only succeeds because you're the king's favorite."

"A small present can do that much damage?"

"Well, perhaps it isn't that small."

Hall waited.

"I have some forty-six trained black dragons, which I have been instructed to provide for your new squadron."

Hal whistled, then asked, "How trained are they?"

Garadice chose his words carefully.

"I don't think I'd walk up to one on a dark night and shout Boh, and I'd make sure they're well fed at all times . . . but other than that, as trained as any dragon by a show-flier before the war."

"Good," Hal said. "Very good. Now we might have something to really shake *Ky* Yasin in his boots."

"There will be more in the offing," Garadice said. "We've had some luck setting out trapping ships like the *Adventurer*, keeping well south of Black Island, putting out lures, and have snared some twenty or so kits, almost yearlings.

"Some, interestingly enough, come from the west, and are a bit war-torn, even though, as far as I can tell, they've never seen man or his wars.

"It makes me wonder what the dragons coming west are fleeing. But that's for another time, when there's peace.

"With several wizards, I'm working with them and hope to have them in shape by the time they're a year older, perhaps less."

Another man sought Hal out, just as he was completing final packing for his trip across the Straits to Paestum, to start his quest.

The man limped up to Sir Thom's mansion, knocked on the door, announced himself, and was taken immediately to Hal.

"I don't suppose you might have room for a crippled flier," Sir Alt Hofei asked, a bit tentatively.

"Great gods, yes," Hal said. "I've never heard of a dragon flier who needed to run footraces.

"Welcome to the First Squadron, my friend," he said, pouring Hofei a brandy. "I was wondering if you were going to decide to serve on."

"Why not?" Hofei said. "There's little joy to be had here in Rozen these days. The time's past, and I missed it fair, when a man in a uniform would never lack for a damsel."

"I don't think it was around very long at all," Hal said.

"That's what the old soldiers say," Hofei said. "A war sucks away all the best things, and leaves nothing."

Hal looked at him closely.

"Are you sure you want to go out again? I'm sure you could find some nice soft posting training new fliers or something."

Hofei shuddered.

"I think being around half-trained glory-boys and -girls, not to mention quarter-trained dragons, might be even more dangerous than finding some Roche fliers to bother.

"No, Lord Kailas. I'm in it for the duration . . . or until they succeed at killing me."

"Then be welcome."

Hal had assigned Farren and Mynta two of the black dragons, in spite of their protests.

"It's simple," he explained. "We want to make as good a show as possible."

"You think a good show's one of those nasty bastards chewing my leg off?"

Hal considered.

"It could be."

"What about you?" Farren said. "I notice you're still on that old beast you had before."

"He's the Dragonmaster," Mynta explained. "He can do as he likes."

"Damned great monster we went and created," Mariah whined.

Two days later, they flew across the Chicor Straits to Paestum, and started looking for fliers.

Cabet was running the squadron and, Hal grudged, doing a good job, even if his attention to the smallest detail was driving everyone slightly insane.

There'd been orders issued by King Asir other than the all-encompassing one Hal had in his belt pouch: the First Squadron was almost overwhelmed with supplies, from new tentage to farriers and wine and beer.

Mariah licked his lips at the thought of all that alcohol going down the throats of the undeserving, and wondered again if he was really necessary on this recruiting trip.

Hal said he was. Farren grimaced, but didn't object, and went to spend some time with Chincha, the dragon flier he was sweet on.

Two days later, the Grand Tour commenced.

It was fairly grim.

They started in First Army's area, which was the hardest fought through, so Hal comforted himself that this was as bad as it would get.

It didn't make him feel better.

He encountered two sets of dragon fliers at the first three bases. The old, experienced fliers were worn out, exhausted. The newer fliers were eager, inexperienced, and fell fairly easy prey to *Ky* Yasin and his black dragons across the lines, or the other Roche flights.

Of the names he had for prospective volunteers, the response, all too often, was: "Sorry, sir. But he was killed a month or two months or three months ago."

Or: "Wounded. Sent home. Won't be back. Hope he makes it."

Or: "Gone missing on a dawn flight. We think we saw his dragon heading north that day, with nobody in the saddle."

Or just a slow shake of the head.

Hal had twenty-seven fliers in all four flights of the First, and needed at least another thirty-three.

He'd thought that wouldn't be an impossible goal, but was starting to wonder.

He had many volunteers—at one base, the entire flight turned out, drawn by the magic of the name Dragonmaster.

Hal put them through two tests in the air—one against either Farren or Mynta, and, if they appeared competent, then against himself.

In neither case did he insist on a mock victory. He wanted to see if the fliers had a feel for the air and, more importantly, for their mounts.

A mediocre flier with a good dragon, and some empathy for the beast, could destroy a superior flier who had no feelings at all for his dragon.

After these tests, he interviewed the prospective volunteers.

He rejected those who were flying out of revenge, or anger, just as he refused those who seemed intent on building a score.

The new fad with the broadsheets was to keep track of the top-scoring dragon flier.

Hal considered it absurd, since he had less than no idea of how many men—or dragons—he'd killed, and wasn't interested in trying to keep track.

The days were bloody enough as it was.

He also rejected those who spouted patriotism. These were invariably either the inexperienced or the fools. Flag-waving didn't last long on the front lines, and, when it vanished, the flier was most likely to be killed in a short while. What gave true tenacity were things like inner strength, in a very few cases, religion, or, the most common of all, fighting for the others in your flight.

They found ten acceptable volunteers in all of First Army, and moved on south.

The situation was a little better in Second Army—they hadn't been as heavily engaged for as long a time as the First, and the fliers weren't quite as shattered.

Twelve more volunteers were picked.

They, like the first, were told to secure their gear, given chits for meals and fodder, and told to make their way to Paestum and report to the squadron.

Mynta muttered that, as adjutant, she should have been left behind at the base to make sure the replacements were slotted in properly.

Hal didn't tell her there would be another change made when they returned—he still wanted an adjutant who'd been trained as a flier, someone who'd have a degree of sympathy for the poor bastards aloft. But this time, he would look for one who couldn't fly anymore. A flier as able as Gart was too good to waste on the ground for even the few hours allotted.

It was desolate winter, the ground gray and muddy below the dragons' wings, the skies dark and foreboding when they weren't storming.

Hal's thoughts were equally bleak, wondering how much longer the war would go on, and what would, what might, happen when it ended. He wondered if he'd be content with his estates, and Khiri, but suspected not. But he had no idea of what might interest him, if he lived.

He also wondered why both sides couldn't just quit, and say this whole nightmare had been a mistake. He didn't say anything, of course. The Dragonmaster's face could only be turned to war.

Besides, there'd been too much blood shed for a painful, inconsequential peace to be declared. There would have to be a winner and a loser . . . and so the war would drag on to a dark and unknown conclusion.

The lines they flew over appeared deserted, although now and again there'd be the moving dots of horsemen as light cavalry foraged or patrolled, and were driven back by infantry or heavy cavalry.

Hal knew there were infantry down there, huddled in their winter shelters or, if they were lucky, in some castle that hadn't been razed or in the ruins of a village or town.

Occasionally they saw other dragons in the air, sometimes on their side of the line, sometimes on the other. Generally the Roche fliers had the odds, and so Hal and his two companions would dive for cover.

Hal had the idea that the Roche had the edge in the air at present, and determined that would be changed as quickly as he could manage.

Yes, there was still a war to be fought, no matter how tired the soldiers were, and so he continued his search.

19

Bedarisi, to a less jaundiced eye than Hal's, might have been charming at one time. It was an ancient city, close on the Roche border.

It had winding streets, old buildings that leaned toward each other, and was known for having the best food in Sagene, better even than Fovant, its capital.

But it was here that the second great Roche offensive had been bloodily repelled, where Hal had seen his first combat as a dragon flier, so he had considerable prejudice against the place.

The city had been smashed by magic and by the soldiers of Deraine and Sagene—the Roche had been driven back on the city's outskirts. There'd been unfought fires that burned whole districts to the ground, and Hal could still smell the acrid reek of the ruins.

The people in the streets were pinch-faced, dressed raggedly, looked hungry, and scurried away from anyone in uniform. There were almost no young women, only a few young men. But everyone on the streets moved like they were aged, even the youngest children.

Another reason for Hal's dislike of the city was personal—there'd been a terrible episode before the war, back when Hal had been apprenticed to a dragonmaster, Athelny of the Dragons, who had great talent and skill with the monsters, but was also a driven and inept gambler. He'd wagered everything, including his show, in a card game with a Sagene nobleman and *Ky* Yasin, who at the time had his own flying show and was pretending to be a civilian.

And he'd lost to the Sagene—a Lord Scaer.

Trying to flee north to Paestum on his one remaining dragon, Scaer's guards had wounded the dragon flier. Athelny had vanished without a trace.

That was another mark against Bedarisi.

But it was the Third Army's headquarters, and it was here that Kailas chose to take a break from the road, and let the prospective volunteers come to him.

He set up shop about a third of a league distant from army headquarters, which was in a large manor house just beyond the city. Third Army officials found an abandoned farmhouse for the trio that hadn't been too ravaged by the battles.

It was Kailas's intent to screen prospective fliers, rest a bit, then move east, and, following King Asir's orders, comb out the Sagene dragon flights.

The volunteers trickled in, and Hal was very sure that someone in Third Army was sabotaging his—and the king's—efforts.

He couldn't figure out who, although he'd narrowed it to someone in army headquarters, who probably resented Kailas's taking "his" reconnaissance elements.

Or, conceivably, the person could have been a traitor for the Roche.

But Hal had expected something like this, and was vaguely surprised there hadn't been more obstructors.

He still managed to get six good fliers, four of them women.

Another volunteer showed up.

"I don't know about this one," Gart said. "He's very new, fresh out of flying school."

"Wring him out, and we'll see," was Hal's response. He was a bit irritated, fingering an invitation from the "Noblemen of Bedarisi," asking him to a banquet before he left the area.

He didn't want to go, but remembered King Asir's caution about being diplomatic, and grudgingly sent a message back that he'd be most pleased.

He'd just finished giving the response to the messenger who'd brought the invitation when Gart came back.

"He can fly, sir," she said. "He's still got a lot of the school ideas . . . but he's fairly good."

Hal, wanting to get a bit of the paperwork out of his system, took Storm up against the man, and was surprised when the man was able to force him into what was called a winding contest—two fliers trying to turn inside the other until either one of them succeeded and was able to make a direct attack on his enemy, or when the dragon's wing folded under the pressures and the beast spun out of the skies.

The volunteer was very much at home on his dragon, and forcibly made the animal bank, its wings almost vertical to the ground.

Kailas heard the dragon squawk in protest and grinned.

He tapped Storm with his left rein, and kicked it with his left foot. Storm obediently ducked, folding a wing, about to turn into a dive.

Hal pulled back sharply on both reins, and Storm squealed, but obediently flared his wings, and the dive was broken off, and Storm climbed.

Just in front of Hal was the volunteer, who'd anticipated wrongly that Hal would continue in his dive.

Hal sent Storm over the man's head, blasted once on his trumpet that he'd killed him, and signaled for him to return to Hal's farmhouse.

Hal brought Storm down just behind the other's dragon,

who was whipping its long neck back and forth, clearly unhappy at being bested.

Kailas slid out of his saddle, went to meet the other flier.

He was vaguely familiar.

The man noted Hal's puzzlement, grinned.

"You don't remember me, do you, sir?"

"No."

"I was your crossbowman, back when the Roche were trying to take Bedarisi."

Hal remembered.

"Right. Your name's . . . Hachir. Married. Used to be a teacher."

"That's me. Also used to be married."

Hal waited.

"After I flew with you, going back to shooting knights off horses got a little tame. Someone said they were looking for fliers, and so I volunteered."

He smiled, a bit twistedly.

"I got a surprise home leave before I went to the school . . . and found out my wife had made . . . other arrangements."

"I'm sorry," Hal said, a bit awkwardly.

"These things happen, I guess," Hachir said, but there was still pain in his voice.

"So I went to the school, graduated second, came back here, and got in some flying time, and a bit of fighting, before the weather closed in. Now the Roche are only accepting a fight on their terms, which means about three or four to one, and over their lines if possible.

"I'm not suicidal."

Hal remembered that Hachir had appeared quite nerveless behind him on a dragon, even though he'd never been in the air before.

"I'll be cold about this," he said. "I can tell you haven't gotten over what happened yet from your voice. I don't need any volunteers who're looking for me to help end their problems."

"As I said," Hachir said. "I'm not that suicidal."

"I hope you're telling me the truth," Kailas said. "Dragons are expensive."

He stuck out his hand, and Hachir took it, grinning.

Now all he needed was another five to be full up.

But he wanted ten or more, if he could get away with it.

Unsurprisingly, the lords and ladies of Bedarisi did not look as if they were dying of hunger. The tables were piled high with the finest foods, and a different bottle of wine accompanied each course.

Hal could have gotten angry, could have stamped out. But what good would that have done?

But the food was tasteless in his mouth.

He pretended hunger, pretended interest in the lord to his left, the lady to his right, who'd made it most clear that her husband was off with the Fourth Army, and she would dearly love someone to see her home after the meal, "considering just how dangerous the streets are these days."

Hal made polite noises, had as much interest in going home with her as he would slithering into a snake's den, and then he saw someone, a small, thin, expensively dressed man, sitting halfway down the right table.

"Who's that?" he asked the woman.

She brightened—that was the first interest she'd gotten out of Kailas the whole meal.

"Why, that's one of our noblest. Lord Scaer. From a very old family."

Hal's smile was tight.

"I think I want an introduction to him."

After the interminable meal ended, the woman obliged.

"I'm surely pleased to meet the Dragonmaster," Scaer said.

"And I you," Hal lied. "Actually, I've heard of you in Rozen."

"Oh," Scaer said. "It's delightful that my reputation has gone before. In what area?"

"I've heard that you're a sporting man," Hal said.

"Well, yes," Scaer admitted. "I do like to hear the rattle of dice and the whisper of the cards."

"Since I plan another day here in Bedarisi," Hal said, "perhaps we might have time for a friendly game or two."

"Certainly," Scaer said, looking at Hal's expensive uniform. "Certainly. I'd be delighted to share a table with Lord Kailas . . . at any stakes you prefer."

Hal was starting to accept the possibility that there might really be a live god or two.

"Innaresting," Farren Mariah said. "But I've a wee bit of a problem with this."

"Which is?"

"I'm not thinking, shrinking, that this business necessarilably has a great deal to do with winning the war. And as we all know, I'm a deep-down patriotical sort, who'd shrink, nay, vanish, at the thought of doing anything not dedicated to movin' the end of the war one day, nay, one minute, closer."

"What he means," Gart said, pouring another round of wine, "is that his curiosity's eating his weather leg off, and he won't help you with any magic until you fill him in on the details."

Hal ground his teeth. He didn't much like indiscriminately telling his secrets.

But Mariah seemed firm, and so he told him the story of Athelny of the Dragons.

"Y'see," Farren said at the tale's end, "you don't give yourself near enow credit for being a duty soldier. I think this Scaer is definitely a villain, and don't it say somewhere in the King's Regularations that we should trample villains?"

"Probably," Hal said.

"Is Scaer a cheat?"

"I don't know," Hal said. "It wouldn't surprise me,

although Athelny didn't need a sharp to clean him out."

"Now, let's us to practical thought. We want to punish this bastardly bastard, in his own style. Now, it'd be easy to stack a deck, or even use a little wizardry to make certain cards come up in that deck at a certain time.

"But assuming this Scaer-face shit is a confirmed gambler, he'd be the first to call for a new deck if he even suspicioned the one he was using happened to be rigged. Hmm, hmm, hmm."

He sat in silence for a moment.

"I have it, I have it fine.

"I think," Mariah continued. "This is one I've not cast nor seen, and all I've done is heard my grandsire prattle about it, and how proud he was for having come up with it.

"It's a bit tricky, but I think, maybe, with different matters . . ."

Again, he lapsed into silence.

"Yes indeedy, I do think," he said. "But what we'll need is a few little herbies here and there. Lord Kailas, do you have any idea where we might find a little vervain?"

"Maybe one of the chirurgeons?" Hal said.

"Of course, of course. Now, you toddle off and get some, since you're the rankest person around, in more ways than one.

"Mynta, dost thou happen to have any beeswax in your traveling gear?"

"I do, for my saddlery."

"If you'll go and procure . . . I'm for whittling a bit of oak off one of those trees out there in the downpour."

It took almost an hour, but the necessaries were procured.

"Now, the spell," Farren said, "assuming it'll work, which is a great assuming right there, is to be keyed to something. Like . . . like . . . ah-hah. Lord Kailas, if you'd beg me the borrow of your little dragon flier's emblem?"

It'd been given to Hal when he graduated from flying

school by Garadice, and become an emblem for all dragon fliers since.

"You'll not hurt it?"

"Sounds like a little weenie girl," Farren said, "wavin' her butt around the street fair. No, I'll not hurt it."

Hal unpinned the emblem, passed it across.

Farren opened a fresh deck of cards, separated the high markers from the rest, laid them flat, face up, on the table.

He consulted a scrap of paper he'd been scribbling on, while he rubbed the emblem in the wax, in the juice of the vervain, and against the oak.

"Now, you think of a word that'll set this off," he told Hal. "And I'll want you to say it, proper loud, but not shouting, when I point, which shall be after I mutter twice."

Rubbing the emblem against the cards, Mariah began chanting:

Your enemy
Turn away
Find another
For this day.

Scaer's luck
Is gone
Long in disarray
And his goods in pawn.

Shun the man
Fortune's foe
Give your best
To the one who sowed.

He repeated it again, pointed at Kailas, who snapped: "Athelny."

"There," Farren said. "That's that."

"And some damned rotten poetry to boot. I think I'm losing my touch. Mrs Mariah's favorite son used to be the bard of the boulevards . . . but now, just another mangy, rag-tail soldier."

He passed the emblem across.

"Rub it on the deal when you want to change somebody else's luck . . . and your own.

"So that's that. Lord Kailas, if you'd to bed . . . you've work to do on the morrow evening."

For the first time in his life, Hal Kailas wished he had the unctuous smoothness of one of the sharpsters he'd seen working the fringes of a dragon show.

He had to force himself to be polite to Lord Scaer, but couldn't manage the cloying friendship he knew to be required.

But he made it through a dinner that was even more painful than the one the previous night, and accepted the fine brandy Scaer poured.

Scaer's townhouse, which he made sure to tell Kailas, was very small, modest, compared to his country holdings which "if it weren't for the damned war, I'd be preparing for the racing season," was, in fact, most palatial.

There were two other men invited to dinner. One of them wore some very flashy uniform of a unit Hal had never heard of.

He asked, found it was a cavalry reserve squadron, kept on standby in case "those damnation Roche dare come back across the border. Plus it lets me get paid for spending time in the saddle."

The other man, Bagseg, was no more than a sycophant of Scaer's, always ready to laugh at Scaer's quips, or prod him into another reminiscence of the "old days."

Hal thought that a bit odd, since Scaer was no more than in his mid-forties.

The idea of a round of cards came up.

The idea met with approval, and they moved into the library, with leather-bound books and scrolls that looked unread, and riding and hunting gear that looked very well used.

Hal waited for almost an hour into the game, making sure to lose a couple of hands, then suggested maybe the stakes were a little low.

Scaer licked his lips.

Hal wondered if Bagseg was feeding Scaer cards or information, wasn't enough of a card player to tell.

He made sure he lost another hand, then, when Scaer was shuffling, touched his dragon amulet, and whispered "Athelny."

Scaer's eyes widened, seeing his hand; then he hastily covered his reaction.

Hal didn't think he was bluffing.

Kailas let his own eyes go wide.

"I think," he said carefully, as if the brandy was beginning to work, "something this good needs to be treated right."

"Like a lusty trollop," Bagseg said.

Hal made himself laugh with the others.

Scaer raised the bet. Hal reraised.

The toady and the horseman tossed their hands in.

Scaer matched Hal's bet.

"Beat this," and laid down a high hand.

The two Bedarisans whistled in awe.

Hal set his hand down.

"Damn!" Scaer said. "I've but seen a hand that precious half a dozen times in my life."

"Just lucky," Hal said, raking in the pot.

"I don't suppose you'd be interested in raising the stakes again," Scaer said.

"Well," Hal said, pretending to think. "I'd be less than a proper guest if I didn't, though it's getting steep for a mere soldier."

Scaer won the next hand, Hal the next two.

Again, the stakes went up, and again Hal massaged the little dragon.

After three more rounds, the cavalry sort pushed back.

"I'm skint," he said. "Spent more'n my wife allows per night, anyway."

He pulled on his cloak, made noisy farewells, left.

Bagseg stayed in for one more round, then folded out, but stayed, watching.

"Shall we make this a final round, Lord Kailas? Hardly any fun with only the two of us," Scaer said. His thumbs were working rapidly against the base of his index fingers.

Hal nodded, unobtrusively stroking the dragon emblem.

Scaer didn't ask Hal if he wanted to deal, and Kailas suspected the fix was in, however Scaer could rig it.

There was no sound but the whisper of the cards sliding across the felt.

Hal picked up his hand. His face showed nothing.

Scaer bet, very heavily.

Hal matched the bet. Almost half of his stake was in the pot. But Scaer had even fewer coins left.

"This is getting expensive," Kailas complained.

"You could always use some of the king's gold you're carrying," Bagseg suggested.

Hal looked at him, and the man shriveled.

"Sorry. Didn't mean anything."

Kailas turned back to the game.

"I'll take one card," he said.

"I'll play these," Scaer said.

Hal shoved the rest of his stakes into the center of the table.

Scaer counted them.

"I'm shy," he said.

Hal shook his head.

"So I'm winner."

"No!" Scaer said, almost shouting.

"We agreed, table stakes, didn't we?"

"Will you take something else to make up the difference?" Scaer said.

Hal pretended to think, looked about the room.

"I rather fancy this mansion," he said. "And Bedarisi might be a good place to live . . . after the war."

"That's absurd!" Scaer stormed. "This place is worth a million, maybe more."

"Play fair, Lord Kailas," Bagseg whined.

Hal said nothing.

Scaer looked again at his hand, stared hard at Hal, then at the huge pot.

"If I didn't believe in what I hold . . . very well then."

"I'll take a bill of sale first," Kailas said.

"Don't you trust me?" Scaer said, his voice ugly.

Hal, again, didn't respond.

Scaer went to a sideboard, found paper and a pen, scribbled, tossed the paper scornfully onto the pile of silver and gold.

Hal picked it up, read it, while Scaer fumed.

"It seems in order," he said.

Slowly, having full faith in Farren Mariah's spell, he laid his six cards out, one at a time, snapping them against the felt.

At each click, Scaer's eyes got wider. He wasn't aware that his mouth hung open.

"And yours?" Hal said.

Scaer looked at Kailas, then hurled the cards against the wall, and stamped out of the room.

Hal picked them up.

"Tsk. Tsk," he told Bagseg. "I'm afraid Lord Scaer is going to need a new place to live."

"Won't you give Lord Scaer a chance to come up with the money to redeem the deed?" Bagseg asked.

"No more than he gave a man named Athelny a chance," Hal said.

Bagseg looked perplexed. Hal didn't explain.

He folded the deed, put it inside his uniform. He saw a pair of saddlebags on the wall, pulled them down, and started filling them with the gold on the table.

"Tell Lord Scaer I'd appreciate his vacating *my* mansion within the week," he said, putting on his cloak.

The charity hospital was very crowded, very busy, and it took Hal almost an hour before the hospital's director was free.

She looked at him, and her expression made it very clear she had little use for soldiers, evidently considering them, and the war, as the cause of all her patients' troubles.

"I want to make a donation," Hal said. "You seem crowded here."

She softened. Just slightly. "We are," she said. "All the wards are full, and we've patients on mattresses in the halls, and my chirurgeons are working themselves to exhaustion."

"First, I wish to donate this mansion to your order," Hal said. He handed the deed across, waited while the woman read it, then took it back and countersigned it. "Sell it, use it, do what you will with it."

"Gods," the woman whispered. "That's Lord Scaer's. Isn't it?"

"It *was*," Hal said. "And you might need some gold to refurbish it into a proper hospice."

The saddlebags went across. The woman almost dropped them from their weight.

"Why . . . why are you . . . who are you?"

Hal thought about it. No, titles weren't right.

"The name's Kailas," he said. "Hal Kailas."

"Why are you . . . I mean, if you don't mind my asking?"

"Taking care of an old debt," Kailas said. "And, by the way, I'd like you to name the place after someone I knew.

"A man named Athelny of the Dragons."

Hal hoped that the bones of the old reprobate stirred a bit in amusement, wherever they lay scattered in some unknown forest.

20

Hal gladly left Bedarisi behind, and moved on into Sagene flying territory. Their fliers did things a little differently than Deraine's. In fact, from what Hal saw, they did everything their own way.

Discipline was a bit more relaxed, but when it was applied, it was far more severe, and with less appeals than Deraine.

When fliers weren't required for duty, they could go and do as they pleased.

The flight roster was taken most casually, but there was always the required number of fliers on their dragons at the appointed time.

The fliers wore pretty much whatever they wanted, frequently civilian clothes when they were off-duty.

The dragons were well-kept, if a little dirtier than Hal would've allowed, just as the enlisted men and their billets weren't always of the cleanest.

But the flights were very aggressive, and would attack any Roche dragons they could.

Tactically, they could do with some lessons, but that would be a simple matter to teach.

One thing Hal thoroughly approved of was the diet. Working with pretty much the same issue rations Deraine had, a Sagene mess cook would improvise them into a masterpiece, using local herbs, garlic, wine, and careful attention.

Naturally, Farren Mariah despised the diet. "Foreign muck," he'd growl. Gart, too, didn't seem that impressed with the cooking, but was more politic about her comments.

At one flight, she was utterly charmed by a slim, well-spoken young flier, and disappeared with him for the night. The next day, she was a bit sheepish, but both Hal and Farren behaved as if nothing had happened.

Hal figured a flier's life, as long as it didn't get in the way of flying, was his—or her—own business. It would be short enough as it was.

Hal had four more volunteers when he came to the Sagene 83rd Flight. He'd been told about the 83rd's best flier, stories both good and bad, and was very unsure about the man.

Once again, the man came to him, lounging into the farmhouse room Hal and his fliers had been given.

The man wore a thin mustache, carried himself like royalty, and somehow managed to have a sneer on every inch of his slender, small body.

"Good morning, Lord Kailas," he said, ignoring Farren Mariah and Mynta Gart. "I'm Rer Alcmaen. I assume you want to talk to me."

"First," Hal said, "you can stand at attention, and salute as you've been taught."

Alcmaen unfastened himself from the doorway, and managed a salute. Somehow that sneered, too.

"Now, why do I want to talk to you?" Hal said.

"Because I'm easily the best flier in all Sagene," Alcmaen said. "Not to mention I'm the high-scorer. Or would be, if those shitheels at army headquarters weren't hells-bent on denying my victories."

"Why do you want to join me?"

"Because I think you'll give me a chance for some action, more than I'll see here with a solitary flight. And you also seem to be close with the taletellers. A little fame never comes amiss," Alcmaen said.

"You certainly know how to win your way into a commander's heart," Hal said sharply.

Alcmaen shrugged.

"I know what I am, what I can do, and expect others to do the same."

Hal stood, picked up his flying jacket and gauntleted gloves.

"Some of us don't," he said, not knowing whether to laugh or snarl at the arrogant little bastard.

It was just as he'd been told. There were other tales he'd heard that Alcmaen was very close to a born liar, claiming everything from being of noble, if illegitimate, birth to having been a spy for Sagene in Roche before the war to the vast estates he'd lost gambling to the beautiful women in Fovant whose hearts he'd broken.

"Why not?" Alcmaen said. "It's always good to have matters in the open."

Hal nodded him out, and slammed the door behind him.

Mariah and Gart looked at each other.

"Hoboy," Mariah said. "He'd better be better than I think he is."

"It'll be interesting to see," Gart said, grinning, "if our fearless leader doesn't decide to go for real blood."

"Five to four he doesn't."

"No bet."

Half a glass-turning later, Hal came back alone.

He slammed the door more loudly than he had on the way out, threw gloves and coat across a chair, thudded back behind his desk and used three words even Gart hadn't heard in her seafaring days.

"Well?" she asked.

"The son of a bitch is almost as great as he thinks he is in the air," Kailas growled. "He beat me three out of three, and didn't seem like he was working that hard."

"So you took him?" she asked.

"I don't see how I have any choice," Hal said.

"How's he going to fit in a nichy little niche in the squadron?" Mariah asked. "Can't see him being the coziest of tentmates."

Hal shook his head.

"He won't be. I'll give him to Richia, let him drive the 34th insane."

He leaned back in his chair, sighed.

"The bastard's killed almost as many Roche as he claims . . . and that's all that counts these days."

"I'll wager a badger," Mariah said, "back when you was a tiddly little cavalryman, you loved to put burrs under your saddle, too."

"I am sorry, Lord Kailas," the Sagene captain, Sir Rhaetia, said, "but I cannot allow you, and your recruiters, on this flight."

"I beg your pardon," Hal said. "But I have the explicit permission of your Council of Barons."

"There are times that a patriot must oppose the commands of his superiors when they've lost sight of the important things."

"Obviously," Hal said, "you're aware that I want to talk to Danikel, Baron Trochu."

"Of course," Rhaetia said. "But it is important to the people of Sagene, to the soul of Sagene itself, that this man, our greatest flier, remains to fly and fight with a Sagene squadron."

Hal thought only a Sagene could say—and mean—something like that without sounding ridiculous.

He thought of arguing, then shrugged.

"Can I at least have the hospitality of your mess? It's getting late."

Rhaetia frowned. Clearly he wanted to say no, but his innate gentility forbade that.

"Very well," he said. "For the night only. In the morning, after the first meal, you must be on your way."

Hal inclined his head.

"Your dragons can be groomed in that tent there, and, at the far end, there's a trio of vacant tents for you and your team. I shall arrange to have a meal served there. But I shall put on guards to ensure you do not try to subvert my orders."

Rhaetia was a man of his word. There were a pair of sentries walking a post around the tents, and none of the Sagene fliers approached Hal.

But at least the food was superb.

"What are we doing to do?" Gart asked. "How good is this man, anyway?"

"The best," Hal said. "At least, unless the taletellers and medal-givers are complete liars."

"You're doubtin' that, ever?" Mariah said. "You should reassure yourself that all they tell is the truthiest truth of all."

"I suppose we'll have to try to get some kind of direct order from the Council," Hal said. "Or let the man stay where he is.

"Hells, come to think about it, we don't even know if he wants to volunteer."

"Yes we do," Gart said. "If he didn't, why would that captain all but lock us up here on the far side of nothing?"

It was an hour later when there was a tap on Hal's tent pole. Hal was still awake, updating his report.

"Come in," he said.

A slender young flier slid in. He was very good-looking, in a feminine way.

"Lord Kailas," he said. "I'm Danikel."

Hal grinned.

"You're welcome, Baron Trochu. How'd you subvert the sentries?"

"It is Danikel, sir. The baron is for other places, other times. As for the sentries, neither of them would deny a request from me. May I sit down?"

Hal shoved over a tack box.

"The amenities didn't go far enough for a suite of furniture."

Danikel smiled slightly.

"My captain is a good man, but there is no holding him back when he makes up his mind.

"I share the same trait, I hope. Which is why I am here. Would you consider allowing me to join your squadron?"

"I would indeed," Hal said. "And I've read enough about your performance that I don't need to put you through the tests I've devised for the others.

"Not to mention doing so might be a little difficult."

"It could indeed."

"Might I ask why you want to fly with me, instead of staying here? Especially when Captain Rhaetia thinks you're the soul of Sagene, and must fly with a Sagene squadron."

"That is a pretty thought," Danikel said. "And I am honored most deeply.

"I wish to join your unit because I think you will give me greater opportunity to kill Roche fliers. And that is all that matters.

"The more I kill—the more I am able to help others kill—the more quickly the war shall be finished, and Roche shattered so they'll never again set foot on my country."

Hal realized he was looking at the exception to his rules about patriotism—this man had seen enough fighting to have become cynical, but most clearly had not. Again, the Sagene thought differently.

"I see," Hal said. "Might I ask a question? You're a baron. Where are your lands?"

"Far west of here, west of Fovant," Danikel said. "May I ask why?"

Hal had been grasping at the last materialistic explanation for Danikel's bloodthirstiness—that his lands might have been ruined in the Roche invasion that started the war. But that was clearly not the case.

"Just curious," he said.

"One request, though," Danikel said. "Might I have two dragons?"

Hal lifted an eyebrow.

"I find I can fly more than any dragon I've yet ridden," Danikel said. "That's one reason for my wanting to move on. Our flight seems to be far down on the list for resupply, and I've been asking for such a favor from Captain Rhaetia for some months. He's tried his best, but without avail."

"Two dragons," Hal said. "I've got quite a few black dragons, and will be giving them to the best of my riders, which certainly will include you. But we're hardly oversupplied. Can you think of a way you can leave this base with the dragon you have now?" Hal asked. "Assuming you want to keep him."

"I do," Danikel said. "Hoko isn't the strongest, but she's used to my ways, and would make my transition easier. Yes, I'll take her."

"This is not going to improve my relations with your good captain, you realize."

"Naturally," Danikel said. "So I expect you should leave tomorrow, as the captain has told us you will. I'll be out on a dawn patrol, and join you somewhere along your route with what little baggage I need. Perhaps you can fly along the eastern highway, and we can link up sometime tomorrow?"

"How, exactly, are you going to handle Captain Rhaetia?"

"I'll leave him a note."

"That will drive him mad," Hal said. "And I'm sure he'll do something such as issuing a warrant for you as a deserter."

Danikel held out his hands.

"I care little about that." He grinned slightly. "What will he do? Make me fight in a war?"

Hal laughed.

"We'll do it that way . . . and travel, very quickly, back into the areas Deraine controls. You might be forgiven, being a hero sort of person. But I'm liable to end up in a Sagene jail charged with . . . hells, I don't know. Dragon-stealing. Flier-stealing. Whatever."

"There shall be no problems," Danikel said confidently.

There were none. Danikel, astride a fairly small, quite young blue-black dragon, swooped down on them an hour's distance from the Sagene flight, and they made it back to Bedarisi within two days.

Hal was now overstrength by nine fliers.

But he wasn't worried about that.

The Roche would reduce the roster in short order, and he would likely find some volunteers who wouldn't work out for one reason or another.

Now, there was only one more army to cover, and he could afford to be very choosy in his fliers.

"You know," Captain Sir Lu Miletus said, "there's a part of me wishes that you came to recruit me for your flying carnival, sir."

He looked marginally less exhausted than he had during the battle for Bedarisi.

"I'm sure," and it took effort for Hal to hold back sirring the man who'd first commanded him in aerial combat, "if you want to go, there'd be a way."

"No," Miletus said. "And don't tempt me further. I've got people to take care of right here. Although I could do with a few more to worry about . . . we're down to nine fliers."

Hal, remembering the lives that had tied him to the cavalry until they had all been killed, nodded, then asked the question he wasn't sure he wanted an answer to:

"Is Aimard Quesney still . . . "

"He is very much still," Miletus said. "Even if he does have trouble keeping roommates."

"And Chook?"

Chook was the enormous cook who'd once driven off a Roche attack, single-handed, with his cleaver.

"Hah. He's immortal."

Miletus's flight was quartered in a former dairy. The big milk barn served perfectly to house the dragons, and there were enough outbuildings for everyone.

Miletus, after making Hal promise to stay for the evening meal and drinks afterward, directed him to a small byre.

He found Aimard Quesney, who was even thinner than he'd been before, and with even more preposterous mustaches, lying on his bunk and reading a book of poetry.

He lowered his book when Hal entered.

"Good gods. It's young Hal . . . sorry. Lord, uh . . ."

"Stick with the Hal," Kailas said. "But you can leave off the young. I don't think I've been that for a couple-three years or more."

"So I've read."

Quesney swung his feet to the floor, sat up.

"And you're forming some sort of a super flight."

"I am. Do you want to join?"

Quesney's eyebrows crawled up his forehead, and he twirled a mustache.

"I guess that's a compliment of sorts.

"I don't suppose you remember the last time we had any words of significance, I cursed you for being a born killer. That's hardly the best relationship to have with one's commander.

"And I've not changed my mind about you.

"In fact, if half of what I read is true, you've gotten much more efficient at slaughter."

Hal, instead of being angry, was slightly amused. "Perhaps

I have. And I certainly see why Sir Lu said you were having trouble keeping shedmates.

"Do you, by the way, know of any other way to end the war than by killing?"

"I'd like to try telling everyone to just frig off and go home," Quesney said. "Or maybe some of us . . . enough of us . . . on both sides . . . frigging off and saying we won't fight on, we're tired of dying and killing . . . maybe that'd have some effect."

"You dream."

"I dream," Quesney agreed. "And until I have the guts to refuse to get on that damned dragon one day, or the bastards succeed in killing me, I'll keep on doing my share of the death-dealing.

"But no, Kailas. I won't join your squadron, nor will I thank you for inviting me to.

"Now, leave me alone, dammit. I was very happy, reading poetry about a world that isn't eyeball deep in blood, and maybe dreaming I was in it, when you appeared and made me think.

"I'm tired of thinking in a world that appears to have abandoned any kind of thought.

"The hells with it all, Kailas. And the hells with you as well. Go on back to your war, and see if killing everything in sight works."

21

Hal could feel it in the wind—winter was drawing to a close.

The war would begin again in earnest.

Other signs were the constant stream of couriers coming in and out of First Army headquarters in Paestum, fast dispatch boats coming across the Chicor Straits from Deraine and mud-spattered coaches from Fovant to the Sagene commander.

Less welcome were the streams of paperwork from headquarters and, worse yet, the Most Important Visitors from anywhere and everywhere, eager to "inspect" the famous—without anything yet on which to base it—First Dragon Squadron, and, even better, a meeting with their commander, the fabled Dragonmaster.

One visitor who was very welcome was Lord Bab, who showed up, and announced that the next time Hal had a Great Idea, he might keep it to himself. Cantabri admitted that he'd mentioned Hal's Special Raiding Squadron in Important Circles, which meant to King Asir. He'd immediately been given orders to form such a unit, at least battalion size, and have it ready for special tasks during the spring offensive.

Hal had offered very mock sympathy.

He had enough troubles of his own.

Somehow, when he'd envisioned this squadron, some years earlier, of dragon fliers who were trained, experienced, and the most dangerous Deraine and Sagene could offer, he didn't think that many of them might well be a shade on the arrogant side.

But so it was.

Rer Alcmaen had no sooner been checked out on a black dragon, requiring almost as short a time as he'd bragged about, when he cozened a fellow Sagene flier into going out across the lines predawn, against Hal's standing orders.

Kailas ripped into him, but halfheartedly, since Alcmaen came back with two victories. Of course, he claimed four, but unfortunately only two were witnessed, and sulked magnificently when Hal refused to send the claim forward to army headquarters.

Alcmaen's boasts had, in turn, fired Danikel, Baron Trochu, who also went out, without bothering to select a fellow flier, and came back with three claims. All of his dragons had gone down within sight of the lines, and were confirmed.

Naturally, the Sagene broadsheets went wild with these five victories, and trumpeted loudly about the true superiority of the Sagene fliers.

These brags meant the world to Alcmaen, nothing at all, it seemed, to Danikel.

But it meant, to Hal, that he couldn't discipline the two without incurring the wrath of the broadsheets and, most likely, King Asir.

Hal damned his new diplomatic nature, went back to work.

The overall problem with his experienced fliers was that few of them thought they had anything to learn.

Hal knew better, but had to pose his lessons very carefully, for fear of throwing pouts into his killers.

He had figured out six rules for living while flying dragons about:

1. Always get the upper hand before you go into a fight. That meant use altitude, surprise, blind angles, clouds. If you don't have the advantage going in, don't fight. Always beware the dragon in the sun, coming at you from your blind spot, and always try to be the dragon in the sun.
2. Your dragon probably knows better than you do. In any event, it can't hurt to pay attention to his or her squeals, honks, and moods.
3. Always have a back door out of a fight. Never get cornered. If you are, try to climb out of it. Never get into a diving or a turning contest with a Roche if you can avoid it—he and his dragon are liable to be better at it than you are, and if you learn that fifty feet above the ground, you are pretty well out of options.
4. Always have numbers before you attack. Never one to one, seldom two to one, and don't get cocky and assume you've got a kill with three to one.
5. War isn't a sport. It's a killing time, so don't think about chivalry, or about "being fair."
6. Finally, the situation makes the rules. All of the first five can be made meaningless in a second, and then you'd best be able to figure, and fly, your way to safety.

All most logical. But Hal had to be very wary of just how he got his fliers to learn them.

"I think," he grumbled one evening to Gart, "I'd just as rather use a godsdamned bungstarter to get things into some of these peoples' minds."

"Howsabout," Mariah suggested, "I winkle up a wee spell.

It'll either make 'em smart . . . or perhaps change the lot into dormice."

"You aren't that good a wizard," Gart said.

"Want to bet?"

Gart considered, then shook her head.

"I'd play hell losing . . . especially as a dormouse. I understand they don't take being beaten with any sort of composure."

Hal was making the armorer Joh Kious a rich man, if not necessarily a happy one, since Kious despised working with a bureaucracy. Even with Hal walking point for him, there was still too much paperwork for the independent-minded craftsman.

He had to hire several men to built the multiple-bolt crossbows for Hal's squadron, and was also busy making modified firebottles. These had originally been thin glass bottles, with a fire-making spell and flammable liquid inside.

Hal had come up with the second generation, working with Lieutenant Lord Callo Goang. This was a long dart, the length of a man's arm. It was cast of cheap lead alloy, both to save money and for ease of breaking. It was made in two parts that screwed together. In the hollow center was more of the flammable liquid, sealed with a spell.

These firedarts were vastly more accurate and handy than the old firebottles, although a good supply of the latter was kept in the armory, in the event of shortages.

Hal had the niggling of another idea for another weapon, couldn't quite get it to appear.

Maybe it'd come to him during the battle.

"Here, then, is my plan," Lord Egibi, Commander of the First Army, said, his white mustaches ruffling slightly in the breeze blowing into the room of the manor house serving as First Army headquarters.

Hal tried to keep his expression neutral, studied the map on the easel.

"It appears to be the same as other offensives we've tried which have failed," Egibi went on. "A frontal assault, all along the Roche lines, intended to finally drive them from the heights they've held for over a year.

"But it isn't . . . quite.

"First, we won't have the usual buildup from our siege machines, which seems only to give the Roche warning. Instead, chosen units will attack, and the Roche will think it's only a raid in force.

"Then, as they move forward, there'll be a great spell mounted against the Roche, and the entire front will attack in unison, as part of the second wave.

"A third element, over here, will be making a flank attack.

"Your opinion, Lord Kailas?"

Hal decided to be politic.

"I'm just a flier, sir. I have no opinion, and wonder only what you intend for my squadron to do."

"I want no special efforts before the day of attack that might give the Roche warning," Egibi said. "Then, on that day, I want you, in force, over their lines. I want you to have complete control of the air, so the Roche have no warning."

Hal nodded, thought.

"I have a better idea, sir."

Egibi waited.

"I would like to make reconnaissances, starting today, of all Roche landing fields behind their lines.

"None of the fliers will have any idea of your grand strategy," Hal continued, thankful that he hadn't used the lesser word tactics. "So, if they're brought down, they'll have nothing to tell their inquisitors.

"Then, on Attack Day, instead of being over the lines, I'll have my squadron over the Roche fields. With any luck, their fliers won't able to get airborne at all."

"Hmm. Interesting," Egibi said. "And certainly it's easier to shoot down a duck frowsting about in a marsh than when it gets into the air.

"Yes. Yes, I like your idea a lot."

Lord Bab Cantabri stormed into Hal's tent.

"What do you have to drink?"

Hal gauged Bab's anger, decided to pour a very strong brandy instead of wine.

Cantabri shot it down, held out the glass for more.

"And what put you into such a charming mood?" Hal asked.

"Have you been briefed by our good lord and master about the upcoming offensive?"

"I have," Hal said. "The day before yesterday."

"Did he happen to point out a certain diversionary attack aimed at the Roche right flank?"

"He did."

"Did you happen to notice what unit is to make that attack?"

"Uh-oh," Hal said.

"Uh-oh is right," Cantabri stormed. "I've spent the last two months carefully building up my stock of killers to be good at everything from creeping through the bushes to swimming across a river and leaving nary a splash.

"And so, for my sweat and their blood, what do we get? The chance to stand shoulder to shoulder, just like we were basic line animals, and march forward until some numbwit with a spear kills us.

"What a godsdamned waste."

"At least you're not part of the frontal assault," Hal said.

"Big godsdamned deal," Cantabri said. "Don't you think the Roche might just happen to have built up their flanks? And that if they see a bunch of warriors pelting uphill toward them they might be able to fight back?

"Or, worse, since my men are lightly armed, putting a few companies of heavy cavalry downslope to wipe 'em out?"

Hal nodded reluctant agreement.

"The only damned chance that I can think of to help is to get some light cavalry elements on *my* left flank," Cantabri growled, "and scare the bastards.

"Not that I think anybody on either side gets scared very easily these days."

It was nice, this high above the earth, Hal thought, as Storm arced around a towering cumulus cloud, and dove through a tunnel in the next one.

Behind him, to the west, bigger clouds promising a storm were onrushing.

But Hal would be finished with his mission before they arrived, although he might get a little wet and blown about going home.

The dragon seemed just as happy to be up here sporting about, no one else in the sky, instead of snarling after enemies as Hal was.

But as soon as Kailas looked down, he was torn back to reality, seeing the bare bluffs of the Roche front lines below him, so fought over that nothing could grow, and there was nothing but man's dugouts and shattered, torn things that had been trees.

He was too high to see the rotting bodies underneath them, didn't want to think about how many more the forthcoming offensive would bring.

Hal prodded Storm on east, and took a map from the pouch clipped to Storm's carapace.

Little by little his fliers had filled in where the Roche dragon fields were.

There was only one "hole," a blank spot some three leagues back of the Roche forward positions.

Two fliers had reported black dragons orbiting that area,

and so Hal had decided to take the last and possibly most dangerous reconnaissance himself.

He was grateful for the spotty cloud cover that let him duck in and out, hopefully not seen by anyone on the ground who might give the alarm about a lone flier, and set a trap for his return.

By now Kailas was a good judge of distance traveled, and as he came up on three leagues, he began scanning the ground below very carefully.

His eye was caught by a bit of a blur, as if he'd gotten something in his eye.

Instead of rubbing it, or looking away, he stared harder into the blur.

Very suddenly, two black dragons came out of that blur, out of nowhere, taking off.

The blur was a fairly high-level spell, cast over what must be a dragon field.

Hal decided he should go lower and make a swift pass over the blur, to see if he could make out any details, hopefully surprising the two Roche dragons below.

This, he thought, would be a decent way to get killed. He ought to be scooting for home.

But duty—or maybe his own pride—called.

He lifted the reins to put Storm into a dive, and two more blacks came out of a cloud at him, less than half a mile away.

Hal swore.

Caught, mooning about as if he were on his first combat flight.

They had a slight height advantage, and were coming in fast, keeping close on each other.

Experienced fliers.

Was that *Ky* Yasin's squadron below, under that spell?

Later for ponderings.

Hal yanked Storm's reins, but the dragon needed no guidance. He'd seen the blacks, and was already banking into them, shrilling a challenge.

Dragon pride was almost as suicidal as man's.

Hal cursed again, realizing he hadn't readied his crossbow when he crossed the lines into Roche territory, a violation of one of his standing orders.

He was thinking, as he cocked his crossbow, and made sure the ammunition carrier was locked firmly atop the weapon, that he wasn't fit to fly with his squadron, let alone command it. He'd been too long away from combat, and had let himself get sloppy.

Hal steered Storm toward the dragon on the right, flying head-on at the monster, fully half again as big as Storm.

There'd either be a collision, or someone would veer away.

The Roche flier's wingmate could do nothing except fire his conventional bow at Hal at a distance when they closed. If he tried to do more, there'd be a good likelihood of collision.

Hal had his crossbow up, aiming.

The Roche flier saw it, flinched, broke at less than twenty yards, pulled his reins to bank away.

Hal fired, as the black's wing almost brushed Storm, and his bolt caught the flier in the side.

He heard the scream as the man contorted, fell from his saddle, spun down toward the ground far below.

Hal forgot him, working his cocking handle and reloading.

He pushed his left knee against Storm, and the dragon veered to the side in a flat turn as the dead flier's wingmate brought his dragon around after Hal.

Now, just ahead, was one of those clouds.

Hal headed straight for it, the back of his mind wishing that the cloud would be as soft as it looked, a fleecy pillow.

It wasn't. Suddenly the world was gray, spattering rain, and Hal couldn't see Storm's head. But at least the wind around him wasn't a gale.

The dragon didn't like clouds any better than any flier did, and blatted a complaint.

Hal kept his mental image of where he was, where the other Roche flier was, counted four, then pulled Storm into a hard bank to the right and up.

He held the climbing turn until Storm was almost headed back the way they'd come, then snapped his reins hard.

He could hear, even if he couldn't see, Storm's wings crack harder, and then they were out of the cloud.

Just below, and to one side, as he'd hoped, was the other flier, pulling his own dragon into a bank, unwilling to follow Hal into the cloud.

He heard the sound of Storm's wings, looked up and saw the dragon, just as Hal fired. The bolt took him in the neck, and he flopped forward on his mount.

Hal turned Storm again.

Somewhere, coming up fast, would be the other two dragons, who surely would have seen Hal.

He gigged Storm again, and they went back, fast, the way they'd come.

Behind him, still below, were the other two Roche dragons.

There was a solid bank of clouds ahead.

Hal thought about turning back, and attacking the other two black dragons, held back his bloodlust.

He'd been lucky once.

He knew too many soldiers who had counted on their luck one too many times.

Storm dove into the cloud, and this one was the other's big brother.

The dragon was caught, lifted a thousand feet, then driven back down by the wind, while rain spattered Hal's face, feeling like rocks.

They were on their side, Storm frantically trying to control himself, and then they were out of the cloud, under it, the world around them gray with rain.

The ground was less than a hundred feet below them, and there was no sign of life as the storm hammered the earth.

Hal went for the lines, climbing to about three hundred feet as he crossed them.

To his right, a catapult spat a long bolt up, missed him by yards, and Hal was safe, on his own side of the lines.

He had seen enough to fill in that last blank on his map. Now to plan the squadron's doings on Attack Day.

He saw Sir Thom Lowess at Egibi's headquarters, looking innocent, and knew the day for the offensive would be very soon.

22

Hal blew one note on his trumpet, kicked Storm, and dove for the still-nighted earth below, out of the glow of the rising sun's arc.

Four dragons were V'ed behind him, all armed with the firedarts, and extra magazines for their crossbows.

Below them was that blur that marked a hidden airfield, that Hal hoped was *Ky* Yasin's base.

Out of sight, other elements of his squadron were attacking other dragon bases.

Hal pulled up into a more gentle dive. He wasn't sure whether he had enough height to dive through the blur and still be off the ground but looking at the trees on either side, he thought he had fighting room.

He felt a strange quiver in his mind as they "struck" the blur, and he felt Storm shake.

Then they were in the open, about a hundred feet over a large patch of cleared forest. Below were the huge canvas domes that were dragon shelters, and, along one side of the field, tents of various sizes that marked the fliers' quarters and ground sections.

"First the dragons," Hal had ordered, feeling his stomach coil within him in self-disgust. "Get fires going in their shelters, and that'll slow them down a bit."

His fliers obeyed, and the firedarts spun downward, punching through the thick canvas and padding. White smoke curled up.

Hal brought Storm up and around, barely twenty-five feet over the ground.

He saw running men, headed for catapults at each corner of the field, paid them no mind. They wouldn't have time to load their weapons, let alone shoot them.

Hal went down the neat line of tents, dropping firedarts as he flew. He deliberately chose the smaller ones, thinking those were the most likely to be fliers' quarters. He realized he'd always rather kill a man than a dragon.

Again, he pulled Storm up, looked back, seeing his four fliers seeding the field with more fire.

One, then two of the dragon shelters gouted flames, and Hal heard the dying screams of dragons inside.

He wanted to vomit, fought control, blew a signal on his trumpet, and his four flightmates climbed away from the sea of flame below.

Hal still didn't know if this was *Ky* Yasin's squadron. He reluctantly decided it probably wasn't, since the base wasn't big enough for a full squadron. But perhaps it held a flight or two of Yasin's since, after all, the dragons were black, and, as far as he knew, hoped, Yasin was the only Roche with the blacks.

There was another base about four leagues distant, and Hal steered his dragon toward it, to give that attacking flight support.

It was two hours before Hal was able to signal his formations to return to their base for a new assignment. They'd done an excellent job of bashing the Roche fliers before they could get in the air.

Hal could only see a half dozen or so dragons in the air as they closed on the front lines, promptly forgot about them.

Below him, the battle raged.

He had no idea how many waves Egibi had sent up the bluffs from the Deraine positions below it.

There was a thin line of soldiery, fighting about halfway up the bluff.

Behind them was a thick spray of wounded and dead.

It looked to be even worse than Hal had worried it would be.

He looked to the flank, to see if he could see how Cantabri and his Raiding Squadron was doing, saw nothing, didn't know what to make of it.

He had his own task.

They closed on their base, landed. Fliers piled off their mounts, all achatter about how they'd leveled the Roche before they knew what was happening.

Hal had accomplished his mission without casualties.

There were men feeding, watering the dragons, rearming them with more crossbow trays, more firedarts.

Other victuallers tried to get the fliers to slow down, drink a glass of wine or beer, eat a high-piled beef sandwich.

But most of them had no appetite, the blood rush of battle humming in their veins.

Hal called them together.

"We did well," he said. "Now, we're going to do better." He pointed to three fliers, including Danikel and Alcmaen, then at Cabet, a man he knew wouldn't get excited or lose track of his orders.

"You four, go high. If any of the Roche fliers get over being hammered, and attack any one of us, take them out."

Danikel nodded dreamily, and Alcmaen grinned, and the four sprinted for their dragons.

"The rest of you, split into pairs. I want you combing the

battlefield. You see any Roche banners, anything that looks like commanders or even officers—kill them. Use darts when you can, and try to stay out of range of their catapults.

"When you run out of firedarts, use your crossbows.

"I don't know how we're doing, but maybe we can give the men on the ground some help.

"Get gone."

Minutes later, Hal was back over the bluffs. He was wondering a bit about this squadron of his. Here he'd put together, with a lot of grief and pain, this great formation, and so far he hadn't fought it as a whole, dribbling it away in sections and pairs.

He'd have to consider that, after the battle.

Assuming he survived.

He came in low, against his own orders, toward the bluffs. It was warm enough for an updraft, and he let Storm ride it toward the top.

He glanced over at the flank, and finally saw movement.

Hal guessed Lord Bab had waited until everyone was fully engaged, then sent his Raiding Squadron into battle.

The Deraine infantry was creeping forward slowly, using ravines, ditches, tree stumps for cover. On this steep ground, there was no way they could bring mantlets or carry shields.

Hal saw a cluster of banners ahead, and pulled firedarts from their canvas bags on either side of Storm's neck, cast them down, didn't look to see what happened.

Ahead was a knot of riders, and they, too, got darts.

Then he crested the bluff, saw a catapult aimed at him, and pulled Storm away, as the gunner lifted the firing lever. The weapon had evidently seen hard usage, for the right prod snapped, and the bow rope whipped back, and cut the gunner almost in half.

Hal saw a man on a horse who looked noble, dropped him with a crossbow bolt, then was over the Roche right flank.

Cantabri's raiders were moving forward not in line, as infantry was trained to attack as if they were on the parade ground, but moving in bounds or slow crawls toward the enemy above them, one soldier covering his mate, one section covering another, one company giving fire support to another.

Hal turned Storm, scattered firedarts over the Roche line, heard screams and saw Roche soldiers start falling back.

Horns blasted below him as Cantabri sent his reserves in, and Hal flew along the line. He reached for more darts, but his bags were empty.

He felt pain, saw an arrow stub buried in his lower arm, the bloody head sticking out. He hadn't noticed when he'd been hit.

Hal took Storm up to a thousand feet, braced himself, and snapped the arrowhead off, and yanked the shaft free.

He was bleeding, used his dagger to cut off a bit of his breeches, and tied off the wound, still not feeling much pain.

He looked over the field, saw his dragons, and other Deraine flights, rising and falling, like carrion crows, diving down for prey.

The field of war justified the comparison. Bodies were piled, stacked, up the rise, a darkening crimson carpet.

But the carpet climbed steadily upward.

Hal was about to turn back for more darts, when a cacophony of trumpets came.

He saw, on the Roche right flank, Cantabri's raiders sweeping over the top of the bluff, and lines of Roche falling back and back.

A roar of pain, rage, he didn't know which, came from below him, and the Deraine and Sagene infantry that had fought their slow way up the bluff came to their feet and charged.

The Roche line broke in two, three, a dozen places, and then they were running over the crest, back and away.

Egibi had won his great victory.

But all that came to Hal, as he looked down at the carnage, was a dull wonderment at how men could stand such pain and, worse, bring it on others.

Storm's honk seemed just as dismal as Hal's thoughts.

23

The butcher's bill for the Battle of the Bluffs was high.

Very high.

84,000 Deraine and Sagene soldiers had died in just the final battle, and an estimated 75,000 Roche. Counting the earlier engagements, a million soldiers were killed, wounded, missing.

The armies of Sagene and Deraine had lost numberless experienced warrants and officers, men who it would take a year or more to train and replace.

Among them was Lord Egibi.

He'd gone forward, to watch his siege engines fire boulders up the slope.

A catapult's beam had snapped, scattering boulders from its net every which way. One took Egibi in the back, and killed him instantly.

Lord Bab Cantabri was named to take over the First Army.

Some of his staff officers tried to throw a celebration, but Cantabri refused to allow it.

"Too many are dead for any of us to feel any mirth," he

said. "There'll be time enough for parties when we take Carcaor and end the war."

He took the Raiding Squadron with him to headquarters, to ensure it would never again be misused as it had during the battle.

Cantabri sent for replacements from Sagene and Deraine, and, as they trickled in, moved on, deeper into Roche territory.

The Roche would take a position, hold it, and fight fiercely, sometimes to the death.

They, too, were bringing up replacements.

Hal thought that if the war continued at this rate, he'd best be having children with Lady Khiri, getting them ready to fight on in this war that promised to last forever.

But at least they were moving, instead of crouched below those damned hills they'd been holding on so long.

It took a while for the squadron to adjust to the change—many of the fliers, and, more importantly, the ground crew, had known nothing but static warfare, having joined after the lines firmed.

They generally moved every fourth or fifth day. The fliers would scout for a new base, looking for a clear field, hopefully on a height, since it was easier for a dragon to take to the air with a bit of an advantage. Then the tents would be struck, and the wagons loaded, and the squadron would lurch forward, in the wake of the front line soldiers.

At the new location, everyone worked, first pitching the dragon shelters, then putting up the work tents for the support elements, finally the fliers and ground staff pitching their own tents.

Hal, in spite of his still-healing wound and rank, worked with the rest.

An advantage of the change that quickly became clear was the increase in looting opportunities. The dragons would fly just in front of the advancing troops, and when they spotted a farmhouse or, better, a village being abandoned, a flier or two would land and ransack the huts, even before the infantry could claim its proper share.

Twice they were a bit too quick, and men were wounded by Roche soldiers, who hadn't retreated as far as it appeared.

But the diet of fresh meat and vegetables instead of the spell-preserved issue rations were more than enough for the danger to be ignored.

There wasn't much fighting in the air. Hal kept his formations strong, and the few Roche dragons they saw generally fled to safety. But there were those who stood and fought. Hal lost three dragons in the rolling advance.

He downed one Roche, as did Farren Mariah and Sir Loren. One-eyed Pisidia had caught two, just at dawn, and slashed them out of the skies. Danikel scored once, but Alcmaen was unlucky, to his increasing fury and the rest of the squadron's increasing amusement.

There was, as yet, no sign of *Ky* Yasin and his dreaded banner. Some of the fliers suggested he'd been promoted to a staff position, out of the field, under his brother, Duke Garcao Yasin, one of Queen Norcia's favorites.

Kailas knew better—not only hadn't they encountered Yasin, but had seen nothing of his Guards Squadron, either, since the Battle of the Bluffs, and then only in limited commitment.

He kept after his men never to relax, reminding them that the war was not over, or even half over, and sooner or later the Roche would come back in strength and there would be blood in the skies.

Hal woke one night with the idea for a new weapon very clear in his mind. Kailas knew that most darkling ideas are worthless and forgotten by the time the dreamer's fully awake, but he'd trained himself, on the off chance that one might prove fruitful, to bring himself awake very slowly, concentrating on the thought.

When he was fully alert he examined what he'd come up with, and decided, with mounting excitement, that it was still good.

The next morning he turned the squadron over to Gart, told her to follow standing orders, and keep patrolling, and he flew back to Paestum.

He met with Joh Kious, made sure his crossbows were being produced without problems, then went to army head-quarters, which functioned as the overseas command for all four Derainian armies.

He wanted a magician, and was pleased that one of Limingo's assistants was available. The man's name was Bodrugan, and, like all of Limingo's people that Hal had met, he was slender, good-looking and, in Hal's mind, a bit effete.

"I'm hardly a wizard," Hal said. "But I understand one of the primary rules of wizardry is that the part remains poten-tially the whole."

"That is so."

"What is wrong with the idea that if we took a boulder, smashed it into fragments about the size of my hand, and put a spell on it so that anyone, magician or not, could recite to make those chunks suddenly as big as the boulder was?"

Bodrugan thought.

"Why . . . nothing at all. A fairly simple incantation."

"Would you be interested in preparing such a spell?"

Hal told him what he intended to use those fragments for. Bodrugan grinned. "I like that. I'm just surprised that nobody else, such as a catapult hurler, came up with it."

"I am, as well," Hal agreed. He set Bodrugan to work, told him to bring the spell, when he had it, to the First Army's headquarters, where they'd know where to find the First Squadron, and thanked him.

Then he went to the provost's office, and arranged for a work crew of Roche prisoners to start reducing a granite boulder Hal had found to rubble. He arranged for the broken-up rock to be brought forward, assigned the highest, most secret priority, to First Army headquarters in the field.

Then the war changed.

Ky Yasin's First Guards Squadron, at full strength, returned to the war.

They hit a dragon flight, not, thankfully, one of Hal's, on noon patrol, smashed all six of the fliers out of the air.

Panic-stricken riders had alerted Hal's squadron, and Gart ordered the flight commanders to split their flights in half, and put them aloft.

When anyone encountered Yasin's blacks, they were to return to the squadron base, and other fliers would go out to alert the other flights.

There'd been a swirling fight in midafternoon that had cost Kailas's squadron three fliers, with three victories.

The flights were just now coming back to feed and rest the dragons.

Hal considered the weather, a bit windy with scattered clouds but fair, and made a hasty plan.

Hal ordered the commanders up, issued fresh orders.

He told Cabet to take his 18th Flight out, in two waves, scattered and not within easy support range of each other, with orders to patrol north-south just over the Roche lines.

"If you're hit," Hal said, "go high, and we'll be coming down to help."

"I'm *quite* entranced with being bait," Cabet said.

"You understand perfectly," Hal said. "And I may need you to do it again, so don't do anything rash like getting killed."

Cabet smiled, without much humor, ran back to his flight.

Within a few minutes, hastily watered and fed, Cabet's dragons were in the air again.

Hal called for Richia and Pisidia, gave them orders, and the rest of the First Squadron was airborne.

Kailas took his three flights up, made the dragons climb steeply, up into and through the clouds, east, into the setting sun, then turned back.

Below and west of him, he saw Cabet's flight, flying slowly, as ordered, to the east.

Hal was as high as was safe. The air was thin, and Storm hissed unhappiness.

Then he saw the Roche.

They came around a great cloud, rising like a mountain, in a formation of threes, each wingman supporting the lead dragon.

A nice, tight formation. Hal approved. The fliers would be paying more attention to not colliding with another dragon than anything else, except that nice, fat collection of Derainian idiots about a thousand feet below.

Hal blasted once on his trumpet, gigged Storm into a dive, out of the sun toward the Roche.

He had not needed to issue the command.

His three flights were already nosing down, spreading out in a loose formation, each flier picking a target below.

Hal ratcheted the loading lever on his crossbow back, chose a target, the leader in the third in the string of V's.

The flier looked up when Hal was about fifty feet above, as Storm screamed a challenge.

Then Hal was on him, fired once, and killed the man, Storm ripping at the other dragon's neck as they closed.

He let Storm dive through the Roche formation, then brought him back up, toward the underside of the Roche dragons. He slammed the loading lever back, forward, shot at another dragon's stomach, didn't see a hit, was up above the flight.

The sky was a swirling mass of dragons, trying to get close enough to rip a wing, or tear a flier out of his saddle.

Hal almost collided with one of his dragons, who didn't seem to see him, banked over, and saw, turning, a flier on a huge black, a pennant flying from the dragon's carapace.

It had to be Yasin.

Hal kicked Storm into a bank, was closing on Yasin, the smaller dragon turning inside him, when another black, a Derainian, cut past him, its rider shouting something.

It was Alcmaen, grinning broadly.

Hal's attack was broken.

Yasin rolled his dragon on one wing, dove away before Alcmaen could fire at him.

Hal recovered, saw a Derainian dragon with two Roche dragons on its tail, thought the rider was Hachir.

He had a slight height advantage, used it to close on the rearmost Roche, shot the rider in his thigh.

The man screeched, almost fell, and his dragon pinwheeled away.

Hal forgot about him, came in on the foremost dragon flier, who had forgotten to always watch your rear until the last minute.

The Roche looked over his shoulder, saw the onrushing Storm, and pulled up sharply, almost colliding with Hal.

As he went past, almost within reach, Hal put a crossbow bolt into the man's side.

The man fell, just as Storm's head snaked out, and tore the dragon's throat out.

Blood sprayed, and Hal was blinded for a second, then rubbed his eyes clear.

Just below him a blue-black dragon, Danikel's, was diving behind a wounded Roche monster. Danikel was methodically snapping bolts into the beast's stomach as he fell.

There was another dragon, about five hundred feet below, trying to flee.

Hal sent Storm down on him, pulled out just before they collided.

Storm's talons tore the other rider out of his saddle, and Hal turned his dragon into a bank, climbing up and away.

Storm wanted to go back and finish the Roche beast, but Hal wouldn't let him.

The sky, so tumultuous with killing a moment before, was empty.

Hal climbed for height, made for his own lines.

He landed, counted the others as they came in.

There were a few wounded men, more wounded dragons. The black dragons were deadly.

There were four missing, including Sir Loren Damian.

But they'd brought down at least seven Roche.

Sir Loren was reported safe in hospital with a broken leg by nightfall.

No word ever came about the other three.

Hal allowed himself one brandy, was leaving the mess tent to write letters to relatives of the missing men as Rer Alcmaen approached.

He saw Hal, grinned most unpleasantly, said, "Sorry, sir. But I thought I had a better chance than you did at that man."

Hal took a deep breath, then stripped off his coat.

"Here now," Alcmaen said. "You can't go and—"

Hal hit him, quite hard, in the gut. Alcmaen whoofed, caved in.

Hal let him drop, bent to pick up his coat, and Farren Mariah was there, holding it.

"Damn shame," he said guilelessly. "Poor bastid went and trippy-tripped over his own flattie footies.

"You best be on your way, sir. I'll help the poor ox to his tent and tuck him in cuddly and put a little kiss on his forehead."

The next morning, Hal waited for repercussions from Alcmaen. It was, indeed, seriously against regulations for a commander to strike any of his men or women.

Not that Hal regretted punching the man for an instant.

But Alcmaen said nothing, then or later.

Hal did notice that the man had quite a few additional bruises on his face, and walked very carefully.

He must have fallen down several more times on his way back to his tent.

24

Evidently, *Ky* Yasin had expected to knock Hal's squadron out of the war immediately for, after the first battle, his black dragons were far more circumspect about looking for a fight.

They patrolled their side of the lines vigorously, and occasionally ventured over the Deraine lines, but only when they had clear superiority and skies.

Cantabri wanted constant reconnaissance flights, preferring Hal's squadron, since he could trust what the First reported.

Hal managed to convince Cantabri he was pounding a square peg into a round hole, that there were other flights not intended for pure combat as his was.

Put up the recon dragons, he suggested, preferably in pairs, and put half a flight from the First with them on the same level. The other half would fly high above, waiting for Yasin or the other Roche units to go after the other dragons. The recon flights were slower, since they generally carried a second man, the expert at deciphering what was going on below them on the ground.

The slow advance continued.

The general battle plan was that the infantry would be sent forward, against the Roche, who wouldn't have had time after their previous retreat to do more than dig scrapes.

The light cavalry would try to drive in the Roche flanks, and the heavy cavalry would wait to exploit the advantage.

Once in a while, there'd be a break, and the Deraine and Sagene forces would make as much as a mile.

But the Roche became experts at counterattack, and all too often the big breakthroughs would be driven back, sometimes almost to their start line.

All very traditional, very expected.

The real battles were going on far behind the lines, as Hal learned when Cantabri called him back for a very private briefing.

"And how goes the war?" Hal asked.

"The war," Cantabri said carefully, "goes as well as it should. But there are problems which you should be aware of, not just because you're my friend.

"The biggest problem is we're having trouble getting recruits. People are feeling, not without reason, that we're pouring men and women down a rathole, and the war is unwinnable.

"Our spies on the other side report the same feeling. At least the Roche have got the big advantage of having heavy-handed goons with truncheons to chivy people into the ranks, although I suppose I'm not supposed to think that way.

"Also, just to dispose of our enemies, Queen Norcia is supposedly carrying on like a harridan, saying that she never dreamed there'd be a day with Sagene soldiers on her soil, let alone the accursed Deraine.

"There's word that she's relieved half a dozen generals, with more promised, if someone can't come up with a way to reverse what's going on."

"That's not too bad," Hal offered. "Maybe there'll be a revolution, and she'll be overthrown for somebody who wants to put a flower in their teeth and dance around the maypole instead of killing folks."

"Right," Cantabri said. "Those sorts are ever so common these days.

"Anyway, back to our side.

"There's talk, and of course you must not mention any of this to anyone, that King Asir may institute some sort of draft."

Hal whistled. "That'll not go well with anyone."

"But if that's the only way to feed bodies into the army . . . I don't know," Cantabri said, shaking his head. "Oh yes. Another piece of wonderful news is that the Sagene Council of Barons is restive."

"That's the sort of thing I'd expect," Hal said. "I wasn't very impressed with the way anyone in Sagene ruled, when I was over here before the war. Of course, I was just a kid."

Cantabri made a face.

"I had the misfortune of falling madly in love back then . . . mind you, this was before I met my wife. The woman was Sagene and noble. So in my mad pursuit, which never went much of anywhere, I spent a fair amount of time over here, traveling around and meeting the nobility.

"Like you, I wasn't much taken," Cantabri said. "Of course," he went on quietly, "I've never been much impressed by a lot of people with titles.

"Not the king, of course," he added hastily. "And now I'm one of them . . . as are you."

"What sort of restive is the Council?" Hal asked.

"There's talk of forming a peace coalition, and maybe trying to open negotiations with Norcia," Cantabri said.

"And what's the matter with that?" Hal asked. "Sooner or later, *somebody* has to sue for peace."

Cantabri started to fume, caught himself.

"True. True enough, I suppose. But I'd rather it be under conditions that are as demeaning as possible to the Roche. I'd rather they couldn't come up with some lies about how they were betrayed into peace, and want another godsdamned war in a generation or two.

"I really don't want my grandsons or their sons to go through this."

Hal nodded agreement, even though children were a long ways from his serious plans, at least at the moment.

"It's a pity that someone like Limingo, or some wizard like him, couldn't come up with a spell that'd make everybody as patriotic as they were back when the war started," Hal said.

"Sometimes," Cantabri said heavily, "magic doesn't appear to have much of an effect, here in the real world, at least not for a whole cluster of people.

"At any rate, that's as much as I've got. I suppose the reason I called you back," Cantabri said, "isn't just to have a shoulder, to cry on.

"What I'd really like—what the army, and Deraine really need—is something spectacular. Something that'll make people realize we're winning, even though it's taking a bit longer than the flag wavers put on, in the beginning.

"You've generally been able to come up with something dramatic in the past.

"This time, young Kailas, there might be a great deal more than an engagement or even a battle riding on it."

25

Hal was busy in the operations section tent the next day when a rather plaintive Mynta Gart came in.

"Uh, sir . . . there's a delivery for you."

"Which is?"

"It appears to be, well, two wagonloads of pebbles."

"Just what I've been expecting," Hal said, putting eagerness into his voice.

Gart looked at him plaintively, wanting an explanation.

Hal, for pure meanness, didn't give her one, but carefully inspected the loads of broken-up granite, ordered them moved to a secure location, and, just because he didn't have any latrines to dig, ordered Gart to put the unit's sinners on guard over the rocks.

Mentally cackling, he went back to his maps, laying out arcs east and south of their location. The arcs roughly represented the range a dragon could fly at one time—six hours, a distance of about forty leagues, depending on weather, load, winds and such.

He found it a bit hard to concentrate. Where the hells was that damned Bodrugan?

*

The wizard showed up two days later, accompanied by Limingo, his superior.

"We had a bit of a problem," Limingo said, "figuring out a way to make the spell universal, but not so complicated that somebody with his mind on other things—say, not having his head eaten by a Roche dragon—couldn't still remember it.

"But we're now adept at turning stones into crags, as soon as I cast an enchantment over your pebbles that's guaranteed to make them ambitious little rocks. Do you have a wizard on the squadron?"

"Barely," Hal said, and sent for Farren Mariah, and, after thought, Lieutenant Goang, who he'd been rather ignoring of late.

Mariah came, was informed he was now Official First Squadron Thaumaturge, protested loudly, was told to be silent and obey his orders by Kailas.

A bit sullenly, he went with Limingo, Bodrugan and Goang to the still-guarded rock heap.

Hal lagged behind, found reasons to go back to the map tent. In spite of everything, he was still a little nervous around magicians.

In about an hour, Limingo and the other two came back to him.

"There," the wizard said. "Your man here can now do the resupply, when you run out of the present pile of pebbles, although the quartermaster corps may raise an eyebrow when he requisitions oil, hemlock, dried yew.

"And, by the way, after the war I've suggested he could do much worse than study wizardry."

"The question remains," Mariah said, ignoring Limingo's words, "just who's about to be playing rocksmasher first before I workies workies workies my wizardry?"

"You," Hal said. "If you don't watch yourself."

"Aarh," Farren said cheerily. "I'll be watchin' myself when the army issues me a mirror." His expression turned dreamy. "Now there's a thought. A nice, full length glass, made of polished silver, that I can hang over my bunk for when I have visitors."

"Shut up," Hal advised. "Now, Limingo, if you'll show us the next stage?"

Bodrugan handed Hal a pebble.

"Now," the young magician said, "you're going to repeat after me, the following—"

"Uh . . . shouldn't we hide our little heinies outside the tent first?" Mariah said.

"Good point," Limingo said.

They went out.

"Repeat after me," and Hal obeyed:

> *Antal, Hant, Wivel*
> *Grow*
> *You were*
> *Now be again*
> *You must*
> *You shall*
> *Antel, Hant, Wivel.*

The tiny rock was writhing in Hal's hand. He hastily let it drop. The rock grew, hurting Hal's eyes to watch. It got bigger and bigger, and Hal had to jump out of the way. It caved in the side of the map tent, then stopped growing.

"Good gods," Hal managed. "I didn't remember that rock being that frigging big."

Goang was looking at the boulder in considerable amazement.

"I thought I'd had some ideas," he said, mostly to himself. "But I never thought about using magic."

Fliers were running toward them.

Hal, trying to recover his calm, looked at Limingo.

"Those words at the beginning and end . . . do they mean anything?"

"They do . . . sort of," the wizard said. "I'm not sure just what, though. Maybe they send out vibrations to other worlds, other forces. Maybe they even call demons. Or maybe they're some sort of a prayer."

"Mmmh," Hal said. He turned to Mariah.

"Get Mynta here. I want her to know that anybody who even breathes about what just happened can count on becoming a spear-carrier within the day.

"And bring Storm out. I'm going to headquarters."

"Ye gods," Cantabri said. "This will work all the time?"

"Limingo said it would."

"And your intent?"

"I'm going to go throw rocks at Queen Norcia in her capital."

"That will drive her even further into raving," Cantabri said. "And certainly won't make her underlings any happier.

"But . . . Carcaor is a long, a very long flight from here."

"More than two hundred leagues," Hal agreed.

"How will you be able to reach it?"

"I'm working on that right now," Hal said confidently. "But I'm sure it can be done. There's wild country between, and all I need is feed for my dragons. I think it'll take about three or four weeks before I'm ready to mount an attack."

"And if your raid succeeds?"

"Then," Hal said, voice hard, "we can train other flights to do the same, not just to Carcaor but to Roche's other cities. Take the war home to Norcia, and all the noblemen who think the war is something at a great distance."

Cantabri considered.

"I'm going to messenger the king, requesting permission for the First Army to refuse its left flank against the Roche, and turn south. For Carcaor. I think it's time to go for the throat.

"Now, perhaps, the end of this damned war is in sight."

*

Now there were many things to accomplish.

Hal's study of the maps of Roche, even though they were frequently sketchy, suggested way stations for his dragons.

His plan, most risky, was to take a flight of dragons toward the capital, Carcaor. Each night they'd fly to the dragons' limits, then land at previously chosen fields, rest and eat, then continue on.

The problem, of course, was that they must not be spotted by any Roche en route.

It was complicated, but not overly so, Hal thought.

The first stage was to seal off the First Squadron's base. No one was permitted out, and anyone arriving with supplies or replacements would not be permitted to contact more than a handful of people.

He thought he was perhaps worrying too much—all that his fliers could know was that Hal had suddenly developed the ability to create large rocks—the map tent was still half crushed.

What he intended to do with that was known only to Hal and Cantabri.

But still . . .

Naturally, the word quickly spread that something was in the works as First Army headquarters again swarmed with dispatch riders.

Someone told the taletellers that the Dragonmaster's First Squadron was closed to all visitors, which of course made them swarm around.

Hal was forced to borrow two platoons of Cantabri's Raiding Squadron to walk guard around the field, which they considered most humiliating and beneath them.

Hal agreed . . . but he knew these men wouldn't talk, no matter what they heard.

Besides, he'd need, he was fairly sure, at least three of them for his plan to work.

A couple of taletellers tried creeping through the woods into the camp, were caught by the raiders, and escorted out. One had a thick ear, and kept peering about as he went, expecting, Hal supposed, to see some sort of secret weapon abuilding.

Certainly he saw nothing in a stupid boulder that must've rolled into the map tent, almost wrecking it.

Three days after he'd told Cantabri what he intended, a sentry reported there was a man on the main road who refused to leave without seeing Hal.

"Have you tried chousting him with a halberd?"

"Thought of it, sir," the sentry said. "But he's a sir, and I don't know shit about the military, but I'll bet if you start whacking sirs and dukes and earls and barons about, you're going to get yourself in trouble."

"Very well," Hal said. "I'll take care of him."

The visitor was Sir Thom Lowess, who sat comfortably in an expensive-looking surrey, laden with boxes.

"Good day, Lord Kailas," he said.

"Good day to you, Sir Thom," Hal said. "And I'm afraid I'm busy, and can't spare the time you deserve."

"I need no time from you," Sir Thom said. "I desire entrance to your camp."

"It's closed."

Sir Thom just looked at him. Hal thought.

"If you come in, you won't be able to come out for at least three weeks," Hal grudged.

"Let me ask you this," Sir Thom said, looking about to ensure there was no one within earshot except the pair of sentries. "If I come in, will my tale be worth my being mewed up for that long?"

Hal hesitated. "Yes," he said grudgingly.

"Then I'm fortunate that I brought sufficient luxuries, aren't I?"

"Let him enter," Hal said to the sentries. "And welcome, I suppose."

*

The most dangerous part of the mission was at the start. That would involve scouting for the layover points, and must be completely hidden.

Hal decided he'd take four other dragons. He'd be happier with less, but he'd need them for the passengers they'd carry.

Since he'd be leading the formation, he didn't want to over-burden Storm, in the event he had to do some rapid maneuvering.

He first chose Farren Mariah, not because he was the strongest flier in the squadron, but because he trusted him absolutely. Mariah had already saved his life once, and Hal hoped he'd never have the chance to do it again.

Second was Danikel, Baron Trochu, since he was not only Sagene, but the best flier Hal had.

Third was one-eyed Pisidia. Hal was learning he was one of the most dangerous killers in the squadron.

Fourth was Sir Alt Hofei, from the prison camp.

Sir Thom was frantic for the full story of what was up, which Hal refused him.

"If I don't come back," he explained, "then I don't have to look like a damned fool as a corpse."

"But what will I say then?"

"Start a story," Hal suggested, "that I vanished into the unknown, in a raging battle with sixteen black Roche dragons."

Lowess looked at him dubiously.

"You wouldn't have made *that* bad a taleteller, you know. Sixteen . . . let's go for ten."

Hal shrugged, and told his orderly, Uluch, what he'd be taking.

In spite of it being summer, flying at height would be chill.

Carcaor lay at the conjunction of three fertile valleys, on the Ichili River, which bisected Roche.

To keep things secret, Hal planned for the reconnaissance flight to keep to the mountains, where they'd be less likely to be seen . . . and where flying might be a little chill.

So high-top boots, sheepskin coats, gauntlets, and lined tied-down caps were in order.

"One of these days," Farren predicted gloomily, "my gods-damned dragon's going to be peckish, see me in this damned coat, and think I'm dinner. Or breakfast."

Chincha, his flying and bed partner, giggled.

"You are, you know."

Farren actually blushed.

Kailas set all four flights to practicing what appeared to be utterly nonsensical flying, half expecting to return to a mutiny.

Hal had asked Limingo for a weather spell to give him some cover. Limingo had said that would be easy, since the Roche magicians would also like a break in the spring balminess that might slow the slow Sagene-Deraine wheel to the right.

It wasn't quite raining, but what Farren called spitting near dawn.

Hal's troops were assembled and fed.

The dragons seemed to realize something unusual was coming, and stamped in eagerness to be away.

They loaded each dragon with two men, the flier and one man from the Raiding Squadron with a heavy pack, plus, slung under their bellies, a butchered sheep wrapped in canvas.

Then they lumbered down the long field, and were in the air, flying almost due east.

Hal had ordered them to keep close to the ground, and give the alarm if they spotted any Roche dragons.

They saw none, and whisked over the Roche lines before any bolts came up, although Hal saw a couple of hastily fired arrows lifting through the mist.

Then they were over the Roche rear lines, and Hal saw confusion and tumult spread as they passed.

He waited until he'd reached open country, then turned his course, by compass, to south-southeast, and went high.

The first leg of his scout would be the longest, which he liked because it would get him farther from the Roche lines, and the possibility of prying cavalrymen, but he disliked because, on the return, if there were casualties or wounded, that could be the killer.

He was fairly certain that first day's destination would not be a problem, since his target had been scouted by a daring cavalry patrol a few weeks earlier.

It was an open, supposedly uninhabited meadow in the middle of a cluster of low hills.

The land below wound past. Most of the farms had been abandoned, a few looted by the Roche, as the armies approached them.

The ground climbed, and now there were trees, growing thicker. Here and there was the smoke from a cottage's cookstore, or bigger plumes from charcoal-makers.

Then there was nothing but trees and, here and there, ponds and small lakes.

The sun was moving down the sky when they found the meadow. They circled it once, made sure it was uninhabited, and landed.

They fed the dragons half a sheep each, ate their own iron rations, and the fliers slept, while the raiders kept watch.

Hal woke well before dawn, and turned the men out.

One raider would stay here, keeping guard, until the raid.

Again, they took off, headed almost due south.

Toward Carcaor.

The first step had gone so smoothly Kailas had to beat back a bit of hope.

He'd learned that elaborate plans never work in war, and wondered why he'd allowed himself to come up with this cockamamie idea.

Probably getting his ear blown into by Lord Cantabri as

being the War's Solution had a lot to do with it.

Or maybe he was turning into a glory hound like Alcmaen.

He gloomed on, while Storm's wings beat steadily.

The land below flattened, and large, rich farms and ranches reached on either side. The farmhouses were manor houses, and cattle grazed quietly.

One of the dragons behind saw all this meat on the hoof, and moaned plaintively.

A pair of bulls looked up, saw the dragons, and went back to grazing.

A good sign, Hal thought. They'd never seen the questing beasts before.

Or else, being bulls, not steers, they simply didn't give a damn, and welcomed those aerial monsters to come down and try their battle skills.

But the war had come here, too, Hal noted. There were few herdsmen in the fields, and the few people about looked up curiously. Hal hoped they thought the dragon flight was Roche, since this was a distance behind the lines.

The maps he'd consulted had gotten more and more slender the deeper they went into Roche.

Hal's goal for the second night had been marked as a hunting camp, a summering place for the nobility of the valley they'd left behind.

But as they circled it, it was evident the camp had been turned into some kind of farm. The open meadows, where stags might have grazed, waiting to become targets, had been plowed and worked, growing what, Hal had not the slightest.

The other fliers had seen this as well, and looked to Hal for guidance. He waved them onward.

His second choice was another hour's flight on, but that put them closer to Carcaor.

Hal hadn't thought it nearly as satisfactory, since all the map showed was a small lake. Where there were lakes, there could well be people.

He found the lake, signaled twice with his trumpet, waved for the others to orbit the lake.

Hal took Storm low, until the dragon's wings sent wavelets across the lake. Some kind of fish jumped, and a few birds took off from the trees that almost overhung the water.

But there was no sign of people, now or in the past.

Hal blasted once, and the trumpet rang across the hills rimming the lake.

He brought Storm down on water.

It had been a while since Storm had made a water landing, and didn't much like the idea.

But he splashed down, and then realized this was a great deal softer than landing on turf.

The dragon blatted in pleasure, as the other dragons came down.

Hal prodded Storm to swim toward a shelving beach, and the dragon waddled up on it, wings whipping, water spraying.

This would do very well for a second base.

The rest of the sheep were eaten by the dragons, and watch was posted again.

But it was very hard to feel any particular threat in this lonely place.

Hal called the raider who'd been detailed as guard/signaler for this spot.

"What do you think?"

The man grinned.

"I like it."

"You won't get lonely?"

"Sir . . . I was a poacher, back before the war. And I've seen animal tracks about. No. I won't get lonely. And I'll stay busy."

Hal doffed and dove into the lake. The others followed.

Farren swam up to him, cavorting like an eel.

"You notice one thing, O my fearless leader?"

"Many things," Kailas said. "Such as you're leaving a disgusting wake. You need to bathe more often."

Farren snorted.

"I'm as clean as any animal that walks, stalks, staggers or wanders the earth, so there'll be an end of insults to the lower ranks, if you please."

Hal suddenly realized something, almost blurted it, caught himself.

"So what am I supposed to notice?" he asked instead.

"All this godsdamned open land, furrow and burrow, here and there."

"So?"

"So why'd these slimy bastards start this war, anyway?"

"I didn't know you needed a reason for a war," Hal answered, turning serious.

"Surely you do. For land, for freedom, for naked women . . . some kind of purplous purpose," Mariah said. "When we win, I think we ought to take a good chunk of it away from these eejiots, since they don't know what to do with it.

"Enough for a decent province, and give it to some deserving lad."

"Named Mariah, by chance?"

"Ah, that'd do for a starter, wouldn't it? Land for all . . . now there's a motto worth fighting for."

"Or," Danikel said, having swum up beside them, "give it to the dragons."

"Now that's an idea," Hal said.

"But it'll never happen," Danikel said. "They're our partners . . . as long as the blood keeps flowing. When that's over, we'll forget 'em. Or put them back in flying shows."

"Why not?" a suddenly bitter Mariah said. "You don't think they'll remember us sojers the turning of one glass after the last bow shot, do you?"

Hal decided this was depressing, decided to follow the lead of Pisidia, who was floating, quite motionless, on his back in lake's middle.

*

The third day's stop was at the same time the least laid out and the one Hal was least concerned about.

Again, it led along a winding valley, with a navigable river at its bottom.

They saw the outskirts of two small cities, avoided them, and flew on, up into foothills.

There'd been little on the maps about this area, but Hal had quizzed Goang about his studies with the hill tribes. This part of Roche he knew, after a fashion, and apologetically, saying he wished he knew more, told Kailas what information he had.

One bit of data had been vital, and Hal hoped the war hadn't changed this, as it had so many other things.

It hadn't.

It was, again, late on a hot and wearisome afternoon when the fliers saw what Hal had hoped they would: rolling hills, with vast herds of sheep grazing on them.

The region was a dragon commissary on four legs.

All they needed to do was find a landing ground near one of the flocks, which were grazed unattended, and close to a stream.

The dragons were in heaven, and got two sheep each.

Then the fliers drove them back, to keep them from surfeiting themselves into a happy coma.

This time, they posted close watch, in the event of seeing a shepherd, but no one disturbed them.

The third guard was let off, with orders to stay well out of sight, but if he was sighted, to make sure he killed both shepherd and dogs.

Then the dragons flew on.

The final day's flight was fairly short, ending not long after noon.

The maps had improved, and Hal had chanced selecting one peak that was marked as having RUINS on its flat summit.

Nothing more.

They saw the ruins as they closed on the jutting peak. Someone had built a castle a long time before atop the crest, and Hal wondered how they'd brought the great stones up the steep slopes.

They landed in an open, once-paved area.

Far below, the Ichili River curved, the river that led south to where Deraine and Sagene had seen a great defeat at Kalabas, and Hal's love Saslic had died. There was a steady stream of trading ships and barges, and so Hal kept below the horizon, even though he'd be no more than a dot to the ships below.

Two bends of the river, and they would reach Carcaor.

Hal said they could expect Roche surveillance in the air, and so took their dragons downslope a bit, to where trees curled.

They were strange-leafed and -shaped. No one could remember having seen ones like them.

The dragons were nervous, without cause, and Hal felt his skin crawling a bit.

He decided it was nerves, being this close to the Roche capital.

The others were just as ill at ease, and no one could offer an explanation.

They fed the dragons and ate.

Hal chanced walking up to the castle, to see if he could determine anything of its purpose or origin.

The walls were smashed in, as if a giant's hand had battered them down. It had to have been winter storms after the place was abandoned, Hal thought.

There were a few open passageways remaining, oddly constructed, very wide and very tall.

Hal went through one, into the keep.

It stretched roofless above him, made of huge monolithic stones, notched for wooden floors here and there.

Whoever built it had fancied high ceilings, Hal thought. Even with thick beam floors, the ceilings would still have been twenty feet high.

He couldn't tell how tall the keep had been—its roof had been torn away, and the keep's stump was jagged, like a skull's teeth.

Hal wondered why he'd thought of that image, decided it was getting on toward dark, and he didn't want to chance slipping in the night.

He went back to the others, who had, in spite of the heat atop the mountain, built a low fire concealed by a pile of rubble.

At full dark, they reluctantly put the fire out, and settled in for the night.

Now, with three of the raiders gone, it was the fliers who stood watch along with the last raider, who was to be left here.

Hal drowsed, had ugly dreams he couldn't remember when he jerked awake.

He fully expected something—he didn't know what—to happen atop this mountain.

But nothing did.

The next morning, they prepared to leave.

Hal wanted to chance flying around those bends, to make sure Carcaor was really there.

But he knew better.

For some reason, he told the raider to stay clear of the castle, and make his watch somewhere below it.

The man glanced up at the ruin, shivered.

"There's no worry about me going near that, sir. No worry at all."

Hal told him they'd be back within a week, and for him to stand firm.

"After all," he said, trying to embolden the man, "you're the furthest forward soldier in this war. Something to tell your children in another time and place."

The man nodded, didn't smile back.

The five dragons took off, and wended their way back toward the front lines without incident.

Stage One was complete.

Now for the battle.

26

Surprisingly, none of the fliers had mutinied, not even Alcmaen, in spite of the seemingly absurd training Hal had ordered before he left.

This had included flying over a secluded field behind the lines, and dropping, from about fifty feet, pebbles at circular rope targets, time after time, with the accuracy logged by squadron members on the ground.

Another task was flying very low over a ruined village nearby.

Very, very low, which meant having to zigzag between a ruined church and a battered grain silo.

Naturally, the fliers turned it into a competition, and Sir Loren Damian, who'd returned to the squadron and insisted on flying with his leg in a splint, was the winner.

He crashed through the remnants of a thatched roof, and rebroke his leg, effectively grounding him for the mission.

Hal thought of saying something to him but realized he couldn't come up with anything worse than Sir Loren was already muttering to himself.

More logical training had included each flight flying in open formation, which made the fliers think there was some sort of aerial parade scheduled, perhaps a celebration of Lord Cantabri taking over First Army.

But that didn't answer the question of why First Squadron had been forced into isolation.

Nor why the formation flying was done at night and through cloud cover.

So the rumors spread, further irking Sir Thom, who was beginning to wonder if he'd outcagied himself by volunteering to be held in seclusion with the fliers.

Hal gave no answers for three days.

He continued the training, but added something—having the entire squadron fly formation.

Now it had to be a parade, the other fliers agreed.

They didn't see the preparations Hal was working out of sight: army victuallers had been combing the area for sheep, hogs and calves. These were taken in herds to other flights on other fields, and butchers assigned.

Everyone knew something was up with the fliers.

But no one except Hal, the magicians, and Lord Cantabri knew just what.

Or so Kailas hoped.

Limingo and Bodrugan were quite busy with a small project Hal had given them. They took two days to complete it.

On the fourth day after his flight into Roche, Hal assembled his squadron, plus Sir Thom.

"My congratulations," he said. "You've been surrounded by what looks like a pack of foolishness for some weeks, with never an explanation.

"Now, you'll get one."

He told them what the magicked rocks were, and that they were intended for use against the heart of the Roche. He said the mission would take eight days, and the people on the ground didn't need to know the details of the flight, nor the target. In time, they'd be told.

Now that boulder still against the map tent got admiring

looks, and comments were made about just how much damage that would do against Queen Norcia.

Hal broke the fliers, and Sir Thom, away from the non-flying members of the squadron, and took them into one of the dragon tents.

The dragons had been moved out, and all that was in the tent was a magical, very precise, model of Carcaor, from the river to the surrounding hills.

"Here's our target," Hal said, and stepped into the model. He went to its center.

"This is Queen Norcia's palace, and here is the Hall of the Barons. Those are our prime targets, as well as anything else that looks impressive or military.

"This model was made by our magic men"—he indicated Limingo and Bodrugan—"from paintings and sketches of Carcaor, and the memories of half a dozen men and women who were familiar with the city before the war.

"Probably it'll have changed somewhat.

"But I doubt if the palace will have moved.

"We will leave the day after tomorrow. I want you to study this model all this afternoon. Our wizards will be giving you a memory spell, so you won't be able to forget what you're learning.

"Tomorrow morning, we'll practice the squadron formation one last time. You'll have the afternoon to rest and think about our target.

"We'll leave an hour after sundown tomorrow night."

There was one further bit of business to take care of, which Hal had been reminded of during the recon flight.

He'd gone to Lord Cantabri for permission.

"Why not?" the scar-faced man had asked. "I should have thought of it myself. Your fliers don't seem to have a long life, and they might as well live what they've got with all the advantages we can give them.

"But I can't knight them. Only the king can do that."

"I don't think," Hal said, "that I've got many fliers that give a rat's nostril about being a sir.

"Unless, of course, there's money or a particularly gaudy medal that goes with it."

Mynta Gart was promoted captain, as were all three of the flight commanders. Farren Mariah was commissioned lieutenant, as were Sir Loren and the Sagenes, Danikel and Rer Alcmaen.

It should have made for a raucous celebration. But not with the mission on the morrow. And not under Hal's controlling eye.

A glass of sparkling wine with the evening meal, then a brandy, and that was enough.

Cabet came up to Hal, looking a bit worried.

"Yes, young Captain?" Hal asked jovially, even though Cabet had to be five years older than Hal.

Cabet wondered what these promotions were going to do to discipline.

"Nothing," Hal said. "Or there'll be a sudden increase in ex-officers."

"If this goes on," Cabet said, "we'll have the whole damned squadron commissioned."

"And what would be the matter with that?" Hal asked.

Cabet started to say something, stopped, frowned, then shook his head and left Hal alone.

Farren Mariah, of course, said he was outraged, that he didn't want to be an officer, that none of his family had ever been officers, whose only real job was kissing the ass of noblemen, but they were proud, independent.

However, when Hal left the mess, he saw Farren, sitting on a wagon with Chincha, and saw his hand continually stroking his new rank tab.

The butchers at the other fields had set to their task, killing the animals intended for dragon fodder, and canvas-wrapping the carcasses, as had been done for Hal's reconnaissance.

"I should ask to fly with you," Sir Thom said. "For this will be a tale worth the seeing. The eyewitness account of how the Dragonmaster singed the Queen's . . . uh, she doesn't have a beard, now does she?"

"No, you shouldn't ask," Hal said flatly. "First, if we run into any Roche dragon flights, you'd weigh me down.

"Second, somebody's got to cover the First Squadron with glory.

"And if you go and do something dumb like fall off, who can we bring in to sing our praises?"

Sir Thom was palpably relieved. Hal hid a grin. He still remembered Lowess's discomfort at being close to the sharp end during the battle of Kalabas.

The greater moon was on the wane, the smaller already set as they took off that night.

Hal was the first away, and he brought Storm, who was carrying the carcasses of a pig and a calf strapped under his belly, around over the field in a slow orbit as the others cleared the ground and formed on him.

There were fifty-nine dragons in the air. Hal thought that was perhaps the most that had ever been flown at once, certainly the most that had ever taken off on a single mission.

They circled the field one final time, climbing for height, and far below Sir Loren's dragon sent up a lonely honk.

Still climbing, they flew toward the lines.

A single Deraine lookout, on a rocky, bare outcropping, saw the dragons, and began waving.

It was a sign for Hal, he decided, but he didn't know of what. He took it as good luck.

They crossed the lines at five hundred feet, flying above the scattered clouds.

Hal flew at the point, followed by Cabet and his 18th flight. On either side flew Richia's 34th flight and Pisidia's 20th. Above the formation flew Hal's own 11th flight, Gart at its head, guarding against the slight possibility there might be a Roche patrol aloft and above them.

But the air was empty, and if they were seen by the Roche below, Hal saw no sign of an alarm.

Hal led the formation on, flying by the moon and by compass, all that night, and into the next dawn.

It was early morning when their first stop came clear, and Hal brought the dragons down toward the meadow.

In its middle was a long yellow cloth panel.

That was the arranged signal the stay-behind raider was to use if there were no intruders. He'd been spell-sealed by Limingo not to reveal that information, even under torture.

The great formation landed, and each flier unloaded and fed his dragon.

Richia came to him, said one flier from his flight had to turn back. His dragon was flying oddly, as if a wing had been sprained.

Fifty-eight fliers.

Hal decided to press his luck, and not wait for nightfall, but get farther away from the front lines.

This second stage would be a long day, for as soon as the dragons were fed and watered, and given two hours' rest, their gear was loaded on, and, protesting, tired, the flight moved on to the next stop.

Again, they crossed the rich valley, and this time were seen by some riders, and a group of farmworkers, who shouted and waved.

Hal had given orders if something like this happened, and so his fliers waved back, and shouted enthusiastically. Hal had a Roche banner rolled and tied against his carapace, and he let it fly free, and heard cheering from below.

They flew on, and saw, once, far in the distance, a pair of

dragons. Hal couldn't tell if they were wild or not. But they saw the formation, and hastily dove out of sight.

It was late afternoon when they came down on the lake, after having seen the yellow banner waiting.

Hal had worried about the dragons wanting to sport about in the water, but they were too tired, and, after being fed, curled under the trees and went promptly to sleep.

The raider they'd left as guard had taken game, set up racks, and had smoked meat for the fliers, an unexpected change from the rations they carried.

As he'd said, he was quite happy in this lonely valley, and said he wouldn't mind staying on until the war ended, if Hal wanted.

Hal tried to sleep, but found it hard, his mind bringing up visions of Carcaor from many angles and their attack, and which would be the best way to approach.

But eventually sleep rolled over him.

He was brought awake by the raider, standing sentry. It was growing dark, and, around the lake, the dragons were coming awake, walking into the lake and thrashing about.

Most of the fliers followed suit, and again they strapped their gear on, and climbed into the skies.

Hal was beginning to have a bit of hope that his overly elaborate plan might be carried off.

His mood was heightened by the flight along the empty winding forest valley. They stayed low, for the area around Carcaor might be patrolled by dragons, although Hal couldn't think of a reason why, since there'd been no threat to the capital.

Yet.

They saw only one person that evening—a young boy, fishing in a bright green rowboat, just at dusk, in the middle of a winding creek. Hal waved, and the boy waved back, and then the formation was gone.

Hal wondered what the boy had thought, and if he'd ever

learn that the dragons were his enemies, or if he'd think they were fellow Roche, and maybe be drawn to flying himself.

He grunted at himself for being a damned romantic, concentrated on his flying.

It was, thankfully, a dull flight, and so Hal was glad to see the rolling meadows marking their third stop appear, just before false dawn.

They landed, and it was a rather bloody paradise for the dragons as they steered panicked sheep this way and that, always ending in a dragon's satisfied gullet.

Some of the fliers got a bit greenish at the sight, and even Hal had to admit a touch of queasiness.

One flier who paid fascinated attention, though, was Danikel. Hal asked him about it, and the man said, very seriously, that the more he knew about dragons the better he'd be at killing Roche.

There was no argument about that.

Hal was glad to see there were no outraged shepherds to deal with.

He decided to press their luck once more, and so ordered the fliers to be roused late the next morning and flew on to their final stop, the crag just beyond Carcaor.

Each dragon carried two carcasses tied in canvas—one for this night's meal, the next for the day after the raid. Hal wasn't sure how that would work out—if there were dragons patrolling Carcaor, or if they'd be able to get out as smoothly as he hoped they'd go in.

But that was for the morrow.

It was hazy that day, which gave decent cover for the squadron. Once again, Hal saw no dragons in the air, wondered if every one the Roche had captured was serving at the front. But that was impossible: they would have to have some way of training dragons—and their fliers—and they'd hardly do that in combat.

The Ichili River was below them, winding toward the

capital, and the crag that would be their final layover loomed.

Hal felt another inexplicable chill seeing it.

He took Storm in over the ruined castle, looking for the yellow banner.

There was none.

Hal thought about finding another base, but it was late in the day. He certainly couldn't raid Carcaor with the supplies still on the dragons, and his boulders and the firedarts he'd brought unready to deploy.

He blew a blast on his trumpet, but there was no sign of his raider.

But there were no signs of Roche, either.

Hal took a deep breath, brought Storm in below the castle, on that open parade area.

Storm didn't seem to like landing there any better than Hal did.

He dismounted, crossbow ready.

But the crag was deserted.

There was a soft wind across the crag, and leaves moved on the weird trees below the crest.

No more.

Hal blew an alerting note on his trumpet, not wanting to, somehow reluctant to disturb the silence.

The dragons came in, and none seemed glad to be on this mountaintop, although Hal thought he might be putting his own feelings on the obviously tired beasts.

He told the flight commanders what had happened, and, even though the fliers needed rest, put a third of the squadron on alert.

Farren Mariah came to him as he was going over the last details of the attack.

"I like your home very little, sir, even though it has a great view."

Hal hesitated, then told Mariah of his own feelings.

"I'd guess the raider got spooked and ran off," Farren said.

"I surely would've considered it. But from what I've seen of Cantabri's killers, there's nothing on the earth or beyond it that would scare them.

"And I'm starting to scare me," he went on. "I think I'll shut my hole and get my head down.

"Although I won't be pissing and whining about having to take a turn on guard.

"I always feel better with a sword—or anyways a good solid tree branch—in my hand."

Hal nodded agreement, found his flight commanders, and made sure they were ready for the morrow, which would come early.

He took the first watch, and would take the last as well.

All was quiet, except for the occasional snore of a dragon, or the rattle of a wing as they moved in their sleep.

The last of the dying moons were setting as Hal came off guard, and curled up near Storm to get an hour or so's rest.

He slept . . . and he dreamed.

Hal was in the minds of several men as he tossed and turned.

A crude savage who traded for furs with the bearded men who came up the river with strange gifts.

One of the traders, craftier than his fellows, for he had a post on the river, and was clearing land beyond it for farming.

A still cleverer man who ended up with his post, and the land.

Then it was as if he were standing at a distance, watching a moving tableau.

There was a town abuilding on the land, after the farmers who'd thought they'd owned it had been run off or killed.

But the river rose, and took the town.

The men rebuilt it on higher ground, and it became a city.

Then something came on them from the heavens above.

Hal couldn't tell, in his dream, if it was a demon, or some

sort of earth spirit. But it was so fearsome that men died of fright just seeing it loom down on them.

It ravaged the city in a night, smashing and killing and, when dawn came, there were but few survivors.

They were stubborn, and there were wizards among them.

They cast spells, and determined that spirit or demon had come from the highest crag in the range that ran alongside the river.

Some peoples would have fled, or tried to placate whatever it was.

These men were different.

Using the labor of many slaves, the last of the native peoples of the region, and magic, they built a great castle, and assigned their strongest wizards to stand guard against the spirit, giving them power and the best of food, drink, men and women as payment.

Time passed, and the demon didn't appear again, nor did the guardians sense any sign of its presence.

They thought it might have died, if something beyond life could die, or perhaps had left this universe for another.

No one knew.

But there seemed little purpose in keeping the watch, and so the castle was abandoned.

Three storms within a year of its abandonment tore at the castle, and smashed it down.

Some people in the city on the river, growing larger and more powerful by the day, said this was a warning, or a sign the spirit still was present.

They were laughed at.

There were more important things to think of for the men and women of the city now named Carcaor—power, and wielding that power to form a great nation.

The magicians had lost their authority, so now barons, and then kings and queens, ruled Carcaor and the lands around that were named Roche.

No one cared about the ruins far above the city, and no one visited them.

Perhaps there was still something there, something sleeping under the crumbling walls.

No one knew.

Hal woke, sweating, feeling like he'd not slept at all.

It was almost time for the last guard, and so he relieved the post he'd assigned himself to, not fancying returning to that dream, and what else it might show.

It took the entire watch for him to come fully awake and rid himself of the dread that pulled at him.

But eventually it was gone, and there were other things to concern himself with as the dragons were saddled and readied for battle.

The firedarts were unpacked from their straw covers, and put in baskets on either side of the saddles. A pouch was hung on each dragon's carapace, holding the ensorcelled bits of that great boulder.

The dragons were fed, and the men flew them off the crag to the river below, to water them.

Then it was time, and they took off again, and circled up and up, out of the canyon, above the crag, and then on up the Ichili River in the dark.

It was bare minutes before false dawn when they rounded the last bend.

Carcaor, still sleeping, with only a few lights gleaming, was before them.

If Limingo and Bodrugan's model was at fault, Hal couldn't tell. The waterfront and warehouses sprawled to his left, along the river, and the suburbs stretched ahead of him, on Carcaor's far side.

The city's center was very obvious, all tall buildings, elaborate parks and palaces.

In the center was Queen Norcia's palace, two golden domes

on either side of the huge entrance.

Hal tooted his trumpet once, and the four flight commanders echoed his command.

The dragons spread out on line, as trained.

Hal steered Storm at the palace.

Dragons had been called "whispering death" by the Roche front line troops. Now their capital was about to experience this death.

He fumbled open the pouch in front of him, took out a small fragment.

For an instant he panicked, not being able to remember the activating spell. But then his battle nerves steadied, and the spell came back.

He chanted the words as the palace closed, finished, felt the fragment squirm unpleasantly in his fingers, as if it were jelly instead of stone.

He tossed it away, and, as it arced downward, past Storm's wings, it grew and grew. Then it was a monstrous boulder.

It hit one of the palace's rooftops, bounced high, and smashed through one of the domes.

Two other great boulders tumbled down from other dragons. One crashed on the palace steps, rolled through four columns, breaking them like toothpicks.

The portico sagged, as another boulder missed the palace, striking short of the palace. But it bounced like Hal's had, and shattered a wall.

Then Hal was past, bringing Storm back around.

Not far distant was the Hall of Barons. Hal saw a pair of boulders destroy its flat roof; then he was leaning forward, a pebble in his hand, and, as he said the spell, he pitched the pebble at the back wall of the palace.

It tore through it, and stones cascaded down.

To one side was a great stable, and a misaimed boulder tore its wall away.

He heard the scream of terrified horses as he came around

once more, and his boulder struck the palace square in the center.

I would hope, he thought savagely, *that it landed on Queen Norcia's bed. With her and her favorite in it.*

He heard dragons scream, saw, in the streets below, a unit of heavy cavalry in formation.

Hal, remembering his hatred and fear of the heavies when he'd been a cavalryman himself, took Storm low, and tossed a pebble at them.

It grew, and tumbled horses and riders aside like bowling pins.

There was a great building, perhaps an office, perhaps luxury apartments, and Storm barely turned aside in time.

Hal glanced back, saw Farren Mariah as he hurled his pebble at the building.

It grew, smashed into its center, and stone crumbled, and fell.

Again and again Hal struck at the palace.

Other fliers were crisscrossing the city center, and Hal almost rammed one, a blue female, recognized Danikel, and saw the fierce look of glee on his face, staring down at Carcaor, not seeing Kailas at all.

The palace was tumbledown, and Hal, with only a few pebbles left, went after large buildings behind it, not knowing what they were, offices or, this close to the palace, apartments for the powerful.

Then the last pebble was gone.

Below, the Roche were streaming out of their homes in wakening panic.

You've not good reason yet for a frenzy, Hal thought, and took a pair of firedarts from their baskets, clung to Storm with his knees, and cold-bloodedly pitched them down into the middle of a mass of men.

The darts exploded, and Hal could hear the screams.

Now have your riot, and that'll teach you to go and play at war, he thought and took Storm over the ruined Hall of the Barons.

Two firedarts went down into the shatter, and flames bellowed up.

Other buildings were afire as well, and fire was licking at the heart of Norcia's palace.

There was no one else in the skies except Hal's dragons, and he went down a broad boulevard, almost below the rooftops of the buildings around him, dropping firedarts as if he was a peasant, sowing a furrow.

Behind him, the inferno gouted.

Then he was dry, with nothing left to kill with, and took Storm high.

Other fliers had spent their weaponry, and were climbing as well.

Hal saw a single Roche dragon, boring in from the east.

A brave man, he thought.

And a fool, as he sent Storm diving down.

The Roche flier looked up, just as Hal triggered his crossbow.

The bolt took him in the chest, and he dropped off his dragon.

There were trumpet blasts from the flight leaders, and the squadron had finished its raid.

Hal took Storm high once more, then back to the west, toward the crag, his squadron in a ragged echelon behind him.

He came around the first bend, and saw the crag, now with ominous clouds rolling around it.

There'd been no sign of weather when they'd taken off, but over mountains things can change rapidly.

Hal was trying to decide if he'd chance staying on the crag through the day, or just feed the dragons and fly on, back toward that meadow, when the ruined castle ahead of him lifted, as if there was some creature digging out from underneath it.

There was.

The creature, brown like graveyard earth, reared, the castle stone cascading off its body.

He was, Hal thought, trying to suppress panic, more than two hundred feet tall.

But it was no bear, for its body, if that's what it was, moved, shifting, as if seen through rippling water.

There was no head, but just fangs, and a mouth, screeching like no animal or legend Hal had ever known of.

It had long talons, and thick arms, reaching for the fliers.

Hal forced his shock away, blasted a command to turn right, away from the monster, the demon, the spirit, into the clouds boiling around the summit.

The dragons were flying as hard as they could, at least as afraid of the spirit as any of the men.

Hal realized he was moaning in fear.

Then they were in the cloud, and the winds caught Storm, and tossed them; then they were in calm for an instant, then winds from another direction took them, and hurled them about.

Hal reached for his compass, but it was under his tunic, and it was all he could do to hang on to Storm's reins.

At least they were headed away from the nightmare, flying north.

He broke out of the clouds, and almost screamed, for somehow the clouds had turned them about, and they were flying straight at the mountain peak and the waiting demon.

Hal had an instant to realize the clouds had been summoned by the monster, wondered if it was a creature of the earth or air, realized it didn't matter.

Behind Hal came the rest of the squadron, drawn by this death dream as if it were a lodestone.

Hal managed to reach for his crossbow, knowing that it was like hurling spitballs at a lion.

From his right Pisidia plummeted past, followed by his flight, diving straight into the monster.

Pisidia was screaming something that Hal couldn't make out, and firing bolts from his crossbow into what might have been the demon's face.

Kailas had his trumpet up, and was blowing a retreat. But the 20th Flight seemed deaf, determined to join Pisidia in death.

The monster reached out, almost casually, took Pisidia's dragon in its grasp, and smashed it down, spinning, spinning, into the canyon and the river below.

The spell, if spell it was, broke, and Hal was able to kick Storm into a tight turn, away from the horror.

Behind him came the others in the squadron.

He saw the creature swatting the air, hitting two of the 20th dragons, and knocking them out of the sky. Then the spell broke for the others in the flight, and they, too, tried to break away after Hal.

Then Kailas was back in the cloud, this time finding his compass, and leaning close over it as the winds tore at him.

The winds, accomplices of the nightmare, tried to turn him, send him back into its maw, but he managed to hold his course.

The clouds were intermittent, rushing past, and he saw, now and again, beside and behind him, other dragons, battling the storm, all following his lead.

Again they were in the clear and this time the crag was gone, hidden behind them. Mountains were below them, clean, honest peaks with no eldritch horrors hidden under ruined battlements.

Hal realized Storm was flying as fast as he could, and would soon wear himself out.

He bent forward, stroking the beast's neck, saying meaningless words in as soothing a tone as he knew.

Storm's wingbeats slowed.

Again, he looked back, and saw the ragged formation of dragons behind him.

Hal forced Storm up into a climb, then a turn, heading back on his unit.

There were trumpet blasts, and shouts, and slowly the panic broke, and the dragon fliers began sorting out their formation.

Assembled, it made two complete orbits while Hal counted his beasts.

Fifty-two were still flying, not including Storm.

He'd lost five dragons in that nightmare over the crag, or possibly one or more in the attack on Carcaor.

Hal turned the squadron again, holding a return course, back for the sheep meadow.

It was no more than midday when they reached it, and landed.

None of the dragons were hungry, nor were their fliers.

Everyone was pale, shaken, jabbering about what they'd seen, whether it'd been real or not.

Hal shouted for a formation, and, reluctantly, the fliers obeyed.

"You will stay silent," he ordered. "We did well today. What that . . . that thing was, I have no idea.

"Right now, you're to eat.

"Then we're going to punish ourselves, and push on. We haven't been pursued or hit by the Roche yet, and I'm hoping we can make our lines before their wizards have time to alert the Roche squadrons there to be prepared.

"Now, to your dragons, and make sure they eat something, even though they're still winded and wound up. We'll be taking off again in an hour. Move out."

He quite deliberately said nothing about Pisidia's death, nor the others of his squadron. A little anger at Kailas's heartlessness might do a deal to break the shock the fliers all felt over the monstrous demon, or whatever it was.

As the fliers finished, he had them shoot down and hasty-dress sheep, then tie them under the dragons.

An hour later, by the sun, he had Storm watered and fed, although the dragon ate little, compared to his usual voraciousness.

They took off, and assembled in formation, then flew on, north and a bit east.

One flier carried the raider who'd been assigned to the meadow with them.

Hal kept careful account of his compass heading, and his estimated flying time as the shadows walked long on the land below.

There was just enough moonlight for him to see the lake below, and bring the dragons down.

None were hungry, but all were thirsty and exhausted.

He ordered the fliers to force the dragons into the lake, and splash them about.

It seemed to help—they came out of the water hungry, and devoured the sheep, while the fliers made do with the smoked game.

Then everyone slept as if stunned.

Hal should have posted a guard, but didn't think anyone, outside of maybe an airborne magician, would find this cleft in the hills.

The caretaking raider was enough of a guardian.

They got up at dawn, and flew hard to the first night's base, the peaceful meadow, arriving in the afternoon.

"An hour's rest," Hal ordered. "And food. Then we're off again, as soon as the sun dips down. I'm hoping we can muscle through the lines by dark. Once we're across, I'll worry about where we land."

There were mutters, but quiet ones. Most of the fliers still had some energy from the excitement of the rage, and none of them, not even Danikel, wanted to face Yasin's black dragons with exhausted mounts.

The dragons were complaining when they were resaddled, snapping at the riders and honking complaint.

But they stumbled into the air, and Hal took them high, feeling for a wind. He found one, blowing due west, and let the dragons glide on it.

Again, he was counting time, and by the early morning, guessed he was closing on the front.

He blew a warning note on his trumpet, and took his fliers in a long dive to less than a hundred feet above the ground.

Hal looked up into the skies as they came across the rearmost Roche positions and saw half a dozen dragons, dots in the sky, waiting for him.

The magicians had alerted Yasin, or other Roche dragon flights.

But they'd guessed he would be high, and Hal had fooled them.

They dove hard for him, but turned away as they closed, realizing the squadron wasn't breaking formation, and that they were vastly outnumbered.

Then the pits and tents of the infantry were below, and they were across the dead ground between the lines.

Hal was trying to see just where they'd crossed, to get an estimated direction toward their base, if possible.

But he was having little luck, as fatigue crawled over his body, fogging his mind.

Storm snorted in surprise, and Hal saw, to his left, a spatter of whirling, magical lights in the sky.

There was someone alive, and awake, over there, and he steered the squadron toward the lights.

Landmarks below became recognizable, even in this dark, and he realized the lights were coming from somewhere close to the First Squadron's home base.

They weren't close, they were in the middle of it.

Hal, believing in miracles, brought Storm in. A handler ran

up to him, caught him as he slipped out of the saddle, almost falling.

"Limingo the magician cast a spell," the man said, unbidden. "Said you were approaching, and would need a guide. I dunno how he knew it."

Dragons were thudding down on the field around Hal.

"We've got food—and fodder—ready," the man went on. "And drink."

Hal nodded dumbly.

But all he could think of was that wonderful cot in the quiet little tent that was waiting.

He stumbled off the field, as two men led Storm away, toward his shelter.

Sir Thom Lowess was there.

"Well, did you do it?"

Hal nodded.

"Do you want to tell me . . ." Lowess caught himself. "Sorry for being a damned fool. Maybe, when you wake."

Hal nodded, pushed past Lowess, and then there was the cot in front of him.

He slumped down on it, managed to pull one boot off.

His orderly, Uluch, was there, trying to help. He pushed him away, reached for his other boot. Then the world swirled, and was gone as sleep took him for its own.

27

Hal woke, undressed, in his cot. It was just a bit after dawn. He hoped he hadn't slept more than the clock around.

Peering cautiously out of his tent, he saw the dragon handlers currying and feeding the still-disheveled monsters, and realized he'd only slept a few hours, although he felt as full of energy as he had before the raid.

He suspected he would run out of energy later that day, but determined to ride the spurt as long as it lasted.

Hal swung out of bed, realized he had a bursting bladder, and walked carefully to the small circular canvas pisser behind his tent.

Vastly relieved, he came back to see a steaming mug of tea, and a plate of crisp bacon and eggs scrambled with chives on a small table.

"Thank you, Uluch," he said into thin air, didn't wait for a reply, but ate, famished.

He went to the bathing tent, came back clean and shaved. A fresh uniform was laid out for him, and he was very grateful he'd been talked into having an orderly.

He came out, and Gart, looking a bit bleary, was waiting.

"I want Storm ready to fly in . . ." And he stopped himself. "Sorry. Dragons need rest, too."

He thought.

"Ask Sir Thom if he'd lend me his carriage. And say that he'd be welcome to ride along with me to army headquarters."

"Yes, sir," Gart said.

"And have the goods of the men who died wrapped up," Kailas said. "Have someone sort through them to make sure there'll be nothing embarrassing go to the family."

Such as love letters to another woman or man, fish skins, and the like. What military goods were in the casualty's locker would be auctioned off on the squadron, generally for ridiculous amounts, and the moneys sent on to the dead man—or woman's—family.

Supposedly there were now pensions for those maimed or killed in battle, but the old habit begun at the start of the war still hung on.

Everyone may have respected King Asir, but almost no one had full confidence in his, or anybody else's, government.

Sir Thom clattered up in his surrey, quite unable to hide his eagerness.

Hal assumed he'd already heard bits and pieces from squadron chatter, but told the story from the beginning on the ride to First Army headquarters. He first swore Sir Thom to secrecy, and knew the man's word was good.

He left out the spirit or demon, not sure if that should become common knowledge.

At headquarters, he told Cantabri everything that had happened, and told him he'd be handing in a written report later in the day.

He also said he'd told Sir Thom the essentials of the raid, leaving out the demon.

Hal asked Cantabri if that should be included.

"No," Cantabri said, then stopped, and thought for long moments.

"Actually, there was a request from the king for you to proceed to Rozen and report directly to him."

Hal thought of civilization, a chance to be under a real roof instead of canvas, a meal not cooked by the numbers, but most of all of Khiri.

"No," he said, then made a quick revision, seeing Cantabri's frown. "Sorry, sir. Of course I'll go . . . if you order me to. But I've been on leave more recently than anyone else in my squadron, and I don't think it would be fair. Plus there's work to be done with the squadron, and I can't forever be running off to . . . to do whatever I do."

Hal had reconsidered what he was about to say at the very last instant.

Cantabri gnawed a lip.

"No," he said reluctantly. "No, it wouldn't. The king won't be pleased, but he'll understand. I hope. He'll damned well have to. But you'll have to get a report ready . . . a good one, with details and color, not just a facts-blurt."

"Yessir," Hal said.

"Now, back to this matter of that demon or whatever it was," Lord Cantabri went on, frowning. "I wish I could keep it a secret, for it surely is a noisome matter. Especially as you don't seem to know whether this monster can be summoned by the Roche . . . or if it appears spontaneously.

"But I doubt if we can gag everyone on your squadron and make them keep silent for long."

"No," Hal agreed, thinking of Alcmaen, Farren Mariah, the dragon handlers. "No, I can't keep it that quiet. They'll be talking on the squadron, and it'll get out sooner or later."

"So I guess you'd best tell Sir Thom. But tell him to keep it silent until someone—you or myself—gives him permission to write about it. That might keep the rumor from exploding completely out of control. Maybe." Cantabri nodded. "That's all."

"One more thing," Hal said. "When do you want the

squadron to return to normal duties? I want to start cycling my men out on leave. Some of them haven't been home for a year or more."

"I'm thinking at present that the First Squadron may never be on normal duties," Cantabri said. "Whatever they are. I'm thinking that I want them as a special duty squadron, like the raiders."

"Thank you, sir," Hal said. "I'll be glad of that."

"You, and the other killers only," Cantabri said. "Because anyone who's sane, and I don't think there's a dragon flier around who is, would realize special duties will increase the chances of their getting killed."

"They're all volunteers," Hal said, a bit of harshness in his voice. "That's part of the bargain."

"So it is, so it is," Cantabri sighed. "As for this leave, go ahead. Say, five at a time. I can't see anything on the horizon in the next couple of weeks, not until we know how Norcia and the rest of the Roche hierarchy took their capital being attacked."

Hal stood, saluted.

"Thank you, sir. But I'll also want to have my men making patrols over the front, just for training." He made a face. "And if you'll excuse me, I've got letters to write after the raid."

Cantabri nodded grimly.

Hal had been too intent on his squadron and reporting for Cantabri to notice the small pile of letters waiting for him, weighed down by a gauntlet.

All, except a plaintive bill from his tailor, were from Khiri.

He should have written those letters to Pisidia and the other casualties of the 20th Flight's next of kin.

But he allowed himself a moment of selfishness, and read the letters from Khiri.

Written almost daily, they were precisely what he needed: a chronicle of her daily life, and the life at Cayre a Carstares, her castle on Deraine's west coast. Nothing to do with the war, but the trivia of summer, and the approaching harvest, and who was reportedly doing what to whom in Rozen.

Except for one:

Dear Hal

I probably shouldn't be writing this to you, since I don't want to worry you ever, but two nights running I've had a most disturbing dream. It only lasted for a moment, but I woke, crying, both times. If you were here, I'd wake you up, and let you tell me what a silly I am. But you aren't, so please indulge me for a moment, and let me tell you about it. Then, if you wish, you can write me, and tell me I'm a silly.

I dreamed I was on this great plain, and the ground was torn up, as if there'd been a battle. There were ruined catapults, and torn tents, and broken swords and lances. But there were no bodies, no soldiers. This landscape stretched on and on, almost to the horizon. But just before it was a city I didn't recognize.

The only thing moving, coming toward me, was a dot that became a dragon. I think it might have been Storm, for it wasn't black like the dangerous dragons you've told me about. But you weren't riding it, even though it was saddled.

That was all there was to the dream. I didn't feel threatened, by the dragon or anything else, but as I said, I woke up crying.

You told me once that dreams have no meaning, that they aren't prophecies or anything. But I worry. Are you all right? Write me soon, please.

Your Khiri

Hal made a face. Certainly he didn't write her as much as he should, as much as he wanted. He didn't have the gift of putting words on paper. But now he found paper and a pen, and decided he would write her a long, cheerful letter, before he turned to the grim matter of the other letters.

*

Pisidia, as it turned out, had not only a wife, but three children as well. That letter was hard, but the hardest was to a Sagene widow, whose only son had been killed by that great monster.

It was with true relief that Hal finished the letters, and turned to the king's report.

"You wish?" Hal asked Lieutenant Goang. He was sitting in a corner of the mess, watching his pilots cavort drunkenly. He was watching them carefully, for a favorite flier game, when drinking, was to somehow suck their commanding officer into their stupid games, such as rubbing ashes on their boots, and having other fliers turn them upside down, so they could "walk" on the ceiling, or riding a horse into the mess or swatting at each other with rolled up broadsheets, blindfolded.

Often enough, Hal, and other flying officers, felt like playing the fool themselves and let themselves get drawn into the idiocy.

But, for some reason, this night Hal didn't feel like drinking and carrying on. Maybe it was the letters, or maybe he was finally letting down after the raid.

"A word with you, sir," Goang said. "An idea."

"Good," Hal said. "That's what I pay you for. Or, rather, the king does."

"I've been thinking of various ideas," Goang said. "But none of them have been worth bringing to you. I think I wasn't thinking right."

"And you're sober, saying that?"

"Yessir. I wasn't considering magic, until we were told about those pebbles."

"So consider magic." Hal decided Goang didn't have much of a sense of humor.

"That's what I've been doing, while you sorts were off being heroes. You're from the north of Deraine, aren't you?"

"I was," Hal said. "But that was a long time ago."

"Was your home around any mines?"

"To put it mildly."

"Did you ever have any disasters? Any mining explosions?"

The memory came to Hal instantly, from when he was no more than six or seven. There'd been screams, and running men, and then the big bellows alarm at one of the mines had started screaming.

There were twenty men trapped, far down.

The village miners started trying to dig them out.

Everyone else did what they could to help. Hal's mother and father set up a kitchen near the mine, and someone else put up a tent for the rescue workers to sleep in, out of the omnipresent drizzle.

But they hadn't dug more than half a day when the ground rocked, and flames spurted out of the pit head. They'd gone up maybe a hundred feet, then died as the blast wave shot out after them.

The twenty trapped men were dead, and another ten rescuers after them.

"Once, twice," Hal said shortly, not comfortable with the memory. "Firedamp, it was."

"Just so, sir," Goang said eagerly. "Gas that explodes when flames hit it."

Hal nodded.

"What would happen if we somehow got some of that, and confined it in a bottle, then set fire to the bottleneck, maybe with a rag?"

"It would explode, I'd imagine," Hal said.

"Suppose we wrapped the bottle with a bandage, with nails, bits of glass, things like that inside it?"

Hal considered.

"A nice, light weapon," Goang went on. "Ideal against troops or cavalry."

"If it worked," Hal said.

"Maybe it would, if there was a spell igniting it," Goang said. "Another idea I've had . . . When you were coming back, even though you were a day early, Limingo sensed it. Or, rather, he told me he'd cast a spell on your saddle, so when it drew near, he could feel it, and have those signs in the air to guide you."

"Damned helpful it was, too," Hal said, realizing he was starting to sound like a curmudgeonly old fart, typical of a unit commander. "Sorry. What would Limingo's magic do elsewhere, since I assume that's what you're driving at?"

"Suppose—I don't know how—but suppose we could get a bit of, say, what *Ky* Yasin feeds his black dragons. Suppose Limingo put a spell on it, and that spell could be passed along to all the fliers, so when Yasin's dragons are in the air, somehow we'd know about it, and be able to get airborne ourselves and maybe above his squadron?"

Hal thought.

"I'm damned if I see how we could do that. But it is a hell of an idea. I'm not sure about the firedamp, either." Hal shuddered. "Most likely it's my own memories stopping me.

"What I think you seem to need now is to talk to a magician. Limingo?"

"Not yet, sir," Goang said. "He's too important and busy to take much time with the likes of me. But I could use his acolyte Bodrugan."

Hal nodded slowly.

"There might be something to either or both of your ideas. I'll see that Bodrugan is sent for, and—YOWP!"

Hal, intent on his thoughts, wasn't watching his pilots. Three of them, led by Mariah, had crept up and jumped on him, knocking him to the floor.

Hal noticed none of them were wearing trousers, and fought futily as Mariah and Chincha started clawing at his breeches.

"This is damned undignified," he yelped.

But no one was listening.

Someone on the squadron wrote home about the fabulous monster his fliers had overcome, and the person who received that letter wrote about it to someone in the army.

The story spread, getting more evil and dangerous by the telling.

Lord Cantabri reluctantly gave Sir Thom permission to write the whole story of the raid.

Hal heard nothing from King Asir about his report, or about anything in it.

He wondered if he'd finally overstepped the bounds, by refusing to hurry to the king's side.

But it didn't matter.

What could Asir do?

Send him to Sagene to fight a war?

Hal thought about it long, then called Danikel to his tent, and told him he wanted the baron to take over the 20th Flight. He'd been pleased with the idea, since that would put a Sagene in charge of a quarter of the squadron, and he never forgot the king's orders to use diplomacy.

Danikel didn't need any time to think.

"Nossir. I can't do that."

"And why not? You'll get your captain's sash, and have more of a say about fighting the war."

"Nossir. I joined the service to kill Roche. Anything else will get in my way."

Hal growled, but sent Danikel away.

He pondered more, and, as much as it would complicate his life, and increase his paperwork, he made Mynta Gart the 20th Flight commander.

Sir Loren, in spite of his objections, became adjutant, and, surprisingly, did well.

*

The first fliers went off on leave. Hal began training the others. There were howls of protest when he brought in hand-to-hand instructors from the raiders, but Hal kept remembering his own captivity, or the fight on the rooftops of Aude, and paid no attention.

Since these were already combat-experienced fliers, he made sure at least one patrol a day went out over the lines. That kept everyone honest, even though he lost a flier on the second day.

But replacements were streaming in, after Sir Thom's tale of the next daring stroke by the Dragonmaster struck the broadsheets.

Everyone wanted away from the drudge killing of the front lines, and somehow thought a death, high above the mud, would be cleaner and more honorable.

Hal doubled the watch on the skies, assuming *Ky* Yasin would be instructed by his brother to take revenge on the First and attack the squadron.

But Yasin's black dragons weren't in the skies as the summer drew to a close.

Hal had his own idea of what training he himself needed. He didn't know whether his squadron would be used with the sorcerous pebbles again, hoped they'd train other flights, since he frankly didn't consider ruining the lives of civilians, and improving the lot of builders, doing that much to end the war.

He admitted arrogance, wanted special duties.

Or else going after Yasin, once the bastard and his damned black dragons made their appearance.

Hal trained one on one with each of the other fliers, made them fly company on him through tight maneuvers, reversed their roles, until he had a decent idea of each of his flier's capabilities.

He also flew the entire squadron as one great formation,

teaching each flight how to cover another, led them in darting sweeps across the lines, putting down all Roche fliers.

He had an idea of a change he wanted to make in the way dragons were fought, particularly when the offensive picked up and they hopefully closed on Carcaor.

But what he wanted to do was fly, by himself, on Storm, out over the gray seas, fly west, thinking about where the dragons came from, what their enemies could be.

But the army was too far south, too far inland, to permit that.

He was starting to understand war. In its simplest form—beyond that of simply killing your enemy—it was denying things to people. The army denied him being able to fly when and where he wanted, he denied the Roche the same thing. Ultimately the army denied its enemy land, freedom and, in the end, its life if there was no surrender.

It was a much cleaner way to think than dwelling on the gore.

Or thinking about the poor bastards below, infantry, cavalry, pioneers, dots who killed and died, without changing the course of the world or the war one degree.

Cantabri summoned Hal, and greeted him with a truly evil smile.

That cheered Kailas immensely—the only thing that seemed to please Cantabri was some reverse to the Roche.

"We finally have word from Carcaor," Cantabri said. "One of our agents crossed the lines last night.

"According to him, Queen Norcia had said, back at the start of the war, that there would be no way Roche, nor any of its people, would be harmed, but that full revenge would be taken on the evil folk of Sagene and Deraine, if they were so stupid as to side with the corrupt Sagenes, and so on and so forth.

"So when your dragons started throwing rocks, it upset the Roche.

"Especially their rulers, after there were protests in the streets.

"I guess Norcia isn't used to peasants and such displaying their feelings, unlike Deraine.

"She—and her barons—overreacted, sending cavalry out to smash these protests.

"There have been more and more of them, and, even better, a few scofflaws who've taken to pegging rocks at anyone seen abroad who looks rich, or wears royal livery."

Cantabri rubbed his hands briskly.

"Nothing better than stirring up a wasps' nest, now is there?

"So now we'll think about how to make matters worse."

Whatever Cantabri had in mind, he didn't say.

Hal considered rocking another Roche city, but realized their dragon fliers would be alerted now, and tried to come up with something new, as well as nasty.

Replacements came in, and Hal wasn't pleased to see they weren't the first flower of youth. There were older men and women now, and some of them didn't look much like the athletic soldiery so beloved of the taletellers.

The war was grinding down everyone.

But that, thankfully, wasn't his concern. The dragon flights were still getting the best, many of them former front line soldiers.

Hal's squadron was ready to fight, at its peak, and almost all of the fliers had gone on leave.

Hal was cursing a mound of paperwork in his tent, when a sentry came running down from his post on the road, shouting incoherently.

Hal came out, buckling his sword on, wondering what the alarm was. He saw, coming into the squadron base, more than a hundred men and women.

They were richly dressed, and the armor of their cavalry escorts gleamed.

There were banners galore, and all of the horses were groomed as if for a parade.

Riding just in front was King Asir.

But Hal wasn't staring at him, unlike the rest of the squadron as they streamed out on to the field.

Four riders behind the king was Lady Khiri Kailas.

28

A cloak was dropped on the ground by two equerries, and the king dismounted on to it. He looked about, at the kneeling fliers and the other men and women of the squadron.

"You may rise," Asir said, and, as Hal got up, he wondered if there was voice training for kings-to-be, so their orders carried as far as they wished.

"I came to visit this squadron," the king said, "for it has pleased me most well. I have authorized, from this time forward, it shall be known as the King's Own First Dragon Squadron, and appropriate emblems shall be made for your uniforms and guidons."

"Thank you, Your Highness," Hal managed.

The king nodded.

"There shall also be medals and promotions given out within the hour, if your commander is pleased to assist me.

"I now wish to converse with him on the matter, in private."

Hal wondered wildly where he could take the king that was not only away from the squadron's ears, but properly dignified.

There simply wasn't anywhere.

Hal must have showed his worry on his face, for the king grinned at him.

"Perhaps, Lord Kailas, we might wish to walk in those woods beyond? Such an pastime might prove relaxing after my long journey."

"Yes . . . of course, Your Majesty."

Hal followed the king, but his eyes kept straying to Khiri, still not sure he really had seen her.

Behind the king and Kailas came six hard-faced men-at-arms, all with the rank sashes of officers, but with the ready, well-worn weaponry of front line soldiers. They kept discreetly out of hearing, discreetly within range of being able to rescue their sovereign if any hostile chipmunks attacked him on his walk.

"Of course," the king said amiably, "you realize I didn't come all this long dreary way through the ruins of war, the first time I've been out of Deraine since the damned Roche attacked us, just to hand out some medals."

"Uh . . ." Hal managed, who'd had no such suspicion, figuring that kings did things like that. "Yessir. Of course, sir."

The king looked at him, lifting a single eyebrow, but said nothing.

"The purpose of my visit to the lines is twofold. Hopefully to build the morale of my soldiers, but also, after I finish waving the flag, to attend a conference with Sagene's ruling Council of Barons, in Fovant. This, by the way, will be the first time any Derainian monarch has been to their capital.

"Briefly, I'll propose that the barons join me in a grand attack, all along the front, with all four armies."

Hal didn't say anything.

"You think that's stupid?"

Again, Hal held his tongue.

"On the truism that he who attacks everywhere attacks nowhere?"

Hal had heard the phrase.

"It's not my place to have an opinion, sir."

"It may be in time," Asir said. "But there is a bit of method to my madness. I see the Roche as being almost to the stage of tottering. If we hit them hard, we might make the front collapse, and end the war much more rapidly than just hammering away here, as Lord Cantabri and the Sagene are doing.

"In any event, this is the course I propose.

"I will want, naturally, to make my visit to Fovant as splendorous as possible. Which means I want to attach one flight of your squadron to my visit. I'll also be taking representatives of my best cavalry and infantry along.

"Your presence will not only give glamour, but give me security from the air.

"I have great respect for the Roche dragons, their fliers, and their spies, and have enough on my mind to not want to worry about what may be coming out of the skies at me.

"Will you join me, and bring your best?"

It was just like Asir, Hal decided, to put the matter as a request, when he could have made it a simple order.

"Of course, sire. And we're deeply honored."

"Damned well better be," the king said. "Now, if you'll give me some names—I propose to hand out Royal Badges of Honor and Heroes of Deraine medals most promiscuously, following dinner—I'll let you go to your lady.

"Since you were such a snitty little duty-minded commander, and did not return with a report on your raid on Carcaor, I figured you might appreciate it if I brought the Lady Khiri on my visit.

"I also, for your information, plan on using her in Fovant, officially at least, since no one, especially the Sagene, believes that a beautiful woman might have a bit of brains, to listen to any idle gossip that might pertain to the war."

"Uh . . . thank you, sire," Hal managed. He named the survivors of the 11th Flight, other noted fliers, his flight commanders, and several Sagene, including Danikel, and through slightly gritted teeth, Rer Alcmaen.

"Good," the king said. "I realize you've listened to what I told you back in Deraine about coddling the Sagene fliers, and heartily agree with your making sure they're on my honors' list.

"That way of thought is one reason that I agreed to come to the barons, rather than invite them to Deraine.

"Now, shall we return to the others?"

Hal barely remembered returning to the formation, calling the men and women to attention, and dismissing them, with orders to reassemble before the evening meal.

Half-dazed, he led Khiri to his tent, later hoping he showed a bit of dignity in not picking her up in his arms and racing toward the nearest cot or, still worse, tossing her over his shoulder and bolting back into the woods, booming like a bittern.

When he came back to himself, they were both naked; his small field desk was overturned, with papers scattered everywhere.

"You're certainly . . . abrupt in your romancing, Lord Kailas," Khiri managed, still breathing heavily. "In certain circles, it would be regarded that I was raped. Or, maybe, that I raped you."

Hal murmured something inconsequential.

"Now, I suppose we should find a way of cleaning ourselves, and investigating all those crashings and thuddings that came from outside."

"Not yet," Hal said.

"Then what are you planning to . . . " Khiri's voice broke off into a moan.

When they eventually were satiated, it was late afternoon. Uluch had managed to fill and heat a half-barrel, and pitch canvas around it, just outside their tent. Also inside the canvas were Lady Khiri's trunks.

The water was tepid by now, but that didn't matter. They washed, dressed, and Hal put on dress uniform.

Hal still felt dazed, but another kind of dazed, as they came out into the approaching twilight.

He barely recognized his squadron's base.

Certainly it was most romantic for the king to appear on horseback, with his nobles, caparisoned for battle, the very picture of a lean fighting monarch.

Asir may have been romantic, but he was hardly a fool, Hal realized, seeing the panoply that spread around him.

There were large tents, small tents, wagons, covered and open, hostlers with spare horses, cooktents, changing tents, dining tents, and everywhere bustling servants in royal livery, very much a tiny city under canvas.

Khiri saw Hal's expression, started laughing.

"How far behind our liege does all this travel?" Hal asked.

"At least an hour, sometimes half a day."

"So you've been sleeping rough—I suppose this must be called rough for a king—since, what, Paestum?"

"Only twice," Khiri said. "And that was when we were caught out. Normally outriders find a place for us to stay—most generally a Sagene nobleman's castle—in the afternoon."

"It must be nice," Hal said.

"It is," Khiri said. "And I say that smugly."

Hal looked about, saw no one was watching them, slapped her buttocks. She laughed more loudly.

Medals were, indeed, given out liberally, which Hal was glad to see, remembering the early days of the war, when no one except senior officers or the suicidally brave got awards.

As Cantabri had said once, "If a bit of tin and ribbon makes a man fight harder, and stand taller in the eyes of his fellows, why begrudge it?"

Hal sometimes wondered if a liberal policy might cheapen the value of an earlier medal, given under stricter circumstances, but caught himself. It was most unlikely, just for openers, that someone who'd won a medal in the early days was even alive to gripe.

That, in turn, made him think of his own mortality, and, once again, of Saslic's words.

The king invited all in the squadron to be his guests at dinner, which made even Mariah gape a little.

Before the squadron trooped into the great tent, Limingo and Sir Thom Lowess had shown up, Sir Thom muttering his usual incantation at good times about "what a story, what a story."

The meal was interesting—the meats were all roasts, and had been cooked in advance, then preserved by magic until needed, requiring only a few minutes of heating before being ready. There were vegetables, gathered along the way or bought in small villages. The only thing prepared from scratch were the desserts.

"Hard as hell," the king said quietly to Kailas, "being a king, sometimes, particularly when you're traveling. You descend on someone, who's honor-bound to give you the best he can manage, eat the whole damned district out of victuals, then move on, like those damned insects down in the south . . . you know, the squiggly ones with wings."

"Locusts, your Majesty."

The tables were lined with various bottles of wine, but Hal noticed no one had more than a glass or two.

He also noticed that the king barely touched the plates of meat covered with rich sauces, and his main course seemed to be no more than bread soaked in milk.

Asir noted his attention.

"Damned stomach hasn't been worth a damn since this war started," he said a trifle sheepishly. "Acts like a Roche traitor. Another good reason to want peace . . . maybe I'll be able to go back to gourmandizing."

That was a price of sovereignty Hal had never considered.

Hal announced, after everyone had eaten, their new mission, protecting the king while he toured the front.

He didn't mention the upcoming trip to Fovant.

The longer that remained a secret, the safer things would be. He, too, respected Roche dragon fliers, and he guessed their agents, although he'd had only one serious encounter with a spy thus far.

Kailas took his leave early, after eating sanely and, with Khiri, went back to his tent.

They made love deep in the night.

When Khiri finally slept, Hal remained awake, thinking about the conference.

He hoped it would produce results, but, selfishly, the thought kept coming to him that he would be with Khiri and also be away from the front.

His life, and those fliers he chose to take with him, would be extended for at least another month.

And that was a royal favor greater than any medal.

29

A day later, Hal and his dragon fliers moved off with the king's entourage, to Lord Cantabri's headquarters and the front.

Hal, paring detachment requirements to the bone, took a full fifteen fliers—a dragon flight—plus each dragon's pair of handlers, Tupilco the veterinarian, and a handful of orderlies and clerks. He would mess on the king, and the cavalry's smith, armorer, and such could handle the other needs.

The fliers chosen were the 11th's original survivors, Gart as second in command and Chincha. The rest were Sagene, including Alcmaen and Danikel. He left Cabet in charge of the squadron.

Those fifty he'd chosen barely counted among the king's company—Asir had at least six hundred retainers with him.

Khiri told Hal that the king was, in fact, traveling very light.

After the king and his retainers reached Cantabri and his generals, Hal made sure he stayed in the air and in the background, wanting as little as possible to do with the high-rankers.

That night, there was an alarum as the guard was turned out. Four men, armored and armed, had tried to break through the cordon around the king. They got as far as the king's tent stables before being seen. One was killed; the others fled, seemingly without doing any damage other than murdering a sentry while getting into the perimeter.

Cantabri, outraged, put his entire Raiding Squadron around the royal household as guards.

The second day was spent resting, and then, for the third, King Asir said he wanted to go forward, into the front lines.

Hal swore the collective gasp from the staffers could have sucked a black dragon down from a thousand feet.

Everyone protested that it wasn't safe, and darted about, gurgling about what would result if something happened.

The worriers were already half apoplectic about the king's habit of riding out just after dawn, with no more than two escorts accompanying him.

Asir didn't listen to either set of objections, and so, early the next morning, Asir, Cantabri, four aides and six escorts crept out toward the lines.

All of them wore drab garments, and were heavily armed. However, the king couldn't let go of being a king, and so a golden, gem-crusted circlet was on his head.

Hal thought that was amusing, hoped that nothing would happen.

He had all his dragons in the air to make sure, at least from his side, nothing would.

Five dragons went high, including Hal. The others orbited the royal group below, in circles as wide as possible not to pinpoint the greatest target the war had seen.

The second line of defense was the rest of Hal's squadron, since they were still within its operating area, and four other flights were on standby.

Hal was watching the lines closely, figuring that the most

likely threat would be from a cavalry patrol who happened to see what was clearly an officers' group—all of the men mounted, not riding in any sort of formation or dispersement—and attack.

There would be enough infantry below to drive back any sort of foot soldiery mischief.

Instead, Farren Mariah, below on the close security, blew an alarm on his trumpet.

Hal saw a great wedge of black dragons driving toward the lines.

He counted thirty of them.

The sky was alive with trumpeted warnings, and the Derainian and Sagene fliers climbed for altitude.

The low element was level with the onrushing Roche, and Hal thought he could see *Ky* Yasin's banner on the leading monster. He wasn't close enough to tell if there was gold trim on the banner, which would denote he had a chance at Yasin himself.

He pointed at the oncoming Roche, blew the attack, and his five dove for the point of the wedge.

Hal hoped it would be Yasin, then decided it didn't matter so long as the attack was broken up.

Rather than hit the lead, dive through and climb back up for another target, Hal brought Storm out of his dive just feet above the Roche formation.

The lead monster was rushing toward him.

Hal loosed a crossbow bolt, missed, reloaded, sent Storm into a skidding half-turn with his knees as the lead Roche dove away.

In the back of his mind, Hal decided that Roche couldn't be Yasin, who'd never been known to avoid a fight.

He came in on the wing of the second dragon, fired. His bolt hit that dragon in the neck, and it scrawked, rolled away, as Hal shot the third through the wing, doing little damage, but annoying the big black.

He reared in the sky, and Storm's neck darted, got that dragon just above the breastbone, and ichor gouted.

Storm let go before the Roche dragon could get him in its death flurry, rolled away and down.

Hal let Storm go inverted through a loop, then climbed back up toward the belly of the Roche flight pattern.

Two fliers, flying close together, smashed into the scattering formation, Alcmaen and another Sagene.

A Roche dragon flopped limply, fell, and his mate went after him.

Alcmaen let that one go, hit another one, and a third.

His aim was very true, hitting one dragon in the guts, the second in its eye. Both went down, screaming.

The bastard may have been a bastard, but he was also a most competent killer.

Hal looked for another Roche.

The formation was scattered, diving away.

He started down after a fleeing dragon, recollected his duty, blew the recall.

Slowly his flight regrouped, assembled, as two other Deraine flights hurtled in, just a little late, to support.

Below, over the king's group, Alcmaen was doing slow rolls, to celebrate his triple victory.

"Congratulations," King Asir. "You made quite a show today."

"Thank you, sire," Hal said. "I would just like to know what made you such a target."

"So would I," Asir said. "I can't believe anyone has eyes keen enough to have noted my crown. They must have just been lucky."

"I suppose so," Hal said, unconvinced. The king didn't realize how hard it was to launch any kind of dragon strike without notice, let alone one the size of that day's attack.

"I particularly noted one flier," Asir said. "I thought I saw him down three dragons by himself. He was the one flying close attendance on me after the battle."

"Yessir," Hal said, trying to sound neutral. "That would be the Sagene flier, Alcmaen."

"Sagene, eh?" Asir said. "I think I might have heard of him."

"He's a favorite of the Sagene taletellers," Hal said.

"I think it might be politic—in the true sense of the word—to make much of him," Asir said. "I'll make him a Defender of the Throne, which he certainly was."

"Thank you, your Highness," Hal said. "He'll be quite pleased with your having noticed him."

He hoped his voice wasn't as sour as his thoughts.

The king spent three more days visiting the lines. Each day, there were black dragons in the air, but they didn't attempt the attack, since Hal had the First Squadron in close attendance.

Asir announced Alcmaen's award, said it would be formally given in time, which meant when they reached Fovant.

Medals given to the ground troops, weighty nods of approval made, the flag correctly waved, the royal column packed, and began its slow journey west, toward Fovant.

Four black dragons flew toward the formation, and were chased away by Hal's fliers. He decided the four had just been reconnoitering a large formation, not knowing what it was.

For the next three days, Roche dragons scouted the formation but never chanced an attack.

Days later, they reached the Bluffs, where the great breakthrough had been made, and continued on.

Still later, they crossed the border into Sagene, and kept on to the west.

As time passed, the countryside grew less barren, not having been fought over since the first days of the war; then they moved deeper into Sagene, where there'd been no battles at all.

The land on either side of them, though, was still picked bare, villages looted, farmland stripped, forests denuded, just by the passage of the Sagene forces toward the front.

Hal barely noticed, being used to the desolation, but the countryside depressed Khiri and other civilians who'd never seen such ruination.

She importuned the king, and he agreed to turn aside, to take smaller, country windings untouched by soldiery, and within a few miles they entered a dreaming land unknown to the sword.

Hal couldn't decide which was the greater pleasure—to fly the high station, drifting through the late summer day, hot and still, baking, the last of the fogs of the Roche northland out of him; or to swerve about down low, Storm chasing birds, not very sure what he'd do with one if he caught the mouthful of feathers.

In either event, he was reminded of the days before the war, when he was advance man for poor damned Athelny of the Dragons, with posters and a small bag of copper and silver, and no one to look over his shoulder.

A long, long time ago, he thought, a bit wistfully, and wondered if, when peace came and if he still lived, he could find such a peaceful life.

He shook his head at the idea: even if he lived through the damned war, he was now Lord Kailas, with estates and tenant farmers and fishermen to worry about and care for.

Hal thought he'd almost like to go back to those days when his stomach couldn't keep his spine and navel from being the closest of friends.

Kailas sighed, put the past out of his mind.

He wished he could ask Khiri to get on behind him, and share this lazy pleasure, a moment of peace in the midst of ruination.

But there was still the army, and its rules, below him, with jealous courtiers watching him closely, wishing him to do something that might usurp his standing with the king, so they might move a bit closer to the throne.

At least he and Khiri had each night together, in Hal's small tent.

And that made up for much as they made love fiercely, as if trying to affirm life and deny the death behind them.

Fovant had been built in a valley, with steep, defensible hills around it, and a river running through its middle, where the great farming region spread out to the west and north.

Rozen, too, had a river. But that was wide, and unfriendly, better for ship and boat passage than for the scenery. Fovant's river had also been navigable, but steep-banked, narrow and deep. The city's builders had concreted its banks and later its bottom, so their river was most civilized, save every century or so when it rose over the banks and the boulevards that wound along it.

The city had been walled for defense from hill to hill, and, for a change, the city builders had allowed for growth, so it was only now that growth had spilled beyond the wide walls.

The city had grown up more than out, and its streets were either broad, suitable for many horsemen, or narrow, twisting, close enough to give a pony pause.

There were many parks dotted through Fovant, from the great one beside the river to tiny vest-pocket patches of green, with no more than a dozen trees.

The houses were mostly stone to the first floor, half-timbered and plaster above that for the most part. Businesses and government buildings were stone, but not hard, cold gray, but in cheerful shades of red.

Hal and Khiri saw it first at sunset, Hal from a greater height, and it gleamed like a city of dreams.

Both of them fell in love with Fovant on sight.

It was not just that Fovant's people thought themselves more beautiful, more handsome, wittier and more cultured than anyone, including their fellow Sagene. It was that, in many areas, Hal and Khiri thought they might be right.

Their opinion wasn't hurt by the Fovant priding themselves on their skills at cookery. Hal and Khiri couldn't remember having a bad meal, from the most expensive banquets to meat and vegetable sticks grabbed on the run from a street vendor.

Sagene's Council of Barons had arranged for King Asir and his party to be housed in a disused palace, just short of the outer walls.

The palace was big enough to hold all of the Derainians, plus the considerable staff the barons had given Asir for his stay.

There was even enough room for the dragons, although dragon tents from the Sagene fliers had to be set up inside the grounds.

A peculiarity of this palace, and one which gave it its name, was that the rulers of Sagene had stocked the grounds with deer. The animals were most tame, and it was common for a soldier to be working at a task and realize three or four deer were peering, as curious as cats, over his shoulder, about to offer advice.

The barons invited the Derainians to hunt the deer as they pleased.

Asir put the word around that killing one of them would be like killing a pet, and he would prefer anyone in his retinue not do that.

Most of the Derainians agreed with him, or felt it improper to go against the king's wishes.

Others didn't.

Hal wasn't surprised to see that Alcmaen was one of the dissenters, and, every couple of days, would lug in a carcass across his horse's withers, as proud as if he'd hunted down a forest bear with a spear.

He'd wanted to hunt the tame animals from the air, from dragonback, which Hal was able to forbid, since it didn't contribute anything to the war effort.

None of this did anything to increase Alcmaen's popularity on the squadron.

Khiri, Hal decided, had put it well, when she said, "That man reminds me of a boy I knew, growing up, the son of one of my father's head servants. He wasn't that ugly or stupid, but no one much liked him. He desperately wanted to be popular, but everything he tried seemed to produce the exact opposite."

"What happened to him?" Hal asked.

"He left a letter, saying he was running away to sea." Khiri shook her head. "We all expected to get boastful letters, lies about how he was becoming a famous ship's captain. But no one, including his parents, heard anything ever.

"I suppose, if he actually did become a sailor, he must have been drowned."

"Or," Hal said, "just as likely tossed overboard by a shipmate whose tolerance he'd pushed beyond the limit." He thought about it a minute. "I guess children can do things like that, not realizing they're making the absolutely wrong impression. But why an adult?"

"Did you ever think," Khiri said quietly, "that there's many of us who never grow up?"

"Like dragon fliers?"

Khiri smiled.

"Some of you."

"Me?"

"I'll never tell."

The first two days were spent in banquets and mutual celebration of the everlasting bond between Sagene and Deraine.

The Deer Park's gates were open to the public, and any

suggestion that better security might be in order was met with raised eyebrows and, sometimes, the hint that Fovant was five hundred leagues or more behind the lines.

Hal thought of the distance Carcaor was behind the lines, and how that hadn't kept the city safe, but didn't say anything.

The best he could do was have the attached raiders outfitted in mufti, and wander about the palace grounds, trying to look innocent and civilian. It didn't work—if hidden dagger bulges didn't give them away, their close-cropped hair and military boots did. But it was better than nothing, he supposed.

The king insisted on going out for his morning rides, and everyone worried.

The king snorted at them, and, probably to show his independence, went farther beyond Fovant each day.

Kailas overheard the officer in charge of the raiders muttering, "It isn't enough that our royal shithead has got to dress himself up in king gear, but he sits his damned horse so well that he really doesn't need the bangles and fripperies. Hell, if I were a Roche sympathizer I'd try to pot the bastard merely for looking noble. But that damned horse blanket of his is better than a godsdamned herald riding in front with a godsdamned trumpet."

The blanket in question was imperial red, with yellow fringes and yellow embroidery with the king's initials.

But Asir was Asir, and most set in his ways.

Hal got used to hordes of children following him around, in awe at being in the presence of the Dragonmaster.

Other hordes, Sagene taletellers, followed Alcmaen and especially Danikel about.

The slender, withdrawn, almost-beautiful young man was becoming a legend in his country, to the barely hidden fury of Alcmaen.

Danikel was credited with a dozen, no, two dozen, no, a brace of dozens of kills. He smiled when asked the precise number, and would only say, "Not nearly enough, since the war still continues."

He got letters by the bale, proposals, indecent and decent, by the cartload.

The fliers were wondering if, perhaps, Danikel preferred men, or perhaps had no sex at all.

He began keeping company with a most beautiful baroness, five years older than he was, with a regal bearing and hair that appeared to have been silver from birth.

But Danikel's life seemed completely focused on his dragons and the war.

The conference began, sealed to all.

But even kings and barons have to talk to somebody.

In Asir's case, it was to Sir Thom Lowess, who, in turn, let little bits drop to Hal.

Everything was going most wonderfully, amicability oozing on both sides.

The only stumbling block was the city of Paestum, long a sore point, being Derainian, on Sagene land. Battles had been fought and lost centuries earlier, but Sagene still thought Paestum rightfully theirs.

Too much Derainian blood had been shed in its defense to ever consider handing it back to Sagene, though.

Asir broke that stumbling block by suggesting that Paestum become, after the war, an open city, belonging to no one and everyone.

There were grumbles from the Sagene, but then cheerfulness came back.

Lowess suggested cynically that the barons took the open city proposal as a prybar in the door that could be used, in the years to come, to make Paestum Sagene once more.

Hal didn't give a damn either way, remembering the

coldness he'd encountered as a broke, stranded wanderer before the war.

Besides, as he kept reminding himself, politics wasn't a soldier's business.

"And what is this?" Hal asked suspiciously, peering about the room.

It was the great room of an apartment that was larger than most merchants' houses. It was on the top floor of a four-story building that overlooked Fovant's river, with four bedrooms, a jakes for each room, the great room, a banquet hall that could've served a dragon flight, and servants' quarters a half-floor below. Outside glass doors was a roof garden that Hal thought he could land Storm in without hurting either the dragon or the plants.

"It's ours," Khiri said. "I bought it as a birthday present."

"But it's hardly my birthday."

"Then it's for last birthday . . . or next." Khiri looked carefully at him. "You don't like it."

"I didn't say that," Kailas protested.

"I've been looking for something like this ever since we got here," Khiri said. "Since we both love Fovant so much, after the war, we'll have a place to stay."

Hal started to say something, stopped himself. It would have been bitchy at best, probably something about he didn't like not being consulted.

It wasn't as if Khiri didn't have more than enough money of her own, which Hal had never an intent of controlling.

He forced a smile.

"And now we do," he said.

"Are you really sure you like it?"

"I'm really sure," he half-lied. "I just never thought about after the war."

He walked to the doors, went out into the garden, looked down at the afternoon strollers below.

Khiri came up behind him, put her arms around him, nuzzled his neck.

"I'm just sorry there's no furnishings yet. Like a bed."

Hal turned, kissed her, cupped her buttocks in his hands.

"And Lady Carstares is suddenly too humpty-hoo to even consider having her little lights screwed out on the floor?"

Khiri looked down.

"At least it's polished wood," she said. "Better than some old castle stone."

"So 'tis," Hal said, unbuttoning her dress.

She stepped out of it.

Khiri wore only a shift under it, her breasts not needing support.

She kicked her shoes off. One arced high in the air, disappeared over the garden wall.

"Oh dear," she said. "I hope it doesn't skull some good and proper Fovanian."

"If it does," Hal said, his voice getting throaty, "they can look for another apartment. This one's vacant."

Khiri giggled, came into his arms.

Later, he wondered why he'd almost behaved like a total shit. Was it worrying about living through the war? Or wasn't he sure he loved Khiri as completely as, say, Saslic? He'd gotten almost as cranky when she'd brought up having children a month or so ago.

The train of thought was making him most uncomfortable, and so he turned away from that, and began nipping, gently, at her nipples.

In a few seconds, they both had something else to think about.

The talks were going very well, and there was distinct optimism in the Deer Park.

An attack all along the front—how could that not break Roche for good and all?

Hal remembered what the king had said about the man who fights everywhere fights nowhere, but that couldn't break his mood.

The endless war, having an end . . .

The other fliers seemed to feel the same, and Hal was reminded that their normal easy cynicism was as much a façade as anything else, little more than a pose youths have always found attractive.

After all, the fliers were all young—even the oldest, Mynta Gart, was just a bit over thirty. Hal suspected Alcmaen was probably older than that, but he was adamantly twenty-five by his claims, and Hal suspected he'd be so long after the rest of his thinning hair vanished.

If there was real pessimism, and Hal suspected there was, it would be among the older men, the infantrymen who were hurled forward, day after day, never being told their place in things, never allowed to see any more of the war and the world than the muddy patches around them.

Hal came into one of the common rooms of the Deer Park's mansion to see a group of his fliers, including all of the 11th Flight's survivors, and Danikel in the background, standing around a great wall map that had the front lines scribed on it.

He'd intended to get a nightcap from the attendant, and nurse it for a few minutes, leaving his fliers alone. No organization is better for having its leader try to be one of the boys, hanging about constantly.

But Farren Mariah saw him, and waved him over.

He got his drink, and obeyed.

"Sir," Mariah said, careful as always to maintain military formality with outsiders close, "we're having a proper go-diddle about after the war, and what our plans are.

"Everybody's bein' most closemouthed about everything, so perhaps, you being the man in front and such, you'll enlighten us with what a proper flier does when peace breaks out."

Hal took a sip of his brandy.

"First," he said slowly, "I'd guess he'd kiss his dragon, then the ground, then his own sorry ass for doing something as surprising as living. That's what I'll do."

There was laughter.

"You're as bad as the rest of us," Mariah said. "C'mon now. Serious as it lays."

Hal thought.

"I'll be honest. Damned if I know. Maybe start a carnival or something. Gods know I can't see sitting around some castle diddling myself until I die of boredom."

"Perhaps you might stay in the army," Sir Loren suggested.

"Perhaps I might find someone with the last name of Damian to be orderly officer for the next two weeks for even *thinking* that," Kailas said. "One war's enough for anybody.

"And why am I in the barrel, anyway? You, Gart. You're far more upstanding than the rest of us."

"I'll buy myself a coaster," she said. "And start carrying cargoes every which way. Maybe even up some of these damned rivers we've flown over. Gods know the Roche'll be needing everything after we whip them."

"I can see it now ... ten years gone," Mariah said. "There'll be this great warehouse, right on the waterfront of Rozen. GART SHIPPING. WE TAKE ANYTHING ANY-WHERE AND MAKE A DAMNED GREAT PROFIT DOING IT."

"Is there anything wrong with that?" Gart asked.

"Of course not," Mariah said. "It's my purest of the pure jealousies that's speaking."

"I know very well what I'm going to do," Sir Loren said, sounding very mystical. "There's a spot on my land, not far from my manor house that, long ago, before there were drag-ons, when men lived like gods and the gods drank with them, was most sacred, and, to this day, is very beautiful. It's a tiny vale, and the gardeners have it planted in roses.

"What I'll do is build a bower, and train roses to climb up

through it. In the bower, I'll have a marble stand made. On the stand, I'll put my crossbow, which I'll have silver-plated, with gold trim."

The fliers were goggling. Sir Loren was known as one of the most antimilitary of the fliers, although he kept his opinion generally to himself.

"And every morning," Loren went on, "just at sunrise, I'll go out, just as the sun's rays strike my crossbow . . . and piss all over the son of a bitch!"

When the laughter died, Hal looked at Farren Mariah.

"What about you? I know you're a city rat and all. Are you going to take Limingo's advice, and study magic?"

Mariah's face was serious for an instant.

"P'raps," he said. "More likely, I'll go into government. Real government, you know, the kind that lets pretty fellers like the Dragonmaster and all those lords and ladies speak to the king for their regions, and meantime these other fellers stay in the background, with good red gold handed out here and there, to make sure things happen the way they're supposed to happen.

"It'll be all over Rozen, if you want to have something done, legal or no, go see Farren. I'll have the urchins write ballads about me, and I'll be surrounded with the wittiest of balladeers and the prettiest of girls.

"P'raps it might not be bad for me to stand for all veterans. Nobody else is going to, once the killing stops."

His voice had become a little bitter, and the fliers were quiet, knowing the truth of his words, not meeting each other's eyes.

"And what about me?" Chincha asked. "When you're out cavortin' with the ladies?"

"Aarh," Mariah said. "I'll buy you a fancy man from Sagene, who knows tricks with massages and like that. You'll not want."

That broke the mood.

"If any of us had any decency," Danikel, Baron Trochu, said from the fringes of the group, "we'd try to pay back what we owe to the dragons."

"What?" Mariah said, pretending outrage, "those smelly bastards out there, honking and slobbering? What do we owe them?"

"Our lives," Danikel said quietly. "Our chances of winning the war. The best tool to beat the Roche back and keep them in hand. And if you think we'll be forgotten about after the war, what the hells do you think'll happen to our dragons?

"Stuck in a cage in an exhibit somewhere. Or part of one of those damned flying carnivals. Giving fat merchants and their squealing daughters rides, up, down, three gold coins if you please, sir?

"Or maybe just taken out and killed, since they're pretty much of an annoyance. Doesn't anybody think they deserve better than that?

"Mariah, if you're really looking for a cause, you could do better than help the dragons."

"And what would that get me?" Mariah said. "Right now, I stink like dragons, true. And that brings the maidens out . . . did before I met Chincha, at any rate. But do you think that stink's going to be so popular when we're at peace?

"No, young Baron. You've got your lands and your peasants to keep you in clover. The rest of us will have to find something else."

Danikel seemingly hadn't been listening to Mariah, but looking at Hal.

"You know what I'm talking about, don't you, sir? Don't we have a debt?"

Hal took a deep breath.

"Yes. I know what you're talking about. And yes, we do owe them."

He drained his snifter.

"And I'm for bed. All this is getting far too serious for me."

Again, there was laughter, and that marked the end of the evening.

But Hal lay awake, listening to Khiri's bubbling snore for a long time that night.

Outside, in one of the barns, a dragon shrilled in his sleep.

30

The cheering started just before noon, and rolled, like a wave, from the gates of the Deer Park to the mansion.

No one needed to know what it meant.

An agreement had been reached between the ruling barons of Sagene and King Asir.

Hal felt his heart leap, went looking for the details.

As matters turned out, there were three levels of agreements. The first, since there had to be something to tell the masses and leak to the Roche, was that Sagene and Deraine had reached a general treaty of goodwill and close cooperation from now until forever, to ensure there would be no stab in the back by the Roche or anyone else.

Paestum, as rumored, would become an open city once the war was over.

Both countries formally agreed there could be but one end to this war: complete and unconditional surrender by the Roche, and occupation, at least for a time, of their lands while a less bellicose regime was installed.

Most civilians thought this an obvious requirement.

Many soldiers did not, arguing that would make the Roche

fight even harder if they knew Queen Norcia and her court would be replaced by something, someone, unknown.

Others snorted, saying they didn't see how the bastards could fight any harder than they already were, and wanted to make sure their children or children's children, wouldn't be attacked by the Roche, or at least not this version of them.

Hal didn't know, seeing good argument on both sides.

The second level of the treaty agreed there would be a massive attack in the far south, in the Fourth Army's area. All other armies would go to full alert to disguise the buildup.

This level was intended for discovery by Roche spies, and was false.

The real treaty included not only the first articles, but the agreement for the general offensive, from all armies, against the Roche, intended to smash their lines from north to south and seize Carcaor.

There were banquets, parades, and general goodwill from all.

King Asir couldn't go beyond the Deer Park without being buried by hurrahing crowds.

Before the goodwill was inevitably worn down, the Derainians packed for their return to the front.

On that last night, Hal jerked awake in the small hours.

A thought, a dream, had come, and he managed to keep from losing it.

He was sitting on the bed, feet on the floor, sweating.

"Whassamatta, love?" Khiri murmured.

"Nothing. Something I forgot to check," he said. "Go back to sleep."

"Ummuck," she said, and obeyed.

Hal dressed hurriedly, went to the planning room, consulted maps. They suggested he wasn't even slightly about to cry wolf.

He went to the stables, and further confirmed his suspicions.

Then he found the officer of the guard, and got directions to Limingo's rooms.

"But my master has given orders not to be disturbed," the servant-acolyte said, pulling himself up from the cot across the entrance.

"King's orders," Hal lied. "Now, go get whatever Limingo needs to wake up."

"But—"

"Move!" Hal said, in a voice that would carry across a parade ground.

The man obeyed.

Hal shoved the cot out of the way, opened the door.

Limingo was not alone—a handsome, tousled, naked young man was getting up, fumbling for a sword.

Hal ignored him.

"Limingo, I think we might have problems."

The wizard started to say something, stopped, then told the young man to get dressed and go back to his quarters.

He pulled clothes on, looking at Hal cautiously, as if expecting Kailas to be shocked or enraged.

Hal felt neither and, in any event, hadn't time for emotions.

By the time Limingo had washed and dressed, his servant was back with a tray with a steaming teakettle on it, and cups.

He poured.

"Now, what's the great alarm?" Limingo said. "I hear no sounds of tumult or disaster."

"If I'm right, you won't, not for three days," Hal said. "Listen to my thread of logic, and please tell me I'm full of shit, so we can go back to bed," he said. "Back on the front lines, we were jumped when the king visited Lord Cantabri, straight out of nowhere by a battle formation of dragons.

"We drove them off, but for the rest of the time we were on the lines, there'd be a dragon or six hovering just out of range.

"When we pulled out, coming east to Fovant, we had a pair or more of Roche dragons—always black, and I'd suspect from *Ky* Yasin's elite squadron—tailing us.

"I was wondering then if there was a spy with us, or if the Roche had some very skilled recon soldiers in the bushes, reporting to a wizard who passed the word along to their dragon fliers.

"But I never saw any sign of their scouts, either afoot or on horseback, lurking about, when I was airborne. I asked the raider captain if he'd seen anything, but he hadn't.

"Isn't it possible that, if you have, say, a bit of the cloth of someone's pants, assuming he's a filthy sod and never changes, you could use magic to track him?"

"Certainly," Limingo said. "It's not that hard a spell, either.'

"Well, let's say somebody breaks into the king's stable tent, and cuts a few strands off that damned royal red blanket he's so fond of?"

"That would work very well indeed, as long as the tracker was only concerned with when the king was a-horseback," Limingo said. He was starting to look a bit worried.

"Remember those four Roche who tried to attack the king the first night after he left my squadron? We killed one, ran the other three off, with no gains. Or so we thought.

"However, I just went out to the stablery, and looked at the king's riding gear. And that blanket has about four or five of its long fringes cut off.

"Do you think maybe that's what those infiltrators were after?"

Limingo nodded slowly.

"Now, let's put another bit into the equation," Hal went on. "Remember how desolate our way was, even after we crossed the border into Sagene, and now some of the king's favorites asked if we could turn away from the main road to Fovant, which we did?"

"Yes." One of the many things Hal liked about Limingo was that he actually listened when you were speaking, and saved his comments until you were through.

"I just looked at the map, and traced the route we were supposed to follow—and the one we'll take back to the areas we already hold.

"Two days after we turned off the main highway on to the byways, we would've passed through a rocky place. Chasms, draws, small but steep peaks. It's called the Pinnacles. Looking at the map, and remembering my days as a cavalryman," Hal said, "I would've loved to have ambushed somebody right in the middle of that, particularly somebody who doesn't have a heavy escort, not needing one that far from the front.

"What do you think about that, my sorcerous friend?" Hal said, with a bit of triumph.

"I think we'd best wake up the king," Limingo said. "And I don't think anybody's going to get a lot of sleep for the rest of the night."

"You're wrong there," Hal said. "I think the only one who won't be getting any sleep is me."

The king looked at the maps Hal had laid out once more.

"I don't normally like guesses about what the enemy is going to do, Lord Kailas. But your suppositions make entirely too much sense for me not to allow for them.

"I suppose now we roust out a baron or two, borrow whatever guard regiment or regiments we can, and have them march east to the Pinnacles and winkle the Roche out. We can use that damned blanket of mine—and I should have known, remembering my father's warning against fripperies—as bait."

"That is one option, Your Highness," Hal said carefully. He didn't like any of it, particularly exposing to the Roche they'd caught on to the blanket trick, having a vague idea about putting the principle to use himself against the Roche.

"But not the one you clearly prefer," Asir said.

Hal made a noncommittal noise.

"What would be your plan, then?" Asir said. "I just realized one thing: there is no way in the world I'll sit on my ass here in Fovant and let the Sagene clean up the mess I've been responsible for."

Limingo looked alarmed.

"An excellent idea, sire," Hal said. "Might I ask which of your sons is the most qualified to be regent?"

The king frowned, then jolted as he got it.

"Kailas, when I suggested you learn a few tricks of the diplomatic trade, I didn't mean for you to get this sneaky."

Everyone knew Asir was not only unmarried, but didn't even have any royal bastards hanging about the palace.

"Very well," Asir grudged. "Perhaps—especially after reaching this covenant with the Council of Barons—I'd best not be out there playing soldier."

Limingo relaxed.

"As for sending the Sagene out," Hal went on, "suppose that I'm wrong, and there's nobody and nothing in the Pinnacles but wild boar and rocks? We'll look more than a bit stupid."

"True. But what can we do?" Asir asked. "And, by the way, do you have any idea how the Roche will mount this ambush? Just with dragons, as they tried the last time?"

"No," Hal said. "I'd guess they might have infiltrated light cavalry through the lines, and had them hole up. They'll have been horrid disappointed that we didn't waltz into their talons, but most likely figure we're going to come back the shorter route, since we've got important matters for the army to implement.

"Another possibility is they've brought infantry across in dragon baskets, like they used back around Bedarisi."

"You and your fliers took care of that rather handily," Asir said. "I'd think they'd be reluctant to try it again."

"Why?" Hal asked. "If everybody thinks that tactic's elderly, doesn't that make it fresh again?"

Asir nodded.

"But you still haven't offered a plan," he said.

"Very simple," Hal said. "I take off right now for the First Army, with orders from you to Lord Cantabri to take, say, two companies of light cavalry, two companies of heavy cavalry, plus as many dragon flights as I can get, and march west to the Pinnacles. The Roche, if they're in there, shouldn't be watching their back as they should.

"Meantime you . . ." Hal caught himself, and saw the king's grin. "Sorry, sir. I meant that as a suggestion, sir. Maybe you could get a couple of companies of heavy cavalry to ride west with you as escort, to keep you from getting any surprises."

That was Hal's intent—to get *Ky* Yasin and his First Guards Squadron between a rock—the Pinnacles—and a very hard place. Which would be them on the ground with Hal's dragons overhead and Derainian soldiers on the ground. With any luck, and assuming Yasin was involved with this elaborate scheme to murder or capture the king, Hal might be able to strike a great blow against the Roche.

The king pondered for a few minutes.

"Very well. Get you airborne and headed west. I'll move east as slowly as possible until I get word you're on the march."

"A better idea, sire," Hal said. "Wait here until I've reached Cantabri, and send a messenger back that we're on the move. *Then* take the road.

"And you could have someone, maybe Sir Thom, write a story about the route you'll be taking, making sure you mention the Pinnacles as maybe being some kind of natural wonder that you're sorry you've missed.

"There's got to be spies here in Fovant that'll report that."

"I'll do it," the king said. "But I feel like I'm being ordered about, instead of kinging the way I'm supposed to." He sighed. "Back and forth, back and forth. It's a great damned pity that our magicians haven't come up with any way to communicate over distances. But I suppose that's an impossibility."

He sighed once more.

Hal got up, saluted.

"Thank you, Kailas," the king said. "If you're right, and there are murderers waiting, I shall truly be in your debt."

"So you're going to fly off, all by yourself, and play hero again?" Khiri said. "Oh well. At least it isn't that dangerous . . . at least not until you start coming back toward us.

"Then you'd best be very careful."

"I'm always careful," Hal said piously.

Khiri just snorted.

Hal took Storm into the air a little before dawn. He wanted to fly east, back to the armies, as quickly as he could, but without exhausting the dragon or himself.

There would be other tasks for him once they reached the First Army and Lord Cantabri.

Flying in a straight line, it would take five days for Hal to reach Bedarisi, where there would be dragon units to leave Storm, but he'd take an extra day avoiding the Pinnacles.

He probably should have taken a wingmate, but there were few enough dragons with the king already, and so he decided to fly solo, and feed both Storm and himself on emergency rations.

Khiri, Limingo and Hal's orderly, Uluch, were the only ones to bid him farewell. Hal turned the detachment over to Gart, and she was the only one to know that Hal was on some other mission than flying northeast, to see what the Sagene dragon training camps were like.

Hal went high, where the air was thinner, and it was easier

flying for Storm, who could glide vast distances with his wings at full stretch.

He landed after dark at a recommended Sagene inn, and was able to husband the emergency rations for a night, feeding Storm on a pair of lambs, and himself on chops with mint.

He was grateful for the warm bed they put him up in, since the late summer was a bit snappish. Storm was curled up behind the inn's stables.

Once again, before dawn, he was roused, and gulped some tea and cold meat. He fed Storm on ten pounds of raw, ground meat, since the dragon didn't seem terribly hungry, then pushed on.

That night, he slept away from the road, in a grassy nook next to a creek. Storm sneered at what he was offered, went fishing in the creek, his long, snaky head hovering like a heron over the water, then darting down.

He caught enough fish for himself, and for Hal to grill a couple over an open fire.

The third day covered the shortest distance—to the immediate north was the main east-west road, and the Pinnacles.

Hal desperately wanted to overfly the crags, to see if he could spot any sign of the Roche ambush, not knowing if it was still set . . . or if, in fact, it ever had been.

He hoped he hadn't made the classic intelligence officer's mistake of seeing an enemy behind every bush, when there wasn't one there, and, sometimes, there wasn't even a bush.

But he held back, and flew low that day, arcing around the Pinnacles. Storm growling at not being allowed to go high.

There was an inn, at a crossroads, and Hal chanced landing beside it.

He ate a gigantic omelet, and Storm munched on a heifer.

Hal allowed himself two glasses of wine, and was nursing the second as his plate was cleared away, when he overheard a pair of teamsters grumbling about the godsdamned bandits in the godsdamned Pinnacles, and how the godsdamned army wouldn't send in some godsdamned troops to clean the gods- damned bastards out.

"They're scar't," one wagoneer said. "Those godsdamned bastids are too strong for a rooty little company. Hells, they've got dragons to scout for 'em. Bet they're not gods- damned bandits at all, but more like, godsdamned deserters."

"Typical gummint," the first said. "Allus too eager for your taxes, but never gonna give anything back."

He snorted, went back to his beer, and Hal drank up his wine and went to bed, feeling a little better that perhaps he wasn't dreaming about the Roche.

The rest of the flight was smooth, if tiresome.

He left a rather plaintive, but exhausted, Storm in Bedarisi, promising to come back for him within days, when he'd rested. Hal wondered if the dragon understood him, decided he was getting a little strange, what they were beginning to call dragon-happy.

He got a brown-orange male dragon that was promised to "be fast, but, sir, I'll warn you, he can be skittish."

Another hand broke in: "He's the Dragonmaster. Not to worry about him."

Hal thought he should have said bushwa, that the Dragonmaster was feeling more than a little delicate, and whoever had said he was a master rider, but stupid pride kept him from it.

The brown was a bit on the high-strung side, but when he realized Hal was proposing to let him fly as hard and fast as he could, settled down and went like the wind.

Now they were over familiar ground, the area fought over by both armies.

Hal realized he'd grown used to the ruin and spoliation. But after having spent a few weeks in something resembling civilization, the shambles came afresh.

He wondered, briefly, what it would be like for him when

and if the war was over. Certainly he wouldn't be able to fit into a civilian niche easily, nor could he see remaining a soldier.

Kailas turned off his thoughts, concentrated on flying fast.

A pair of dragons came in on him as he was closing on the First Army headquarters. He didn't recognize them, nor the flight banner on both dragons' carapaces, but they knew him, and asked a shouted question about needing an escort.

Hal called back that things were fine, but the riders must have recognized his rather harried appearance, and dropped in on his flanks.

They waved farewell as he brought the brown in, just short of Cantabri's command tent.

Sentries ran up, challenged him, saluted, and obeyed when he asked to be taken to Lord Bab at once.

Cantabri listened, took a few notes, consulted three maps, and asked for his top aides to be sent in, plus the liaison officer with the Sagene forces.

Hal listened, a bit enthralled, having forgotten what it was to be with quiet competence.

Within an hour, two battalions of heavy cavalry had been told off, with orders to draw two weeks' supplies and march east toward Bedarisi. One of them was a crack Sagene unit.

They would be the slowest to move, next to the infantry, and therefore had been the first to be put on the march.

The foot soldiers came next, a full regiment of conventional infantry. Supporting them were four reserve transport companies, to carry the infantry and its supplies in wagons.

Next were three battalions of light cavalry, with the same orders.

With them went Cantabri's raiders. "They'll march at the stirrup, and their rations'll go with the cavalry."

Hal nodded. That meant the footsoldiers would hang on to a horseman's stirrup, and keep pace with him, half trotting, half being carried. It was hard on horses and men, but it doubled the pace the raiders would be able to travel. They well earned their jaunty uniforms and tough reputations.

"I'll depend on them to at least pin the Roche until the heavies can arrive," Cantabri went on. "Then we'll wipe them out.

"Now for you, Lord Kailas," Cantabri said. "I would like your squadron to move east as my long range scouts. Do you have any additions?"

"Yessir," Hal said. "We'll need to send a flier—two of them—east, looping around the Pinnacles, to alert the king that he should begin moving slowly in four or five days say, when we're on the other side of Bedarisi.

"I'd also like to draw from the other flights on the front," Hal said, "and bring my squadron at least up to full strength.

"I'm assuming Yasin is in command of those dragons, since he seems to be fond of anything smacking of dirty deeds, and I'd like a chance to wipe him—and his unit—out for once and for all."

"That would be a desirable end," Cantabri said. He nodded to an aide. "Has there been significant air fighting lately?"

"Nossir," the aide said. "And I've been wondering why."

"I'd guess the explanation might be that their best is behind our lines, looking for a chance to take out King Asir," Cantabri said.

He thought, tapping fingernails against a map.

"That should do it, for a starter," Cantabri said. "Now, all of you—except Lord Kailas—out. I assume he's got things for my eyes only."

Hal waited until the tent was empty, reflexively checked to make sure the posted sentries were the only ones close to the tent's canvas.

"I do, indeed, sir," Hal said. "The treaty has been agreed on with Sagene. We'll have full cooperation with the barons. And both parties agreed the only peace will be unconditional surrender."

Cantabri looked wolfish.

"Good," he said. "Now, with an offensive to plan, I should remain here with my maps. But I'll allow myself a bit of privilege first."

It was a forced march to Bedarisi, where Hal reclaimed the rested Storm.

The formation went on east, moving as fast as it could. Stragglers were simply abandoned, told to catch up or return to the First Army, it didn't matter which to Cantabri.

Hal, his First Squadron, and the augmentation kept airborne. Hal hadn't briefed anyone on what the mission was, any more than Cantabri had told anyone but unit commanders.

The weary messengers sent to Fovant returned, reported that the king's party was moving out of the city.

"Deceptions," Cantabri told Kailas, "are under way by the king's party."

Hal, while Storm drifted above the formation, considered what those deceptions might be.

He had the idea that Limingo, with a couple or three of his bedmates, plus a small cavalry escort and two dragons, was marching west to meet them, toward the Pinnacles. The wizard not only had the king's blanket on his mount, but had cast a deceiving spell around the group so no Roche spies could see what they were about to attack.

For some unknown reason, Hal pictured the blanket, and Limingo, on a rather contrary and braying gray mule, an image that amused him, and one he never bothered to correct.

Two days short of the Pinnacles, Cantabri gathered his men in a great natural arena.

His speech was short, and pointed:

"Derainians! Our king is being stalked by a Roche enemy. We are marching to the rescue.

"Sagene! Your barons have agreed to a great plan that will end this war.

"We must not let anyone stand in that plan's way.

"Two days from now, we shall encounter the Roche, and ambush them where they would have waylaid His Royal Highness.

"There are moments in history where one man—or one company of men—can make a difference.

"This is one of them.

"Years gone, you will tell your grandchildren you were here, and no one will be able to say he did greater fealty to his country.

"For Sagene!

"For Deraine!"

The men cheered until the hills gave back the echo.

Hal insisted on flying the first reconnaissance over the Pinnacles.

The Roche camp, fairly well concealed, was hidden just where Hal would've put it himself, assuming that no one would be looking for Roche this far behind the lines.

It looked as if there was a small flight of dragons, about ten monsters, and about two companies of infantry, around 150 or more men.

They were quartered under trees, and the transport baskets the dragons had brought them in were hidden in a draw nearby.

Hal wondered how the Roche were going to lift out their infantrymen after the ambush, or if they were proposing a suicide operation.

That didn't make sense—the Roche weren't known for their stupidity.

But that wasn't his problem, nor that of any other Derainian. Better if every Roche died in place as far as Kailas was concerned.

Before they had left the front, Cantabri had a large-scale map of the Pinnacles cast by a wizard, and used that for the final briefing. Some officers were worried that their camp was less than a league away from the Roche, but Cantabri was confident of surprise. The Roche wouldn't be looking to their rear.

Hal hoped he was right.

That night, the raiders went out on foot, and came back with a clear scout of the terrain.

A dragon was stationed on a peak, in a shallow cave. A raider officer, with a glass, and the flier waited with it.

They reported that Roche dragon scouts went out that dawn, flew west, looking for the king.

They came back, landed. There was no particular excitement around the camp, so the raider officer flag-signaled to another raider to the east, who sent the word to Cantabri's camp.

They waited another night, and then most of a day as the Roche dragons went out once more.

The Roche hurtled back at speed, late in the day, and it was clear to the watchers the king's column had been sighted.

There would be two choices for the Roche—either ambush the king at dawn, when the column was rousing, or immediately, near dusk.

From the bustle that was signaled back, it was evident the Roche commander had decided to attack what he thought was Asir's column immediately, not taking a chance and betting on fatigue and hunger to fight on his side.

They definitely wouldn't be watching their rear.

Cantabri ordered his forces into attack.

The heavy cavalry went straight up the main highway, planning to divert up a wide draw that wound into the Roche camp.

The light cavalry and the infantry took a winding herdsman's path the raider scouts had found, moving at the trot.

A league—an hour before the fight would begin.

One turning of the glass.

Hal would begin the attack.

He took his dragons off after half an hour, swept once back over the camp, forming an arrow formation and drove for the Roche.

They came in over the Roche camp, a fairly defensible nest in the rocks, just as the Roche were getting ready to move to the main highway and their ambush positions.

Hal took Storm in low, and a black dragon fairly leapt into the air at him.

Kailas had an instant to recognize the dragon's banner on its carapace as being, in fact, Yasin's First Guards Squadron. Then he put a bolt in its rider's chest, another shot into the dragon's throat, and it scrawked, pinwheeled, and thrashed down to the ground, knocking another two dragons sprawling.

The Roche infantry froze for an instant, then rigid discipline returned. They formed extended lines, knelt, and brought up their bows, ready to destroy the dragons.

The Roche dragons were trying to get into the air, but Hal's formation swept across the field, dragon riders spattering down crossbow bolts.

Hal suddenly remembered when he'd used bowman mounted behind the fliers, cursed that he'd not had time to use the tactic again.

A dragon in front of him was hit, tucked its head down as if entering a rainstorm, and crashed, rolling, bouncing across the field, killing half a score of Roche as it and its rider died.

Then the light cavalry and the raiders came into the nest, still on line, not pausing to reform into a battle line, but spreading out as they came.

They hit the Roche hard, smashing them back, into knots. But the Roche held firm, trying to reform as the cavalry came back on them.

The Roche dragons were all in the air, and banked hard away from the field.

Hal sent his dragons after them, and there was a low-level melee that sent four Roche and one Derainian dragon down.

Trumpets blared, and Hal chanced a quick look back at the Roche base.

The heavy cavalry had come on the field, its ponderous chargers moving from the walk into the trot, long lances coming down.

The Roche men held for an instant, then broke, running, scattered.

As they broke, the light cavalry and infantry swarmed after them, swords slashing.

The Roche dragons clawed for altitude, but Hal's squadron denied it to them.

The black monsters fled low, across country, heading east, back for their own lines, abandoning the men on the ground.

Hal sent his dragons after them, and there was a long pursuit in the dusk, dropping a dragon here, and there.

None of them carried the fringed banner of *Ky* Yasin.

No more than a handful of Roche were able to escape their harriers.

Finally, Hal blew the recall, and they turned back to the Pinnacles.

Hal wondered if the Roche dragon fliers had also panicked and fled, or if they'd been under orders to abandon the foot soldiers, fliers being vastly more valuable than any ground troops.

Ordered or not, that tasted very nasty to him, and he wondered if the flight also rang sour in the mind of Yasin. Hopefully it had, and would eat at him, possibly clouding his judgment in the future.

It was near dark when they came in on the battlefield, the dragons' wings cracking as they braked for a landing.

It was strewn with bodies, and there were only a few wounded. The Roche hadn't asked for quarter, and, generally, none had been given.

Hal landed, reported to Cantabri.

Lord Bab was a bit angry. There'd been no ranking prisoners taken, and so no one to tell Lord Bab—or the king—just what had been intended by the ambush, whether capturing Asir . . . or just killing him.

The formation's support units came up the road, and the Sagene and Deraine forces moved down to the highway, to rest, and wait for the king.

Skirmishers were still busy on the battlefield, stripping arms and armor from the dead, and, supposedly, succoring the Roche wounded.

Hal doubted if there would be much of that.

"So that's that," King Asir said, after full reports had been made. "If we had time, I would have liked to have visited that field myself.

"But we've wasted enough time as is.

"Now, let's get back to the lines, and get this damned war over with."

31

It took almost three weeks for the Grand Offensive to be mounted. By the time the banners waved and the bugles blew, Hal had revised his opinion of the plan's validity.

With almost a month of rumors and whispers, it was inevitable that the Roche would realize *something* was going on.

Their spies went to work up and down the line, and Derainian and Sagene counterspies went after them.

Roche dragons overflew the lines, trying to see what was happening below.

Hal and the other dragon flight commanders had patrols out from dawn until nightfall.

There were snarling fights in the skies as a Deraine or Sagene formation would attack a Roche scout. Roche reinforcements would hurtle to the rescue and Derainian support would be airborne within minutes.

The sky would be a great melee of death, dragons pinwheeling about, men and monsters falling, screaming, into death, and then, as if on a signal, there would be nothing but clear, blue, peaceful summer heavens.

Hal killed his share, probably more, but didn't bother keeping a count. He was too busy trying to keep his own men and women alive and fighting.

Alcmaen and Danikel did keep score, or rather Alcmaen did. He claimed seventy-five kills, although only forty were allowed.

Hal had decided that if people were going to make numbers important, the only way he'd allow them was with a witness. Naturally, Alcmaen always came back from a flight claiming a victory, although too many of them were accomplished with no other allied flier in sight.

Danikel didn't bother with numbers, but his chief handler did, and gleefully reported that Baron Trochu somehow always remained in the lead.

The supposed rivalry got out to the taletellers, and the First Squadron's base had at least one or two of them, generally Sagene, fawning over Danikel and Alcmaen on a daily basis.

At least they weren't bothering Hal.

Khiri had gone back to Deraine with King Asir and his company, so he didn't have her on his mind, as much as he would've liked to.

Then the orders came by courier, and, from the Chicor Straits to the Southern Ocean, Deraine and Sagene went on the attack. There was no subtlety here, no room for it, as the allied divisions stolidly marched forward against the Roche.

The Roche fought hard, but slowly fell back.

But they never broke.

A formation would be hit hard, and retreat. But the Roche would leave ambush teams in any cover that presented itself, who, as often as not, fought to the death.

The Roche, fighting on their own soil, poisoned the wells and used magic to blanch the soil when they could.

Their sorcerers sent spells against Deraine and Sagene, which were sometimes caught and stopped in time. Other times, demons would ravage and tear until Derainian wizards could cast a counterspell, then another spell aimed at the Roche magicians.

No one envied the wizards—a magician could be in mid-spell, all calm about him, and then fire would raven him, and anyone within range.

To Hal and the other dragon fliers, the world below was almost meaningless. Their war was in the skies. But it was still fascinating, if distressful, to see a green land slowly being turned muddy brown as the armies fought and marched across it.

The days were a blur of flying, fighting, killing, and the nights blank unconsciousness, with not a flier wanting to remember if he dreamed or not, and, if he did, what his dreams were.

The days were bad enough.

Hal remembered a new flier who reported in one morning with a dragon he'd been trained on. He was sent aloft on a noon patrol, in a supposedly safe sector. But a flight of Yasin's black dragons was waiting, and neither flier nor his mount came back.

What bothered Hal was that he couldn't remember the flier's name, and had to look it up in the records.

That first time was troublesome. But after the sixth time the same thing happened, Kailas almost got used to it.

Brandy might have helped somewhat.

But Hal couldn't allow himself that luxury.

Bodrugan and Goang returned from Deraine. They'd managed to procure large glass carboys, journeyed to a mine, and somehow managed to trap the deadly firedamp gas in the carboys.

Now all that remained, Goang told Hal, was to put the gas in smaller containers, put the containers in some sort of sack with nails and broken glass, come up with a bursting spell, and Hal would have his anticavalry weapon.

A week later, the pair asked for Hal and a dragon to try the thing out.

Bodrugan said, apologetically, that the spell was still a little complicated, so he'd prefer to ride behind Hal, and cast it himself.

"Of course," he assured Kailas, "when it works, we'll have a much simpler incantation."

It was a misty day, and there were no more than two or three pairs of dragons assigned missions, so Hal summoned the squadron to witness the great event.

Bodrugan had a wicker basket with half a dozen small bottles inside canvas sacks.

They put a target in the center of the landing field, and Hal took Storm off.

He took the dragon up to about a hundred feet, then turned back toward the field.

"Now," he said over his shoulder, "I'll bring it down to about fifty feet, and then come in over the target. Are we safe that low?"

"Yessir," Bodrugan said. "I mean, I'm almost certain, sir."

"Wonderful," Hal muttered, and only dropped to seventy-five feet.

"Start incanting," Hal said, and he heard Bodrugan muttering behind him.

The target was below, then directly underneath, then past.

"I'll take Storm round again," Hal said, "and give you a longer approach. Do you want me to give you a release point?"

"Thank you, sir," Bodrugan called back. "I'd appreciate it."

This time, the muttering started earlier.

"And five and four and three and two and . . . drop!" Hal shouted, and the bag dropped down toward the target.

It struck the ground about ten feet short of the marker.

And nothing happened, at least as far as Hal could tell.

They tried again, and again, until there were no more sacks.

Hal brought Storm in for landing, trying to decide if he should be angry or amused.

He settled for amusement, especially when Farren Mariah reported, "The bottles smashing, crashing, sounded just like geese farts on a muggy day when they struck . . . sir."

Hal kept back laughter until Bodrugan and Goang had shamefacedly picked up their sacks and gone back to Goang's tent to figure out what went wrong.

Mariah watched them go.

"Ah," he said. "That's what 'tis to be a knight of the dragon, privy to all kinds of secrets and magics.

"You should've asked me to do the spell, sir.

"Give a *real* wizard from the depths of the city a chance."

Hal told him he was welcome—in his off hours—to work with the pair.

Mariah made a face.

"Nawp, nawp, nawp, as my grandfather used to say. Once a spell's been spellt and spillt, there's no place for somebody to come in behind the goat."

The firedamp never did work.

Hal was called to Cantabri's headquarters for consultation.

The king had decided there should be dragon flights devoted solely to casting the sorcerous pebbles, and had named a pair of nonflying but high-ranking lords—Gurara and Hakea, one Derainian, one Sagene—to command these flights.

They weren't nearly as dunderbrained as might have been expected. By this stage of the war, there was little room for fools.

The pair had already gotten flying volunteers, had Limingo on standby and wanted Hal to help them develop a training curriculum. This Hal did, starting with the idea that perhaps these casting flights should have two fliers aboard—one solely to fly the dragon and watch for intercepting enemy, the other to do the casting.

They also wanted a couple of fliers who'd been on the Carcaor raid, and Hal grudgingly loaned them a couple of Derainians.

Then Cantabri proposed a flanking attack on a fortified Sagene position, and needed Hal's entire squadron to give his plan a bit of surprise, and Kailas put the matter in the back of his mind.

Hal called Chincha in, told her she was being commissioned and would take over the 11th Flight. Hal had been trying to run both the flight and the squadron long, and had forced himself to let go.

"But . . . but there's fliers better suited," Chincha stammered.

"Such as?" Hal asked.

"Farren, for one."

"You think he'd take the promotion?"

Chincha considered, slowly shook her head.

"But he's going to cast a kitten when he hears about this."

"Tell him, from me, that he should consider adopting a more mature attitude toward life and such."

Farren Mariah, as Hal had known he would, found the whole matter hysterically funny, and it didn't affect his relationship with Chincha at all.

Chincha took the whole matter very seriously, and tried to spend all day and night at her duties.

That was something else Hal had known.

Moving was always painful. The fliers would establish a base, and fly from it as long as they could. But eventually the armies plodded on east, and it was time to move.

Hal or one of the flight commanders would find a new location, near to the front lines, and then the tents would be struck, the wagons loaded, and the squadron would creak into motion.

At the new base the tents were repitched, various holes dug, and paths made.

Then it would take days for a new routine to be established—just where the mess, the farriers, the jakes, and such, were. Generally two or three mistakes, usually involving garbage or worse pits, were made in the learning.

The replacements complained bitterly about the discomfort, but there was generally a veteran around who'd remind them that it might be a little uncomfortable, particularly when it rained, but it wasn't even close to being as bad as it was for the infantry.

Nothing was that bad.

Some of the replacements never bitched, and Hal knew that they'd come from one of the line formations, and were most grateful that they could get out of a warm, dry bed before going out to be killed.

Someone in the commissary department made a mistake on one move, and didn't check the fresh meat that was bought.

Everyone, dragons and men, got embarrassing cases of the runs, promptly dubbed the "Roche gallop," and Hal was forced to take the squadron off the duty roster for three days, although Mariah insisted they should still be flying: "Just sit farther back in the saddle, and you and your beastie can come in on our foes and both poop 'em to death."

Then he grimaced and set out at a rapid trot for the nearest jakes.

Sir Loren called the hoary old army joke after him to be sure and cover his flanks.

One good thing that came out of the enforced idleness for Kailas was figuring out how he might use the locating spell the Roche had used against the king for his own ends.

But he still wasn't precisely sure how to do it.

*

There were four fliers in the room, part of a shattered manor house, listening to Lord Hakea and staring at the map he kept touching. His companion, Lord Gurara, sat behind the fliers.

The fliers were Hal and his four flight commanders: Chincha, Gart, Richia and Cabet.

"Yarkand is the key," he said once more. "It's one of Roche's most important trading cities. There's the major highway from Carcaor to the front, plus this north-south highway, and these two coming in from the northeast and east.

"The city is mostly stone, very ancient, so knocking down as much as we can will stop passage, not to mention ruining Yarkand as a warehousing center and replacement depot.

"It's packed with refugees and soldiers trying to get forward, so the attack should be a serious shock to Queen Norcia and her barons.

"We'll hit them with almost a hundred dragons, the biggest raid of the war so far."

"It's a long flight," Hal said.

"It is," Hakea said. "My casting flights will lift out of here not long after midnight, and I calculate, if the winds are right, that we'll reach Yarkand about midday.

"We'll want you to join us when we get over the Roche lines."

"Then we—or rather you—cast our rocks," Richia said, a bit doubtfully, "and then we fly back, getting back over our own lines about . . . ?"

"Midnight."

Richia whistled, shook his head, eased his bulk to a more comfortable position. "A long damned flight," he said, almost to himself.

At least, Hal thought, the two commanders were going on the mission, even though they weren't fliers, but flying as casters.

"We've been training for this mission for two weeks,"

Hakea said. "And if everything goes well—and your squadron, Lord Kailas, keeps any attacking dragons away—this could be a major step toward ending the war."

The flight commanders looked at Hal

"We would have appreciated a chance to rehearse this attack with you," Kailas said.

"There wasn't the time," Hakea said. "Besides, you have enough duties on your plate already."

"I mean no offense," Hal said. "But this scheme is more than a bit chancy."

"It has been approved by the king himself," Gurara said stiffly.

"Then," Hal said, getting up, feeling weary, "there's nothing left to discuss except the details, is there?"

32

Things went wrong from the beginning.

Hal, and the rest of the First Squadron, were to take off three hours before dawn, since their dragons would fly faster than the casting monsters, and fly east on a compass heading until they reached Yarkand.

No one had allowed for a heavy summer fog.

Hal was roused a little after midnight by the watch, reporting the fog rolling in.

He ordered his squadron commanders wakened, then washed his face, and walked out on the field. The fog was dank, thick, and he could barely make out the dragon tents half a hundred feet away.

Now Hal was forced to make one of those decisions never seen in romances—one man, alone, staring up at the night sky and trying to decide what the weather would be at dawn and, more importantly, later, over Yarkand.

Not to mention, of course, whether the casting dragon flight commanders would abort or continue the mission.

For once, Kailas chose the safe option.

No one argued with him, when he announced it, but he

could feel a swell of disapproval from the other flight commanders and pilots.

There was one way to check his decision to proceed, and so he took his squadron up, as scheduled, but with a slightly different compass heading.

The squadron took up a series of vees behind him, flying very close, but still barely able to see Kailas through the roiling fog.

The new dogleg took the squadron over one of the casting dragon bases. He blasted instructions, and the dragons climbed, hoping to get above the fog. Hal dove down, counting as he went. His palms were quite sweaty when he broke out at less than a hundred feet, almost over the base.

It was pitch-black, but he could see the dragon tents were open, and empty.

So at least one flight had obeyed orders, and was in the air, heading for the target.

Hal went back upstairs, climbing and climbing, and then broke into a starry sky, and saw the circling bulk of dragons not a third of a league distant.

Hal flew to them, and blasted the follow-me signal.

He took a slightly adjusted compass course east.

Toward Yarkand.

He couldn't see anything below, and couldn't tell when the squadron crossed the lines into Roche territory.

Hal was navigating by compass, and by his time in the air.

There were no other dragons visible, at least, none flying above the fog.

At dawn, they were deep inside Roche.

Hal thought they were well ahead of schedule, and chanced diving down on a deserted lake, and watering his monsters.

They wanted to eat, rest, were denied, and blatted their unhappiness.

Hal paid no attention, and the squadron flew on, very high, to ease the strain on the beasts.

Then the sun burned the fog away, and they could see clearly, league after league below of yet-unravaged Roche countryside.

Every now and then, Hal saw, far below, someone spot the dragons, and panic.

Their interest wasn't in killing farmers or burning villages, though.

Two hours before midday, he saw his first dragon. It was a Sagene beast, and was flying slowly toward him, to the west. The dragon was favoring one wing, and there was only the flier on its back.

Hal flew close enough to see rips in its side, and the flier was swaying in the saddle.

He straightened, seeing Hal and recognizing the uniforms, waved, shouted something Hal couldn't make out.

They flew on.

Now the navigation was easy—they found the main east-west highway leading to Yarkand, and followed it, curving through low foothills.

Then a wide valley opened, and there was Yarkand.

It was a city under siege, not uncommon, but the first time this had happened only from the air.

Sagene and Derainian dragons swooped and dove around Yarkand, and Hal could just see buildings struck by the mag-icked boulders crash into ruins.

But the battle was not going to the casting dragons.

Someone had talked, or sorcery or spying had found the plan out, for, tearing at the Deraine and Sagene forces were half a hundred black dragons.

As Hal watched, two of them attacked a single Derainian, one ripping at its wing, the second, coming from above, lock-ing a deathgrip on the dragon's neck.

The three monsters slammed together, then apart.

But the two blacks recovered, spinning, and climbed for the heights. The Derainian dragon, its neck flopping limply, rolled over on one wing, and fell toward the earth.

The Sagene and Derainian casting dragons were trying to fight back, but without training or experience.

A line of casting dragons was coming up on the center of the city. From above, black dragons dove down, shattering the formation. The already-cast pebbles became boulders, smashed here and there in the city's heart.

Other casting dragons were trying to flee to the west, skimming the rooftops.

That was enough for Hal.

He blew the attack, and the First Squadron's sixty dragons dove into battle.

The Roche fliers had been intent on the battle, and were hit by surprise.

Black dragons screeched, flopped in the sky like fledglings, and died, or their fliers were torn from their perches by dragon claws or shot out of the saddle by the Derainians.

Hal looked for a Roche who looked like a leader to take out, saw a dragon, just above him, and the gold-fringed banner on its carapace, kicked Storm into a climb, toward the monster's stomach.

He hesitated, still reluctant to kill a dragon, then aimed his crossbow at the dragon's side, and pulled the trigger.

The bolt shot home, just as Hal recognized the dragon's rider.

Ky Yasin.

Hal grimaced, angry that he hadn't held his fire until the better target presented itself

Yasin's dragon keened, rolled, and Storm was on him, ripping with his fangs at the other monster's neck, horns stabbing upward as his talons dug on.

The black dragon recovered, stabbed with his horns at Storm, almost took him in the throat.

Hal had another bolt in the trough, aimed carefully, fired at Yasin, just as Yasin's arrow whipped past him.

Kailas missed, and Yasin jerked his reins to the side, and the black tucked and dove.

Storm, eager for the kill, ducked, almost tossing Hal, and dove after Yasin.

Ahead of them was a great square, and Roche soldiers were setting up catapults.

Yasin pulled out bare feet above the stones, and catapults sent long bolts aloft.

Hal, shouting at Storm, pulled the reins, again, and, reluctantly, Storm banked, flying down a boulevard, below building roofs.

Hal brought his dragon back up and back in a climbing bank, looked for Yasin, didn't see him.

He swore—he'd missed another chance at the bastard.

His mind reminded him that Yasin had also missed, but that didn't matter that much, with the blood dinning in his ears.

He climbed up to a thousand feet, saw the black dragons still attacking the Sagene and Derainian beasts who'd given up the attack and were trying to escape east, back toward the front.

Hal let Storm climb higher, blowing commands on his trumpet—break off . . . assemble on me . . . cover the other dragons.

Reluctantly, his squadron obeyed, going for height, then, as they saw targets, going in, sometimes from below, sometimes at the same height, against the Roche blacks.

It was grim, as the casting dragons fled, and Yasin's beasts, faster, less weight-burdened, savaged them.

The day wore on, dragons attacking, being attacked.

Hal saw, all too often, one of the casting dragons torn out of the skies and, worse, one of his own fighters.

He saw no sign of Yasin, guessed that his dragon had been wounded seriously enough to break off action.

Hal took Storm into a patch of cloud, brought him back and around, and surprised a black harrying a wounded casting dragon.

He aimed carefully, shot the Roche flier out of his saddle,

and the black broke off, flying back toward his base. Hal nodded in satisfaction—a dragon he didn't have to kill.

He heard a high scream that had become too familiar that day, saw two dragons clawing at each other, stabbing with their horns.

The Derainian black was a bit smaller than its enemy, and the Roche monster pulled away, and its long tail whipped the other.

Again the scream came from the Derainian beast, and now Hal recognized its flier was Farren Mariah.

Hard hit, Mariah's dragon dove for the ground, open farmland, with workers in the field.

Mariah tried to pull it up, but the dragon was too badly wounded.

Its wings flared, and it slammed in, hard, went limp.

Mariah sagged in his saddle, then bleared up.

The workers had recognized the Derainian uniform of the flier, and, waving scythes, hoes, were running toward Farren, shouting rage.

Farren pulled himself out of the saddle, drawing his sword. He stumbled, nearly fell, in shock.

There were at least a dozen farm workers running toward him, too many for even a warrior to deal with.

Hal's standing orders were to avoid suicidal acts and sentimental bosh.

What he was going to do was clearly in those categories.

He sent Storm spiraling down toward Mariah, and his motionless dragon.

Hal came in behind the running workers, and Storm's talons slashed at them, and his tail whipped back, forth.

Then Storm was on the ground, and the graceful killing beast became a waddling behemoth.

"Get on!" Hal shouted.

Farren hesitated. A worker hurled a rock, hit Mariah in the chest.

Hal shot the man down, recocked his crossbow as Farren came back to himself a little, and stumbled toward the dragon.

Another farmer threw a spade, which narrowly missed Mariah, then the small man was beside Storm, weakly pulling himself up behind Kailas.

Hal shot down the nearest farmer, gigged Storm into motion. He ran ponderously forward, and there was a farmer in front of him, waving a scythe.

Storm trampled him, and his wings thrust down, and he was in the air.

A rock thumped Hal's leg, but he paid it no mind, bent over Storm, talking to him, getting him to climb.

Then there was a flashing shadow overhead, and a Roche black dragon dove on them, jaws widen.

Hal sent a bolt fairly blindly at the beast, and made one of the luckiest shots of his life.

The bolt thudded directly between the dragon's fangs, into his throat.

The Roche dragon screamed, its talons clawing at its mouth, then it rolled on its back and dove straight into the ground.

"I suppose we're even-out for my saving your ass back in Aude, then," Mariah said. "Sir."

"Damned right," Hal growled. "Now here, take this damned crossbow and keep the Roche off my ass."

The Derainian and Sagene dragons flew on, limping, exhausted, wounded.

Then, ahead, was the brown, mucky, bare ribbon that marked the front.

Derainian dragon flights were waiting, and Yasin's squadron, almost as weary as the Derainians, broke off, flying back into their own territory.

The casting dragons were escorted back to their fields and, eventually, the remnants of Hal's squadron found its base, and succor.

Someone helped Farren Mariah down.

"Are you all right?" Hal asked.

Mariah nodded.

Then Hal noticed tears in the man's eyes.

"There's no godsdamned reason I ought to feel this way about a godsdamned smelly beast," he said fiercely, and stamped away toward his tent.

Hal had no idea how much damage had been done to Yarkand, and didn't much care.

The day was an unmitigated disaster.

Forty casting dragons were lost, including both commanders of the flights. Three or four fliers managed to work their way to the lines afoot and across the lines.

Of the sixty dragons in Hal's squadron, twenty had been either smashed from the skies or were gravely wounded enough to be retired.

As usual, most of the casualties were the newest replacements, although three experienced fliers had gone down.

Hal tried not to think about the magnitude of the catastrophe, and busied himself with letters to the next of kin, pleas to Garadice, back in Deraine, for replacement dragons, requests for more fliers.

He was interrupted by a courier, with new orders.

Hal, and the survivors of the squadron, were to withdraw from combat and proceed, with all expediency, to Deraine and Rozen for further orders.

The command was signed by King Asir.

33

Hal went to Cantabri while the squadron packed, and asked him if he had any idea what was going on.

Lord Bab shook his head.

"Nary the slightest, and I'm not pleased to be losing you in the middle of this offensive, especially after we got our head handed us trying to level Yarkand.

"We need to come up with a counterstroke that'll destroy whatever triumph they're feeling, and you're generally a good source for that.

"All I've gotten about your recall to Deraine was a formal notification from the king, with no explanation, and I've learned when His Highness does something this abruptly you're wasting your time protesting his decision."

"True enough," Hal said. He thought of the disastrous invasion of Kalabas, which had been the king's great idea, and hid his wince.

"The only thing I can tell you is that King Asir has had some secret plan abubbling ever since the conference with the Sagene barons, something that's got little to do with this offensive," Cantabri said. "And he's not talking about it with anyone."

"Well," Hal said. "I guess I'm off. Try to have a nice war without me."

"I suppose it's a measure of how things have improved," King Asir said, "that I am able to greet you openly, instead of having you snuck in through the back gate."

Hal made a wry face. "Possibly, sire. But I don't know about improvements, since everyone who hears of my summoning no doubt thinks it's because you want to tear an enormous strip off me for Yarkand."

"Oh dear," the King said in what appeared to be honest bewilderment. "That's not the case at all. The notion was entirely mine, and it was catastrophic enough that I certainly don't want anyone dwelling on it.

"I must start learning that repeating something generally leads to a debacle. Not to mention that your raid on Carcaor was mounted secretly and swiftly, and I'm afraid the commanders of my casting unit were rather lumberous, if there's such a word.

"Pour us both a drink, and I'll explain what my scheme is.

"I think it's good, but I've not exactly been the best strategist in this war, so I would honestly appreciate it if you tell me I'm once again playing the fool."

Hal hid his surprise at the king's honesty, went to a nearby sideboard, while the king walked to a large map, covered with a sheet of cloth.

Kailas hesitated. All of the spirits were in crystal containers, without labels.

"Oh," Asir said. "It's confusing when there's no markings on the chart, isn't it. The brandy is the second from left, the old brandy is third from left, and all the way on the right corner is the *really* old brandy, twenty years in the cask. Which I'll have, and so will you, for it's unlikely even a lord with elaborate properties and wealth will ever be able to find something that rare.

"Yet another thing the damned war has ruined.

"You might want to fill another glass with charged water to chase the alcohol with. There is a bit of a bite in the aftertaste."

Asir waited until Hal handed him a pair of glasses, then pulled the cover off the map.

There was no legend, but it was clearly part of Roche's north coast. There was a broad river delta, a city at its mouth.

Asir noted Hal's change of expression.

"No," he said. "I'm not proposing another river invasion. I learned my lesson at Kalabas.

"That is the River Pettau. It's a distance from the Zante, where you were a prisoner. It's in fact around the peninsula to the east of the Zante.

"The Pettau, we've discovered, is one of the main trading passages for Roche, to the eastern lands, which appear most unsettled.

"I'll make a confession here. It is one of the failings of my family that we have little interest in matters that don't concern Deraine, which is why we've never had much of a navy, and have made few explorations beyond the lands we have always dealt with.

"I might also add, speaking personally, that I have never had the slightest interest in war, thinking it a matter for men who are bloody-minded and like to dress strangely.

"That was utter stupidity on my part, and may account for the mistakes I've made. But I'd prefer not to dwell on that, but on the subject at hand: my, and Deraine's, ignorance about our world.

"That ignorance, once the war is over, will not be allowed to continue," Asir said grimly.

"Now, stare at that river, because, unless you think my plan is idiotic, you and your squadron will be committed to the area.

"Good brandy, is it not?"

Hal came back, realized he hadn't touched his snifter, and tasted the brandy. It was mellow fire, that went down easily, then warmed the throat with a gentle flame.

"Yes, sire," Hal said. "It's very good."

"Back to the subject at hand. I desperately want peace, as quickly as possible, for three reasons. The first, of course, is that I'm losing the finest Derainians, and we'll be paying for these deaths for the rest of this century. Second is the same concern for Sagene. And the third might surprise you.

"That's my worry about Roche. I proposed the General Offensive because I hoped Queen Norcia and her damned barons would see the light, and sue for peace.

"Thus far, there's been no such light on the horizon.

"Roche is our enemy, but if the war continues, and we reduce the country to a wasteland, we'll have done ourselves a great disservice.

"If Roche falls into complete anarchy, then who knows what can happen to our own land?

"And what about invaders from the east, from beyond?

"Roche as a desert, or if it falls back into a web of feuding petty baronies, such as it was three hundred years ago, would be a catastrophe for everyone."

Hal had never thought of that. His mind growled at the concept—it would suit him fair well for Roche to be reduced to barrens. But he grudged the king might well be right, yet another reason he was glad soldiers stayed out of politics, if they had any brains.

"In the middle of the conference in Fovant," Asir continued, "it came to me that I had no other position in mind if the General Offensive failed . . . or succeeded too well.

"Quite suddenly I came up with one, and, in the final days of the conference, discussed it with Sagene's Council of Barons.

"They thought it a good idea, one which might accelerate

victory and, best of all, one that wouldn't significantly increase the slaughter. At least, not for our side.

"When I returned here to Rozen, I very quietly began building small, light ships, almost boats, that can hold a platoon or so of infantrymen, and reconditioning and converting fishing boats. I also set about finding the men and women to man them, preferably people with knowledge of the Eastern Sea, which the Roche call the Wolda.

"Briefly, I propose to mount a blockade on Roche. Sagene's fleet will cover the Southern Sea, Deraine the north."

"What about land caravans from the east?" Hal said.

"I don' t know, " Asir said. "I can theorize that they're not that important, since, before the war, Roche had few large trading cities along its eastern border.

"The Roche main trading routes are from the south, up the Ichili River, and, in the north, down the Pettau.

"Roche is fairly independent, but Sagene raiders have seized baled cotton, and rice. From the north come furs, dried fish, and, most important, dragons from Black Island.

"The southern blockade is the easiest to deal with, geographically. The problem is the Pettau. I've had small craft scouting its mouth, or mouths, which come off this huge delta. The river's mouth is constantly changing, and most sea traffic is shallow-draft barges or hulks.

"They travel through the Wolda hugging the coast, sheltering behind barrier islands, enter the delta from the east, in any of several passages, move to the head of the delta, then upriver to the city of Lanzi, where cargoes are either broken up or continue on upriver to smaller cities.

"At first, I thought I might be able to blockade the north with the vessels I'm building for deployment close onshore, sailing, when they see a target, within the barrier islands.

"Roche ships will be seized when it's possible, burnt when it's unhandy to try to capture them intact.

"Then I had a better idea, thinking of you."

Hal waited.

"As I recall, your flight did an outstanding job of inter-dicting traffic on the Ichili, during the siege of Aude, correct? I even remember your dragons were known as 'whispering death.'"

"So I heard, sir."

"I propose your entire squadron, once it's built back up to full strength, as a reconnaissance unit for my small ships, and as a raiding, a casting, unit by itself.

"The rest of the northern blockade will be handled by the fleet, big ships out at sea, smaller ones hugging the coastline.

"If we can't fight the damned Roche into submission, then we'll starve them!"

Asir tossed back his brandy, set the glass down, and looked ferociously at Hal.

"Well? What do you think of the idea?"

Hal had been dreading the moment.

"Sir," he said, "does my answer have to be final right now?"

"No," Asir said, a bit grumpily. "You can have a few days."

"Thank you," Hal said. "I can give you my first reaction, which is that I like the idea. I don't mean I like the idea of starving women and children, but anything that ends the war soon can only be good.

"I don't see any holes, any problems, but I'd like to with-hold my final answer until I've gone over the maps, particularly the one of the River Pettau."

Asir's mood had changed again. "I'm sorry I growled," he said. "I should have known you'd at least tell me your first thoughts. Not like some of my damned courtiers, who wouldn't say shit if they had a mouthful.

"Go on. Your squadron won't get here for another week, and I give you leave to join your wife.

"Oh. One other thing that might help. If you think the

blockade is feasible, you'll be rebased here, in Deraine, somewhere on the east coast, although I think you and your
dragons will be spending time at sea, which you've done
before.

"Now, get gone, and I'll talk to you in a week."

Khiri met Hal at the castle, and their lovemaking was a roil of
ecstasy.

They talked about what they should do for the promised
week, decided they'd stay at Sir Thom's city mansion, where
Khiri had been living when she first met Hal.

She was clearly most curious about what had brought him
back to Deraine. Hal refused to tell her, not having been given
permission by the king, for two days.

Then he noted the taletellers were filling the broadsheets
with stories of the brave Sagene navy, and the even braver
Derainian mariners, and of the recently discovered evils of the
Roche traders in the primitive lands to the east.

Hal figured the hells with it. If the king's campaign to ready
the civilians for the war to be continued on a pair of new
fronts was already under way, what was the problem with
telling his wife, who'd certainly proven herself not to be a
babbling gossip?

She listened carefully, sat silently for a time, then asked, in
a small voice, "That'll mean civilians—women and children—
will starve as well as the lords and soldiers."

"It does, I'm afraid," Hal said uncomfortably.

"That doesn't seem right, since they didn't start the war,"
Khiri said.

"No," Hal agreed. "But I can't think of a way the king could
do this without hurting some innocents. What of the Derainian
women and children who've lost brothers, fathers, sons?"

Hal thought of Khiri's father, dead at the war's beginning,
her brother, and someone who might have become her lover,
killed in battle.

Khiri shook her head. "That doesn't make what King Asir is going to do right, does it?" Before Hal could reply, she went on: "And I know very well that the queen and the Roche barons and soldiers will be fed first. Won't they?"

"I suppose so," Hal said.

"Oh," Khiri said, and rather ostentatiously changed the subject.

The next day, she said she had some business to attend to, regarding one of her estates, and didn't invite Hal, which was most unusual.

He started to get angry, since he wasn't exactly the originator of the blockade, decided that wasn't right, and called for a horse to be brought around.

Something had been pulling at him for a time, and so he sought out Garadice, head of what was, archaically, still called the King's Remounts. Garadice's son had trained with Hal earlier in the war, and was killed during the siege of Aude, and Garadice, still mourning his only child, busied himself with replacement dragons and the dragon training schools for both beasts and men.

Garadice was headquartered at what had been the King's Own Menagerie, but now was turned over to the reeking dragons. Dinapur, father of his dead love, Saslic, had been head of the menagerie, but, to Hal's relief, wasn't in sight.

Garadice took him into his common room, and ordered tea brewed.

Hal hadn't seen Garadice since the dragon-stealing raid on Black Island. His beard and hair had whitened, and there were new lines of determination and fatigue on his face. He'd aged but Hal supposed he had as well.

"I assume you have business," Garadice said. None of us seem to have any interest except the war these days ... although, if you've come just to socialize, that'd be a blessing, uncommon as it is."

"No, I have business. Of a sort," Hal said. He told

Garadice about what Danikel had said, during the Fovant conferences, that once the war was over the dragons would be discarded or even killed, and no one would give a damn, any more than they would for ex-soldiers.

"I've read of that young man," Garadice said. "Quite the hero . . . and now I see someone who's got more than a bit of brain."

He sat down heavily, staring down at his teacup.

"I'm afraid he's dead right. There's no provision for a crippled dragon, any more than there is for a broken-legged horse. Dragons either heal—and the gods be blessed dragons are tough, almost as tough as a man—or they're gotten rid of.

"If they're so seriously injured they can't recover . . . well, the unit vets are issued poison."

"I know that, sir," Hal said. "But what about the others that're not that seriously injured. Say they can't fly. I know they're taken off the station . . . I've seen enough of that. But I've never wondered what happens to them."

"They're put out to pasture behind the lines," Garadice said. "At one time, they were just killed, but I put a stop to that. Now, we have rations continuing for them, and they're cared for by wounded soldiery who volunteer. I'm glad to say I had a hand in setting that up.

"But once the war is over, all military funding will be sliced to the bone and further . . ."

He broke off, and shook his head sadly.

"Man is a long ways from being an ideal master. If he can't eat it, or make use of it, there's no use for it and it, whatever it is, beast or whatever, is put away."

The two sat looking at each other; then Hal thanked Garadice for his time, got up and left.

He went to the king's castle, sought out an equerry he knew, and asked who would be a reliable sort to draw up a will, or such. He got a name, an address, and rode into the heart of the city, thinking how truly inept he was at handling personal business that the army didn't take care of, let alone the rather more complicated affairs of a lord owning villages and great expanses of land.

The legal counselor was awed at meeting the Dragonmaster, and offered any help he could provide.

Business complete, and feeling a great deal of satisfaction, he rode back to Sir Thom's estate, and sought out Khiri.

He explained that he was having papers drawn up to take care of crippled and maimed dragons, to be paid for with a small deduction from his estate's profits. Since Khiri was his heir, he hoped she didn't mind, and, if he, well, failed to make it through the war, he wanted her to know what was in his mind.

"I certainly don't care for myself," she said. Then she looked at him a bit oddly. "But wouldn't your money be better spent, say, founding an orphanage? Or even a poorhouse for widows?"

"Why?" Hal asked, honestly bewildered.

"Because," Khiri said, in the voice of an adult speaking to a small child, "they're people. Dragons aren't."

"But nobody's taking care of the dragons," Hal said. "And there're lots of orphanages and poorhouses."

Khiri looked at him for a time.

"It's your money," she said. "You can do with it what you like."

Hal was not that unhappy to be told three days later that his squadron had arrived in Deraine, and he was to return to duty.

34

"Now this, young Lieutenant, is an example of what is called irony," Sir Loren Damian said to Farren Mariah. "Since you have ambitions beyond getting yourself eviscerated in this war, ambitions that I've heard include public leadership, learn to use irony whenever possible.

"It'll make the masses think you to be educated, and hence fall into line and obediently do your every wish."

"Aarh," Farren Mariah said, then considered what lay before them again. "But 'tis a bit of all around turn around. To think this is where we all began, and where we end up now."

Where, was the old monastery named Seabreak, where Hal and the other founding members of the 11th Dragon Flight had begun their training.

Gray stone against a gray sea and foggy skies, it looked no more inviting than it had almost ten years before.

Perhaps someone in the army had sensed the gloom, because Seabreak was no longer used as a dragon fliers school either.

Hal thought *that* was not frigging likely. Armies aren't known for being mood-sensitive.

But this would be the new base for the First Dragon Squadron in the blockade.

It might have sounded odd for Hal's unit to be based in Deraine, rather than in Paestum or the conquered fringe of Roche. But Roche, east of the Zante River, curved out, and the farthest reaches of the country that would be Hal's operational area were a closer flight from Deraine.

Not that anyone would have objected if it had been longer—what little comforts war can provide are easier to get hold of closer to the mother country.

"At least one thing," Mynta Gart said. "We know where the back door to the mess is."

She looked down, toward the heaving sea. Three frigates were moored there, plus two light corvettes, and the familiar *Galgorm Adventurer* dragon transport and a newer sister ship, the *Bohol Adventurer*. Her expression was unreadable.

"Are you sorry you didn't stay in the navy? Hal asked quietly.

She hesitated.

"No, sir. I don't think so, anyway." She forced her mood to change. "I wouldn't have met fine, upstanding gentle souls like Farren."

Mariah looked offended.

"O Captain Fearless Leader Lord Kailas, sir, I gotta lodge a complaint on being picked on by my superiors."

"Not nearly enough," Hal said. "But since you've problems with the present company, I'll put you in charge of divvying out the buildings."

"The student huts are for fliers, right?"

They were the best thing about Seabreak—four-person cottages scattered around the estate.

"Right," Hal said. "But first we make sure the dragons have enough. I don't think we'll have to pitch the tents."

They didn't. The dragons fit comfortably into the large horse barns the religious order had built before the war. The explanation Hal and the other students had made up was the order, which seemed to have vanished, worshipped some sort of horse god. Or else their acolytes were most wealthy.

There was also more than enough room for the humans in the squadron.

It took about two weeks for replacement dragons and men to trickle in, and then Hal sent a courier to Supreme Army Command in Rozen to say that he was ready to go to back to battle.

There were five men on the single-masted sloop, in peacetime a patrol boat for the Roche fisheries, now a guard ship on the inner passage that led from the Roche border west to the Pettau River.

Their duty was to keep watch for any Derainian intrusion and summon reinforcements from their nearby headquarters, garrisoned with a half company of marines and a very small hooker.

One man was at the helm, another in the prow, keeping watch, although the Roche were local sailors and utterly familiar with the passage, with its tidal vagaries and shifting sands.

The other three were forward, arguing about what the proclaimed blockade might mean to them.

They'd pretty well decided that the Derainians would try some sort of big raid, end up going ashore and finding little in the way of loot or enemies, and henceforth keep an almost-useless patrol far offshore.

None could see getting worried about anything. War may have been boring, but they were sitting quite comfortably on the trade route from the east, and anything they couldn't catch or their wives make could be traded or purloined from the small coasters headed for the delta and Lanzi.

One of them heard a sound, like the rasping of silk, looked up, and shouted an alarm.

Three black dragons dove out of the lowering cover toward them.

The sailors had just time to see the fliers wore Derainian uniforms when a crossbow bolt whipped through the helmsman's leg. He groaned, let go the wheel, and stumbled back, just as a second bolt took him in the chest.

He fell on his back, lay still, just as the lookout was hit in the body by another bolt.

One of the arguing men ran for the wheel as the sloop yawed out of the dredged, marked channel.

He, too, went down.

The two survivors dove for shelter, one behind the upturned ship's boat, the other behind a bulwark. The bulwark wasn't heavy enough to stop the next round of bolts, and two took him. He stood, screaming, stumbled forward and went over the side.

The survivor stayed where he was, even as the sloop ran into the shallows, hard aground, then lurched sideways, its mast cracking overside.

The dragon riders didn't wait for the tide to take and wreck the sloop, but flew on, down the waterway, looking for another target.

Hal looked down at the ocean, and thought of the few hours it took to fly from Deraine to beyond the Zante River, as opposed to the days he spent as an escaped prisoner in that damned boat he'd killed for, tossed by the seas and hoping he was headed somewhere friendly.

From up here, the water looked friendly, bobbing white-caps in the still-warm sunlight.

He knew if he was down there, conditions would be a deal less inviting.

Ahead of them, the barrier islands rose out of the sea.

Hal blatted an alert to the other three dragons in his flight, not that there should be any need to bring them to the alert.

Two of the dragons carried passengers—earnest young women with drawing boards firmly lashed to their saddle rings.

Hal touched Storm's neck with a boot, and the dragon obediently turned east by northeast, flying, at about three hundred feet, above the sandy islands that were covered with brush and scattered trees bent by the near-constant offshore wind.

The dragons flew as slowly as they could, and the artists busied themselves drawing.

Hal considered how much of war never appeared in the romances, tasks such as this, making maps for the ships that would keep the inshore blockade.

At least there weren't—yet—any Roche catapults or dragons to worry about, and he relaxed in the sun.

As much as he could ever allow himself, which was not much.

Too many dragon fliers had eased off, when they absolutely knew it was safe . . . and gone down to a very surprised death.

Hal thought about after the war, then grinned, remembering a story of Farren Mariah's.

"Ah, it'll be a grand, grand homecoming when somebody flinches and we're struck with peace.

"I'll land my dragon in the street outside my house, where my mother, the always-delightful Lady Mariah and my sisters, those she hasn't succeeded in marrying off to some dunderbrain with money, are waiting, having made all my favorite dishes.

"I'll whip out my sword in one hand, dagger in the other, then run, zigging and zaggetying through the gate and the yard, ducking any archers lurking about, kick open the door, flash up against the wall inside, and then bellow, 'Ma! I'm home!' "

*

It was raining, a dull soaking rain that had started before dawn, and looked to last for days.

Below Hal and his three dragons, eight coasters, under full sail, scattered among tiny islets.

The wolf was in the fold.

Four of the new shallow-draft raiding ships and three corvettes had been guided into the inland passage by Hal, and then led into the convoy.

Some of the Roche coasters gave up, and ran aground, their crews leaping into the shallows and running ashore for shelter. Others, stouter, more foolhardy, or, most likely, with captain-owners aboard, packed on sail, and tried to flee upchannel.

But there was no safety this day.

The sleek corvettes and raiding ships ran at their heels, and sorcerous firebottles were hurled from the Derainian ships.

Perhaps the Roche knew about pirates, who would dare everything before ruining their chances at loot.

The Derainians cared nothing about grain or furs, and so the ships roared up in pitch-fed flames.

There were three Roche warships based in Lanzi, and now they were coming out, after a Derainian corvette who'd chanced pursuing his merchantmen almost into the harbor itself.

They were fast, almost as fast as the corvette, and knew their waters far better.

The Roche sailors sensed a victory, something to savor after the weeks of their convoys being savaged by ships that struck and ran.

But the sailors weren't anticipating the full flight of dragons that dropped out of the clouds, casting pebbles that sent waterspouts climbing into the sky.

Two pebbles, now boulders, smashed into one ship, and the rest of Hal's flight came in low, with firedarts.

That warship took flame, and the others fled.

But they had bowmen aboard, and one Derainian dragon was hit three times in the chest.

Screaming pain, it climbed for the heights as the rest of the flight closed in about it.

Somehow the dragon kept in the air in the long flight back across the Eastern Sea toward Seabreak.

They were in sight of land when the dragon's indomitable will broke, and it spun down, into the waters.

Hal took Storm low, saw his flier swimming hard away from the dying dragon, went around again, shouting to Storm to go down, down to land in the waters, trying to rescue the flier.

But there was nothing to see but heaving gray waves, and the sinking body of the dragon.

"All right," Hal said. His fliers were drawn up in front of him, some still in the throes of their hangovers after the fliers' traditional wake for the dead flier.

"We're going to make things easier . . . and harder.

"All of you who've no experience landing dragons aboard ship are going to learn. Half of the squadron—the half that isn't on patrol—will practice.

"Here's the change. From now on, one flight will be assigned to each of the *Adventurer*s. They'll be offshore, with the navy's great ships.

"The other two flights will be here, resting. Every three days, a flight at sea will interchange with one on land.

"You won't like it and the dragons will hate it.

"But if you're hit—like poor Patric was—you stand a chance of living, if you can get away from Roche to one of the dragon ships."

If the water hadn't been so cold, and the wind so gusty, and the seas so sloppy, it might have been funny watching the newer fliers learn how to bring their dragon down to the barge tied alongside the *Adventurer*, stall the reluctant beast until it thudded down, then was led up a heavy ramp on to the ship itself.

But it was, it was, and they were, and, on a regular basis dragons and men went overboard.

For the dragons it wasn't that upsetting. They honked displeasure, and either tented their wings over their head, as dragons had done for no one knew how long making the great passage east from unknown lands, or the more intelligent ones clambered aboard the barge or took off from the water.

Two of them actually swam to their unseated riders and waited until they hauled themselves back into their saddles before unfurling their great wings and thumped across the ocean into the sky.

Those beasts instantly became priceless.

Hal chanced a passage over Lanzi, seeing if a convoy was in port, wondering if he dared go after the small boats that would bring the cargoes upriver, as he'd done during the siege of Aude.

He was half looking for Roche dragons, half watching to see if the Roche had brought in any catapult units.

Lanzi was a wonderful city, he decided. Very ancient, very rich, with twisting cobbled lanes, houses and businesses that climbed for three or more stories, leaning crazily toward each other, gay banners flapping in the wind from the sea.

The gray world about the city may have inspired the Lanzians to paint their buildings in the rawest of bright colors.

Even the wooden parapets were painted, many with vivid murals.

Hal decided it would be a city he'd like to show to Khiri, when the war was over.

*

Below Hal, a fishing village was afire. It was true that a handful of Roche marines had been quartered on the village, which made it technically a justified target. But Hal doubted if the fishermen had been given much choice by the Roche soldiers when they arrived.

The village had a clear view of one of the deepest passages into the delta, and the watchmen would have ample time to see the Derainians, and take a small boat, or even use signal flags, to warn any merchant shipping approaching.

And so one of the raiding ships, guided by the dragons, ran up on the beach, and armed sailors poured out, with orders to seize the marines and tell the fishermen they'd best become neutral if they didn't want to be treated as soldiers.

Hal had no idea what had happened, but suddenly flame had poured out from one hut, then another, then a third.

He sent Storm low, saw women and children being pushed into a group, some scattered bodies, and then the boats onshore burst into flames as well.

By the time the raiding ship was kedged out into deeper water, the oil-soaked boats and buildings were burning down into ruins.

He saw no sign of the civilians, wondered if they'd fled, or been taken somewhere as captives. Or . . .

Hal didn't think he wanted to know for sure.

In theory, having a personal life makes a warrior more vulnerable.

Hal decided there might be merit to the idea in the abstract, but he'd take the chance.

Besides, it didn't seem anyone was going to make it out of this war alive anyway.

It was very nice having Khiri show up from time to time. She was never obtrusive, taking rooms at the tiny inn in the closest village, as did some of the other wives, and gave Hal someone to talk to about things other than soldiering.

Fliers and groundsmen found lovers in the surrounding villages, or else visited Rozen and brought back friends. Every now and again someone—Hal studiedly kept from finding out who—imported a bevy of whores from the capital, and so most everyone had someone to cuddle as the nights grew colder.

Some of the dragons came into season, and Hal arranged for them to be mated with dragons from Garadice's host, which also gave the dragon fliers some time off in the capital.

Hal had worried there'd be problems with Khiri as the blockade tightened, but she never brought up the subject again.

He noticed she wasn't quite as much of a flag-waver as at the start of the war, but then, who was?

The squadron still suffered losses. But only one, the flier shot out of the sky over Lanzi, was the result of direct action. There still were no Roche dragons to worry about.

The casualties came from poor judgment but mostly from fliers getting lost, and not being able to find the *Adventurer*s, or even Deraine.

Hal remembered what he'd come up with, years ago, before the raid on Black Island, and sent to Rozen for a magician. Bodrugan showed up, and cast a spell on the ever-loathed salt meat served aboard ship, so that a flier thinking of it would be drawn toward the fleet.

Another spell was cast for fliers trying to return to Seabreak.

An instantly beloved dish on the squadron was tarts, made from the small apples of the district.

Those apples were used as the base for the second spell.

Losses dropped, and fliers used the second spell as an excuse to visit the area's farms, ostensibly to refresh the spell with new apples, actually to court the farmers' and workers' daughters and, naturally, wives in some instances.

It was still dangerous up there, but a deal less so than if the squadron had still been down south, back with Cantabri's slowly grinding offensive.

The squadron was grounded by an early storm. The two *Adventurers*, unhandy pigs at sea as they were, had been brought back from the blockading squadron, and the dragons and their fliers had nothing at all to do for a few days.

The more experienced fliers spent their time drinking, maintaining their gear and sleeping. The newer ones still had energy enough for gaming, gambling and wenching.

The storm faded, but daylong, low-level fogs still clung to the sea and the shores of Roche.

Hal was fuming about the war's hiatus one day, watching some very bored fliers play a game of quoits, when the idea came.

Just after dawn the next day, he had two flights in the air. Seabreak vanished into the fog, and he set a course by compass for Roche.

Every now and again the wind scudded the fogbank open, but there was nothing but roiling ocean below.

He kept track of the time, and on the mark started looking down and around.

There was a long clear patch below, and Hal spotted a smallish, uniquely shaped island below.

That gave him a location from his map, and he took the flights north, following the invisible inland passage below.

Ahead, he saw things sticking through the fog, thin spikes that were masts, with yards vanishing in the mist and topsails here and there.

Hidden in the mist below were Roche coasters, happily believing they were invisible to any enemies.

But their masts gave them away, so many quoit pegs sticking up through the mist.

Hal, flying as slowly as he could, flew along the convoy's

course, back and forth, casting pebbles and then firedarts as he went. Other fliers behind and on either side did the same.

Mostly he heard nothing but splashes as the pebbles grew into boulders and slammed into the sound.

But there were also crashes as a boulder smashed into a ship, and screams to be heard.

He cast until he'd run out of pebbles and darts, then brought the flights up, and set a return course for Deraine.

Whispering death had struck once more.

Kailas was brooding quietly in his hut about the blockade. It was very effective, but not a complete closure.

When he flew over Lanzi, he could still see coasters coming in and leaving, and river boats taking cargo inland.

Winter was almost here, and the weather would keep the dragons grounded, and probably drive the Derainian ships to seek shelter, while the Roche coasters could still bring in their goods behind the barrier islands.

He'd been scheming for several days, without product. His fliers knew he wasn't that happy, and why.

There was a knock.

"Enter," he said.

Danikel, Baron Trochu entered.

Hal offered him some tea from the pot on a trivet.

"You've got a problem?" he asked.

"No, sir," Danikel said. "An idea."

"I could use several."

"I think I've got a way to seal off the blockade. The only thing is," Danikel said, "it'll most likely kill off some thousand Roche children and women."

He smiled wryly, his face boyishly innocent.

35

Hal's plan of attack was sent off, by courier, to the palace, with a note that it would be implemented within the week unless it was countermanded by the king.

No response came.

That had been somewhat expected—the king, after all, ruled in the end by popularity, and Danikel's idea was one guaranteed to cause civilian deaths, not just in the course of the attack, but in the winter to come.

Danikel's plan was simple: burn the city of Lanzi to the ground, warehouses, docks, shipping, businesses, inns and houses. With no receiving and distributing point, either for incoming or outgoing trade goods, it would be difficult to move goods promptly into the heart of Roche.

Especially with many clerks, warehousemen, longshoremen and other trade experts hopefully being dead.

It was a simple plan . . . and an ugly one.

Roche had already lost access to some of its richest farming land, first with the assault that took the Bluffs, then with the General Offensive. Now the screws would tighten further.

Hal had no response from Rozen, and so, as he'd promised, the plan was set in motion.

Two flights were issued large amounts of firedarts—there should be no need of the casting pebbles on this attack.

They were dispatched to the two *Adventurer*s, once again at sea off the River Pettau.

The other two flights were similarly armed, and put on standby.

The flights aboard ship flew out in the late afternoon of the set day, and the other two, at Seabreak, were airborne an hour after the first two.

Hal flew with the first element from the *Galgorm Adventurer*.

They took off, orbited the blockade fleet once, forming up, then made for land.

It was chill but clear as they flew up the delta. Fishermen and boaters saw the thirty dragons overhead, and went for any shelter they could find.

None of the Derainian or Sagene fliers paid them the slightest mind.

The waterway grew wider, and then they saw Lanzi ahead, ancient buildings along the city's canals and estuaries.

Hal heard trumpets blast ahead of them, and men running for catapults.

He blew a single blast on his own trumpet, and the two flights formed parallel lines, the dragons flying close.

Then he was over the wharves, and aiming as best he could while hurling the firedarts.

Again and again he made his throws, then the swamps of the city's outskirts were below him.

He blew two more blasts, and slowly the lines wheeled back over the city.

Here and there, he saw fire start to spurt, taking easily on the ancient lumber, especially along the waterfront where, for generations, fish oil had soaked the warehouses.

Again, he sent firedarts cascading, and then they were over water, and he was out of ammunition.

Hal set course back down the main shipping channel, into the delta and the open sea.

They were still in sight of land when the other two flights of his squadron from Seabreak flew past, toward Lanzi.

Then the blockading ships were ahead, and the flights broke apart, and, in line, dropped down for landings on the pair of *Adventurers*. There was beer waiting, and steaming roast meat on buns, but Hal had no appetite.

The dragons ate greedily from barrels of salt beef, then fresh firedarts in netting were loaded aboard the dragons, and they were airborne again, flying back toward Lanzi.

Once more, they passed the rest of the squadron, coming back empty.

Hal took his flights upriver. Now there was no need to check his compass—a pillar of smoke curled above the doomed city.

He circled wide to attack Lanzi from a different quadrant.

Once more they flew their course, seeding death and flame.

One of the newer fliers was gawking down at the boiling fires, didn't notice a catapult tracking her. Her dragon was hit near his hindquarters, screamed, snapping at the bolt, pitching his flier off, down into the roaring blaze, then followed her into a fiery death.

Hal brought the dragons back over Lanzi, dropping the last of the firedarts, then set a course back to sea.

Once more, they saw the other two flights, shuttling back to feed the fires in the dusk.

Hal kept his dragons in the air, and didn't land on the ships.

The other two flights would, and replenish and spend the night.

Hal and his dragons at least had the comfort of Seabreak.

The fliers were very quiet that night. No one seemed

interested in drinking. Perhaps it was because they'd been told they'd be returning to Lanzi the next morning.

Or perhaps there were other reasons.

They took off in midmorning, laden with the old-fashioned firebottles. The two flights on the *Adventurer*s should have been well on their way.

It was a still fall day as they sighted land, and then the two flights coming away from the city.

This time, there wasn't a smoke cloud to follow, but a writhing great flame that rose higher than his dragons. For an instant, he was reminded of the great demon that still waited outside Carcaor.

He signaled, and his dragons climbed to a safer altitude, above the flames.

Today, no one was interested in shooting at dragons.

All that existed below was fire and agony.

Hal steeled himself, went in over Lanzi, scattering firebottles as he went.

He saw, below, a fire wagon hurtling up a street. A gout of flame reached out from an alley, almost casually, and licked up wagon, horses, men.

Below him, as he swung back, still adding to the fire, was a small lake. There were bodies floating in it, and he saw, his stomach churning, that the water was boiling.

He had to bank sharply as fire came up at him.

Hal saw a wizard, easy to define in his robes, acolytes flanking, evidently casting a spell.

But the fire was stronger than magic this day, and the flames took him and his assistants.

Hal realized he could hear nothing—the fire was roaring like a great beast as it ravaged the city. The center of Lanzi was a mass of flames, and Hal blinked, seeing a stone building melt and pour across a street.

It was as hot as a still summer day over the city. Hal was sweating, not just from the heat.

They were over the docks then, and the fire had taken the warehouses and ships. There was a handful of boats on the river, and the flames were reaching them as well.

Out of ammunition, they went back downriver, seeing people fleeing the city below them.

They landed on the *Adventurer*, and Sir Loren came up to him.

"Sir, there's three fliers who came back with their firebottles. They've refused to go back over Lanzi."

Hal wanted to sympathize with them, but couldn't.

"Tell them to make their own way back to Seabreak," he said, his voice sounding like it was coming out of a metallic throat, "turn in their dragon emblem, and tell them to stand by. They'll be off the squadron as soon as I return."

Hal and his two flights spent that night on the ships. Kailas was totally exhausted, but couldn't sleep.

At first light, he took his two flights, freshly rearmed, back over Lanzi.

There were still flames, but there was little left to burn.

He saw a scatter of river boats up from the city, sent Storm down on them.

The sailors dove overboard when they saw him coming.

He coldly fired their ships, then led his dragons back out to sea, and to Seabreak.

Lanzi had been completely destroyed.

True to his word, forcing callousness, he ordered the fliers who'd broken—his three, and four from other flights—off the base, and back to the replacement companies.

What happened to them when they got there, whether they were grounded, or given another chance, mattered not at all to him.

He gave his fliers one night to drink themselves into sodden forgetfulness, if they could. The next morning, he put them into hard physical training and flying.

No one would be permitted time to brood about what had

happened, even though he knew Lanzi would always be at the back of their minds.

There were no celebrations of this victory, no boasting, not even from Alcmaen.

What had happened to Lanzi quickly spread across Deraine, but in a very muted manner, without celebration.

Even the normally jingoistic broadsheets dealt with the horror with circumspection.

Possibly even the most rabid taleteller realized that something different had come to war, something even more terrible than the traditional sacking of a city. If men could ruin a metropolis from afar, without bloodying their hands, would common decency, already mostly a fiction on the battlefield, completely vanish?

It was a question never asked, never answered.

Now the feats, mostly made up by the taletellers, of the Dragonmaster and his squadron were muted, and the stream of love letters to Hal from strangers dropped away.

But there were exceptions. The adulation the Sagene had for Danikel seemed to redouble. Hal wondered if they had known the idea for leveling Lanzi had come from him would have lessened their adulation. On consideration, he thought not. Sagene, he'd noted, hated hard, and, after all, it was their country that had been invaded to start the war.

Kailas got a new group of supporters, members of groups with strange names like Deraine First, Derainians Supporting Our Men and Women in Uniform, Sorrowing Mothers for the War, Derainians for Decisive Action, and so forth. Those letters he threw away unanswered and unopened. There were also single letters, almost all from men, most of which began with: "Dear Lord Kailas . . . I never had the privilege of serving the colors, but what you've done strikes a chord . . ." Those too, after the first handful, went into the trash bin.

Hal supposed everyone thought there were two merciless

monsters in Deraine's ranks—himself and Lord Cantabri.

He tried to push it away, but it bothered him, like it bothered the others who'd been in the attack.

Strangely enough, Khiri, who he expected would have been most upset by what had happened, with her husband as the cause, seemed to know nothing of the matter. She never brought it up on her periodic visits to Hal, and seemed more passionate, more caring than before.

Perhaps Hal should have brought it up with her, and exposed his heart, but he didn't, grateful for what appeared acceptance of the realities of the day, and feeling far too tired to look behind the surface.

The blockade continued, and Hal and the King's First Squadron returned to the normal duties of scouting for the inshore blockade, and chivying any ships they found.

Lanzi remained a ruin, with only a scattering of people who returned to its desolation, evidently having nowhere else to go.

Now Kailas took his whispering death further upriver, where small boats met coasters in camouflaged inlets, hastily breaking down cargo into deck loads, and scurrying south, away from the dragons.

It was still dangerous—Hal lost two dragons to the weather, two more who just disappeared—but now it was becoming routine.

Hal considered, decided that it was time for him, and his fliers, to return to the real war. Any collection of dragon flights could handle the blockade. Enough people had told him the First Squadron was to be used for special duties and the most hazardous tasks for him to believe it.

Besides, he now had a target worth pursuing, one that was very capable of striking back.

Not sure of who he should importune, Kailas sent a request directly to the king.

He was owed a favor.

36

The streets of Rozen were a-tilt with cheering crowds, dancing trollops, blaring bands, amateur and professional, and happy drunkards.

It must be a famous victory, Hal thought, reined in his horse and tossed a vender a copper for a broadsheet. It was only a single sheet, which meant whatever had happened occurred just recently.

It was, indeed, a famous victory.

Queen Norcia Overthrown!
Barons Take Charge
Of Roche, War

"Holy shit," Hal said in astonishment, then read on.

According to the broadsheet, the barons had been most unhappy with her conduct of the war for some time. That was news to Hal. Not that he doubted it, but he wondered how some hack had gotten intelligence that no one, up to King Asir, seemed to possess.

The head of the conspiracy was the queen's onetime

confidant, Duke Garcao Yasin. After Norcia had been deposed, a caretaker government had been formed by the dukes and barons of Roche, under Yasin's direction.

There was nothing in the story about whether Norcia had survived the overthrow, who the caretaker government was caretaking for, nor even whether Norcia had any offspring, legitimate or not.

In any event, Yasin had issued a proclamation saying the war would be pursued more vigorously, with victory over the invaders, Sagene and Deraine, being the absolute and only acceptable goal.

So they wouldn't be suing for peace . . . at least if the broadsheet was correct.

Hal smiled, thinking his own thoughts.

This sudden change boded well for his mission.

"I suppose I do not stand particularly high in your esteem at the moment, Lord Kalabas," King Asir said formally, not turning away from the window he was staring out of.

Hal decided not to answer the question.

"King's aren't supposed to be cowards," Asir said. "But all too often, we are. That was why I didn't endorse your plan to destroy Lanzi, and have distanced myself from the results.

"But now . . . now, with Norcia toppled from her throne, which was directly caused by your action . . . now I not only look the coward, but the fool as well."

Hal managed some meaningless noises.

"So, before we go on any further, might I ask why you asked this meeting?"

"Yes, sire," Hal said, deciding to keep it brief. "The block-ade is running very smoothly. I think a conventional group of dragon flights will suffice to continue the pressure.

"I wish to have my squadron deployed, back to the First Army.

"If you allow this, I intend to devote the squadron's full

efforts to the destruction of *Ky* Bayle Yasin and his First Guards Dragon Squadron. He's the best they've got, and now, if the broadsheet I read is correct about his brother, he will be even more in the public's eye. His destruction—"

The king held up his hand, and Hal shut up instantly. Asir turned, and Hal was puzzled to see relief on his face.

"Thank the gods for one thing," the king said. "I was afraid you'd come here to tender your resignation."

"Why would I do something like that?" Hal was honestly puzzled. Maybe it was growing up mean and poor in a corrupt mining district, but Kailas had never expected much from his bosses, whether they were kings or no.

The king blinked.

"If I had the time, which I do not, with this latest confusion from Roche going on, I would pour us both a drink. But I don't, and won't.

"I'll figure a way to reward you for the action that led to the change, which can only be good for us, since no group rules as efficiently—or sometimes inefficiently—as a single person, king or queen. We could have hoped this would be a regency for peace. It is not.

"So the war will go on, and we can anticipate it shall be with growing savagery. So be it.

"The Roche have had at least two chances. We can afford no more generosity.

"Now it will continue to the bitter end, until Carcaor lies in ruins, like Lanzi.

"I assume you have a plan to hound Yasin and his dragons to their deaths. Good. Go to it, sir. And I'll see you when the war is over."

37

Hal turned the task of packing and moving the squadron back to Cantabri's positions over to Sir Loren, and went back to Rozen. He sought out Limingo the wizard.

He thought he knew how to finally trap *Ky* Yasin, but needed a magician's help.

To his disappointment, Limingo turned him down.

"Your theory sounds perfectly valid," the magician said. "So your plan should work excellent well. But the casting of the spell won't take a great deal of ability. I'll lend you Bodrugan, who should be quite competent, and is clawing for a chance to get back to the front."

Limingo noted Hal's expression.

"I'm not turning arrogant on you . . . I'm up to my eyebrows in another task, one that might be a bit more important in the long run."

Hal made understanding sounds.

"Have a seat," Limingo said. "I was going to send for you in the next couple of weeks anyway, since the matter pertains to you.

"One thing that has troubled me is that damned great demon—if that's what it is—you and your dragon fliers aroused when you raided Carcaor. Assuming that apparition wasn't something spontaneous, which I certainly don't think, that means that the armies will almost certainly have to confront—and destroy—whatever it is when they close on that city, even though we have no idea whether it can leave its mountaintop and that damned castle it inhabits."

"I know," Hal agreed. "And I've been trying to think of what we might do."

"Well," Limingo said, "I happen to have a bit more information than you do. You remember that raider you set atop that mountain to stand guard until you returned with your dragons?"

"I do," Hal said. "Poor bastard must've gotten eaten by the demon . . . or been done away with however demons kill people."

"Not quite," Limingo said. "Three weeks ago, he wandered across our lines in the south. Somehow he managed to travel all those leagues without getting killed or captured.

"The problem is that he's quite raving mad.

"They returned him to his unit, which thankfully is under Lord Bab's direct control. He remembered the man, and what had happened to him, and sent him, with a pair of minders, on to me."

"Mad, you say?"

"Babblingly so," Limingo said. "I've set a team of secretaries on him, so that everything he says, no matter how nonsensical, is recorded and transcribed."

"What does that give us?"

"So far, nothing," Limingo said. "But I'd like to send on a copy of his ravings, to see if you can find anything in it."

"So the man lived," Hal mused. "I wonder what he did—if anything—to escape being killed by the demon."

"I don't know yet," Limingo said.

"Have your writers try to draw him out about what happened," Kailas suggested.

"That might make him worse," Limingo said.

"Or it might give us something to work from," Hal said. "We'll have to take our chances that the man lives."

Limingo looked at him thoughtfully.

"The war is getting to us all, isn't it?"

Hal didn't respond.

Bodrugan was more than delighted to get out of Rozen. He listened to Hal's plan, and nodded.

"Of course," he said. "the spell will essentially be the same as the one Roche cast against the king to ambush him in the Pinnacles. That won't be the hard part at all. What will be a bit . . . difficult, shall we say, is actually belling the cat."

"Don't remind me," Hal said.

Hal reported to Cantabri, who said he was more than delighted to have Kailas—and the First Squadron—back.

"And it's good to be back," Hal said. "Lanzi left a pretty sour taste in my mouth."

He realized he wouldn't have admitted that to anyone except another butcher like Cantabri.

Lord Bab snorted. "If you figure a way to have a war without killing people—and that includes civilians—be sure and let me know."

That was the unanswerable.

"How long until your squadron arrives?"

"I figure about a week, with Sir Loren chivying them along," Hal said. "When I left Rozen, he was still beating up assorted quartermasters to replace lost, worn and stolen."

"That's time enough for you to take charge of a delicate matter for me," Cantabri said. "I want you to head a court-martial."

"Very well," Hal said, not liking the idea much. "But why me?"

"It's a fairly simple case of refusing to obey orders," Cantabri said. "But the culprit just happens to be a dragon flier."

Hal grunted.

"He's not the first," Cantabri said. "But he managed to make his refusal to fight a public issue. A couple of those damned taletellers reported the matter, so we can't handle it quietly as we have in the past by breaking him to the ranks and putting him in the front lines to get killed when the next battle rolls around."

"Do you happen to know his name?" Hal asked, hoping he wouldn't know the miscreant. But, considering the size of the dragon corps, he assumed he'd know.

"I do. And what's worse, he's a longtime flier, decorated, and has led flights. He's a rotten apple named Aimard Quesney."

Cantabri noticed Hal's expression.

"You do know him."

"Very well, sir." Hal told him about Quesney, how he'd been one of the first to fly with Hal in combat, been his tent-mate and someone who'd prized war flying as somehow cleaner than dying in a mucky infantry charge.

Cantabri hmmphed loudly.

"A godsdamned romantic! How in the hells can somebody be a flier, a fighter, from almost the beginning and still have blinders on?"

"I don't know, sir," Hal said. "But he cursed me roundly back when for figuring a way to kill Roche fliers—as if I hadn't, no one else would've—and then, more recently, when I tried to recruit him for First Squadron. He's an exceptional flier."

"I don't give a damn about that very much," Cantabri said. "Very well. You're to take care of him. Give him a nice, fair trial, try to keep his lip buttoned and the trial over with in no more than a day, then convict and hang him before other fools start thinking of him as an example."

Hal stood, and saluted.

As he went out of Cantabri's tent, something came crashing in on him.

He, too, was a godsdamned romantic.

There was no way he was going to officiate at the murder of Aimard Quesney.

The question was, what could he do to change what looked like an immutable decision?

38

"The court will come to order," the bailiff said.

There was silence in the conference tent.

"The court martial of Aimard Quesney is now in session," the man went on. The words came easily to him—he, Quesney's counsel and the prosecutor were the only ones with any trial experience.

Hal, hastily briefed in military legal procedure, sat at the center of a table. On either side of him were his fellow judges— Lord Myricil, a beribboned if elderly infantry officer, and Tzimsces, an eager-appearing, young quartermaster captain.

In front of him, at another, smaller table, was Aimard Quesney, and the officer assigned to defend him.

Behind them were the assembled witnesses, including Captain Sir Lu Miletus, Quesney's commanding officer.

On the table in front of Hal and the other judges was an unsheathed sword. At trial's end, if the point were aimed at Quesney, he was guilty; if away, innocent.

No one in the tent thought there was any possibility of an acquittal.

"Lieutenant Aimard Quesney is charged with failure to

obey a lawful order in the face of the enemy, to wit fly in combat against His Majesty's enemy, the Roche."

There were other charges—insubordination, improper behavior, and such that courts have always used to make sure the net they'd casting is sufficiently broad and fine-meshed.

"This case is a capital one," the bailiff said, "so it is emphasized the matter is an extremely grave one."

Everyone in the court looked appropriately grim, except for Quesney, who grinned wryly.

"The head of the court is Lord Kailas of Kalabas," the bailiff finished, "and all matters of procedure and evidence will be subject to his ruling."

The prosecutor stood.

"May it please the honorable members of this court, the king's representative, myself, will attempt to prove that—"

"You can stop there," Quesney said.

Wide eyes and shock spread through the tent.

For some reason, Hal wasn't surprised, nor bothered.

"The defendant will be silent until permitted to speak at the proper time," the bailiff said.

Hal held up his hand.

"A man on trial for his life might be permitted a few liberties," he said. "I'm sure the King's Justice can allow for that."

Now the shock grew larger.

"Lieutenant Quesney," Kailas said, "I assume you have something to say?"

Quesney looked perplexed, then took a deep breath.

"I do. I assume that the court is bound and determined to find me guilty of refusing to fly into combat.

"I say this considering who the head judge is, a man who brought death to the skies, and then to the innocent people on the ground.

"If this were a proper court, that is, one determined to decide whether or not I was right in refusing to kill any more men and women, it would exclude Lord Kailas as being prejudiced on the matter, since he is, with all due respect, sir, the bloodiest-handed flier in any of the three armies."

"Sir!" the bailiff snarled. "Sit down, or I shall be forced to have you gagged!"

"Gag me if you will," Quesney said. "But this court should be prepared to delve into the matter of uniformed homicide before judging me."

"You are hardly helping your case," Myricil said calmly.

"If you want to be hanged," Tzimsces added, "we're more than prepared to help you in your quest."

Hal rapped sharply with his knuckles.

"I gave Lieutenant Quesney permission to speak," he said, "and have not withdrawn that permission. I would request the members of this court to honor my authority."

Again, Quesney gave Hal a surprised look. Evidently Kailas wasn't behaving like the hanging judge the flier had expected.

"To simplify matters, and allow others to go back to their licensed murder," he said, "I concede freely that I disobeyed orders several times to fly, and will refuse any future orders given me, so all these assembled witnesses can be permitted to go their own ways."

Quesney's defender looked hopeless.

"Treasonous bastard!" hissed Tzimsces.

Quesney looked defiant.

"Perhaps I've gone loony," Hal wrote. *"Or perhaps . . ."* He stopped writing, considered what he was going to say next, went on:

. . . this is to compensate for some other things that I've done.

But there is no way I'm going to hang Quesney, in spite of Cantabri's near-order. I don't think it has anything to do with the fact we shared a tent and he gave me advice when I was a new flier. There's been several who've done that. So I don't feel particularly indebted to him.

Nor do I feel that he's any particular example of virtue—he's at least as obnoxious in his self-righteousness as any street-corner priest.

Maybe—and I think I'm guessing—maybe he stands for something beyond this damned war and killing, something that should be protected.

Or, more likely, I'm just getting softheaded in my old age.

Gods, but I miss you, and wish that I was with you, and all was quiet.

"So you decided, all on your very own," the prosecutor asked Quesney, "to declare peace with the Roche."

"No," Quesney said. "Not peace. But I was tired of killing."

"All of us are tired of killing," the prosecutor almost snarled. "But we are still patriots who know our duty."

Quesney shrugged, made no response.

"You're not on trial," Hal reprimanded. "Stick to the point."

The prosecutor nodded.

"Sorry, your lordship." Then, to Quesney:

"Perhaps I might ask why you enlisted in the service of the king in the first place?"

"Because I wanted to fly," Quesney said. "And, frankly, because I wanted to do my part in the war, to drive the Roche back to their own lands."

"Your own part," the prosecutor asked. "As long as it didn't involve killing? Perhaps you're a bit unsure of what war is all about."

"Your lordship," Quesney's counsel said. "Lieutenant Quesney is being unfairly chivied."

Hal thought.

"No," he decided. "I'll allow the question. I'd like an answer to that."

"I'm not a fool," Quesney said. "Of course I knew—

know—war is no more than killing. But—I'll be honest—I hoped to be able to do my duty to my country without . . . without . . ." Quesney's voice trailed off.

"Without having to bloody your own hands?" the prosecutor sneered.

Quesney was staring at the wooden duckboards of the tent.

"I guess I wasn't being very smart," he admitted. "But I went along with things as long as I could . . . and then something broke."

"So you made out your own peace treaty," the prosecutor said. "Wouldn't it be convenient if all of us could do the same when we've decided we've fought enough.

"If we did, what do you think would happen?

"Do you imagine the barons who now rule Roche, and their soldiers would just smile happily, and go back to their farms and jobs?"

"No," Quesney said. "But . . . but someone's got to do *something* to end this war before it destroys all three countries."

Hal remembered what King Asir had told him.

"Doesn't it seem to you that *something* is in the hands of the barons who quite illegitimately now rule Roche?"

"No," Quesney said. "They're part of the whole killing machine—as much as Lord Kailas is, as much as I was."

"I see," the prosecutor said. "But you aren't now. That seems most arrogant of you."

"I don't mean it to be," Quesney said, and Hal could hear the honesty in his voice. "But I had to do something . . . and this was all I could figure out."

"Let me ask you, Lieutenant. What effect do you think your refusal, as an officer, to obey lawful orders will have on other soldiers?"

"I would hope that it would make them refuse to keep on with the killing . . . on both sides."

"You therefore advocate disobedience to the king's orders?"

Quesney hesitated, then nodded.

"That, sir," the prosecutor hissed, "is the highest of high treason!"

"He surely seems determined to hang," Myricil said to Hal. The three judges had decided to eat together, and discuss what testimony there'd been in the two days of trial.

"And I think we should oblige him," Tzimsces said. "If we didn't have a firm hold on what the taletellers say, his nonsense could be all over the armies in a day! Gods know what effect that would have on the average trooper, who, as we all know, isn't guilty of thought when he can avoid it."

"I have a bit more faith in our soldiery than you seem to," Hal said. "But you do have a point."

"You certainly can't say Quesney's a coward," Myricil said. "You and I, Lord Kailas, know there's a point where any of us can break. Quesney has just reached that ... and gone beyond. Or perhaps, if we accept his viewpoint, he's suddenly become the most moral of men."

"As the prosecutor said," Tzimsces said, "if we allow Quesney to spout his drivel, then we create the precedent for any of us to decide we've had enough war, and just go home.

"We have a duty to the king—and to Deraine—to deal with the man most harshly." Tzimsces sipped at his wine. "Although I'll grudge that the man is clearly mad.

"A pity, for a man with his record."

Myricil nodded, smiling grimly.

"A warrior gone wrong, without doubt. And I agree about his mind having left him. We live in a terrible world, gentlemen. I do not wish to be the one who orders Quesney's death as a reward for his services to Deraine.

"Aimard Quesney no long wishes to chance death, which certainly is an indication of being able to reason logically, particularly considering how deadly this war is to dragon fliers. Therefore, he cannot be insane, for an insane man would wish to continue on, until he is killed. What a predicament."

It came then to Hal.

"I think, Lord Myricil, that you have the solution to our problem."

Hal ordered the court-martial recessed for the day, and set to on Myricil and Tzimsces.

It was dusk before they wearily agreed with Hal's suggestion.

"Thank heavens I'm not a career army man," Tzimsces said. "For I fear there'll be no promotion this side of the ocean for the three of us after King Asir hears of this."

"Don't worry about it," Hal said. "The king seldom remembers things like this for long."

"I'm glad to hear you say that," Myricil said. "For when, when the war's over, I come begging on your doorstep asking for a crust of bread, we can debate whether you were right or not."

"Actually," Hal said, "it's not the king I'm afraid of, but Lord Cantabri."

"We have unanimously decided," Hal announced the next morning, "that this court no longer needs to sit. We have reached a verdict."

Both defense counsel and prosecutor started to yammer.

Hal thudded the butt of his flier's dagger on the table, and only then did the men in the tent notice the sword that should have been set between the judges and Quesney was gone.

"Our decision, justified by military code and precedent, is that the defendant, Lieutenant Aimard Quesney, cannot be held responsible for his actions, due to his clear impairment of mind."

Quesney was on his feet. "I never thought you'd be capable of—"

"If you do not sit down," Hal said coldly, "I shall order you to be removed, to be tied and gagged, and then returned to this court."

Quesney's mouth was open, but he saw the look on Hal's face, and slumped back down in his chair.

"We further order him, since he is evidently a threat both to himself and to the public order, to be removed to a proper place of detention in Deraine, for an attempt to restore his sanity and then determine, at that time, whether he wishes to obey orders or to continue to disobey, in which case this court shall be reconvened and the trial shall continue."

Two guards brought Quesney into the deserted tent.

Hal eyed him coldly.

"You wished to speak to me?"

"Yes, you bastard," Quesney growled. "You silenced me, and you made my stand into a joke! How dare—"

Hal was on his feet.

"Silence!"

Quesney shut up.

"You two," Hal told the guards. "Outside."

"But sir, what if the prisoner attempts to escape?" one said.

"Then I shall cut his frigging weasand out myself."

The two saluted, left the tent.

"Now, I have less than no interest in hearing what you have to say," Hal went on. "Except for answering one question.

"Are you such a fool that you really want to have a rope strangle you? Remembering that your last letter will be held until the war's end, and there will be no one permitted to transcribe your last speech, no matter how noble.

"All you'll be is one poor damned fool in some unmarked grave somewhere within the borders of Roche.

"You have a family.

"What a memory to leave them. Now, answer my gods-damned question."

"No," Quesney said. "I'm not a madman, contrary to what you decided. Of course I want to live, and—"

"That's enough." Hal came close. "I put the guards out because I don't want any witnesses to what I'm going to say.

"You're going back to Deraine. They'll find somewhere to mew you up with women who think they're the king, men who scratch all the day and night, children who're in some private world of their own.

"That's a horrible damned thing to do to a man who's at least as sane as I am. Maybe saner. But it'll keep you alive. You'll live to see the war out. Stay mad until the war's over, when no one will care about a peace-spouting idiot, and you'll be quietly released from the asylum. Nobody'll be reconvening any damned trial, and no one will care about punishing you. Then you can, if you want, start prancing back and forth in front of the king's palace, shouting about what a murdering bastard he is. Or you can come to my estate, and do the same.

"If I'm still alive then.

"Or you can go around from town to town, preaching about the evils of war, and maybe enough people will listen to keep this kind of shit from happening ever again.

"I don't think you can succeed—people seem to like cutting each other up and down too much. But you can try.

"Because," and Hal spoke with great emphasis on each word, "you . . . will . . . be . . . alive!"

Without waiting for a response, Hal turned.

"Guards!"

He looked at Quesney.

"Now, get your sorry ass out of my sight . . . And when this is over, drink a dram to my memory. I've wasted enough time on you. I've still got a war to fight."

39

Lord Bab Cantabri considered Hal coldly.

"You know," he said, "I was not a terribly bright child. Some say nothing has changed from that day to this."

Hal tactfully kept silent.

"One of the dumber things I used to do, when I'd done something bad, was not to stay out of my father's way, like any sensible lad should have done, but seek his presence out. Maybe I thought he wouldn't have noticed whatever sin I'd committed, or maybe I wanted to be punished.

"In any event, not the brightest thing I've ever done, since the beatings I incurred were no gentler than if I'd kept myself hidden in the stables for a day or so.

"Now, let us consider your case.

"You and your fellow idiots commit a travesty of justice with Lieutenant Quesney, in spite of my rather clearly expressed wishes for him to be found very damned guilty. Which were also the king's wishes.

"Very well. If it had just been three idiots, I could have sent all of them off to, say, the tip of Deraine to watch for icebergs or such.

"But not with the Dragonmaster one of the crew.

"So I decided, until I cooled off a bit, I would do without your presence, to keep me from saying, or worse yet doing, something meritorious, such as hanging you by your balls for a week or so.

"I was quite pleased with my insight and my forbearance.

"Then you seek me out with this—no, I won't insult it—this plan.

"Are you trying to attract my lightnings?"

"No, sir," Hal said. For some unknown reason, he was having a hard time not laughing.

"I fully agree with you that *Ky* Yasin has been an unutterable pain in the ass for far too long, and he and his Guards Squadron should be dealt with harshly.

"Especially since his brother now seems to be atop the Roche group of barons that insist on keeping this damned war going.

"Clearly your plan—assuming this sorcerer of yours develops a spell—is promising.

"If I were a vindictive man . . . What is the matter, Kailas? Are you choking on something?"

"No, sir," Hal said. "A raspy throat from dawn flights."

Cantabri snorted.

"To go on. If I were vindictive, the thought might have crossed my mind that one of the virtues of your plan is—I assume you're planning on implementing this yourself—that you'll be behind Roche lines, with an excellent chance on getting yourself killed."

"I don't plan on that."

"But it could—notice I said could—have been a sidelight that might—notice I said might—have cheered me.

"But it didn't. We do need you, even if you seem to have the sappiest of ideas from time to time, which I assume comes from the thin air you breathe when you're atop your dragon.

"All you need from me is approval for your plan—which I

grant—and two men from my Raiding Squadron. This I also grant. I'll send them along to your squadron at once.

"You'll also need an order from me commanding every godsdamned dragon leader in the armies to become your scouts to find Yasin's base, without asking any questions.

"This, too, I'll give, although I'm a bit surprised you didn't think of just how good a flier can be at disobeying orders if he doesn't want to follow them.

"Now, get your ass back to being invisible. I haven't forgiven you totally yet."

"Yes, sir."

Even though winter was coming in strong, Cantabri kept the army pushing forward, very slowly driving the Roche back and back, east and south, toward Carcaor.

Hal guessed there'd be no winter quarters this year, at least not unless the Roche forced a stalemate.

Now that we're prepared to bell the cat ... at least when Bodrugan finally finishes his spell, Hal thought, and we actually have our foolish mice who'll attempt the feat, all we need to do is find the bugger.

Once Yasin's landing field was located, he planned to take in himself and the two raiders for the operation. That would require three dragons.

He pondered the reality of war, where the tail kept getting bigger and bigger. In this case, not a tail, but a head, someone to carry the warriors. Hal had considered the dragon baskets, that were about as dangerous to monster and master as they were to the passengers, thought wistfully of a *really* large dragon, able to carry, perhaps, a dozen men on its back, then wondered where in hell they'd find men—or women—with muscles and guts enough to tame it and pushed the whole matter away.

He would take Sir Loren, Farren Mariah, and Chincha.

Hal put the three fliers off the duty roster, told them to stand by "for Special Duties."

"So I'm for it again, and again, and again," Mariah said.

"What makes you think that?" Hal asked innocently. "I could have asked for the three of you to, say, fly three of the king's popsies around."

"Narh," Mariah said. "First, you didn't ask us to volunteer, which is the biggest clue right there. Second, I didn't know the king had—popsies—at least out in the open—let alone three of 'em.

"And, come to think, if we were toot-toot-tootling tarts about, the king would've specified all women fliers, instead of virile young sorts like myself," he finished.

"And," he added reluctantly, "Sir Loren, I suppose, although nobody I know's measured the length of his thingiewhacker."

"All you're going to have to do is fly somewhere," Hal said, "escorting me with a passenger on your back, land on a nice, quiet hill, then wait for me, and the passengers, to take care of a nice, simple job."

"Nice, quiet hill," Mariah said. "I'm on to your shame-game, Lord Kailas. How far back of the lines is this nice, quiet hill?"

Hal looked at him, didn't reply. Mariah nodded.

"Just what I thought. I'll go help Chincha make out her will."

The two raiders arrived, and Hal wondered if Cantabri wasn't trying to arrange his death, after all.

One was a baby-faced sort named Gamo, who looked far too young to be in any army, let alone be a purportedly deadly warrior in the raiders. The only thing that might be a give-away was his calmness, and the easy way he carried his sword and dagger.

The other, Hakea, was a chubby, sleepy-eyed peasant, who Hal thought should have been trudging the fields behind an oxen.

But if they were what Cantabri had given him, they were the ones he'd go in with.

Bodrugan still hadn't come back with the spell. Waiting, Hal set out, alone, on Storm, visiting other dragon flights on the front.

He took flight leaders aside, and gave them one simple instruction: if you're attacked by Yasin's black dragons, try to find out where their base is.

No one needed to know why the Dragonmaster wanted the information, and any clever sorts who figured out the obvious could damned well keep their mouths shut.

Don't advertise the knowledge, don't attack the base, don't fly over it more than once.

He continued the analogy of the cat in his own mind—the last thing to do is wake it up from its nap, when it might be hungry or cranky.

Contrary to Cantabri's cynicism, he didn't have to use the lord's direct order. There was a reason—almost all the fliers on the front, Sagene and Derainian, had either faced Yasin's killing machine, or had heard of it.

All of them wanted the huge Roche black dragons destroyed, but none of them particularly wanted the honor of taking them on.

Again, the analogy of the cat came to mind . . .

Hal had thought, with almost every flier with the First and Second Armies looking, they'd find where Yasin and his dragons lived in a few days.

But it took two full weeks, and showed, yet again, Yasin's cleverness.

As well as the cleverness, and luck, of the Sagene fliers.

A pair of Yasin's dragons, on patrol, had been tracked by a Sagene flier back of the lines, and then the dragons dove hard toward a narrow draw—and vanished.

No one—yet—had been able to move dragons around by magic, so the tale made no sense.

Against orders, the Sagene flight leader sent two of his fliers to make a sweep over the area, just at dusk, when all sensible dragons were returning to their roosts.

Again, a flight of three blacks carrying Yasin's guidon were seen in the same area, and once more they dove for shelter, impossibly, up a narrow draw.

And were gone.

The two Sagene dragons chanced a lower pass, and at first saw nothing.

Then luck intervened.

One of the Sagene fliers happened to be color blind. He'd managed to join up and make it through flying school without his minor disability being discovered.

Then the disability became a prize, when his flight commander discovered that a color-blind man was almost impossible to fool with camouflage.

So it was here.

The draw was in fact a fairly broad valley. A base had been prepared on the valley floor and then heavy wires had been strung across the valley.

Treetops were hung on the wires, their greenery kept alive by magic, then, once more with sorcery, were being artfully faded through fall coloring.

But the magic either hadn't been renewed often enough or wasn't quite artistic enough, for the color-blind flier looked down, saw something very false, looked harder and saw a long, huge dragon shelter to one side of a leveled, rolled field, and, he was almost certain, tents, huts and sheds on its other side.

That was enough for Hal, when it was reported to him.

The entire area was proclaimed a no-fly zone at army level.

Now it was Kailas's turn.

"It wasn't the spell that took so long," Bodrugan said. "It was where it was to be applied."

"I'd suggested that it be attached to Yasin's guidon," Hal said. "If you'll recall."

"I recall quite well," Bodrugan said with a bit of asperity. "But I didn't think it was a particularly good idea. Suppose Yasin decided to change his banner if his brother renamed the squadron? Suppose the bits we'd somehow managed to ensorcel got blown away?

"So I bethought myself of other places to apply the spell. None of them were particularly good—I thought we could spray the dragons themselves, but that sounded most shuddersome in the execution, not to mention risky.

"Then, a week ago, a Roche dragon flight was overrun by a cavalry strike. I got myself forward as quickly as I could.

"Of course the dragons and their fliers were long gone, and those of the ground workers who hadn't been slain had fled as well.

"But most of their apparatus remained, and so I was able to spend two hours wandering about before the cavalry was forced to fall back and abandon their conquest.

"Makes you wonder what good all these fools farting about on their horses do, in the long run.

"But I found a possible place for the spell. The most expensive piece of a dragon's gear is the saddle, correct?"

"Of course," Hal said. "Just like it's that of a horse."

"I propose that we work our way into *Ky* Yasin's base, find the tack room, and use the spell on the dragons' saddlery. Also, I'll make up enough so that we can cover the bridles and such as well."

"What happens," Hal asked skeptically, "when all the saddles that you've treated get lost in action or just get torn up with wear and tear?"

"That is the second part of my scheme," Bodrugan said. He held out a small can.

"This is the standard issue oil for the Roche leathers, it seems. I've cast the spell on half a dozen tins I found in that dragon base.

"We'll leave them lying about, and every time an earnest worker rubs his flier's tack, well, the spell will be renewed."

"Ingenious," Hal said. "Remembering how long our oil lasts, if the war lasts beyond the supply you've worked on, we'll all be dead."

"That, too, doesn't matter," Bodrugan said. "For Yasin and his men will have gone before, which is all that matters, isn't it?"

Hal ignored that for the moment.

"So the way the spell will work," Bodrugan said, "and work it shall, for I've tested it, is each flier, or each flight commander, or however you decide, will have a small wooden plate. On the plate, mounted so it can spin freely, will be a pointer. That pointer will always indicate two places. The first is Yasin's base. Since that's stationary, the flier can ignore that. The second will be any of Yasin's dragons with gear that's been ensorcelled who're in the air. Isn't that perfect?"

"I guess so," Hal said. Then something came back to him.

"Uh . . . a question. You said, a bit ago, that 'we' will work our way into Yasin's camp."

"Of course I'm going," Bodrugan said. "You don't think I trust a mere dragon driver to make sure my spell is properly in place, do you?

"Besides, that young raider—the one with a face like a depraved child—is quite striking, don't you think?"

"You have a plan afoot," Danikel said.

"Perhaps," Hal said cautiously.

"Without a Sagene flier to accompany it."

"As a matter of fact," Hal lied, "I'd just realized that, and, needing another dragon, was about to ask for volunteers."

"Which I am," Danikel said. "And it's a good thing I came to you. Would you rather have had Alcmaen?"

Hal briefed his fliers and the two raiders.

He'd had two men make up a sand model of the area from a hasty map, which showed not only the hidden valley, but the hilltop Hal proposed landing on, and leaving the dragons, about half a mile from Yasin's base.

They sat digesting their orders for a time.

"I suppose," Farren Mariah said, "that you've come up with some alibi."

"I don't understand," Hal said.

"Let us suppose that we slip into Yasin's camp, and get discovered. If we just take to our heels, toes following promptly along, Yasin might figure our intent. Shouldn't we be there for some other purpose?"

"That's taken care of," Kailas said. "We'll carry firebottles, and if we're surprised, we'll use them to fire that dragon shed. Or try to, anyway."

"You think Yasin'll believe you went along just because you love the bright flicker, flicker of the flames?"

"I won't be carrying any identification," Hal said grimly. "Nor will anyone else. And I have no plans on being captured again."

There was silence for a moment; then Gamo stood.

"If I may say something, Lord Kailas?"

"Go ahead," Hal said.

"I want to make one thing clear," Gamo said. "Once we're on the ground, until we get back to the dragons, I am in charge. You others know flying and magic, but raiding is Hakea's and my specialty. I want that very certain. If not, my partner and I will be forced to return to our unit."

Hal saw his expression, and suddenly there was something quite chillingly lethal about the man's baby face.

"Well, hickety-doo," Mariah said. "A mere warrant dictating to a bunch of ossifers. I love it."

"I'm sorry," Hal said to Gamo. "I should have made that very clear in my orders. You, of course, are in charge on the ground."

Gamo nodded, sat back down, studying the table.

"We'll leave tomorrow," Hal said. "At full dark."

The dragons glided in out of the cold night, wings spread, and thudded down onto the hilltop.

Hal, Bodrugan and the two raiders slipped off their dragons, and readied their gear.

Storm was looking about, nostrils flared, scenting the enemy dragons not far away. He opened his mouth to shrill a warning perhaps, and Hal tapped him on the snout.

Storm snapped his jaws shut, looked unhappy, or so Hal defined his expression in the dimness, and curled up.

The raiders shouldered their packs, and moved down the hill. All of them wore black, with darkened faces. Bodrugan had cast a nonreflective spell on their daggers and swords.

Hal had chosen the night carefully, when both moons were out.

Both Gamo and Hakea hadn't liked that at all, preferring to wait until the dark of the moons.

"That may be fine for you raiders, with eyes like bats," Hal had said. "But not for us fliers, who need all the help we can get."

"Whyn't you think of stayin' back, sir," Hakea rumbled, "and let us just go in and piddle that magic about?"

Hal had just looked at him, and Hakea shrugged and said no more.

The four went down the hill to its base, and crouched, moved across rolling brushland toward the draw.

Hal, from his cavalry days, thought he knew a bit about sneaking around.

But the raiders put him to shame.

Hakea, that hulking peasant, suddenly became an eel, slipping from shadow to shadow.

Gamo simply became one of the shadows.

Bodrugan must have done some hunting, or perhaps was just a moonlight wanderer, for he, too, moved without stumbling or crashing through brush and into stumps.

They went across the meadow, to the opening of the draw. They crouched, while Gamo watched, for long moments. Finally he nodded in satisfaction, and motioned the others to the far side of the draw. He moved like an ape Hal had seen once in a menagerie, bent over, keeping below the brush, creeping very slowly.

There was a nest of boulders outside the draw, and Gamo led them behind its shelter. He pointed out, and Hal saw, on the other side of the narrow canyon, slight movement.

A sentry.

Then he spotted two of them, and heard the murmur of conversation.

This far behind the lines security could get a little sloppy.

They went into the canyon, staying on the slope, away from the floor, where no patrols would likely travel.

Then they were under the cover of the false trees. The landing field reached out in front of them, and the huge shed was to their left.

Gamo looked at Hal, waiting for orders.

Hal thought.

If Yasin were logical, he most likely would have built the most essential supply sheds closest to the dragons.

He saw three such.

He pointed to them. Gamo nodded, and they crept off.

It was cold, getting colder, and frost was forming.

They'd have to be out of here by dawn, for their passage through the dying brush around the field would leave streaks in the frost.

There were still lights on, here and there, mostly across the field in the squadron's quarters.

No one seemed to be about.

Hal smelled the acrid musk of the dragons in the long bay, heard a long, bubbling monstrous snore from inside.

Gamo stopped outside the first shed.

Hal sniffed, wrinkled his nostrils. Blood and offal. That would be the dragons' butcher shop.

He pointed to the next shed, and then went on.

Hal smelled nothing, but Gamo must've, for Hal saw a grin flash in the moonlight.

The door of the canvas and wood shed wasn't locked, and they slipped inside, closing it behind them.

Gamo reached into Hakea's pack, took out a small bull's-eye lantern and lit it. He opened one panel, and Hal saw hanging saddles, bridles, other leather workings.

Bodrugan had seen as well and needed no orders.

He unslung his pack, and took out four small sprayers, such as women used for perfume.

Each man took one, and sprayed the hanging gear, and the saddles on their stands.

Hal's went empty, and he went to Bodrugan's pack, and took out half a dozen tins of leather oil.

He stacked them on a shelf, and their mission was successful.

All they had to do was slip away without wakening the cat.

Hal was beginning to have hopeful feelings as they left the shed that they'd get away with it clean, and then there was a surprised snort as a skinny man came out of a door in the long dragon shed, saw armed men in the moonlight, guessed they weren't there with good intents, and opened his mouth to shout an alarm.

Gamo snaked out, and his hand rose, fell.

The thin Roche grunted, went down, began making snoring noises.

Gamo motioned to Hakea, who came up, and knelt, his knee on the Roche's throat. The snoring stopped.

Hal had the idea this wasn't the first time they'd dealt with a surpriser in such a manner.

Hakea rose, lifted the body over his shoulder, and they went back out of the valley.

The sentries were quiet now, hopefully sleeping.

None of the Derainians made a sound as they crept out of the draw, and across the rolling ground to their hillock.

Farren Mariah rose from behind a rock, crossbow in hand.

"Any problems?"

"None," Hal said.

"Who's that?" He indicated the body across Hakea's shoulder.

"Someone who was where he shouldn't have been," Hal said.

"What I suggest, sir," Gamo said, and Hal noted the way authority had reverted to where it should be, "is we take the body out with us, and dump it in some lake. They'll think he deserted or, as like, not even notice. I've seen the Roche don't seem to give much of a hang about their help," he said.

They remounted the dragons, and took off along the far side of the hill.

Hal had the body across his knees and noted, with disgust, the man had voided his bowels in dying.

They saw silver in the moonlight, dropped down over a chill-looking pond, and Hal pushed the corpse over.

He felt a moment of pity. If the man had a family, they'd never learn what happened to him and be forever wondering.

Then he remembered the sentry he'd dumped in a river when he was an escaping prisoner, and forgot about the dragon handler.

There were bigger things to consider.

Such as the morrow, and the surprise he hoped to bring *Ky* Yasin and his fliers.

40

The dragons were trundling out of their sheds in the gray chill, when one of the field sentries announced a courier to Hal. He bore a rather sizable package, coming from Limingo the wizard.

Hal puzzled, then remembered he'd promised to look over the poor mad raider's ramblings that'd been transcribed.

But not right now.

Storm squealed at him, and, obediently, Hal clambered up into the saddle.

He popped his reins on the dragon's back, and Storm staggered forward, great wings spreading. He hopped, then leaped, and was in the air.

Behind Hal, the rest of his squadron lifted up, and began circling the field, reaching for altitude.

As Storm climbed, Kailas looked down at the tiny needle and board secured to Storm's carapace.

It pointed steadily in one direction, the direction of Yasin's base.

Kailas tapped the rear of the needle with a fingernail, but it stayed in one place. That meant Yasin's dragons hadn't taken off yet.

Hal blasted on his trumpet, and, still climbing, the squadron followed him east and slightly south.

Hal's course would, hopefully, intersect Yasin's flight on its way to patrolling the fighting ground.

He took the dragons as high as he could, until he was struggling to fill his lungs.

Storm's wings moved slowly, sluggishly, at this height.

Hal saw one dragon fall off on a wing, and pinwheel downward to thicker, safer air. But only one.

He forced on east. His course, if he'd set it correctly, should intersect with Yasin's, no more than a league beyond his field.

Now there was nothing to do but wait, and listen to the leathern creak of Storm's wings, and the faint sound of the other monsters behind him.

It was cold up here, even colder than the late fall weather below on the ground.

For some reason, Hal's mind turned to Aimard Quesney, who he hoped was now safely tucked away out of harm's way in Deraine.

He wondered what Quesney would think of this latest devise, almost certainly knew the flier would rage about Hal finding yet another way to bloody the skies.

The sky had lightened as they climbed, although the ground below was still nighthung.

They'd crossed the lines without Hal realizing it.

His target lay on east.

Now there was the peep of the sun, glaring at him.

Yasin's advantage.

Hal squinted, looked ahead and down.

He thought at first it was his eyes, then picked out small black dots ahead and below.

Dragons.

Storm had seen them as well, and snorted.

No Roche saw them, which Kailas had counted on. It would have been insane for any Derainian or Sagene formation to be east of the front this early in the day.

Hal chanced a blat of warning, looked back, and saw answering waves from his flight leaders.

He forced calm, counted, watching the blots get larger and larger below.

Then he could wait no longer. He didn't need his trumpet. The lift of an arm was enough to take the squadron diving down, in four V flights, on Yasin's black dragons.

Hal found it momentarily amusing that he, and everyone else, still thought of Yasin as being a black dragon unit, strange because there were now almost as many blacks with Kailas's squadron.

But the menacing label remained.

Hal swore at his mind for fripperies, coming up with nonsense to avoid thinking about the death they were plummeting toward.

Hal steered Storm toward the dragon at the head of the formation, hoping it was Yasin. He had a moment to realize it wasn't, its guidon unfringed.

Storm had that dragon by the throat, tore it down, bones snapping loudly.

Hal snap-fired at that flier's wingman, hit him in the chest, then was below the formation as the rest of his squadron tore into them.

Hal pulled Storm up, letting the speed of his dive convert into energy, lifting him back up through the formation.

He had his crossbow reloaded, aimed at another flier, missed.

Storm lay over on a wing, turning, skidding as a Roche dragon came in on him. Hal tried to aim at the flier, couldn't get a clear shot, sent his bolt into the dragon's throat. It tore at itself, trying to rip the bolt out, spinning, falling, and was gone.

The two squadrons were a spinning, swirling melee. Storm went after another dragon, rolling almost on his back, Hal swearing, clinging desperately with his knees to the saddle, and there was a Roche dragon almost touching him. Storm's talons ripped at the Roche, and ichor gouted, and the beast fell away.

Hal had control, was forcing Storm into a climb, and a Roche flier fell past him, silently, mouth opening and closing like a beached fish, and he was gone.

A Roche dragon, wing torn, was trying to escape. Hal closed on it from behind, shot the flier out of his saddle, forgot about the beast.

Another dragon, this time one of his, tumbled past him, dying, falling to the ground far below, and then the sky was almost empty.

Hal blew the recall, and obedient to his own order, turned back toward their own lines.

As he flew, other fliers assembled on him.

Hal could hear them shouting, cheering as they flew.

Hal realized he had a grin as broad and stupid as any other flier.

They went back before dusk, this time circling around Yasin's base and coming in from the east. Also, Hal forbade the flying of any squadron symbol. He wanted Yasin to think that he was being hit not just by one squadron, but by all the dragon fliers of Sagene and Deraine.

Hal's fliers had claimed five dragons down in the morning, and six more at dusk, for a loss of three dragons.

That night, his fliers wanted to celebrate, which Hal allowed, within reason. That meant beer only. No one should fly in the morning with a thick head.

Hal went back to his tent, tried to sleep, couldn't.

Muttering to himself, he lit a lantern and decided to leaf through the madman's ravings.

He wasn't sure what he was looking for, so started near the end:

Down, away, stumbling, not fall, come after me, abandoned, alone, silent like mousie like they taught me like they left me no squeaking, crying . . .

That was enough for that night. Hal decided he'd try again tomorrow or the next day.

The squadron was stumblingly weary. Not only was the drive against Yasin's squadron nearly constant, but they were constantly called for other duties, in spite of their supposed special status.

Exhaustion killed.

Hal now was used to writing letters to Sagene and Deraine, bemoaning the death of a flier, when, in truth, they'd been nothing more than names on the status report.

With an exception.

Danikel seemed beyond exhaustion, beyond fear.

He flew not only his detailed tasks, but whenever he could.

He and his blue dragon, Hoko, were in the air all the time, always across the lines, in spite of Hal's admonitions.

Kailas thought of grounding him, didn't know how he could, short of chaining him to his tent post.

Danikel never seemed to change, never seemed sleepy or tired.

He was buried under fan letters from Sagene, which he smiled at, but seldom read and never answered.

With one exception.

A letter came every day—or when the mails were on time—in a woman's hand, in gray ink, the addressing quite calligraphic.

He never told anyone who the letters came from, burned them after reading them twice and answering them.

Hal couldn't decide if they came from the baroness he'd been keeping company with in Fovant.

Danikel was beyond being the darling of the Sagene taletellers. Now they were referring to him as the very spirit of Sagene, the warrior soul of the country.

And day by day, his death toll mounted, although Hal never heard him claim a specific number of kills.

Alcmaen was nearly beside himself, left far behind in the count, but Danikel paid him little attention, treating him kindly, as a not particularly bright younger cousin, which further increased Alcmaen's rage.

Then, one morning, a clear day, Danikel didn't come back from his predawn patrol.

He'd told his dragon handler that he thought he'd "nip back of the lines, and see if any of Yasin's people were out this early," nothing more specific.

Hal checked the hospitals, sent orderlies to see if any of the front line units had reported a falling dragon.

None did.

Nor was any body recovered.

There were no claims from the Roche for a time.

Little by little it crept out: the soul of Sagene was missing, lost in battle.

The taletellers wailed like peasants at a village chief's funeral.

After a few days, word came from the Roche.

Danikel had been downed, in mortal combat, by one of *Ky* Yasin's fliers.

Hal didn't believe it—the claim was made very weakly, with no confirmation or interviews with the black-dragon flier who claimed to have killed him.

Hal thought it was the Roche taletellers' invention.

Alcmaen said, three days later, that he'd seen the Roche flier across the lines, and, in a terrible battle witnessed by no one, had killed the man and his dragon.

Even the Sagene taletellers had trouble with that one.

The gray-inked letters stopped coming, with never a query from their writer to Hal about the flier's death.

It was, other than the periodic wails in the broadsheets, as if Danikel, Baron Trochu, had never been.

The half ring around Carcaor was slowly closing.

The Sagene blockade of the Ichili River was closed, and almost nothing was coming upriver to Carcaor. Deraine had sealed off the River Pettau and the Zante, and its navy was slowly making its way south toward Carcaor, capturing or isolating each Roche riverine city as they came. Each league they captured meant less foodstuffs and war materials for the beleaguered barons in the capital.

Yet still the Roche fought on, as if determined to destroy their country if they couldn't win.

Once again, Hal varied the squadron's tactics. This time, all the fliers had tiny magicked compasses, and flew out by themselves. Again, they held the heights, and waited over Cantabri's battlefield.

As they waited, Hal saw Roche formations break and fall back. The Sagene and Derainian troops, probably as exhausted as their enemy, stolidly moved forward.

When Yasin's black dragons flew into sight, the squadron hit them from all directions at once, as if the Roche were magnetized.

They took out four dragons that morning, Hal having killed three of them. Yasin's squadron fragmented on the first attack and fled.

Little by little . . .

Hal had the squadron stand down for a day. The fliers might have been up for more slaughter, but the dragons were wearying.

He started to catch up on the always-present paperwork, then stopped.

If he'd told Limingo he'd go through the madman's ravings, it was to find something that might suggest a way to defeat that demon.

And the time for confronting that spirit was drawing closer.

He sighed, pulled the manuscript over, and started reading, this time from the beginning.

Kailas forced attention, and then, abruptly, the babblings seized him:

Ruined, ruined, all is ruins, ruined stones, moving, lifting, coming toward me . . . brown . . . a bear . . . jelly . . . jelly bear . . . reaching . . . duck away, duck away, do not take death . . . spear . . . thrown . . . hit . . . through it . . . jelly, jelly, jelly, run, trying to run . . . screaming . . . crying . . . mother . . . a boy not wept . . . clawing at me . . . nor dashed a thousand kim . . . attacked . . . trapped . . . mother, this place stinks . . . death . . . the dagger, dagger, my grandfather's . . . sharp . . . a bit of rust on the blade, blade, iron, old iron . . . tunic flaming . . . embers . . . crumbling, reaching bear . . . and I threw it hard into jellyness . . . screaming . . . stupid so slight a hurt . . . jelly bear screaming at so slight a hurt . . . in back and away and chance to run, run from jelly, run from death—

Hal had it.

Maybe.

But it was worth a try.

Maybe.

If he could just figure out how to make his idea work.

41

Limingo rubbed his eyes wearily.

"All right," he told Hal. "I concede that your more careful reading—and thinking—seems to have given us a clue. I surely wouldn't have noted that your raider carried an irregular weapon, least of all what it was made of. And certainly cold iron is legendary proof against demons. So we have a bit of knowledge now, thanks to our poor mad friend."

"But not much more," Hal said, staring out of the ruined building Limingo had taken over for what Kailas thought of as Magic Headquarters. "If iron hurts that whatever it is, well and good. What we need is a big piece of iron to kill it, I guess, but I don't have the foggiest idea of how to deliver it, point first, into our demon. Maybe cast a big godsdamned spear out of iron, land some raiders who're a lot braver than I am on the rock, and, when and if the demon appears, they charge him and we give medals to the suicidal."

"Not good," Limingo agreed. "Not to mention the things we don't know, such as whether that demon was brought up by the destruction you wrought in Carcaor, or by your presence the night before in that castle.

"Plus, we don't know if the barons know about this demon, and if that's why they're being so foolhardy in refusing to surrender. Or if they're just pigheaded Roche like everyone believes."

"You know," Hal said carefully, "perhaps there is a way to hit that demon—if he appears—with my big spear. Maybe if we cast just the spearhead, and then fletch a wooden shaft like an arrow—maybe fletching that goes all the way up to the head—and then somehow rig it under a dragon, and come in against him—or it or whatever it is—very godsdamned fast, and use the dragon's speed to launch the spear, and . . . and there's too many godsdamned maybes in this."

He slumped back, looked out at the icy rain coming down.

"It's nice to have a roof over my head for the moment," he said. "My squadron and I are still out there with tents."

"It could be worse," Limingo said.

"It could," Hal said. "At least we've got tents. I saw a couple of foot soldiers trying to use a tree to rig a pretty small piece of canvas."

Limingo shook his head.

"This war's gone on too long."

"It has," Hal agreed, getting to his feet. "I used to be able to spring up like a goosed lamb. Now I'm a creaky old man."

He pulled a long waxed coat on, and shivered.

"But I suppose I'd better get back to my blacksmiths and start figuring out just how damned dumb I am."

The war had ground almost to a halt as the weather got worse. It took the hardest of officers to get the men out of whatever shelter they'd figured out, into the freezing muck, and stumbling toward the Roche positions. Horses stamped, and refused to come out of their stables, and lashed out at their grooms.

The dragons, accustomed to cold weather, were a little more cooperative, but not much more.

The Roche held as best they could, but they couldn't stand firm for long.

They were out of almost everything—fresh food, dry clothing replacements, and even their fighting supplies were now rationed.

Out of everything—except raw courage.

"That's about as cockermaymie a contrapatrapashun as I've ever seen," Farren Mariah said. "And I'm not even mentioning the dropping mechanism. I've seen amateur hangmen come up with better."

"Thanks for the compliment," Hal said. "Now, go get your dragon out. There's a spear and contrapashun for you, too. And the other squadron commanders."

"Why me all the time?" Mariah wailed.

"We all need to have an example set for us," Sir Loren said. "Whether good or bad is immaterial."

Storm didn't like the setup any more than Mariah did. The spear's head was about a yard wide, and the shaft twelve feet long.

Hal had come to the measurements by experimentation—dropping models off a nearby rise, and making note of which fell point first most readily. But then he cut the weight out of the head, since the spear would have to be cast from a flying dragon.

One of Hal's ropemakers came up with a cradle front and rear that was tied to the unhappy dragon. When a rope was pulled by the flier, the cradles came unhooked, and the spear fell free.

All that remained was to see if the contrivance worked in the air.

For a while, it appeared as if it didn't at all, generally falling from the dragon and dropping straight down.

Spears were recovered, and weight was drilled off the head, added to the shaft, and that helped matters.

But it still required a flier to have his dragon at full speed when he released the spear. Then, if everything went well, the spear would wobble through the air, and hit the earthen bank it was aimed at.

After two days, everyone in the squadron had taken at least three shots.

The best shot was Hachir, the former crossbowman, and the second was Farren Mariah.

But no one knew if the weapon would work against the demon.

"Since we know somewhat less than nothing about our demon," Limingo said, "and since the time for his appearance looms near, I've set my young man, Bodrugan, to watch the mountain. With Lord Cantabri's approval, he, and half a dozen raiders and equipment, have been flown to another mountaintop to watch.

"I have dragons from another flight—sorry, Hal, but you appeared busy with other things—making unobtrusive fly-pasts morning and night to receive their flag signals.

"So far, everything on the mountain appears quiet. One strange thing—the ruins of that castle you reported the demon came from, further destroying the ruins, now appear undisturbed."

"I like that but little," Hal said.

"I imagine," Limingo said dryly, "our Bodrugan likes it even less."

Hal continued harrying Yasin when his squadron came out. But the war in the air was almost at a standstill as winter's first storms raged.

In spite of the weather, Cantabri lashed the armies back into motion.

Hal's squadron was detailed for another special duty—they

landed teams of raiders to the east and south of Carcaor, with orders to hold their positions and stop any movement past them.

Other, stronger teams were told off to support these teams if they were attacked. Dragon flights were moved in to fly in these backup teams, and supplies for the teams.

Then, one gloomy day, Hal landed a team on a plateau, happened to look southwest, and saw the flurry of a cavalry patrol moving through the freshly fallen snow.

He glassed the patrol, and saw they were Sagene.

Carcaor was surrounded.

42

The armies of Sagene and Deraine occupied Carcaor's suburbs on the west bank of the Ichili River. Reinforcements were rushed forward, and troops were fed and resupplied, getting ready for the final assault.

Perhaps Cantabri shouldn't have allowed the pause, for it gave time for old soldiers to talk about the horrors of the Comtal River crossing years earlier that led to the siege of Aude. And somehow there were stories—no one knew how they got out—about some horrid wizardly weapon the Roche had.

Everyone who knew of the demon swore they'd said nothing, but someone had.

Balancing those stories were the terrible ones of what it was like in the encircled capital. There were whispers that bodies had been found with steaks carved from their buttocks or thighs. The soldiers were on the scantiest of rations, no more than half-ground grain baked into flat breads. Civilians were simply starving while the barons continued to dine on their hidden luxuries.

Then flat-bottomed boats started arriving from the north and south, and were readied for the assault on Carcaor.

Roche wizards sent firespells and storms against the boats, but the spells were largely quashed by the Sagene and Derainian magicians.

Hal moved his squadron up to the river, made himself ready to support the crossing.

Cantabri summoned him one day.

"We'll be forcing the river in two days," he said without preamble. "And I want my soldiers to keep crossing and not get stranded on the other side without any backup. That means your task is first to cover the river against any dragon attacks. Your second task will be to take on the demon . . . If he appears, which I assume he will.

"Any questions?"

"No, sir," Hal said.

"Then I'll see you in the victory parade."

Hal was making last-minute adjustments to Storm's harness, and making sure he had enough bolts and firedarts ready when Farren Mariah came up, looking carefully from side to side.

"What now, Lieutenant?" Hal asked.

"We don't have to worry our little nogs about what happens today," Farren said. "At least, not you and me."

"Oh?"

"I set a small spell up at dawn," he said. "And it said for sure and certain you and I and Chincha would live through the day. Barring certain things."

"How damnably reassuring. What sort of certain things?"

"Well, it got confused, but we're safe as long as we fight well, and stay clear of magic."

"Gods," Hal said, dripping sarcasm. "Now I can truly relax. You're sure of your magic."

"Sure as cert," Mariah said. "I cast that spell three times."

"What happened the other two?"

"Aaarh, you don't want to know, boss."

The soldiers had been formed up by boatloads, hidden from view across the river.

Hal, flying overhead with his squadron, diving in and out of the intermittent cloud cover, heard the shout of orders and the blast of trumpets, and lines of soldiers debouched from shelter to the boats waiting at the river's edge.

They pushed out into the current, and rowers heaved mightily.

The line grew ragged against the Ichili's swift current, and then the boats were in midstream, then into the shallows safely.

The soldiers leapt out, and Roche fighters came to meet them.

There was a flurry of fighting; then the Roche were pushed back, as the boats shuttled back for another load.

This time, they'd barely loaded and left the west bank when many of them began to twist and roil in the water. A few overturned, and there came up screams.

Hal took Storm low, to see what was going on, and saw strange creatures pulling at the boats. Some of them were driven away by alert archers or spearmen, but more came up from the depths to take their places.

It came to Hal—these were like the monsters of wizardry created back during the attack on Kalabas.

Some boat coxswains panicked, and turned back. Others tried to follow their orders, and the creatures tore at them.

On the far shore the Roche soldiers had gained heart, and were coming back on the invaders.

Step by step, the Sagene and Derainian infantry were being pushed back toward the river.

Hal caught himself, reached behind him, into a case strapped to the back of his saddle. He came out with a firedart, sent Storm diving down.

He waited until the dragon was no more than fifty feet above the river, reflexively pulling out of its dive, then leaned over and pitched the firedart close to a beleaguered boat.

It hit the water not five feet from the boat's gunwales, exploded, and the fire spread over the water, smoking greasily.

The creatures attacking the boat, who might have been bloodred seals with fangs and arms, rolled away from the boat and disappeared.

Hal took out another firedart, found another target, and then his squadron was down with him, and the Ichili was spattered with flames.

The boats straightened out, continued on their course, and Hal heard a warning blast from somewhere.

Above him, out of the clouds, dove Yasin's decimated but still deadly squadron. Now it was their turn to have the advantage of height.

A dragon was hurtling down toward Storm, and Hal sent Storm back toward the water.

He watched, waited, as the dragon closed, till he could see the tight grin of its flier, anticipating a victory.

Then he sent Storm rolling out of the way.

The Roche dragon tried to recover, had too much speed, and slammed into the Ichili.

Hal sent Storm climbing, into the heart of Yasin's squadron. At its head, and he absolutely knew without knowing how, was *Ky* Yasin.

He went for him, fired, and put a bolt in Yasin's dragon's foreleg. Then Yasin was gone, and it was a mad swirl over Carcaor.

Hal managed a quick glance down, saw the boats coming back across with another load, untroubled.

The magicians of Sagene and Deraine must've produced their counterspell.

Then there was a dragon just above him, and he put a bolt in its belly just as the dragon's tail flailed at him.

Storm had the tail in his jaws, tore sideways, and the Roche dragon screeched, was gone.

There was another, wounded dragon converging on him, and Hal aimed closely, hit the flier in the head, knocked him out of his saddle.

They had the heights then, the snarling fight about to begin, and Hal heard repeated blasts from a trumpet.

He looked, saw an unknown dragon, its flier blowing a horn frantically, and waving his free hand.

Hal knew that prearranged signal.

The flier had seen Bodrugan's flags from his mountaintop. Either the demon had appeared or Bodrugan's magic said he was about to.

Just as Yasin's fliers dove away upriver to reform, Hal was blowing the recall, and going for the squadron base.

The dragon handlers heard his signal, and had the spear cradles ready.

Hal put Storm down almost next to one, and, in seconds, the cradle was tied around the dragon.

It seemed as if every nonflier in the squadron was helping, but Hal had no time for thanks, taking Storm up ahead of the others.

Storm didn't like the cradle or the heavy spear suspended under his belly, but confined his protests to a high whine, then concentrated on reaching for the sky.

At full speed, Kailas drove Storm downriver, toward the grim mountaintop and its ruins.

Then he rounded the last bend in the river, and saw the ruins, just as they shook as if taken by an earthquake, and then cascaded off the sides of that great brown demon, rearing from his underground or otherworldly lair.

This time he was taller than two hundred feet, and this time he didn't stay on the mountaintop, but strode forward, impossibly walking down its near-vertical side, toward Hal and the river.

Maybe he had been called by Roche wizards, or maybe the bloodshed in Carcaor was his summons.

A dragon hurtled past Hal toward the demon. It was Alcmaen. Hal grudged him courage, when he should have been screaming in terror.

Alcmaen's spear came undone, and wobbled toward the demon. But he was too far away, and the spear dove toward the river.

Alcmaen tried to bank away, but was too close, and the demon swatted both the Sagene and his dragon down, crumpling them as if they were paper.

Hal banked around the demon, toward his side, and was coming in for an attack when a black dragon was in front of him, and a crossbow spat a bolt at him.

Yasin's fliers had taken advantage of the break in action, and were coming back on them.

Mariah was just above the demon, coming straight down, and released his spear. It took the demon somewhere in the chest, and the whole world rang with the monster's scream.

Two other dragons dropped their spears, both missing, as Hal turned Storm, into the face of a surprised Roche flier.

Storm tore at the beast's side with his double horns, and it fell.

The demon was swaying, expanding, very unsolid.

Its chest was pointed to Hal's side, and Hal hoped, as he sent Storm in again, that its attention was elsewhere.

He was close, very close, and Storm was whining in fear.

Hal pulled at the cord, and the spear arced away, and took the dragon in its chest.

It stumbled back, fell against the rock wall it had just descended, and Hachir came in and dropped his spear. It caught the demon in the belly, and it collapsed, fell forward into the Ichili, and then, very suddenly, there was nothing there as another flier's spear went through nothingness to clang against a boulder.

Nothing but onrushing Roche dragons.

Hachir was banking back toward Hal, and a dragon carrying Yasin's guidon dove on him.

Hachir rolled out of the way as Yasin recovered, climbing.

Hachir went after him, and the two vanished into a cloud.

Hal was bent over Storm's neck, calling for everything the dragon had, and they were climbing after the two.

Then one dragon came out of the cloud—Yasin's.

Hal saw no sign of Hachir or his dragon.

Yasin brought his dragon around, and dove on Hal. He was aiming his crossbow. Hal ducked, barely in time, and shot back, missing.

Both dragons circled, bare yards above the cliffs, as their fliers reloaded. Yasin aimed quickly, fired, missed, as Hal aimed his crossbow.

He was suddenly the crossbow, the bolt, and moved his aim a little left. Yasin saw his death approaching, sat frozen as Hal pulled back on the trigger.

The bolt shot forward, and *Ky* Yasin flew into it

He screamed as it hit him in the chest, and his dragon dove straight down, toward the Ichili.

It struck hard, a gout of brown water lifting.

Hal took Storm very low.

But there was nothing but ripples.

Then a dragon's foreleg rose above the water, sunk again.

Ky Bayle Yasin was gone.

Athelny of the Dragons was avenged, as was Saslic and all the other dragon fliers who'd been killed in this war.

Hal Kailas wondered why he was crying.

But it didn't matter. No one could see.

He took Storm back upriver, his squadron forming on him, to Carcaor.

The city was in flames.

Heavy lighters were on the east river's edge, and were loading cavalry.

The palace in Carcaor's center was a firestorm, like Hal had brought to Lanzi.

Soldiers were streaming across the river and through the city's streets.

Charging horsemen rode past them, shattering the few Roche formations that stood fast.

Then there was nothing but running men, and other men after them, killing as they ran.

White flags exploded through Carcaor.

The war was finally over and done.

43

It was stormy, and the winds from the nearby whitecap-tossed Western Ocean promised a gale this night.

But it didn't matter.

Hal—and Storm—would sleep warm this night, warm in Cayre a Carstares, Lady Khiri's castle.

The war was truly over.

Lord Bab Cantabri found it very difficult to make peace, since Roche's ruling barons had either been killed, took their own lives, or fled.

Not that it mattered.

Once the Roche realized their leaders were gone, it was if a solid bar of steel was suddenly revealed as rusted through.

Carcaor was the last holdings of the Roche, and now it was gone, as well.

There was some looting, some murders by the conquering Sagene and Derainian soldiers, but not that much.

They were almost as weary as the Roche.

There would be some kind of victory parade sometime in the next few weeks. Actually, there would be two of them, one in Rozen, one in Fovant.

Hal didn't give a diddly-damn if he was in either.

The war was over, and he was no longer a soldier. He supposed they'd send him some papers one day or another.

Many of the soldiers had felt the same, and had gone home on their own ticket, not waiting for any discharge or bonus, content with their lives.

That had been the case with Hal's squadron.

He'd been surprised so many of the old fighters had survived—Farren Mariah, Mynta Gart, Sir Loren Damian. Even some of the newer ones had made it—Chincha and Cabet. Richia had been killed in the final struggle with Yasin's black dragons.

Hal wondered what the death count was for the ten years and more of war. Two million a side? Three? More?

He also wondered what would happen to Roche, now completely shattered.

But not that much.

That would be for others, for diplomats and such, to worry about.

All that Hal wanted was to sleep, and then, maybe, go looking for the boy who wanted to be a dragon flier, who'd been dragged into the army so long ago.

He wondered, if he found him, he'd recognize him.

Hal shook his head, took himself away from the dark mood coming on.

Below him was Cayre a Carstares.

Storm gave a happy honk, swung around, and lowered toward the ground.

A dot came out of a building, ran to the center of the keep. Khiri.

And that was all Lord Hal Kailas of Kalabas, the Dragonmaster, needed or wanted.

For a time.

About the Author

Chris Bunch became a full-time novelist following his twenty-year career as a television writer. A military veteran, he was the *Locus* bestselling author of *Star Risk, Ltd.*, and such popular works at the *Sten* series, *The Seer King, The Demon King,* and the *Last Legion* series. He passed away in July 2005.